D0271629

CROSSING THE RIVER

BY THE SAME AUTHOR

Fiction

THE FINAL PASSAGE
A STATE OF INDEPENDENCE
HIGHER GROUND
CAMBRIDGE

Non-fiction

THE EUROPEAN TRIBE

CROSSING THE RIVER

Caryl Phillips

BLOOMSBURY

KING ALFRED'S COLLEGE
WINCHESTER

823.91
PH/

01455486

First published 1993

Copyright © 1993 by Caryl Phillips

The moral right of the author has been asserted

Bloomsbury Publishing Ltd, 2 Soho Square, London W1V 5DE

A CIP catalogue record for this book is available from the
British Library

ISBN 07475 14976

10 9 8 7 6 5 4 3

Typeset by Hewer Text Composition Services, Edinburgh
Printed in Great Britain by Clays Ltd, St Ives plc

For those who crossed the river

Acknowledgements

I have employed many sources in the
preparation of this novel, but would like
to express my particular obligation to John
Newton's eighteenth-century *Journal of a Slave
Trader*, which furnished me with invaluable
research material for Part III.

I

THE PAGAN COAST

II

WEST

III

CROSSING THE RIVER

IV

SOMEWHERE IN ENGLAND

A desperate foolishness. The crops failed. I sold my children. I remember. I led them (two boys and a girl) along weary paths, until we reached the place where the mud flats are populated with crabs and gulls. *Returned across the bar with the yawl, and prayed a while in the factory chapel.* I watched as they huddled together and stared up at the fort, above which flew a foreign flag. *Stood beneath the white-washed walls of the factory, waiting for the yawl to return and carry me back over the bar.* In the distance stood the ship into whose keep I would soon condemn them. The man and his company were waiting to once again cross the bar. We watched a while. And then approached. *Approached by a quiet fellow.* Three children only. I jettisoned them at this point, where the tributary stumbles and swims out in all directions to meet the sea. *Bought 2 strong man-boys, and a proud girl.* I soiled my hands with cold goods in exchange for their warm flesh. A shameful intercourse. I could feel their eyes upon me. Wondering, *why?* I turned and journeyed back along the same weary paths. *I believe my trade for this voyage has reached its conclusion.* And soon after, the chorus of a common memory began to haunt me.

For two hundred and fifty years I have listened to the many-tongued chorus. And occasionally, among the sundry restless voices, I have discovered those of my own children. My Nash. My Martha. My Travis. Their lives fractured. Sinking hopeful roots into difficult soil. For two hundred and fifty years I have longed to tell them: Children, I am your father. I love you. But understand. There are no paths in water. No signposts. There is no return. To a land trampled by the muddy boots of others. To a people encouraged to war among themselves. To a father consumed with guilt. You are beyond. Broken-off, like limbs from a tree. But not lost, for you carry within your bodies the seeds of new trees. Sinking your hopeful roots into difficult soil. And I, who spurned you, can blame only myself for my present misery. For two hundred and fifty years I have waited patiently for the wind to rise on the far bank of the river. For the drum to pound across the water. For the chorus to swell. Only then, if I listen closely, can I rediscover my lost children. A brief, painful communion. A desperate foolishness. The crops failed. I sold my children.

I

THE PAGAN COAST

The news reached him after dinner. A well-liveried domestic entered the drawing-room, bowed and thrust forward a silver tray on top of which sat an envelope. Edward seized the letter and dismissed the servant with an elegant flick of his wrist. He levered himself upright and began to read. It was true. Nash Williams, sent to Liberia under the auspices of the American Colonization Society, having undergone a rigorous program of Christian education, and being of sound moral character, had disappeared from the known world. After seven difficult years in Liberia, in which he had worked with unswerving application to his own and his God's tasks, in which he had apparently won the respect not only of the African natives, but of the free colored men from America, and of the few whites in the inhospitable clime, after seven long years this former bondsman who had been an inspiration to priests and educators alike was nowhere to be found. The worst was feared.

Nash Williams was a teacher of remarkable gifts. He was a man who, in a country in which fewer than two hundred heathens had been converted in almost twenty years, could lay claim to being responsible for at least fifty of the successes that were reported back to America. The reputation of his mission school was legendary, a fact all the more remarkable given the isolated position it occupied near the known head of the St Paul's River. The few letters he had sent back to his master, whilst full of the usual childish requests for tools, seeds, money and other necessities of life, positively bristled with the spirit of faith, courage and purpose. Then, a little under a year ago, and at the same time as a saddened Edward was mourning the loss of his wife, Nash Williams had conveyed, by means of an intermediary, an abrupt message making it plain that he had no desire ever to hear again from his former master, and informing him that his own communications would now cease. A disturbed and worried Edward, judging it best, at this juncture, not to communicate directly with Nash, had word and money sent by means of a packet out of New York that Madison Williams, an older and somewhat haughty former bondsman, should immediately journey from his place of abode in Monrovia and secure news of Nash's whereabouts and, if possible, his general state of health. Madison had, at an earlier time, borne Nash some feelings of ill-will, having reasoned, and to some degree correctly, that his master's affection for himself had been usurped by this younger interloper. But Edward trusted that the passage of time, and a change of climate, would have healed these old wounds, and that Madison would not resent the task with which he was now being entrusted. However, the letter before Edward bore the disturbing news of Madison's expedition. Not only had Madison failed to locate Nash, but he had been blocked at every turn by native intransigence, their crude vulgarity sometimes taking the form of aggression. The details set forth in Madison's sad letter let it be known that he considered himself fortunate to have escaped with his life intact.

Not that the American Colonization Society was ignorant of the dangers that would accompany their policy of attempting to repatriate former slaves on the west coast of Africa. This was, after all, a continent belonging to the native African, and to nobody else. But they hoped that the natives would see reason, and that the prospect of welcoming home their lost children might help to overcome any unpleasant cultural estrangement that the African heathens might temporarily experience. The American Colonization Society was sure that benefits would accrue to both nations. America would be removing a cause of increasing social stress, and Africa would be civilized by the return of her descendants, who were now blessed with rational Christian minds. And so on January 31st, 1820, the ship *Elizabeth* left New York for the west coast of Africa on what was to be the American Colonization Society's inaugural voyage. Some weeks later, eighty-six former slaves, half of whose number were women and children, arrived unsuccessfully in the British territory of Sierra Leone. Sadly, a mysterious malady, later understood to be malaria, soon dispatched all but a fortunate few of this initial batch of pioneers. Two years later, in 1822, a second and more successful expedition deposited settlers on the Grain Coast, at the part of West Africa that would soon become known as Liberia.

Being chosen for colonization was regarded by most slaves and their masters as reward for faithful service. A skilled worker, who was also a converted Christian with a sound moral base, was considered a prime candidate. But reports from early settlers told stories of great hardships. The initial work of clearing the bush, constructing shelters and building fortifications against native attacks resulted in a heavy toll of life. The wet and miserable climate, which between April and November could produce over two hundred inches of rain, ushered many to an early grave. From December through until March, the poor, unfortunate newcomers, having survived the floods, now labored in unbearably high temperatures, and endured a humidity of stifling proportions. But it was the African fever, or malaria, which most affected the lives of the settlers. The severe chills, producing a sensation of cold as fearful as any American winter, and the accompanying delusions which infected the imagination, combined to introduce a deep misery. No longer were these unfortunate creatures pioneering in the welcoming bosom of their native land, with a clear blue sky for a roof and a fertile soil beneath their dusty feet. They were being tossed upon the stormy seas of fever, and when the storm diminished many found they had been driven clear out of this mortal world.

By the second decade of emigration, very little had changed. Pioneers still arrived, their innocent faces etched with a passionate desire to do God's work, but sadly they soon found themselves unable successfully to weather the twelve-month seasoning period, and friends and relatives were called upon to be the messengers of melancholy intelligence to those they had left behind in America. One who arrived in this period, and one of those most determined to survive and pursue the task that he had been prepared for, was Nash Williams. Neither climate nor native confrontation, disease nor hardship of any manner would deflect him from his proper purpose. Word soon reached his former master that on many occasions he had to be prevailed upon in the harshest terms to cease working in the rain in the best interests of his health. On receiving this news Edward Williams felt moved secretly to reach for his pen and address the first of his two letters to his former slave. A portion of this first letter contained the following words of wisdom:

Before you left America, I reminded you of the sacrifices that our good Lord Jesus Christ made for us all, and urged you to consider the situation of Christianity in this new country that you inhabit. You were kind enough not only to dwell upon my words, but to convey back to me in the form of a letter information as to the unlettered and heathen state of the masses. For this both my good wife, Amelia, and myself are grateful. Such information will no doubt prove vital to those slaves whom we are now preparing, in order that they might one day join you on the pagan coast. However, I am somewhat dismayed to hear (from a source you will no doubt guess) about your continued insistence upon attempting to carry out tasks, without recourse to aid from other fellows, that would strain five men, both physically and mentally, either Christian or native. Christ's sacrifices were many, but surely your acquaintance with the Good Book will have revealed to you that they were calculated. Even He could not do everything in one day. You are fortunate in being blessed with a *fair* mind and strong body and (although I say so myself) doubly fortunate in that your former master was of a progressive persuasion. Do not disappoint me, or yourself, by falling short of the high standards that you have already set yourself. Only yesterday the children gathered about Amelia and asked after your well-being, and then said prayers for you. Our whole experiment depends greatly upon your success. Your resolve may be firm, but we are all flesh and blood. I hope that you understand that I speak to you in order to assist in your development. May I suggest that you study the Good Book for further guidance.

Sadly, this letter was uncovered by Edward's wife, Amelia, and not conveyed. However, never again did Edward receive intelligence that his former bondsman Nash had either disobeyed his instruction, put himself in unnecessary mortal danger, or done anything that might lead Edward once more to consider reaching for the pen and composing lines of disapproval.

In 1841, having received the letter from his former slave Madison, and having fully digested its discomfiting contents, Edward Williams rose from his chair in the drawing-room and immediately set about making plans to journey to Liberia in order that he might determine for himself what had befallen the virtuous Nash. His plan was to travel alone by the first ship that was sailing for the coast, and he foresaw no reason for there to be a delay of any kind. Being now a widower, he would have to endure neither harsh nor reproachful words from his lady wife, Amelia, who would no doubt have been gravely suspicious of the motives which lay behind his projected expedition. At first, and much to Edward's surprise, the idea of this scheme did not win the consent of the officials of the American Colonization Society. Though full of admiration for the enthusiasm of Edward Williams, and sympathetic to the ardor he continued to display towards his black charges, they were at pains to point up to him the many dangers to which he might unwittingly be exposing himself. Edward persisted in his communications with them, and eventually, but only after much altercation, they chose to relent their opposition and grant cautious support. At first they had insisted that the mysterious disappearance of a single settler was something they could reasonably expect to occur on a regular basis. Such was the peril of dispatching good men to heathen shores at the edge of civilization, and encouraging them to make this African land their home. But Edward had argued that to abandon men as remarkable as Nash could only reflect adversely on the future of the Society. He reminded the Society that, on his own initiative, he had borne the not inconsiderable expense of sending this man to college in Virginia, in order that he might be thoroughly prepared and trained for the life of a missionary. And further, he had encouraged all of his former slaves, including Nash, to avoid Monrovia, and like wind-driven seeds to scatter themselves about the land in the hope that there might be a widespread distribution of the message of the Lord. Only Nash had heeded his words. He had settled up-river in native country, having taken to his bosom a good Christian wife from Georgia, one Sally Travis, now deceased. Edward reminded the Society that, together with his wife, Nash had operated the most successful of the mission schools for natives. In fact, Edward had reminded them of this fact at every possible juncture, for, according to his closely argued deposition, this was not simply the sacrifice of one missionary, a victim of untreated fever or ill-advised wanderings into the interior. Edward was adamant that the disappearance of Nash could signal a humiliating defeat for the Society's ideals as a whole, and he was determined to reach the territory of Liberia and investigate matters with his own eyes. Finally, the American Colonization Society, having listened with patience, came to realize that indeed there was more virtue in assisting Edward Williams than in impeding him.

It was customary at this time to set sail from Virginia or New York, but Edward had determined to leave on the first available ship, irrespective of its port of departure. He spread before himself a map of the known world, and stared at the inelegant shape of Africa, which stood like a dark, immovable shadow between his own beloved America and the exotic spectacle of India and the countries and islands of the Orient. He would travel for an undetermined length of time, although he had been led to believe that twenty-eight days was not at all unusual for such a journey. Fortunately, he was already armed with some knowledge of what rigors he might reasonably expect to face, both on the passage and after arrival, through the evidence of those letters from his former slaves which Amelia had permitted him to peruse. They spoke of problems and difficulties which would inevitably tax the health of a man of Edward's fragile constitution, but common sense and restraint would be his guides.

Born in 1780, the son of a wealthy tobacco planter, Edward had inherited his father's estate in his twenty-ninth year, and with it the sum total of three hundred slaves. A rich man of unrivalled wealth, he could simply have luxuriated himself and slipped quietly into a premature retirement, but he also inherited from his father an aversion to the system which had allowed his fortunes to multiply. Edward soon took the unusual initiative of encouraging his slaves to acquire the generally forbidden arts of reading and writing. When, some years after his windfall of slaves, he became aware of the formation of the American Colonization Society, this seemed an ideal opportunity to divest himself of the burden, or at least some part of the burden, of being a slave-owner, a title which ran contrary to his Christian beliefs. His wife, though initially not sharing fully in his unusually philanthropic fervor, had slowly come to tolerate the strange behavior and desires of her husband. But, sadly, she was no more. And now the chief player in his game, the most successful of his Christian blacks, was lost somewhere on the dismal coastline of Africa. Day and night a troubled Edward mused over Nash. Had that dark face, charged with belief and propriety, been somehow changed in the humid and barbarous climate? He could not believe that Africa could have distorted Nash's faith, and encouraged him to turn his back on his God. And why now, after all these years of patience, had he suddenly chosen to break off with his former master? This troubling conundrum, which each night kept Edward awake and tossing first this way and then that, threatened to tear apart his very soul. He knew that he had little choice but to travel to Liberia, not simply to discover the truth surrounding the fate of his Nash, but in order to confirm that his life's work, and more importantly his own life, had been of some worth.

On the evening of November 3rd, 1841, the *Mercury* set sail out of New York harbor. On deck, Edward Williams knelt and prayed both for the soul of his dearly departed Amelia, and for the success of the journey he was embarking upon. As they passed out beyond the stillness of the river and into the sea, he leaned over the rail and watched his beloved America recede from view and eventually vanish behind the horizon. Sadly, within a day of their departure, thick black clouds appeared overhead and they hit upon a terrible storm in which the ceaseless rain cascaded down from a perpetually dark sky. Edward remained below and listened through the planks to the moaning of his fellow passengers, a parcel of Louisiana blacks headed for the coast, who lay about the boards stricken into various stages of mortality. They were a week out of New York, and the storm had still not abated, when the mast came crashing down. The sailors were men of experience, but for some time it appeared as though the ship would have to be abandoned to the wind and waves, for there seemed to be no end to this tempest. All who were able were summoned on deck to help repair the ailing vessel, but by this time Edward had contracted the fever and was unable to bestir himself in any way. He lay below and listened to the painful creaking and straining of the wood, as the squalls grew ever more violent. Mercifully, midway through the second week, the storm finally blew itself out, but soon after the true and unbearable force of the sun's heat was upon them. Long, sunstruck afternoons assailed the ship, the sky forever clear and without even the slightest stain of a cloud, the air still and bereft of any breeze that might flutter a sail or distort the mirror of the sea. The journey was now in danger of becoming prolonged past the supply of food and, more crucially, water. Sadly, despite the efforts of the ship's surgeon, Edward's ghastly condition, his body roaring with fever, showed no sign of improving. The Captain, a man renowned for his sagacity, resigned himself to the inevitable loss of his most illustrious passenger.

At last, on the evening of December 14th, 1841, the *Mercury* limped into the harbor at the British settlement of Freetown, Sierra Leone, the Captain having thought it politic to acquire fresh supplies and immediate medical help for those, like Edward, who lay between life and death. Natives came on board and bore Edward, perspiration flowing down his forehead, his body racked with chills and fever, into a crudely constructed rowing boat. Through the haze of illness Edward could hear, in fact almost taste, the sea, which stretched out all around him, melancholy and still. By straining his half-closed eyes, it was possible for him to discern the shoreline, where torches burned in the moonless dusk. The short journey seemed interminable, and was made worse by the descent of a thick mist which soon turned into a light rain. On reaching Freetown, Edward was clumsily lifted on to a rudimentary cart that was to be pulled by a solitary mule. The black driver yelled at the dispirited beast, and Edward felt the cart lurch, the wheels spin idly in the mud, but the whole contraption remained painfully static. After much bellowing and inconvenience to Edward, he was eventually, by these impossible means, transported to a mission hospital whose only virtue appeared to be the number of white faces which inhabited this otherwise insanitary place. Here Edward lingered for some days, his hand in the hand of his God, until the tide turned and washed him back upon the shores of this earth.

After a week, in which his body grew accustomed to solid foods, and in which he learned how to walk again without aid, Edward was impatient to commence upon the final measure of his journey. It was at this juncture that the British doctor informed him that his ship, the *Mercury*, had set sail without waiting for those passengers who had been discharged. It appeared that some trading dispute had broken out between Sierra Leone and Liberia, which meant that all exchange, commercial or otherwise, between the two territories had, for the time being, been suspended. Apparently, the *Mercury* was not welcome in Sierra Leone as long as she flew openly and with pride the American flag. Edward felt desperate, and made immediate and hourly cross-examination of the doctor as to how he might reach Liberia. He was keen to impress upon this man the seriousness of his intent, but the doctor was powerless to help beyond offering up the suggestion that either Edward attempt the passage overland, or he wait in Sierra Leone for this diplomatic squabble to subside. In response to Edward's enquiries as to the general health of the Liberian experiment, the doctor simply shrugged his shoulders. What could he say? He had never been to Liberia, but neither would he want to travel there. Here, in the Crown Colony of Sierra Leone, he was British. There he would be nothing. He touched Edward lightly on the arm, in that manner which doctors soon accustom themselves to in order that they might assuage the fears of their patients. His advice was to wait. He assured Edward that these disputes tended to be short-lived. There was little to be gained by worrying excessively.

Monrovia, Liberia
September 11th, 1834

Dear Beloved Benefactor,

I am exceedingly happy to take up my pen and embrace this precious opportunity of addressing you a few lines. I trust that God in His mercy will spare you to read these words and many more. My family and I were blessed with a safe and prosperous passage over the briny deep, and delivered safely to this African land. Accordingly, I thank God that I remain alive to have the pleasure of writing to you from distant shores. Though we are separated by wide waters and steep mountains, you, my dear father, are forever with me in my mind. That we were only seventeen days at sea speaks of the fine weather that we were fortunate enough to have bestowed upon us. Further, the ship happily improved her numbers, for there was one birth at sea. This is the first opportunity I have had to send to you a humble communication since our arrival here. I do so in the hope that my crude lines might find both yourself and your wife in fine health, thanks be to God. We are all well, with the exception of young York, upon whom the sea-sickness vented itself with uncommon fury, and whose childish body has yet to recover equilibrium. Fortunately, my wife Sally is of a more rigorous constitution and dutifully nurses him while I attend to more pressing matters. Among the other emigrants of our ship with whom you will be familiar, only old Nancy and big Mabel were ill at ease on the sea. The rest are somewhat well, and earnestly salute your noble person, although many are now touched up with the African fever.

Galloway Williams is dead. He died only a day since. His wife, Constance, who arrived in this country aboard the same packet as myself, was only last week delivered of a fine son, but alas the Lord saw it fit to take the child. He could not have taken it at a better time, the child being but an infant, but He soon after took to Him Constance also, to be with the child, and now Galloway to afford his wife some support in the hereafter. The Lord giveth and the Lord taketh, blessed be the name of the Lord. The burden you placed upon us of repeating the Ten Commandments, which we considered a form of punishment, has proved of the utmost importance in meeting the pain of these trying times. As a father you cared for us, and we hope that the Lord will reward you for your kindness.

Liberia is a fine place to live in. I was at first astonished to see the bushes that grow in the streets, and the boldness of the nature all about, but my person is now accustomed to these strange sights. Thank God I have been spared to reach here in good health and by His permission do still enjoy it. The town of Monrovia is well-watered and timbered, and if a person could have a little capital he would do very well. A colored person can enjoy his liberty in this place, for there exists no prejudice of color and every man is free and equal. Although, dear father, I am greatly desirous of seeing you again before we leave this world, I doubt if I shall ever consent to return again to America. Liberia, the beautiful land of my forefathers, is a place where persons of color may enjoy their freedom. It is the home for our race, and a country in which industry and perseverance are required to make a man happy and wealthy. Its laws are founded upon justice and equality, and here we may sit under the palm tree and enjoy the same privileges as our white brethren in America. Liberia is the star in the East for the free colored man. It is truly our only home.

Sadly, there is amongst some emigrants a tendency for lying about and doing nothing. True, it is very hot hereabouts, but after the industrious man achieves acclimatization, there is no excuse for not applying himself with unwearied dedication. Those who won't work and who get along by stealing are becoming something like the natives.

Of the money you lodged for me with Mr Gray, I have not seen one cent of it as the *gentleman* denies all knowledge of the matter. Why he does so I cannot say, but it is so. I informed him that as I am determined to obey your instructions and proceed to the country in order that I might establish a school, I shall require capital. He countered with the knowledge that it would be a deathly and ruinous undertaking to go up there, the native population being uncivilized so that during sickness with fever I would most certainly be robbed of whatever articles of value I might possess. Indeed, the scantiness of the Christian population beyond Monrovia is somewhat surprising, but I am resolved to lead by example and carry the word of God to the heathens.

My resolution has occasioned something of a rift to develop between my good wife, Sally, and myself. She remains steadfast in her belief that the Lord, having blessed me with a reasonable portion of health, will surely regard the exposing of my person to the rigors of the country as both eccentric and foolish. Her concern was initiated by the most recent bleeding from the nose that I suffered. The climate agrees with my health in many respects, but in some respects it does not. This rainy season that we presently endure will, I fear, eventually prove the most injurious portion of the year with reference to my constitution. I have already suffered several bleeding attacks, but this most recent one, which commenced shortly before noon last Sabbath morning, lasted two full hours. It then ceased its red passage, only to recommence at six in the evening, whereupon it determined to set its course clear through until midnight. Sally offered up a volley of prayers to Him that orders all things to His own glory, and clearly He set a favorable ear to her pleading, for the discharge and discomfort soon ceased their labors.

Father, some emigrants hereabouts, having previously embraced religion and displayed the patience necessary to resist the temptation of the evil one, now dance to the discordant tune of drunkenness. I am, however, happy to report that not only my wife but those of our immediate acquaintance remain steadfast in our beliefs. I have attended worship at every opportunity, and find the people very friendly, as does my wife. Her anxieties concerning our impending journey into the interior merely reflect her unease upon receiving alarming stories of the primitive state of affairs beyond this Monrovia. Rest assured, dear father, for she remains a true Christian.

Please give my true love to all my friends, and urge them to conduct themselves in such a manner that they might reasonably expect to meet me in Heaven, that is if I am not fortunate once again to lay eyes upon them in this world. In particular, Aunt Sophie, George, Hannah, Peter Thornton, Fanny Gray, Aggy and Charlotte, Miss Mathilda Danford, Henry, Randolph and Nancy. Above all, please give my love to my dear mother, but you who have done more for me than natural father, or any other, must keep the greater portion of my affections for yourself. Please read what follows in the presence of all your servants so that they might know from one who is free, and in no manner in bondage, thus in no way obligated to express such sentiments, what quality of master they are blessed with: –

There are those servants who, having served their master for more than fifty years, are not rewarded with their liberty, but are instead sold at auction to the highest bidder. How good the Almighty is to have blessed you with such a master as this, for there is not another under Heaven such as your master. I have found since my arrival in Africa that many of your master's ways and fashions, burdensome though they were while in America, have served to form the basis of my character and have enabled me to survive this seasoning period with relative ease. Under his tutelage my understanding has been enlightened, so I beg of you servants to pay attention, attend school, and seize the opportunity to learn, for not all masters are so inclined to place the wisdom and good sense of the Bible at the disposal of their colored property.

And now to you, dear Father. If they should refuse to attend school or heed your words, you must punish them, whether young or old, for as I have already observed in these parts, too much pleasure brings on sin and ruin. I humbly remind you once more that you should convey my love to my own dear mother, who has been happy in your service for the greater part of her ancient life. Should she be visited by a change of heart, and desire to live out her final years in the bosom of Africa, or should she simply move past useful labor, I trust that despite her unlettered state you would allow her liberty to undertake such a journey. Dear father, I have recently read again the very kind letter you gave me as I set out for college some years ago. It gives me more pleasure than I can express to think that I have one such as you as both advisor and friend, and as I pursue my calling of teacher, I pray that the Lord will not abandon me, for without Him we are nothing and can do nothing. I praise His holy name that I was fortunate enough to be born in a Christian country, amongst Christian parents and friends, and that you were kind enough to take me, a foolish child, from my parents and bring me up in your own dwelling as something more akin to son than servant. Truth and honesty is great capital, and you instilled such values in my person at an early age, for which I am eternally grateful to you and my Creator. Had I been permitted simply to run about, I would today be dwelling in the same robes of ignorance which drape the shoulders of my fellow blacks. Words cannot express my gratitude for the care you displayed towards me during my younger days, for as the Scripture says, train up a child in the way he should go, and when he is old he will not depart from it. I am ever hopeful that we might see each other's faces again in the flesh, but if the Lord has ordained it otherwise, then I trust that we shall be amongst that number that John saw surrounding the Throne of the Lamb, where sorrow, pain and death are neither felt nor feared no more.

I look up to you as a son to a kind father and will ever expect assistance as long as we hear from each other.

Presently I stand in need of help from you by the first chance, for I have not received one cent from your man, and the Society agents hereabouts seem determined to clasp what little there is to their own bosoms. Will you be so kind as to send me some mustard seed and some flax seed for stomach complaint? Father, will you please send me a pair of spectacles for my own use, and a further pair for my wife, Sally? I am very much in want of clothing; you may send some coarse cloth, and shoes. Further, my wife begs of you a spinning wheel and cards to keep her employed. I plead with you, sir, on behalf of myself, to aid us. The amount of four to five hundred dollars would be of little consequence to a man such as yourself, but in this hard country it can overnight alter a man's fortunes. Anything further that you choose to send, whether dry goods or provisions, will be very acceptable, for this is no different from other new countries. Mr John Sawyer asks if you would be so kind as to send a pair of drum heads. He says he entrusted them to the care of the Captain, but they got wet and the mice made a hole in them. This tale is his own.

I wish you to be so kind as to try to remember my best regards to all enquiring friends. You might remind them to try and serve the Lord, in the hope that He might provide a way for them to reach these lands of civil and religious privileges. At present I have no more to say about myself which can be interesting to you. So, dear sir, receive the kindest wishes of this humble servant. I bid you adieu and do remain your most sincere and affectionate son until death. Dear Father, I trust that the Lord will continue to guard and protect you from all harm and dangers in this sinful world. My prayer to God is that He will bless and preserve you long in life, and at death – having finished your course and performed the work assigned to you – receive you into Heaven where you may sit at the right of God. I hope we shall meet there to part no more. Your affectionate son.

Nash Williams

Saint Paul's River, Liberia
October 22nd, 1835

My Dear Father,

This letter leaves me in not a good state of health. I have had the fever, but now embrace the present opportunity of writing a few lines, my intention being to forward them to you by means of the Liberia packet which sails in a few days. I sincerely hope that my letter might find yourself and your wife in better circumstances than those which presently assault my person. It is to be hoped that you may live a long number of years, blessed by the Lord in many ways, and do more good on earth.

I am no longer of Monrovia, having relocated into the heart of the country. Before I left that place I wrote to you on two occasions by Mr Andrews, and once more directly, but I suppose my communication was transmitted into several hands and you did not get it, which is often the way. You know best. I am unable to give you intelligence as to the progress of others for we live so far apart, some few in this direction, but most in the capital town. I am truly now a pioneer of sorts. I am striving to do all the good I can amongst these natives, who form a most dominant majority. To this end I am even speaking a little of their crude dialect, which is very hard to learn. I can, if truth be told, understand it better than I can speak it, but with practice this state of affairs will regulate itself. Since receiving the land, I have not had the opportunity of doing much, but I have made some significant improvements. The first of these has involved the construction of a primitive school building under the watchful supervision of myself. The natives worked with glee, and now this heathen village has a mission school where I am able to instruct in writing intelligibly, in the Bible, in arithmetic, and in geography. I labor purposefully as a teacher in the hope that these heathens may one day soon become lettered. Come Sabbath, our school is transformed, by the simple method of my decree, into a small Baptist church where I preach and provide the multitudes with the opportunity of hearing the Gospel.

The second of my significant improvements relates to efforts to till the soil. I have made a start of farming, and cleared some fifteen to twenty acres of my land, and have planted it down with coffee trees, and cotton, and potatoes, and cassava, and much more kinds of plants such as this Africa affords. I have been led to understand that this land is exceedingly rich, and will eventually yield up everything in abundance. That is, if the seed is properly planted, and taken care of by keeping it clear of grass and weeds. With common industry, a man can raise more of everything than he can use, and have much to sell besides. I soon hope to be in the prosperous situation where I might expect to exchange the results of my labors upon the land for foreign produce. I am led to believe that a little of this trading occurs in Monrovia, but I am now, for good or ill, a man of the country. I will enclose with this letter some paw-paw seeds which are dried in ashes. Perhaps they are cured incorrectly. If they do not produce the required result, I shall procure a variety, fix them as they should be, and forward them by the next chance.

I will share with you a few words about the animals in this place. I have been visited by a cunning leopard in the past few days, who has taken off with both goats and hogs, two of each if my count is correct. I watched out for this creature but could never see him. Leopards often visit Monrovia, where they walk the streets at night committing great depredations. Here, far removed from what passes as civilization, their task is made considerably easier. Recently, I killed a snake of nine feet in length, and the proud possessor of a tremendous girth. He was black and red in color and basking on the margin of the river with an air of unfettered superiority. In addition, we have quite a variety of handsome birds, although their names still elude me.

As you know, an industrious man who is free from debt of any kind can live in tolerable comfort, yet when a man becomes involved in debt, whether it be his fault or not, he often suffers much from this circumstance. A little aid from you, dear Father, would do me much good at this time. 'Giving doth not impoverish.' I would be glad to plague you a little to see if you would send me out some trade goods that I might in the due passage of time answer with coffee, ginger, arrowroot and other materials that I will presently crop from my land. Good white shirting, shoes, stockings, tobacco, flour, port, mackerels, molasses, sugar, and a small flitch of bacon and other little trifles as you find convenient to send. Though cotton is raised in this country, there is at present not so much as to be able to manufacture clothes. If you could send some good strong cloth in order that shirts, pantaloons and other clothes be made available for the modesty of the natives hereabouts, I should be most grateful. A half-keg of 10*d*. nails and a half-keg of 4*d*. nails would be very acceptable. I also need some borax but cannot get it in this country. Please mark the box with my full name and direct it to the Saint Paul's River settlement, where full knowledge and appreciation of my Christian work grows with each merciful day.

Since the passing of my wife and child, my wants are few, and of course they are easily supplied in this land of darkness. I have nothing to fear. America is, according to my memory, a land of milk and honey, where people are not easily satisfied. Things that seemed to me then to hold so much value are now, in this new country, and in my new circumstances, without value. All that I now wish for is enough to give me comfort and some small happiness whilst I dwell in this world, for I have learned, by means of sad experience, and by close study of the scripture, that we carry nothing out of this world when we go hence. In addition to my latest bout with the African fever, I have also a complaint in the hip which you may remember occurred before I left America as a consequence of being thrown from an unruly horse. I hope to meet in Heaven with my dearly departed Sally and my only boy, York, and thereafter dwell with them for ever. This blessed hope, to meet where there will be no further trouble, no vainglorious toil, no more parting, and to sing the praises of God and the Lamb for ever and ever! Surely the religion of Christ is my greatest comfort in this dark world. I pray that the Lord may bless, protect and defend you through life by his unerring counsel, and that when the voyage of life is over and He has no more for you to do on earth, He will take you to live with Him in glory.

My glorious asylum in Liberia remains under the protection of a wise God, who promises to be a God of all nations, provided they obey and dutifully serve Him. Although a country with some inconveniences, there remain many privileges to be enjoyed, for any man can live here that will work, although the quality of man that is these days choosing to make this new country his home leaves me with some cause for concern. Two months past I paid a visit to Monrovia to try to force the hand of that scoundrel who clings to what is rightfully mine. There I encountered others of a similar mind to Mr Gray, unchristian in their behavior and vulgar in their demeanor, whose only visible occupation seemed to be to prey upon poor unfortunate creatures such as myself. True, there are many fine, charitable societies abounding in Monrovia, and churches of all denominations, but I fear that unless the agents of the Society exercise a firmer grip, the affairs of this young country might yet slide out of course. I chanced to spend a part of one morning in conversation with Ellis Thornton Williams, of whom you no doubt have fond memory. You will be pleased to hear report that he has settled in the country to the north of our capital town, and cleared land and planted a fine crop of rice, corn and cassavas. He has on his farm about two dozen Congo boys, the greater number of them having been rescued from the dungeons of a slaver by a British man-of-war. He has very near ninety acres under cultivation, is blessed with a brace of fine sons, and is in tolerably fine health. This chance meeting served to lift my spirits, for by this time I was convinced that the character of all our Monrovian people of color was rotting in this African heat. My conclusion is that a man's spirit and wholesomeness is more pleasantly watered and nourished among the heathen natives of the country, for there one can daily observe the evidence of Christian work which marks out the superiority of the American life over the African.

Now a few words to my dear beloved mother which I trust you will be kind enough to read to her:–

Dear Mother, your advice to me when a child remains in my breast as fresh and as full of wisdom as the day you delivered it. I pray that God will spare you to behold your son's face once more. I am sorry to inform you of the death of Solomon Charles, whom I believe was known to you in earlier times. Beyond this sad occurrence, there is little further in the way of news. When Sally was asked by your son, 'How stands it between thee and thy God?' her answer was, 'All is clear. I am willing to go.' Yes, these were her words, but two days before her death. Mother, how stands it with Uncle Daniel? Is he still living, or should I expect to meet him in Heaven? Since I have been in this country, I have been stricken with the African fever on many occasions. I am still not full with health, but I am somewhat improved. Yesterday I moved amongst the natives who labor about my land. They are good workers, although they require a stern and watchful supervision. Now dear mother, I must come to a close in the knowledge that God and Mr Edward Williams will take care of you. Give my respects to all, white and black. I remain your affectionate son, Nash Williams.

Dear Father, I wish you to be so kind as to remember my best respects to my old fellow servants, and any other enquiring friends. Hoping that they will behave themselves to you. If they fail to do so, you must remind them of the many kindnesses that you have showered upon my humble person. You are ever present in my affections. Perhaps you might dispatch some books for my school. Valuable readers are a most necessary part of my mission. Also, I would be glad to learn my true age. When I write again I shall try and send you some curiosities. I subscribe myself a servant of God, and the friend of my fellow men. As this letter will reach you, I hope, by Christmas, I will conclude by wishing your good lady wife and yourself a Merry Christmas, and sincerely hope that you both enjoy many more. Farewell, dear sir, and receive the kindest wishes of your humble servant and affectionate son.

Nash Williams

Saint Paul's River, Liberia
March 10th, 1839

My Dear Father,

I am taking this favorable opportunity of writing a few hasty lines in the hope that they might be conveyed to you by the departure of the vessel *Mathilda* which will presently leave these shores for America. Your letter reached me on Feb. 5th, and was read with great joy. I declaimed it aloud to the people here and its kind contents caused some tears to flow. I am sad to learn that your brother has been called to his long and happy home, but reassured by the information that his was only a short illness of ten to twelve hours. That your good lady wife, Amelia, still enjoys rude health must be a great blessing to you. I would be happy if you could give her my regards, and inform her that there are many in this dark country of Liberia for whom she represents the highest achievement in womankind.

Why, dear Father, you chose to ignore my previous letters, you do not indicate. I must assume that this represents your either not receiving them, or your finding their contents so ignorant and poor in expression that you rightly deemed them unworthy of response. Whatever your reasoning, I am overjoyed to receive news of my friends and family, with the one obvious exception. What news for yourself? Mr Lambert has taken an Alabama woman by the name of Bertha, and her son Prince, to live with him in his brick house in Monrovia. It seems he is doing well in business, although this illiterate woman chooses to behave herself improperly. And perhaps you have already heard, by means of some other source, that old brother Taylor and sister Nancy have both lost all religion. The former has in addition turned out to be a great and scandalous drunkard. He is accused of habitual intoxication, much nocturnal revelling, lewdness, and in fact everything that characterizes the immoral man. You may correctly deduce from the above that I have severed all connections with this man. They say that his decline was occasioned by the misfortune of losing his youngest son to a sore mouth.

Of the two new arrivants that you recommended to my care, first good news and then sad. Young Solomon Williams is now comfortably situated here with us. He is working the fields for seventy-five cents a day in the hope that he might one day purchase some farmer's tools to commence farming for himself. When he first approached my presence, I had no knowledge of him, save the name he bore. After a little discourse I recognized the fellow. At first he tested his freedom, and acted like a young horse out of the stable, but I soon reined him in. He is now learning his trade finely, and is upon the whole a very proper boy. He suits me well, and may one day (if he continues in a sober fashion) make a useful man for our young country. Of the second arrivant, only sad news. After surviving a difficult voyage of forty-nine days, marred by an outbreak of smallpox which took the lives of some thirty persons, he soon departed, but his end was peace. He was taken sick on a Monday and his end was Wednesday. His illness, though severe, was of only three days' duration when it terminated fatally, his chief complaint being of a pain in the head. He lay in Monrovia and, according to sources, the Reverend visited him each day, and questioned him concerning his soul's salvation, and whether the way from earth to glory was clear or not, to which he would always answer the same, that his hopes were anchored in Jesus Christ. He was, come Wednesday, perfectly sensible of his death as he fell asleep in Jesus's arms, never more to have earthly communion with our kind, trusting to that day when we may meet again and grasp hands in friendship in our Father's kingdom where there shall be no further parting to endure.

You are not aware perhaps that I have recently established myself and my school in a new settlement. It is somewhat further up the same Saint Paul's River, but located in a very good place. I continue to make all the improvements I can, and I have quiet hopes for the future. I have now fourteen boys in school and two girls, all of whom are making some progress in reading the word of God. They are all native children, and I willingly labor amongst these little heathens, doing all I can according to your wishes. Last November I took a young American woman, a recent emigrant from Maryland, as my assistant and teacher. But alas she was soon sacrificed to the climate and called home to rest. I have every reason to believe that her journey was a peaceful one. Hers was the third death in the mission in a matter of weeks. We lost a boy with consumption, his malady lingering for a cruel length of time. The other unfortunate one died speedily, being seized with stomach pains at five in the morning, yet he caused such a commotion as to raise the whole village. By dawn he was no more, but his sad demise convinced a handful of our *scholars* to run off, for the native people among whom we live are still very superstitious. If someone dies suddenly, they are sure that somebody must have bewitched them, and off they will go to the grand devil man of the village who will, in exchange for some small trifle, tell them who it was that bewitched the person that died. This person will then be fed some poison in order to dispatch him for his wrongful deed. This appears to me not an entirely unjust method of administering justice, and one from which we of the so-called civilized world might learn something valuable.

Indeed, the natives are a much-maligned people in this dark and benighted country. Some of our less respectable emigrants find cause to torment and exploit these creatures, rather than try to fuse into their souls the values of American civilization with which their good masters labored to anoint them. In our neighboring settlement, a Mr Charles, an American, his money grown short due to the ruin of his smallholding near Monrovia, *borrowed* two native boys, informing their fathers that he was going to teach them English. Instead, he cruelly carried them to a slave factory and sold them for the equivalent of twelve dollars. In conversing with the natives, I often ask them how it is they cannot read and write like the white man (they call us all white man), and I generally receive reply that their gods had asked them to choose between the land and their livestock, or books, and they had chosen the former. At this juncture I often protest, and talk about the ingenious nature of native embroidery and craft, my contention being that our God has blessed the native with as much sense as any white man if only they would put this in exercise. The native is generally resigned to finally admitting that this *white man* does talk true, for I think they have become much fond of me.

Sadly, not all *masters* will converse in such a manner with these natives. Only last year, in an attack spurred on by revenge for native depredations upon settlers, the strongest and most populous native town on this part of the coast was taken, burned, and the natives powerfully routed, for they can be very savage when they think they have the advantage. At times like this, it is strange to think that these people of Africa are called our ancestors, for with some of them you may do all you can but they still will be your enemy. For many months now, there has been no sound of war amongst the neighboring tribes, and the affairs of the country appear quite smooth. We are all truly grateful that the war horn is heard no more, and the natives continue to display some friendship, for in this way we might avoid foolish loss of life. It was intended that Africa should be a land of freedom, for where else can the man of color enjoy his liberty? Not in Haiti or in Canada. This land of our forefathers, where many delicious fruits grow, is determined still to attract the noblest minds. If you hear any speaking disrespectful of it, I would be grateful if you would tell them to hush their mouths, for a lazy man, be he a gentleman or otherwise, will not prosper in any country should he determine that he will not work. Further, in this republic the practice is to address me as *Mr Williams* and not *Boy*. There are a few white people out here, and they are polite, moving to one side and touching their hats. In Monrovia, I have had occasion to call at their dwellings and to range over the subjects of the day, religious and otherwise. The white man never calls me by anything but my name. I am *Mr Williams*.

Sadly, I do not enjoy the same happy intercourse with the black emigrants hereabouts. Some emigrants, who styled themselves as lay ministers of the Gospel, asked permission to enter my new settlement and to preach the word of God. They gained admission with my blessing, and with that of the agents of the colony, as my present settlement lies beyond the furthest position in the interior to which we are generally encouraged to travel. However, our relationship soon soured as they took pleasure in forever recounting the number of hopeful converts who resided with them in their previous settlement, and how these converts were now filled with the Holy Ghost, their confidences awakened, and how they had become more friendly by the day. It was as though they made this continual assault upon my person in order to insult what they assumed to be the so-far modest achievements of my present mission. It appeared that amongst their biblical attachments were Methodist, Baptist and Presbyterian sentiments, and that so ill-schooled were they that clearly they could not distinguish one variety from the next, but I refrained from raising this subject. That they had truly embraced religion, that they displayed the patience to resist the temptations of the evil one, I did not doubt, but their criticism of my *dictatorial* manner and their suggestions on the moral value of my behavior proved too much, and, soon after their arrival, I ordered them to withdraw. They did so, but not before they had spread malicious gossip abroad that a child recently delivered to a native woman bore a strong and suspicious likeness to one Nash Williams. I countered, suggesting that this would appear only natural in that we shared the same ancestry, but in the minds of some emigrant farmers, a brace

33

of whose number chose to leave my settlement, it appeared that the seeds of damage that these *ministers* had so wilfully scattered, were now finally beginning to bear some fruit.

Soon after the expulsion of my *ministers of the Gospel*, it became clear that I would have to look for one who was willing and able to help me in my labors amongst the heathen flock. To this end, I traveled to Monrovia, where I engaged a young lady who was recently arrived from America, being formerly the property of a Mr Young of Pennsylvania. She informed me that she had come out to Africa last September, and had passed through her acclimatizing fevers very well. She seemed, to my eyes, ably prepared for the business of mission work, having been raised up in one of the best Christian families of America. The young lady returned with me up the Saint Paul's River, and although clearly a little disenchanted at first casting a glance over our small Christian empire, her eyes soon accustomed themselves to the more primitive conditions of the interior, so much so that she now acts and behaves as though she has known nothing else. I expect to be wedlocked to her in a short time, if life lasts and all things hold out. Perhaps you would be so kind as to send out something to start on in the way of making a living as a newly married couple, for you know that my time is not consumed in speculative affairs which are likely to result in my achieving worldly gains. The colony is not now as flourishing as it was, trade is dull, and the past season very unfavorable to the growth of all our main staffs of life.

As respects coffee, these days it sells at fifty cents per pound, but it grows wild and often natives and monkeys take it. Loaf sugar sells at twenty-eight dollars per hundred. Fresh beef will fetch twelve cents per pound. Cattle sell at fifteen dollars each, sheep two dollars, goats a dollar, hogs at different prices according to size from one dollar to fifteen, ducks at one dollar each, and fowls at two dollars per dozen. Laborers can be hired for twenty cents per day, and a person might have good common people to work the ground and make it as productive as that in America. But one word of explanation as to why such as I, who plant and work the land with application, still struggle, is to be found in the maxim that it is several years before farm land will pay. It has always been so, and so it will remain. There are some that have come to this place that have got rich, and done well, by using the natives as slaves. But invariably this means that the poor, unskilled people who come from America have no chance to make a living, for the natives do all the work. There is little chance for farming at Monrovia, for it is all stones. Out here, in the interior, there is good land, but unless one wishes to administer one's province in an uncharitable and cruel manner, the times are hard for all who would till the soil honestly.

Dear Father, perhaps you will please send me one bonnet and an umbrella, if you please. And some cloth to make one white frock, as there is none to be found in this country. These things will not prove difficult for you to get, for there is plenty in America and nothing here. Can you please send some valuable books, such as history, and a dictionary, and writing paper and quills or steel pens. Also flour and pork, and other articles you may think will be of service to me, including a hoe, an axe, some trowels and some hammers. If you, or any of your kind family to whom I am already under so many obligations, shall send anything for me, it shall not be misplaced charity, for provision is scarce.

I was very sorry to hear that my mother was dead, but I take great consolation in knowing that she has gone home to rest and we have nothing to do but to prepare to meet her. I am further consoled by your heartbroken intelligence that she died with Jesus in her soul and Heaven in her view, and her confidence well-anchored in the Lord. I have been in Africa a long time and I wish to come home as soon as possible. I wish you to write to me by the first emigrant vessel and let me know on what terms I can come back, and if I will be interrupted by white people. William Young left here shipped aboard a storeship, and I have heard from him twice. He is in Cincinnati acting as a porter in a merchant's store or warehouse, so it must be possible to successfully return. I would like very much to see you once in the flesh, and this may prove my last chance to cross the Atlantic. It is naturally my full intention to return to Liberia, for it is the best country for the black man that is to be found on the face of the earth. Older nations, with different styles of government, may be slow to acknowledge all that is due to us for whom the golden sun of liberty is newly rising. But Liberia is doing her part in improving human affairs, and stands now tall and proud with other regions of the civilized world.

Will you please be so kind as to let my friends know that I am well? I would inform them myself, but I am no longer sure of their circumstances. I think they would come over were they not afraid of the fever, but every person that comes to this country must naturally go through a course of sickness before they can expect to enjoy health. I wish you to be so kind as to remember my best respects to Lucy and Fanny Thornton, should you see them, and any enquiring friends. I intended to send some of all kinds of seeds on the first chance I have. I do not recollect of our losing anyone, besides those already mentioned, since you last had the pleasure of hearing from me, and all who know of you join with me in thanking you for your unspeakable kindness and goodness towards us which shall never be forgotten. It will not surprise you to learn that Mary Williams Lewis still distributes tracts on temperance, and remains an advocate for the cause of refraining from the use of ardent spirits. Those that take the pledge under her guidance are not known to take one more gill of spirit, for her doctrines are so-framed as to make the believer steadfast in the knowledge that he does this not only for himself, but for his country.

You must write to me by the first opportunity. I would send you some fruit, but the passage being expected to be long, I thought it would certainly spoil before it reached you. When I write again I will try to send some curiosities. You must excuse my bad writing as it is late. You give away no hints, but I really think some hard feelings against me on your part forms the reason I have received just one letter from you up until this present time. You know I will write to you as long as I can find a piece of paper. I beg to close by subscribing myself to be sincerely yours in the bonds of affection. I remain yours in love.

Nash Williams

Saint Paul's River, Liberia
Oct. 2nd, 1840

Dear Father,

I trust that these few hasty lines which I set down with respect find you in good health and fine spirits. Why your heart remains hard against me is a mystery which has caused me emotions of great distress. But so it must be. I can never guide your hand. I was greatly disappointed on the arrival of the last emigrant vessel by not receiving a single line from you. You chose to comment, in your only letter to this date, that you still have affection. But why do I not receive letters more often? I am so situated that I cannot see every vessel that comes on the coast, but my name and settlement are broadly known in this region. I like this place very well, but my greatest desire is that I may see you once more in this world. I have followed your counsel as much as possible. You need not be afraid that I shall forget or neglect them.

Did I tell you of my partiality to a young woman hereabouts? After a short courtship I put my addresses to her, and I expect to be somewhat true to her till I die. We were married on the first of March, she being a native woman, and one of the best in Africa. She faithfully discharges the office of mother to a child I possess by another, less successful, connection, and she remains an industrious woman who performs all the duties relative to house-keeping, including making clothes for her *family*. This *family*, above whom I reign as head, join me in sending love to their good father whom they have never seen. My son, whom I have taken the liberty of naming Edward in the hope that he might emulate your esteemed self, will soon be in need of materials to help speed his skills in reading and writing. You will therefore send me something. Anything you may choose to send will be acceptable, and the sum of three hundred dollars, being of no consequence to a man of your wealth, would suffice. I would be very thankful for some newspapers, and if you wish I will send to you a few of ours. I hope, dear Father, that you will send me a few working tools such as axes and hoes, for the like are very useful, but very hard to get here.

The fever in these parts is not so bad now as it used to be, for it would seem that the older the place gets, and the more it is cultivated, the better the fever is. Having long passed through the acclimatizing process, and having watched others do so with equal success, I am glad that I can say that I love this country more than I did at first. The seasons here remain quite different from those in my old country, yet the weather seems to get cooler. This year we have been blessed with little rain, and the sun has parched up most of all of the crops in the fields, so if you would be so kind as to send me out something, I would feel much obliged. Anything, I do not mind what it is, for I feel sure that it will make a valuable contribution.

Farming is now our main occupation, the numbers at the mission school having fallen off in a dramatic manner. I have my fields planted with potatoes, arrowroot, cassava, and considerable corn. In addition, I have a large number of cotton bushes, and a variety of other vegetables. I have also planted a large piece in rice, and together with the natives work from morning till sunset clearing and planting. I should be much obliged to you if you would send me a mill, for I have tried to cut a stone for that purpose, but found it beyond me. I am not in such a prosperous situation as might be expected, for it remains difficult to exchange produce for foreign produce, and besides, we make up just enough to sustain us from starvation. I have fowls in plenty, of all kinds. I have also hogs and goats. My horned cattle are only now beginning to increase, and some of the more skilled natives have, under my influence, made fences to secure them. They would, before this, often run out into the woods where they would quickly become lost. Keeping this rich land in order, and clean of grass and weeds, is my main task. But any man who will use common industry can raise much that he will eventually employ.

If, dear Father, these lines should find you in the land of the living, I will be more than glad to hear from you. I have written many letters to you at different times across the breadth of the last few years, and yet you seem reluctant to engage with me. I have come to the conclusion that you have repudiated me for reasons that perhaps owe their origins to some form of shame. Is there perhaps someone who has poisoned your mind against me? If these lines should find you in health, please return me an answer by the shortest way. My pleas with you to aid me, on behalf of all of this settlement, have been ill-received, for you have made nothing available to ease my present circumstances. Like all new countries, this is a very hard one, and some kindness on your part would have been pleasing to me. Should you have chosen to send me seeds of all description, I would have gladly made some use of them. I have given you full accounts of this place, so you can be in no doubt as to the often troubling nature of affairs hereabouts. That you have chosen to ignore my request that I might once more visit America to pay respects to my departed mother, and to cast my eyes upon old friends, has caused my heart to suffer in a great deal of pain. I have little opportunity for intercourse with familiar emigrants in these parts, for most of those who know of you are scattered all about the country, some few up here, but most down in the capital. So daily I wonder about those names across the water who, hearing no news, I constantly fear may have already departed this life.

Only last week I chanced to go into Monrovia in order that I might visit with old friends, both white and black. But not only could I not discern any news, it would appear that my present domestic arrangements have caused some offense to those who would hold on to America as a beacon of civilization, and an example of all that is to be admired. Are we not in Africa? This is what I constantly asked of the blacks. But it appeared they felt I merely sought to justify

my *native* style of living. I counter-rallied and made it plain
that I have nothing to justify, for amongst the emigrants I
am indisputably the proudest holder of my race, but I soon
found myself effectively shunned by my fellow Americans,
many of whom privately mock African civilization whilst
outwardly aping the fashion and posture of persons returned
home. I realized that it would be beneficial for my health
were I to cease conversation, withdraw, and return for ever
to the safety of my Saint Paul's River settlement.

Sad to report, but before my retreat from the capital I
was able to ascertain that these days the chief topic of
conversation is that ancient immovable, slavery. Hardly a
week passes on this coast of Africa without some report of a
sea-bound slaver, and its unfortunate cargo, who have been
afforded protection by the unfurling of the Star Spangled
Banner. Without the hoisting of this emblem, the British
man-of-wars would quickly, and happily, take these ships
captive and liberate their black inhabitants. To most colored
men, who reside here in liberty, and would expect liberty
to encompass all of Africa, this dark land of our forefathers,
this American protectionism is a disgrace to our dignity, and
a stain on the name of our country. The hoisting of some
other banner would be scarcely less insulting, but that they
choose to sport our national flag, this is surely too much.
But sadly, there is still more to be said on this subject of
slavery. It appears that slave-dealers are establishing slave
factories within the territory of Liberia, cunningly situating
them further down the coast in the hope of avoiding prying
eyes. The Governor recently ordered one such villain away,
telling him he had no right to deal in slaves in that territory,
and instructing him under threat of penalty that he must
remove his factory in so many days. However, contrary
to his agreement, he would not do so, and so the factory
was broken up and forty puncheons of rum turned loose
on the ground. There are those in Monrovia who profit
handsomely from this *business*, and who would choose to
ignore the existence of such evil deeds and their correction,

but the problems of slavery continue to plague us, yes, even here in the bosom of liberty.

The rains are still with us, and the sky continues to open its heart and shed tears upon all the known earth. Master, you took me into your house as a young boy and instructed me in the ways of civilized man. Under your tutelage, I acquired whatever rude skills I now possess in the art of reading and writing, and more besides. Why have you forsaken me? There are many things I cannot discuss with my native wife, for it would be improper for her to share with me the memories of what I was before. I am to her what she found here in Africa. If this is to be goodbye, then let it be with love and respect in equal portion. I must close these hasty lines by saying I remain your affectionate son.

Nash Williams

Just when Edward's recovery appeared complete, he was seized again by another severe fever and the accompanying shivering. He dragged his wretched body back to the safety of his bed, and, as the British doctor applied a cold towel to his head, he closed his bloodshot eyes. Sadly, Edward's stubborn fever refused to break, and merciful sleep eluded him as his mind ranged back and forth. When sleep did come it was soon destroyed by demons which prodded at his memory as though it were an open wound. Accordingly, at night he chose instead to lie perfectly still, the towel now hot and burning his brow, his stubbled aspect irritating him to the point of madness, and he simply stared out of the window and up into the black African sky. The thick heat of this devil's climate clung to him like a woven blanket, and he was constantly visited by that unwelcome guest, thirst. Edward prayed earnestly, and with devotion, that he might be spared these days and nights of sad affliction, and that his health be soon restored to him.

Some two weeks later, his gait betraying little of his recent bout of illness, Edward was once more able to walk about unaided. The doctor informed him that he was now acclimatized, and whilst he must continue to be ever vigilant with regard to the many diseases which abounded on the African coast, his worst fears were over. Edward secured temporary lodgings down by the harbor, and then set about making enquiries as to how he might obtain a passage to Liberia. A Dutch sea captain, who chanced to be drinking in the same tavern as Edward, informed him that whilst he was battling with the fever, whatever dispute it was that had occasioned the cessation of civilities between Sierra Leone and Liberia had been successfully concluded. Apparently, he would simply have to await the arrival of a ship that would agree to transport him. Edward thanked the gentleman, and listened as the sad, drawn-out sound of a bugle being blown from the parapets of the British fortress signalled the end of the day. As the last note drifted away and across the sea, Edward emptied his tankard, gathered up his cane, tipped his hat, and retired to his rented rooms, where he slept and dreamed soundly, and passed a blessed night without once breaking sweat.

The following afternoon, Edward engaged the services of the first mate of an American trading vessel. The experienced *sea dog* advised Edward that they would be setting sail on the evening tide, which meant there would be little time for Edward to occupy himself with spiritual preparation for the journey ahead. He simply hurried back to his rooms, gathered his belongings, paid the landlord, and employed a sturdy native to convey his boxed personal effects to the ship. The moon shimmered on the wrinkled face of the sea, and a stern breeze bellied out the sail. Edward settled in, and decided that he would pass most of his time sitting out on deck amongst the bales of luggage, breathing deeply of the salty air, and staring at the gleaming shoals of flying fish which leapt to either side of the ship. His inner being was filled with a strange tranquility, and a deep peace fell upon him at least the equal to any he had ever known in his life, although the origins and purpose of this strangely contemplative mood eluded him. In his mind he would rehearse scenes from the life of Christ, yet found that even in Christ's moments of greatest adversity, such as when betrayed by Judas, or when being led to the Cross, his Lord's face never lost its purity and compassion. Edward wondered if this peace were not perhaps the herald of his impending demise, but when this thought fought its way into his mind, he redoubled his strength and immediately banished it.

There was simply no way of Edward discovering whether the man with whom he most eagerly desired an audience, namely Madison Williams, had received the letter informing him of Edward's intention to set sail for Liberia, and giving him notice of the anticipated week of arrival. Following the souring of Edward's relationship with this difficult man, when it became clear to all that a junior slave, Nash, had supplanted Madison in the master's affections, Madison, a strong, proud man, both of character and stature, had withdrawn from the house and, in the privacy of the slave village, intensified his efforts to acquaint himself with the Bible and with the skills of reading and writing. After nearly two years, in which Madison rejected Edward's many overtures towards him, perhaps recognizing that they originated in Edward's guilt at having surrendered to his own changing passions, a sober-looking Madison had presented himself at the house and requested an audience of his master. When Edward appeared he announced that he now considered himself sufficiently educated, and properly acquainted with God's ways, to have earned his freedom and subsequent transportation to the new African territory of Liberia. Edward, who had long desired the opportunity of bestowing upon Madison a gesture of good-will, hurriedly agreed to Madison's request and asked if there were anything further that he might do. Madison shook his head firmly, bowed and withdrew. Soon after, he made his preparations to depart for Africa. His subsequent letters to Edward, though brief, had remained polite. Through them, Edward was able to discover that Madison had settled in Monrovia and was eking out a living as a small trader selling palm oil, rice, camwood, and animal skins to passing European and American ships. As this short voyage unfolded, Edward arrived at the uncomfortable conclusion that, perhaps because of the warmth of their first encounters, or perhaps this and the additional fact that the passage of time had served to sever Edward's links with many of his other former charges, Madison had now become the only person in Africa whom he felt he could trust. Indeed, it had been to Madison that he had immediately turned when faced with the unpleasant details of Nash's abrupt and final message. He would now have little choice but to place his entire confidence in this man.

Edward's first sighting of Monrovia came at dawn, but it certainly did not occasion his heart to leap with joy. In fact, Edward felt himself suddenly overcome with an ill-feeling of foreboding. The morning sea was beautiful and calm, and held in her embrace a number of small offshore islands. Beyond these rushed the boiling surf, where the low waves bit at the shore and foamed white, but thereafter was misery. Edward stared at the gathering of low, square huts, seemingly built of sticks and mud, walls leaning drunkenly to the north or south of vertical, clumsily thatched and adorned with grass, or a flattering crown of corrugated iron. Behind these dwellings he could see only a forested horizon which appeared to mask a huge, roaming jungle in which nothing stirred, and whose only sound was a mournful roar of silence. As Edward clutched the rail and watched, it would have been impossible for any onlooker to have guessed to what depths of loneliness he had now sunk. He looked up into the sky and saw rain clouds beginning to form and flow through the sky like huge ships, although by now he had come to understand that, in this zone, rain was little more than a precursor of the heat to follow. Back on land there was neither a whisper, nor a sign of movement from the ragged cluster of abodes which lined the shore. A despondent Edward leaned forward and set his face towards the bottomless ocean.

Within the hour the ship had anchored off the African port of Monrovia, and the passengers and freight were being gingerly reunited with *terra firma* by means of a fleet of small launches. As his ill-made craft picked its leaky way through the surf, Edward noticed the fishing boats, their nets suspended from tall poles and drying in the sun before being once more thrown to the deep, and he reached the conclusion that these vessels of commerce seemed far better equipped for sea-faring than his present mode of transportation. Fortunately, the low wind merely ruffled the surface of the ocean, otherwise he was sure that both he and his boxes would have succumbed to a watery end. Once on shore, Edward clasped a handkerchief to his mouth and nose to ward off the fetid African air, but the sudden mist of mosquitoes could be combated only by his swatting them against his skin, until his forearm was decorated with a series of red blotches. Suddenly, natives and colored Americans were everywhere, anxious to greet the arrival of this new ship, and in their wake they created a veritable din. Edward examined them, particularly the natives, their semi-clad bodies ensnared by large corded muscles, but amongst their numbers he was unable to recognize any who had about them a demeanor which suggested that they might have been sent by Madison to greet him. And then the weather, being predictable in this region only in its excesses, suddenly, and without warning, changed, and the rain teemed from the skies. At moments such as this it was customary for a Christian gentleman to acknowledge that such a downpour, whilst causing inconvenience to the human being, inevitably bestowed much satisfaction and benediction upon God's shrubbery, his crops, and his trees. However, the sudden outburst served only to irritate Edward and, following the example of others about him, he abandoned his boxes and marched with some purpose towards the shelter of an overhanging palm tree, whose branches hung limply as though they had been exhausted by the heat of many days. Edward examined the stout grey trunk, and fingered the grainy ridges which ascended as though a series of healed wounds. The rain began now to increase in volume, and Edward realized that he was effectively marooned until the wind chose to rise and blow the clouds to some other part of Africa.

When the rain ceased, Edward entrusted his belongings to a

colored American boy, whom he guessed to be not in excess of twenty years, and whom he observed to be a decent specimen. The boy asked of his *master* in which direction they were headed. Edward, who still carried within his bosom some idle hope that he might recognize a former slave from among the throng at the dockside, now found himself in the lamentable position of having to ask advice from his employee. Under questioning, it appeared that this boy was aware of decent lodgings where white people could comfortably accommodate themselves. Edward had presumed that such places would be difficult to locate, for the idea was that Liberia would be established as the country of the free blacks, and Edward had imagined that those white men who dared the seas to arrive in Liberia would have little choice but to join with the more civilized negroes in the sharing of all manner of facilities, even those most basic to mankind. He had further presumed that this policy would no doubt prevent some *opinionated* white men, both traders and seamen alike, from tarrying too long in Liberia, if they chose to visit at all, but it had been argued, by those of a liberal disposition, that perhaps these were not the quality of men that this new country wished to attract. However, Edward's employee assured him that lodgings for white gentlemen were indeed available.

The young colored boy, his person severely burdened by Edward's effects, led his *master* through the unkempt and overgrown streets of Monrovia. Edward could not help but notice what appeared to him to be appalling conditions, and he kept his handkerchief pressed close to nose and mouth against the truly foul smell which cleaved the air. Others, however, both white and colored, appeared unconcerned by this atmosphere, which led Edward to speculate as to whether or not he might, in the fullness of time, become similarly familiar with the unwholesome character of this Africa. The boarding house to which the bondsman led Edward bore some similarities to the one in Sierra Leone where he had recently dwelt. A wooden, two-storey affair, a thin coat of white paint and a small veranda bestowed upon this simple building an air of majesty. The colored boy stopped and lay down his boxes, as though unsure of his choice, but with a friendly nod of his head Edward made it clear to the boy that these premises were acceptable.

The room was sparsely furnished, but with good taste. Edward eyed the mosquito net, which draped itself purposefully about the bed, and imagined that this would no doubt prove the most important item in the room. The window gave out on to a small courtyard where the clamor of commerce might, according to the black innkeeper, prove a trifle deafening in the daytime, but come the evening there would be neither sound nor song to disturb the slumber of his new guest. The man withdrew and left Edward together with the boy. It was at this juncture that Edward thought it politic to ask after the young man whether or not he was in possession of either a wife or a girl. To this the boy smiled shyly, then shook his head. Edward examined the young man, his perfect shape, strong torso, powerful legs, and then sat down on one corner of the bed. The bondsman remained standing, although he moved uneasily from one foot to the next as though unsure what was expected of him. And then Edward, sensing the young man's discomfort, simply leaned forward and asked after his name. The boy averted his eyes, and, keeping the screen of his lashes low, he whispered the single word, 'Charles.' 'I see,' replied Edward, rising to his feet. 'Charles, I will be taking a short rest. Perhaps you might try to locate for me the whereabouts of one Madison Williams, a former slave on my plantation and now, according to his testimony, residing hereabouts.' At this juncture, Edward produced a piece of paper and held it out. However, before Charles could take it into his grasp, Edward withdrew the paper and made proper enquiry as to whether the young man could read. On receiving assurance that he could, Edward once more proffered the paper, which Charles took into his hand. 'Once you have located Madison Williams, you will inform him that I desire to hold an audience with him at his earliest convenience, is this clear?' Charles nodded his head and bowed silently. Then, without taking his eyes from his employer, he backed out of the room and gently closed in the door behind him.

Some hours later, Edward heard a light knocking upon his door, and he jumped from the bed, startled by this unadvertised interruption to his slumber. Realizing that it must be Charles returning with news of Madison, he called to the black retainer, ordering him not to stray from his present position. Edward pulled about himself a loose gown, and then gently cracked the door and ushered in a sheepish-looking Charles. Edward thought it best to say little, and to give the chance to the young man, which proved to be the correct decision. No sooner had the door been pushed to behind him, and Edward guided him into a chair, than Charles immediately set forth on his tale of disappointment. Apparently he had, with little difficulty, located the house of Madison Williams, but when he arrived there he discovered the abode to be in a state of abandonment. It was not that it was either broken-down or weather-beaten in its appearance, but merely that it looked as though whosoever had formerly occupied the premises had departed in some haste. By standing on the tips of his toes and staring through the window, Charles was able to see that everything had been left in a state of disarray. It was at this moment that Charles was apprehended by a well-dressed man, in the company of his lady wife, who, pointing an umbrella in the direction of the younger and less worldly man, demanded of him an explanation as to his behavior. Charles had stammered a little before blurting out the information that he had been sent by his *master* to convey a message to one Madison Williams. On hearing this, the well-dressed man let it be known that Madison Williams had indeed left suddenly, to go up-river to attend to some business, the full nature of which the gentleman was unsure about. He was polite with his information, and further explained that he imagined that his friend, Madison, would be returning to Monrovia in the next day or two, for it was unknown that he should be absent from *home* for any protracted period of time. Edward listened carefully to all that the animated Charles related, his eyes never leaving the young man's face. At the conclusion of the tale, Edward stood, reached into his pocket and pressed a coin upon Charles, who in turn muttered his thanks and made ready to take his leave. Edward informed young Charles that he expected him to visit at Madison's house three times each day, morning, noon and evening, until the fellow returned. When he did so, Charles was to inform him immediately that his former master requested an audience with him as soon as possible. In the mean time, should Charles want for anything, he was to make it his business to appear at Edward's lodgings, at any suitable hour, and reveal to Edward, without fear or embarrassment, the full nature of his needs. At this, Charles expressed gratitude, promised to do as instructed, and retired from the room.

The evening was suddenly upon him. An overheated Edward, sweat sliding from his armpits and down his sides, examined his ashen flesh, observing with some distaste his stomach, where the skin was wrinkled like paint. After the departure of Charles, he had once more fallen asleep, but this time he had choked on a succession of unpleasant dreams and awoken in a fury, the sheet knotted about him as though he had fought with the bed in his sleep. Certain that further sleep would elude him for some hours yet, he dressed quickly, pausing only to inspect his ageing body and to listen as a rat ran across the thin boards of the ceiling. Then, satisfied that he was attired in a proper manner, he stepped out into the streets in search of some innocent amusement. In this Africa it appeared that both dawn and dusk were brief and ambiguous, as though there were little time to waste, and Edward soon found himself enveloped in gloom. In the distance, he heard the quiet engine of the sea continually renewing itself, and echoing across the night. Then he momentarily stiffened with fear as a dog whose sick-eye ran with water stepped casually out of the darkness. The ribbed mongrel hobbled awkwardly and eyed Edward in the hope of some morsel of food, but Edward glared back and thought about tossing a stick, for he considered it undignified to beg, and for this reason he found dogs repellent.

Pausing at the first tavern, Edward glanced through the open door and was pleased to discover the place mercifully free of clientele. He entered, removed his hat, and sat at the nearest table. He signalled to the boy with his cane, and he came quickly to him, over-delighted in a childish manner to see custom in the form of a white gentleman. Edward made his demands known and settled back to cast his mind forwards and backwards across this problem of his former slave, Nash. That he had banished not only Nash, but many of his other slaves, to this inhospitable and heathen corner of the world disturbed Edward. The boy arrived and delivered a foaming tankard of beer to Edward's table, and Edward rewarded him with a generous coin. The buffoon smiled and capered into the corner, and Edward supped carefully at the beer, his elbow bending like a stubborn hinge. Perhaps, thought Edward, this business of encouraging men to engage with a past and a history that are truly not their own is, after all, ill-judged. The light in the candle flickered, shadows danced against the white stone wall, and Edward drew again on his beer. It occurred to him that perhaps the fever, the sleepless nights, the complex welter of emotions that he had been subjected to since his arrival in Africa, were nothing more complex than manifestations of a profound guilt.

In a vain effort to banish the despair of this moment, and hopefully ensure a peaceful night's sleep free of demons, Edward raised his hand and once more summoned the boy to him. An hour or so later, his person much refreshed by consumption, and risking offence by leaving a tankard unfinished, Edward struggled out and picked his way down to the harbor. Once there, he gazed upon the tranquil sea, the moonlight sparkling on the water so that it looked like a liquid case of jewels. And then his attention was seized by the echoing of heels upon flaggings, and the loud protestations of a woman who declaimed lunatic phrases as though speaking some foolish part she had written for herself. Judging her an Irish whore by dint of her accent, Edward stared at her as she trembled in her cloud of wounded indignation, the thick powder on her face channeled with tears, her mouth set in a twist, and he felt pity and despair in equal part.

The following morning the braying of the traders and the incessant barking of dogs roused Edward from a troubling sleep. He fetched a deep sigh and cast a glance towards the small window, through which he could see that the clear, unclouded blue of the sky promised a murderously hot day, at least the equal of those he had already endured. He turned in the bed, careful not to disturb the mosquito netting, and realized that last night he had forgotten to pinch out the candle. A lump of misshapen wax overflowed the shallow dish. Then, a series of stifled coughs rattling through his body, Edward stepped urgently from the bed and first poured and then drank a glass of water. Perching on the edge of a chair, he soothed his dry throat with a further glass, and wondered if the boy Charles had left any message for him. Abandoning his desire for more slumber, he dressed quickly and sought out the innkeeper in order that he might make enquiry of Charles. Having located his host, he was informed by him that there was neither message, nor had there been any visit by Charles or any other, which caused Edward momentarily to panic and wonder whether the black bondsman had for some reason chosen to abandon him. Choosing not to dwell upon this unpleasant thought, Edward enquired after a club in which he might discover the company of white men and share with them some words, reasoning that if he was to be expected to pass yet more time in this savage environment, then he ought at least to be exposed to some of the pleasantries which civilized company can bestow upon a man's otherwise wretched African existence. The negro innkeeper, his face suddenly closed and his eyes lowered, informed Edward that he knew of a colonial club whose members were, as he termed them, *masters*.

Armed with directions to this place, which lay not too far off, Edward set forth across the town, the sun hanging above him like a bright lamp. He could feel small beads of sweat forming on his forehead and trickling down his temples, and others sliding about the bridge of his nose and then down and under his chin to his collar. He pulled out a handkerchief and dabbed furiously at his face as he walked. Having located the door to the club, Edward raised the brass knocker and struck it three times with force. A black man, clearly of American origin, answered and asked after his business, to which Edward answered that he had been given to believe that this was a Gentleman's Club for white people. As a visitor, he simply craved some companionship and some information as to how things went in these parts. Edward was surprised to discover the degree of hostility that this experience occasioned in his soul. Never before had he had to explain or ask anything of a colored man, and to have to do so now, and in order to gain access to the company of other white men, he found extremely difficult. The colored man listened carefully and then announced that he would soon return, a reply calculated to check, not encourage, enquiry. He closed in the door and left Edward standing in the street like a beggar.

Some moments later, the door was opened by the same fellow, and Edward was ushered into the comfortable and well-appointed vestibule of the brick house. Only when he surveyed the prints, and other wall décor, did it become apparent that this must be the abode of one of the principals of the American Colonization Society. Edward followed the servant into a drawing-room that was cluttered with books and papers, and well-finished with couches and loungers. Three white men, their skins grown dark through familiarity with the sun, rose as he entered, and hands were proffered and enquiries made. The already uncorked wine was poured into a glass, which was then thrust into Edward's willing hand. Thereafter followed an engrossing session, in which a cautious Edward shared his circumstances with those that came and went, and sought from them similar stories all relating to the common question of how it was they had come to find themselves adrift and washed up on this furthest shore of civilization. Anecdotes and faint memories were traded, and some attempts were made to swell them into order with dates and places. Edward stayed for lunch, then coffee, but thought it wise to retire before dinner, for by now he was fearful that news of the personal tragedy that had recently enveloped his name might somehow have crossed the waters and reached the ears of these gentlemen. He reasoned that before the confessional urge took hold of any tongue, he should request his cane. Edward stood, thanked them most warmly for a splendid day, and made ready to return to his lodgings.

Slightly merry on account of the good wine, a contented Edward asked the innkeeper after Charles, only to be informed that up until this very moment there had been no sign of the young bondsman. Edward returned to his hot and airless room with a bottle of claret, his mood rudely transformed by this news. Slipping into an involuntary sleep, he found his mind populated with images of Amelia, her face decorated with pond-like sores where flies and other creatures drank greedily. As dawn began to break over Monrovia, Edward awoke in a sweat and thrashed the covers off himself. Tears misted his eyes, for indeed his love for Amelia had festered and become stamped with a self-pity that was near-cousin to self-loathing. He simply craved to be offered the uncon-ditional love of a child, could she not understand this? He looked ashamedly at the mauve contusions that decorated the several folds of his skin, and realized that the years had descended and smothered him like a fog. What else now but to submit to the indifferent squalor of old age, and give himself up to his fears? Edward let his feet fall over the side of the bed and brush the wooden floor, then he decided that if Charles did not show himself by the end of the day, he would go in person to Madison Williams's home and make enquiry. In the interim, he would do the next best thing, which was to spend another day in the company of his civilized countrymen.

As Edward dressed, his mind turned back again upon Amelia. Clearly she would have hated this Africa that Edward now felt marooned in. It had struck him, while at the club, that the lack of civilized white women in these parts would only have served to drive home her suspicion of all things African. Not only would curious, perhaps desperate, white eyes have traveled the length of her body, but black eyes would no doubt have made her the object of much unwanted attention. Edward ceased his wardrobe, fell to his knees, and prayed to the Lord that he might be forgiven for his indifference towards Amelia, for in truth no harm or misery had been intended. That she took it upon herself to sabotage her husband's friendship with Nash by destroying the colored man's letters was a painful discovery for Edward, but had he not found it in his heart to forgive her? Her accusation that in the wake of Nash's departure he was now making a fool of himself by lavishing an excess of affection upon a new retainer, was this not again met with forgiveness? That she had subsequently chosen to flee his home, then her mind, then this mortal world at the instigation of her own hand, was a tragedy the responsibility for which could not reside at Edward's doorstep. Surely his dear father understood this? A half-dressed Edward reached for his Bible, and clumsily fingered the pages until he reached the relevant verse. Thereafter, his wretched body burning with faith, he began to recite aloud.

Late in the morning, having left instructions with the inn-keeper that he should, at all costs, delay Charles if he chanced to arrive during Edward's absence, a somewhat despondent Edward stepped out into the street and followed much the same route as the previous day. When he arrived at the club, Edward seized the brass knocker and rapped three times, and the same colored man soon appeared before him. Only this time the man informed Edward that the members, having last night convened an extraordinary meeting which lasted into the small hours, had decided that Edward was not welcome, either as a visitor or as a member, should he choose to linger on these shores. Edward stared at the liveried servant and asked if he might be blessed with a reason, but the colored man, clutching self-righteously at his lapels as though they were a badge of some importance, simply eyed him with the manner of one who is happily charged only to deliver decisions and not to share with the unfortunate recipient the highways and byways that were explored in order to reach the proffered conclusion. Edward tarried a moment, scratched the skin under one eye, then, realizing that he was making little headway, turned on his heels, anxious that he should avoid having to suffer the ignominy of the door being slammed in his face.

Edward reached the inn, his mind in a daze, and discovered Charles standing with a travel-weary but finely dressed man whom he instantly recognized as Madison Williams. Immediately, Edward's gloom abated, and he shook hands firmly with his former slave, who, by all appearances, appeared to be well suited to the life of a free man. Edward dismissed Charles with a proffered coin, but the young man looked a little forlorn and asked if there might be some other way in which he could be of service to the *master*. Clearly Edward's curt dismissal had stung the young man like a lash, and the hurt that was now painted across his boyish face begged the older man to be kinder to him. Edward relented, and told him that he could, if he so wished, return tomorrow, and with this news a somewhat chastened Charles smiled, nodded cheerfully, and took his leave. Anxious not to waste any more time, Edward ordered the innkeeper to prepare food and wine for Madison and himself, which they would take in due course. With this request made, they retreated into Edward's room, and Edward signalled that Madison should make himself at ease in the more comfortable of the two chairs.

As Madison sat opposite him, Edward could not help but note that his former slave's person became suddenly very grave, the flesh frowning on his brow. Madison leaned forward. He spoke slowly and carefully, as though anxious that he should not be misunderstood. 'Master, Nash Williams is dead.' Edward recoiled slightly, as though he had been struck. 'The fever called him home. And he is burned according to local custom. This much I found out in the place from where I am happily returning.' A long silence deepened. Edward stared back at Madison and made no attempt to dam the tears which now flowed down his face. Eventually Madison stood. At this signal, Edward drew a hand across his cheeks. 'I shall return,' announced Madison, 'with more news.' Without waiting for further instruction, Madison withdrew and closed in the door behind him. Some moments later, the innkeeper knocked at the door with the requested food and drink, but Edward simply called for him to take it away and sank further into his grief. Nash Williams, the boy he had brought from the fields to the house, the boy who won his love, freely given, who would force on to him all the pain and confusion which finally proved too much for Amelia to bear, this Nash Williams was no more? And he, Edward, having traveled half the known world once again to be with him, what was he to do?

Edward spent the remainder of the day, and the full length of the night, sitting upright in the chair, his anguished mind questing in every conceivable direction, but forever stumbling into blind alleyways which proved to be swept clean of any meaning. In the morning Madison returned and found his former master in the same position in which he had left him, though Madison observed, by virtue of Edward's vacant stare, that there had been a considerable decline in his mental state.

He sat opposite Edward, but his former master gazed back at him as though he were not there. Madison spoke quietly and at length about Nash's final country settlement, and about the many problems which Nash had to face by choosing to live among the natives, but Edward remained silent. For some time, they simply stared at each other, each one a prisoner of their innermost thoughts. And then Madison reached into his pocket and pulled clear a letter. He informed Edward that this letter had been placed into his hands by Nash on the understanding that Madison would personally give it to his former master, and to him alone, even though it was understood that this would mean crossing the sea and returning to America. Edward looked more intently now. 'Did Nash not know I was coming?' Madison narrowed his eyes. 'You chose not to write to him.' Madison paused. 'And by the time I discovered him he was merely a few hours this side of death.' Edward dropped his gaze. Then he whispered, 'I want to go to where Nash lived.' Madison bestowed a scornful glare upon his former master. 'I have to go there.' Madison said nothing. He held out the letter. 'It is for you.' He paused. 'I promised Nash that I would deliver it to you personally.' Edward took the letter and looked at the envelope. He squeezed it gently. 'I have to go to where Nash lived.' Madison climbed to his feet.

Saint Paul's River, Liberia
Jan. 3rd, 1842

Dear Father,

Despite my earlier protestations, I resort again to pen
and paper in a final attempt to engage with you. I find
the process humiliating, and I fail to see what hurt I
ever inflicted upon you that could justify such a cruel
abandonment of your past intimate, namely myself. There
is much to report, but being unsure of how it might interest
you, if at all, it is my intent to be brief.

My three wives (I have considered a fourth, but the
expense is at present beyond me) are faring well, as are
the children. Six in total, all of whom receive lengthy
instruction in reading and writing which sits well upon
their shoulders. In addition they receive, from their mothers, instruction in the African language, as I do. I feel
the necessity of being able to understand properly the
words of the natives in whose land I reside, and the
inconvenience, self-denial and hardship I suffer on this
count is clearly worth-while if it facilitates my being able
freely to communicate with those hereabouts. That children
learn faster, and with less inhibition than their elders and
betters, is daily proven as we sit together and try to drink
up these strange words and sounds. That my present family
does not conform to what you might reasonably expect
of me will no doubt disturb you. However, despite their
heathen origins, my wives send their best respects to you,
but nothing further, for you would scorn their poor marks
were they to attempt written words. They had no school
to attend, and have suffered accordingly, but not in their
generosity of heart, or in their ability to act out the role
of dear and gentle mother to their precious children. They
know also how to administer to the needs of a husband, for
as I chanced to mention in an earlier communication, the

climate of this country does not suit old sores. Two such
fellows have long since taken up residence on my left leg,
and although I am obliged to suffer a little for want of a
cure, my wives seek all the while to ease my discomfort
with as much care and attention that I might reasonably
expect from an American-born woman. Some months ago,
I was quite afflicted by the death of my youngest child, a
fine boy of about nine months. A large and healthy child,
he was taken ill quite suddenly, and died thereafter. I am not
able to say what his sickness was, for this remains a mystery
even to those closest to him, who continue to grieve.

Perhaps you imagine that this Liberia has corrupted my
person, transforming me from the good Christian colored
gentleman who left your home, into this heathen whom you
barely recognize. But this is not so, for, as I have often
stated many times over, Liberia is the finest country for
the colored man, for here he may live by the sweat of his
brow, although everything remains scarce and high, such
as provisions, clothing, etc. There are still many out here,
and more arriving with each ship, who are not prepared for
freedom, and who get on poorly because there is no one to
act for them, and they are totally incapable of acting for
themselves. But this is not the fault of the country, for
although not free from famine, war, sickness and death,
and other troubles incidental to mankind, I still proclaim
that it will compare favorably with any other part of
the habitable world. Persons coming to Africa, white or
colored, should always remember that this is a new country
and that everything has still to be created. Things can be
both inconvenient and uphill, and many hardships will no
doubt be experienced, but such problems are common to the
first settlement in any country. We, the colored man, have
been oppressed long enough. We need to contend for our
rights, stand our ground, and feel the love of liberty that can
never be found in your America. Far from corrupting my
soul, this Commonwealth of Liberia has provided me with
the opportunity to open up my eyes and cast off the garb of

ignorance which has encompassed me all too securely the whole course of my life.

These days I am happy simply to raise my crops. The land is rich and produces the familiar American garden stuff, cabbage, peas, beans, onions, tomatoes, etc., as well as the native produce, which it does in abundance. The school is no more, and shall never again occupy a position of authority in any settlement of which I am a part. This missionary work, this process of persuasion, is futile amongst these people, for they never truly pray to the Christian God, they merely pray to their own gods in Christian guise, for the American God does not even resemble them in that most fundamental of features. The truth is, our religion, in its purest and least diluted form, can never take root in this country. Its young shoots will wither and die, leaving the sensible man with the conclusive evidence that he must reap what grows naturally. It has taken my dark mind many years to absorb this knowledge, and while it would be true to assert that the man I love is Christ, and I love him as one might love an intimate, having no means to return to America, and being therefore bound to an African existence, I must suspend my faith and I therefore freely choose to live the life of the African.

If it please you, I wish you to remember me kindly to my colored friends. Inform them that should they choose to come out to this country, then they must bring everything for housekeeping, farming and carpentry, etc. They will need them, for they cannot be got here nor, unless their master chooses to be bonded to his promises, can they be obtained by means of purchase from the packet. It only remains that I request of you that you do not come out to Africa, for I fear I will surely disappoint you. I suppose I shall never again see you in this life, but if the Lord so deems it, I might yet cast my eyes upon you on the pleasant banks of deliverance. Perhaps in this realm of the hereafter you might explain to me why you used me for your purposes and then expelled me to this Liberian paradise. I believed fiercely in all that you related to me, and fervently hoped that one day I might be worthy of the name I bore, the learning I had been blessed with, and the kind attentions of a master with the teachings of the Lord fused into his soul. That my faith in you is broken, is evident. You, my father, did sow the seed, and it sprouted forth with vigor, but for many years now there has been nobody to tend to it, and being abandoned it has withered away and died. Your work is complete. It only remains for me once more to urge you to remain in your country.

Nash Williams

Madison Williams appeared at the rooming house and enquired of the innkeeper as to the general well-being of his former master. The innkeeper slowly shook his head, and informed Madison that for three days now he had neither seen nor heard from the gentleman. Sadly, he presumed his guest to be still in a state of distress. Madison thanked him for his intelligence and, acting upon the innkeeper's suggestion, he made his way to Edward's room. He knocked, but there was no answer, so he knocked again, this time more briskly. From inside he heard a muted cry to enter. Madison opened the door and, peering through a gloom that belonged to neither night nor day, he discovered Edward prostrate upon the bed, and Nash's letter scattered about the floor.

The room had a heavy, musty smell, the drapes having been pulled against the world for three whole days. Edward, as though suddenly conscious of his lamentable appearance, heaved himself into an upright position, rubbed a hand into his face, and then, with some difficulty, stood and made some efforts to stretch. Madison remained standing by the door, unsure as to whether or not he wished to witness this spectacle. Then, through a small chink in the drapes, a slither of light hit Edward and, taking this as a signal, he drew back the coarse material and flooded the room. Madison lifted his arm to his face and awaited his cue, but for the moment at least Edward chose to remain silent. He carefully positioned himself at the foot of the bed and, as he pulled on his leather shoes and strapped them into place, he observed Madison out of the corner of his eye. Madison chose to ignore him, and instead looked all about himself, studying the sparsely furnished room. There was something about the small room, the many hours of darkness having cooled the air and created a welcome respite from the familiar heat, which suggested to Madison that whatever business had to be carried on in these parts had been concluded. Madison knew, without his former master saying anything, that Edward was ready to leave. He expected an announcement.

Edward cleared his throat and spoke slowly, but forcefully. 'I wish,' he began, 'to be taken immediately to where Nash Williams conducted his affairs.' Madison looked hard at Edward. Detecting Madison's opposition, Edward repeated himself. 'I wish you to conduct me to the Nash Williams settlement.' Madison nodded once, careful to make his nod an acknowledgement of his understanding the words, and not an agreement to act upon them. 'Well?' asked a suddenly animated Edward. 'When do we leave?' 'Perhaps in a day or two,' suggested Madison. 'How long do you wish to tarry there?' Edward snorted in disbelief, and then laughed out loud. 'A day or two! We leave today. And I will tarry there as long as I desire.' Madison adjusted his posture, and then explained to Edward that should they leave immediately they would inevitably have to spend this coming evening in a settlement between the capital and Nash's own former place of residence, for the distance was simply too great to be covered in what remained of this day. A river canoe would have to be engaged, and a navigator found. Supplies would have to be purchased. Precautions taken. Madison listed off the various stages of preparation that still needed to be passed through, but even as he spoke he could see that nothing was going to deflect the smiling Edward from his chosen course. The man's mind was fevered with determination.

The river wore a rutted frown where their slow progress had disturbed her sleep. To either side the somber banks, cluttered with trees, shrubs and vines, were pressed by a thick, brooding undergrowth that was heavy with years. As dusk approached, the heat still hung low like a ceiling above their heads. Madison uttered some words in the local language and the native helmsman, a reed of a man who could clearly boast no association with books, and whose liquor-stained breath announced his common mode of recreational activity, began to paddle towards the northern shore. The mosquitoes redoubled their attentions, and Edward crushed another against his blotched arm and asked if this place was to mark their journey's end for this day. As the canoe neatly avoided the clean stones, and fetched up on a muddy shelf, Madison replied that he knew of a settlement hereabouts where, according to his calculations, they should receive a peaceful welcome. However, he advised Edward that perhaps he ought not to mention the true purpose which lay behind their visit, for there were those who would not consider a pilgrimage to the site of Nash Williams's demise an honorable journey.

Madison followed a stamped-in path through the tall grass, and Edward, ignoring the irritating bite of a nail in his boot, and the native tracked close behind. A little more than one hundred paces from the river bank, Madison stopped suddenly and pointed through the bush towards a village. Tall brown huts were huddled together within a clumsy fence, and a faint wind lifted human voices and stirred Edward's curiosity. Choosing not to speak, Madison edged forward through the drooping foliage and into the heart of this village which, much to Edward's consternation, was soon revealed to be, not a native settlement, but one populated by Americans who spoke English. The primitive nature of the conditions shocked Edward, who until now had not the slightest notion of the poverty-stricken rural existence which enveloped those Christians who chose not to settle in and around the capital town of Monrovia. Men, women and children appeared to be living alongside hog, goat and fowl as though family members, and Edward had never before witnessed such scenes of squalor, not even on the worst-run plantations in his native America.

Night fell quickly, the sky bereft of stars, the moon hidden behind drifting clouds. Fires were lit and the bush closed in as though a cloak were being draped around them. Madison left Edward alone with the native, and withdrew to negotiate for some shelter in which they might pass the night. An exhausted Edward slumped to the ground and removed the offending boot. Madison soon returned and informed his former master that there was only one small hut available, and they had been encouraged to share it. However, continued Madison, if his former master wished, he would happily sleep outside with the native. Edward would have none of this. Madison sat down on the dirt beside Edward and reached for a gourd of water. He drank deeply and then enquired if Edward were hungry, for the settlers would soon be roasting a goat. Pleading excessive fatigue, Edward insisted that he simply wished, if possible, to retire. Madison put the gourd to one side and, sensing the white man's discomfort, he helped him to his feet and together they crossed the strangely quiet village until they reached their lodgings. Once there, Madison deposited Edward at the mouth of the wooden hut, and then he moved off to relieve himself in the bush. Edward watched Madison's dark, glistening, sweat-filmed skin until his former slave was swallowed up whole by the blackness of the night.

When Madison returned, Edward was already undressed and basking in the glow of the lamp. Two straw cots lay next to each other, and an uneasy Madison looked around at the personal articles which littered the hut. In order that he might mask his discomfort, Madison spoke quietly as he unbuttoned his clothes. He asked Edward if there were any real purpose to their visit in a practical sense, or if this was nothing more than a tribute to Nash? Or perhaps a promise that was being kept? Edward listened intently to Madison, his eyes fixed upon his former slave. Madison removed his shirt. And then Edward shared with Madison his intention of taking the children of Nash Williams back to America and offering them the possibility of a proper Christian life amongst civilized people. Madison turned away and said nothing in reply. Outside the hut the nocturnal screeching and sawing began to build towards its terrifying nightly pitch. Edward asked the semi-clad Madison if he thought the children would return with him, and how many there were, and how many wives did Nash truly possess? Madison drank in all of these questions, and then turned back and stared directly into the face of his former master. Half of Edward's face lay shrouded in thick shadow, the other half changed hue and shape according to the nature of the dancing flame. As Madison moved to answer this volley of questions, Edward reached up his hand in a gesture of silence, and then leaned forward and took Madison's hands in his own. He spoke softly to Madison of how far he felt from home, from those like himself, and how he desired to be once more among his own people, both white and colored. Madison stared back and said nothing in reply. And then he felt the pressure increase upon his hands, and Madison took this as a signal to speak. 'No,' he said. The word echoed around the small hut, its weight and purpose obscuring the sounds of nature without. And then, after what seemed an eternity, Edward Williams gave up Madison's hands and lay back on his straw cot.

Shortly before noon the following day, the native helmsman leapt nimbly from the canoe and hoisted it up and on to a narrow strip of shingle. On the river bank lay scattered the rusting remains of tools and old field equipment. Edward and Madison waded ashore. They stood at the water's edge and listened to the strange creaking of the trees. Then Edward watched as his former slave found a secure footing and hoisted himself, by means of a strong vine, up and on to the summit of the muddy bank. With some aid from both the native and Madison, Edward was able to follow. There, spread before him, he could now see the litter of brown cones that constituted the final Nash Williams settlement. Madison took the lead and ushered Edward forward and into the unkempt filth of the place. Everywhere he turned, Edward's eyes were assaulted by natives who squatted idly, their bodies resting awkwardly on their foundations, like their infantile shacks. Edward attempted to paint his face with a thinly benevolent smile, but realized that he was ill-equipped to disguise his true feelings of disgust in the midst of this specter of peopled desolation. A seemingly undisturbed Madison shepherded Edward through the dried and drying mud, until they stood outside of the *house* of Nash Williams. Madison pointed at the straw grass hovel, encouraging his former master to enter, but Edward stepped back in revulsion. What could possibly have occurred in the Christian soul of his Nash Williams to have encouraged him to make peace with a life that surely even these heathens considered contemptible? Again Madison gestured to Edward that there was nothing to block his path should he choose to step forward and enter, but Edward recoiled. His eyes climbed to the sun, which had now reached its highest point in the sky, and for some moments they stood together in silence. Then Madison pulled an over-large handkerchief from his pocket, and dabbed at his damp brow. Edward looked across at his former slave, and hoped that this man might usher him towards some understanding of the disorder that lay hereabouts. But Madison had about his person an air of nonchalance. And then it struck Edward with a terrible force. He was alone. He had been abandoned. Madison would not even meet his eyes. 'Madison?' His former slave ignored him. Recognizing the hopelessness of his predicament, Edward opened his mouth and drew deeply of the foul air. He decided that he would sing a hymn, in order that he might calm his beleaguered mind. The natives stared at him, and watched as the white man's lips formed the words, but no sound was heard. Still, Edward continued to *sing* his hymn. The natives looked on and wondered what evil spirits had populated this poor man's soul and dragged him down to such a level of abasement. Their hearts began to swell with the pity that one feels for a fellow being who has lost both his way and his sense of purpose. This strange old white man. Madison turned away.

II

WEST

Curling herself into a tight fist against the cold, Martha huddled in the doorway and wondered if tonight she might see snow. Beautiful. Lifting her eyes without lifting up her head, she stared at the wide black sky that would once more be her companion. White snow, come quickly. A tall man in a long overcoat, and with a freshly trimmed beard, chin tucked into his chest, looked down at her as he walked by. For a moment she worried that he might spit, but he did not. So this was Colorado Territory, a place she had crossed prairie and desert to reach. Hoping to pass through it quickly, not believing that she would fall over foolish like a lame mule. Old woman. They had set her down and continued on to California. She hacked violently. Through some atavistic mist, Martha peered back east, beyond Kansas, back beyond her motherhood, her teen years, her arrival in Virginia, to a smooth white beach where a trembling girl waited with two boys and a man. Standing off, a ship. Her journey had been a long one. But now the sun had set. Her course was run. *Father, why hast thou forsaken me?*

Lucy would be waiting for her in California, for it was she who had persuaded Martha Randolph that there were colored folks living on both sides of the mountains now. Living. According to Lucy, colored folks of all ages and backgrounds, of all classes and colors, were looking to the coast. Lucy's man had told her, and Lucy in turn had told Martha. Girl, you sure? Apparently, these days colored folks were not heading west prospecting for no gold, they were just prospecting for a new life without having to pay no heed to the white man and his

73

ways. Prospecting for a place where things were a little better than bad, and where you weren't always looking over your shoulder and wondering when somebody was going to do you wrong. Prospecting for a place where your name wasn't 'boy' or 'aunty', and where you could be a part of this country without feeling like you wasn't really a part. Lucy had left behind a letter for her long-time friend, practically begging her to come out west and join her and her man in San Francisco. It would make the both of us happy. And although Martha still had some trouble figuring out words and such, she could make out the sense in Lucy's letter, and she reckoned that's just what she was going to do. Pioneer. She was going to stop her scrubbing and washing. Age was getting the better of her now, and arthritis had a stern hand on all parts of her body. She would pioneer west. Martha pulled her knees up towards her and stretched out a hand to adjust the rags around her feet. She blocked up the holes where the wind was whistling through. Stop. The doorway protected her on three sides, and she felt sure that she should be able to sleep here without disturbing anyone. Just leave me be. But she felt strangely beyond sleep. As though her body were sliding carelessly towards a kind of sleep. Like when she lost Eliza Mae. Moma. Moma.

Martha unglued her eyes and stared up into the woman's face. 'Do you have any folks?' It had started to snow now. Early snow, huge, soft snowflakes spinning down out of the clear, black sky. 'You must be cold.' It was dark and, the woman aside, there was nobody else in sight. When they had set her down here, they had told her that this was Main Street, as though this information freed them of any responsibility. But she did not blame them. A few saloons, a restaurant, a blacksmith, a rooming house or two, indeed this was Main Street. 'I have a small cabin where you can stay the night.' Martha looked again at the woman who stood before her in a black coat, with a thick shawl thrown idly across her shoulders and a hat fastened tightly to her head. Perhaps this woman had bought her daughter? Was Eliza Mae living here in Colorado

Territory? There was no reason to go clear to California if Eliza
Mae were here in Colorado Territory. Eliza Mae returned to
her? 'Can you get up?' The woman stretched out her gloved
hand and Martha stared hard at it. Eliza Mae was gone. This
hand could no more lead her back to her daughter than it
could lead Martha back to her own youthful self. A small
cabin. This woman was offering her some place with a roof,
and maybe even a little heating. Martha closed her eyes. After
countless years of journeying, the hand was both insult and
salvation, but the woman was not to know this. 'Please, take
my hand. I'm not here to harm you. I just want to help.
Truly.' Martha uncurled her fingers and set them against the
woman's hide-bound hand. The woman felt neither warm nor
cold. 'Can you stand by yourself?' Inside of herself, Martha
laughed. Can this woman not see that they abandoned me? At
least they had shown some charity and not discarded her upon
the plains. But stand by herself? Martha Randolph. Squatting
like a filthy bag of bones. Watching the snow. Don't know
nobody in these parts. Barely recognizing herself. No ma'am,
she thought. I doubt if I'll ever be able to stand by myself again.
But no matter. I done enough standing by myself to last most
folks three or four lifetimes. Ain't nothing shameful in resting
now. No ma'am, nothing shameful at all. She squeezed. The
woman's hand squeezed back. 'Can you stand by yourself?'
Martha shook her head.

I look into his eyes, but his stare is constant and frightens me.
He shows no emotion. 'Lucas?' He turns from me and scrapes
the wooden chair across the floor. He sits heavily upon it. He
lifts his hands to his head and buries his face in his cupped and
calloused palms. Eliza Mae runs to me and clutches the hem
of my dress. The light in the lamp jumps and the room sways,
first one way and then the next. I pull Eliza Mae towards me
and hide her small body in the folds of my dress. Lucas looks
up. He opens his mouth to speak. His face is tired, older than
his thirty-five years. The weight of yet another day in the

field sits heavily upon him. But not just this. I run my hand across Eliza Mae's matted hair. On Sunday I will pull the comb through the knots and she will scream. Outside, I can hear the crickets, their shrill voices snapping, like twigs being broken from a tree. 'Master dead.' Eliza Mae looks from me to her father, then back to me. Poor child, she does not understand. 'Lucas, we going to be sold?' Lucas lowers his eyes.

The sun is at its highest point. The overseer is looking across at me, so again I bend down and start to pick. Already I have the hands of a woman twice my age, the skin beaten, bloodied and bruised, like worn-out leather. The overseer rides his horse towards me, its legs stepping high, prancing, almost dancing. He looks down at me, the sun behind him, framing his head, forming a halo. He raises his whip and brings it down on my arm. I don't hear the words that fall from his mouth. I simply think, Master dead. What now? I bend down and again I start to pick. I can still feel his eyes upon me. And the sun. And now the horse is turning. It dances away from me.

I stand with the rest of the Virginia property. Master's nephew, a banker from Washington, is now our new master. He has no interest in plantation life. He holds a handkerchief to his face and looks on with detachment. Everything must be sold. The lawyer grabs the iron-throated bell and summons the people to attention. Then the auctioneer slaps his gavel against a block of wood. I fall to my knees and take Eliza Mae in my arms. I did not suckle this child at the breast, nor did I cradle her in my arms and shower her with what love I have, to see her taken away from me. As the auctioneer begins to bellow, I look into Eliza Mae's face. He is calling out the date, the place, the time. Master would never have sold any of us. I tell this to my terrified child. Slaves. Farm animals. Household furniture. Farm tools. We are to be sold in this order. I watch as Lucas soaks a cloth in cold water. He comforts me and places it first on my forehead, and then on that of his child. Last night he came to me, his eyes grown red with drink. He confessed that death would be easier. This way we are always going to be wondering. Always worrying. His voice broke and he choked back the remaining words. Then he took me in the circle of his arms and laid me down. Until the old horn blew to mark the start of a new day.

Farmers have come from all over the county. A fun-seeking crowd, ready for haggling, but amongst them I see the lean-faced men. The traders, with their trigger-happy minds, their mouths tight and bitter. I try not to look into anybody's eyes. The auctioneer is dressed formally. Dark vest, colorful cutaway coat. He continues to yell. Now, as he does so, he motions towards us with his gavel. Then he slaps this instrument against the wooden block with a thud. Now again he gestures towards us. My throat is dry. Eliza Mae moves restlessly, so I take her hand. She cries. I pinch her to quiet her. I am sorry, but it is for her own good. The auctioneer beckons forward the traders. They look firstly at the men. A trader prods Lucas's biceps with a stick. If a trader buys a man, it is down the river. To die. That much we all know. The families in need of domestics, or the farmers in need of breeding wenches, they look across at us and wait their turn. I am too old for breeding. They do not know that I would also disappoint. My Eliza Mae holds on to me, but it will be to no avail. She will be a prime purchase. And on her own she stands a better chance of a fine family. I want to tell her this, to encourage her to let go, but I have not the heart. I look on. The auctioneer cries to the heavens. A band strikes up. A troupe of minstrels begins to dance. Soon the bidding will begin. 'Moma.' Eliza Mae whispers the word over and over again, as though this were the only word she possessed. This one word. This word only.

Martha leaned against the woman and peered into the small, dark room. Still cold. Through the half-light, she saw the single bed, the mattress rolled back and revealing an ugly grid of rusty wire. Then she felt the woman's gentle touch guiding her across the room and into a hard-backed wooden chair. Like a child. Martha sat and watched as the woman first lit the lamp and then quickly made up the bed, stretching a clean sheet tight like a drumskin across its length and breadth. Having done so, she helped Martha the two paces across the room and set her down to rest upon the corner of the bed. Martha's right eye was clouding over, but she could make out the woman's motions as she now attempted to fire some life into the pot-bellied stove. She failed, and bestowed a sad smile upon Martha. Girl, don't worry. Don't worry yourself. The woman reached for the pitcher and poured a glass of water. 'Here, take it and drink. Are you cold?' Martha dragged her tongue around her swollen lips. Then she took the water and held the glass between both hands. She swallowed deeply, and as she did so the woman knelt and began to remove the wet rags that swaddled Martha's feet. No. Please. Martha closed her eyes.

She could only once remember being this cold. That was on that miserable December day that she had crossed the Missouri, riding in the back of the Hoffmans' open wagon. When they arrived on the western shore, Martha, by now gaunt and tired, having traveled clear from Virginia with only the briefest of stops, stepped down into the iciness that was a Kansas winter. Did they buy me to kill me? All her belongings dangled in a bundle that she held in one hand. She no longer possessed either a husband or a daughter, but her memory of their loss was clear. She remembered the disdainful posture of Master's nephew, and the booming voice of the auctioneer. She remembered the southern ladies in their white cotton sun bonnets and long-sleeved dresses, and the poorer farmers who hoped to find a bargain, their bony mules hitched to lame carriages. The trader who had prodded Lucas with a stick bought him for a princely sum. But Martha held on to some hope, for Lucas was a man who never failed to make friends with dogs. He charmed them with his dark, gentle voice. Lucas was not a man to let his body fetch up in flinty, lonely ground. Eliza Mae was sold after Martha. The

Hoffmans could no doubt detect in their purchase a powerful feeling towards this girl, so they had bundled Martha into their wagon and left quickly. They had made their transaction, and the festivities would run their natural course without them. Goodbye, everybody. Once they had passed out of sight, the woman offered Martha a lace handkerchief, which Martha ignored.

Within the year, the Hoffmans had decided to sell up and leave Virginia. They had decided to settle outside of the city of Kansas, in a part of the country which was young and promising for pioneers. Good roads provided easy access to the back country, and new arrivants were permitted to purchase land from the United States government at a cost of two dollars an acre. Mr Eugene Hoffman intended to do a little farming on his five-acre homestead, and he had ambitions of building up a herd of forty cattle and a dozen or so hogs. Cleo Hoffman, her training having prepared her for a life of teaching music, mainly the piano, was equally optimistic. Deeply religious people, they were sadly without children. In this Kansas, Martha sometimes heard voices. Perhaps there was a God. Perhaps not. She found herself assaulted by loneliness, and drifting into middle age without a family. Voices from the past. Some she recognized. Some she did not. But, nevertheless, she listened. Recognizing her despair, Mr and Mrs Hoffman took Martha with them to a four-day revival by the river, where a dedicated young circuit rider named Wilson attempted to cast light in on Martha's dark soul. Satan be gone. The young evangelist preached with all his might, but Martha could find no solace in religion, and was unable to sympathize with the sufferings of the son of God when set against her own private misery. She stared at the Kansas sky. The shield of the moon shone brightly. Still she heard voices. Never again would the Hoffmans mention their God to Martha.

And then one morning, Mr Hoffman called the graying Martha to him. She knew this would eventually happen, for the crops were not selling, and once again the cattle had come back from market. A merciful market where nothing would sell. Martha had overheard them arguing with each other at the dinner table. Mr Hoffman looked at Martha, and then down at his hands which were folded in front of him. 'We have to go west, Martha. To where there is work for us. Kansas is still too young.' He paused. 'We are going to California, but we shall have to sell you back across the river in order that we can make this journey.' Martha's heart fell like a stone. No. 'We shall do all that we can to ensure that you are rewarded with good Christian owners.' No. He continued to speak, but Martha did not hear a word he uttered. Across the river to Hell. Eventually she asked, 'When?' She was unable to tell whether she had cut him off by speaking. Mr Hoffman cleared his throat. 'Next week, Martha.' He paused and looked up at her. 'I'm sorry.' This appeared to be his way of apologizing and dismissing her at the same time. It was possible that he was sorry. For himself. Martha was not sure if she should or could leave. Then Mr Hoffman climbed to his feet. 'You can leave, Martha.'

That night, Martha packed her bundle and left the house. For where, she was not sure (don't care where), being concerned only with heading west (going west), away from the big river (away from Hell), and avoiding nigger traders who would gladly sell her back over the border and into Missouri. The dark night spread before her, but behind the drifting clouds she knew the sky was heavy with stars. (Feeling good.) And then Martha heard the barking of dogs, and she tumbled into a ditch. (Lord, give me Lucas's voice.) She waited but heard nothing, only silence. (Thank you.) Eventually, Martha climbed to her feet and began to run. (Like the wind, girl.) Never again would she stand on an auction block. (Never.) Never again would she be renamed. (Never.) Never again would she belong to anybody. (No sir, never.) Martha looked over her shoulders as she ran. (Like the wind, girl.) And then, later, she saw dawn announcing its bold self, and a breathless Martha stopped to rest beneath a huge willow tree. (Don't nobody own me now.) She looked up, and through the thicket of branches she saw the morning star throbbing in the sky. As though recklessly attempting to preserve its life into the heart of a new day.

The woman poured Martha another glass of water, which Martha held tightly, as though trying to pull some heat from the wet glass. Still cold. She stared at Martha, who noticed now that this woman had the defensive, watchful eyes of a person who had never lost control of herself. The woman loosened her shawl, revealing a gold necklace at her throat. Still cold. 'Should I leave you now?' Beneath the hat, Martha could detect a shock of gray hair, but she was unclear as to whether or not the woman was trying to conceal it. Then somebody moved outside, their shadow darkening the line of light at the bottom of the closed door, their weight firing the floorboards. No. Martha's breath ran backwards into her body. For a moment, she was unsure if she would ever have the power to expel it and then, against her will, she burst in a quiet sigh. Eliza Mae. Come back for her? 'Shall I leave you now?' 'No.' Martha released the word, without quite understanding why she had done so. Then, as the woman sat on the edge of the mattress, and Martha felt the bed lurch beneath her, she regretted the generosity of her invitation. The woman was making herself at home.

I put down the plates in front of these men and stand back. They do not take their eyes from me. 'Thank you, ma'am.' The one with the blue eyes speaks quietly. The other two are in his shadow. They all dress alike in fancy attire; silver spurs, buckskin pants, and hats trimmed with rattlesnake skin. These three unshaven men, who sit uncomfortably in my restaurant. My other customers have left. They have driven away my customers. The truth is, there was only one other customer. These days, I am lucky to set eyes on more than six or seven a day. Colored men don't appear to be riding the trail like they used to. Coming in here with their kidneys and lungs all ruined, spitting blood, arms and legs broken over and over. Even the toughest of them lasted only a few years, but now it looks like their day is done. 'Anything else I can get you?' They still haven't touched their food. 'When's he due back, ma'am?' I run my hands down the front of my dress. They are more worn than ever, not just from the cooking, but from the washing and cleaning. It is almost ten years now since I arrived in Dodge and set up laundering clothes, then cooking some, then doing both when Lucy agreed to come in and help me out. 'He'll be back at dusk.' My mind turns to Lucy in the back. Waiting for me. Needing my help. We have a large order of washing needs finishing up before morning. 'Dusk?' He lets the word fall gently from his lips, as though he were the first man to coin such a term. I nod.

There used to be four of them when they last came up the trail. I don't remember the fourth man, but I know that there used to be a fourth. They arrived as four, but left as three. This time they have arrived as three and will leave as three. They tried to cheat Chester while playing poker in the saloon bar, but Chester, in his gentle manner, sneaked a little piece of chewing tobacco into his mouth and pointed up their ways. According to the sheriff, the fourth man, the scoundrel amongst them, he drew the first gun. The sheriff let Chester go. Gunplay is second nature to Chester. Their food is getting cold. One man picks up his fork and chases the potatoes through the gravy and around the plate a little. I know he wants to eat. He is waiting for the signal with mounting hunger. I tell the man that I have to go out back now, but he simply stares at me with those blue eyes. I tell him that I have clothes to wash. I offer him this information almost as a gift. He looks across at his friends, who can barely restrain themselves. They want to eat. He waves a dismissive hand in my face. Then, as though it is not important, he reaches into his pocket and throws a few bills on to the table top. He tells me that they will leave when they have finished. That they will wait out front for Chester.

I lift the dripping pile of clothes out of the boiler and drop them into the tub. I feel Lucy's eyes upon me, but I will not turn to face her. I am hot. I wipe my brow with the sleeve of my dress, and then again I bend over and try to squeeze more water from the shirts. She puts her hand on my shoulder, this woman who has been both friend and sister to me. She puts her hand on my shoulder and presses. She says nothing, and I still do not turn around. I continue to knead the clothes between my tired fingers. 'Martha,' she begins. 'Martha, child.' I turn to look at her. I drop the clothes and wrap my wet arms around her, and she pulls me close. I begin to sob. She says, 'You must go to Chester and warn him.' I listen to her, but we both know that it is too late. Even as she insists that I should leave now, she clasps me tighter.

I stand in the street. I see him in the distance, the dust clouding slowly around him as his horse, frame bent, head low, ambles out of the sunset and into the shadow that marks the beginning of the street. And they see him too. All three of them. They jump down from the rail. Lucy stands in the open doorway and looks on. I had only been in Dodge a few weeks when he came to me with his clothes to be laundered. He came back every Tuesday afternoon, as regular as sunset, but he barely spoke. Tipped his hat, always called me 'ma'am', never asked me for no money, or no credit, or no nothing. And then one day he told me that his name was Chester, that he was a wrangler on a ranch just outside of Dodge, that nobody could *top off* a bad horse like him, that he could smell loneliness like a buffalo could smell water. I told him, I didn't need no help, I just needed some companionship, that's all. He looked at me with a broad, knowing look, a look that could charm the gold out of a man's teeth, and asked if I wanted to move in with him into his store. I asked him what he sold, and he told me that he didn't sell a 'damn thing', but, there was plenty of room if I wanted to open up a business. He said that if we were going to prospect for happiness together, then he figured we ought to try and make a little money, too. I told Chester that I didn't think I could make him no babies no more. He smiled and said, 'I got babies some place that I ain't been no kind of father to. Figure it's best if I don't bother with no more baby-making.' He paused. 'I guess you noticed I ain't one to dress to impress the local belles.' Then he laughed some, till the tears streamed down his sweet chocolate face. That same afternoon, I pulled off my apron, pulled on a clean, calico dress, pinned down my hair with a bandana, and moved everything to Chester's place, which turned out to be a proper store. Chester said he won it in a card game from a storekeeper who had headed south to Mexico with everything he owned in his pockets. He claimed that, to begin with, some folks didn't take to the idea of a colored owning decent property, but by and by people let him be. He sat amongst the lumber stores, merchants, watchmakers, carpenters, blacksmiths, mechanics, medical men, and lawyers, trading nothing.

I soon set up in business concocting stews and soups for weary, half-starved colored men who had long since spent their trail rations. Vegetables and livestock, grown and raised in and around Dodge, appeared on the market. Beans, potatoes and onions at twenty-five cents a pound, beef at quarter the price, and large, plump turkeys at less than two dollars a piece. War came and war went and, almost unnoticed, the Union toppled. For a week or so, all lines were forgotten as Dodge toasted the victors in liquor until most folks could no longer hold a glass. I was free now, but it was difficult to tell what difference being free was making to my life. I was just doing the same things like before, only I was more contented, not on account of no emancipation proclamation, but on account of my Chester. I look down the street and see him coming yet closer, his shoulders square, his head held high. For ten long years, this man has made me happy. For ten long years, this man has made me forget – and that's a gift from above. I never thought anybody could give me so much love, even without trying, without appearing to make any effort, without raising no dust about it. Just steering and roping, and whatever manner of business he felt like seeing to in the days, watching the sunset at dusk, and a little whiskey and cards at night. Always there when I needed him. I glance at Lucy, whose face is a picture of fear. I want to tell her, 'Don't worry, Lucy.' And then the shots ring out and Chester slumps from the saddle, but his foot gets caught up in the stirrup. His horse stops and lets Chester fall respectfully to the ground. Three brave men with pistols smoking, and Lucy screaming.

Lucy brings the candle to my room and sits on a wicker chair. She has not yet stopped crying. I have not begun. 'We can go up to Leavenworth,' she says. 'I hear that the colored troops in the Fort are always looking for somebody to wash and clean for them. And plenty of colored folks still figuring to come across the Missouri and into Kansas.' I stare back at her, but say nothing. 'We can't stay here, Martha.' I know this. I know that I will never again be happy in fast-loving, high-speeding, Dodge. Not without Chester. And the restaurant. 'We can take our business to Leavenworth, establish a laundry.' I nod in agreement. Then I ask her. 'Lucy,' I say, 'did I ever tell you that I had a daughter?' She looks back at me in astonishment.

Again she asked Martha if she was cold, and this time Martha could not hold back the sad confession that, despite this woman's efforts, her body remained numb. Too late. The woman smiled, then stood and stoked at the stove, but her gesture was one of idle hope. Too late. On top of the stove sat a great iron kettle which reminded Martha of the one back east, twenty-five years ago, in Virginia, which rang like a bell when you struck it. And if you put the tips of your fingers against it, you could feel the black metal still humming long after the kettle had ceased its song. Martha used to catch rainwater in it, the same rainwater with which she would wash Eliza Mae's matted hair. Keep still, girl. Such misery in one life. She looked at the palms of her hands where the darker skin had now bled into the lighter, and she wondered if freedom was more important than love, and indeed if love was at all possible without somebody taking it from her. Her tired mind swelled and surged with these difficult thoughts, until it pained her to think. The woman finally stopped her stoking. Martha could feel the tears welling up behind her eyes. 'Can I help?' No, you must go. 'Are you all right?' No. Please go. 'I'm sorry about the stove.' No. No. No. Martha stifled a sob.

It seemed another age now, although in truth it was only two months ago that Lucy, her hair in a wrap, had come to her in the small, two-roomed cabin that they shared, and broken the news of her impending marriage. It had been a dark night, the solitary light from a candle teasing the two friends with the twin possibilities of both warmth and security. Not that Lucy's news came as any surprise to Martha, for she had long been aware of her friend's feelings for the colored man from the dry goods store. Tubs and boilers no longer had a hold on Lucy's mind, and now she would be escaping them by marrying this man who had built himself a storey and a half house from the profits of selling that boom-town, sure-fire money-maker at a dollar a pound: nails. Martha took Lucy's hands in her own, and told her that she was pleased, and that Lucy must not, under any circumstances, worry over her. With this said, she encouraged Lucy to begin packing if she was going to leave, as planned, in the morning. Lucy levered herself out of her chair and began to address herself to the tasks at hand, while an ailing Martha sat basking in the glow of the candle and watched her. These days, Martha's old body was overburdened, and seldom did she pass an afternoon without a few cat-naps. By evening her feet and ankles were so swollen that she had to use both hands to pull off her shoes, and her undergarments now grew strangely tight during the days, her underskirt band often cutting into her waist. She desperately needed to rest, but she had determined that Lucy must never see the evidence of her malaise. And certainly not now. Lucy was to leave with a clear conscience, but not before Martha had herded her into the picture-making man's studio and ordered her to sit still. She watched her friend as she continued to gather up her few belongings, and Martha began to laugh quietly to herself.

A week later, the man came into the cabin outhouse, his arms burdened down with a bundle of heavy flannel shirts and coarse pants that needed laundering. Such visits were becoming less common, for either men seemed to be getting accustomed to giving their own garments the soap and water treatment, or Martha had serious competition from some place that she had not, as yet, heard about. The conversation that he struck up with Martha was a generous one, in that he desired to know if she could possibly manage this load by herself. Well, excuse me, mister. Was there anybody else in town to whom he might turn? Feigning ignorance of what he might be implying, Martha took the clothes and assured him that they would be ready for him whenever he needed them. This was just as well, he said, for he would soon be leaving for California with a group of colored pioneers. He informed her of this fact as though it were something that one ought to be proud of, and with this announcement delivered, he tipped his hat and wished her good day. After he left, Martha thought long and hard about her own prospects. The many years of her life with Lucy in this two-roomed cabin were now at an end, and although this Leavenworth had suited her, despite its numerous saloons, billiard parlors, and houses of joy, Martha felt that she must leave. Not that Leavenworth was either violent or dangerous. In fact, the townsmen had established a liking for law and order, and introduced codes that were rigidly enforced by deputies and marshals, which meant that in this town the fast gun was not the law. But although Leavenworth was free of the turbulence of Dodge, and in spite of the fact that her years here had been peaceful, if somewhat lonely, Martha had a strange notion that she, too, must become a part of the colored exodus that was heading west. Lucy had left behind a letter, not so much inviting

Martha to come out and join her and her future husband in San Francisco, but begging her to do so. Martha unfolded the square of paper and decided to look it over one more time. Then, when she had finished, she blew out the lamp and sat quietly in the dark. Eliza Mae was once again back in her mind, not that her lost child had ever truly vanished. Perhaps her girl-child had pioneered west?

When, some days later, the man returned for his clean and well-ironed garments, Martha eyeballed him directly and announced that she, too, would be coming along. She deliberately did not ask, but he, with equal deliberation, did not respond. So once again, Martha informed him of her decision, and only now did he put down the clothes and begin to explain why this would not be possible. He advised Martha that this was to be a long and difficult journey, with at least twenty wagons, and they would have to cope with what the Indians called 'crazy weather', both blizzards and heat. Martha simply stared back at the man, forcing him to continue. 'We'll be following stream beds most of the way, but you never know.' He shrugged his shoulders. 'And we'll likely be called upon to walk, for the wagons will use every ounce of space for food, water, tools, and so on.' Martha found herself borrowing courage from this conversation, the way she had seen some men do from tequila. 'My role will be to cook for you,' she said. 'I won't be a burden, but I don't have no savings.' She went on, assuring him that she knew about wild and dangerous country, and had many times seen horses and oxen shot that had broken their legs, and watched as the trailriders made soup out of their hides and bones. She claimed that she had been aboard wagons that had fallen clean apart, that she knew sagebrush and sidewinders like they were her kin, and the shifting sands and whirling dust of the cactus-shrouded world would suit her just dandy. 'I'm afraid of nothing,' said Martha, 'least of all Indians or hard times. Colored folks generally got to be obligated to white folks to get clear to California, but you colored pioneers are offering me a chance. You let me work my fare out and I'll cook, wash clothes, and powerfully nurse to the sick and ailing. And I ain't fussy about sleeping on no bare ground. I done it plenty of times before, had the beaten hardness of the earth for a bed and the sky for covering.' The man looked blankly at her, but Martha, anxious that she should not be fooled, pressed on and asked after him when they proposed leaving. 'The day after tomorrow,' he said, his voice low, his expression now one of confusion. 'I'll be ready,' said Martha, tearing at her apron. 'And you just tell your people that you done found a cook.' He smiled weakly, then turned and left, his arms laden with clean laundry. My daughter. The energy of youth once more stirred within her. I know I'm going to find my child in California.

But the woman who now stood above Martha, casting pitiful glances, was not her daughter. Eliza Mae? 'I'll leave you now,' she said. 'But you must expect to receive me in the morning.' You must expect to receive me? Did she mean by this to suggest that Martha had some choice over their arrangement? That she could, if she so wished, choose not to receive her in the morning? Martha watched the woman back slowly out of the cold room. Thank you. She left Martha alone. Sickness had descended upon her and she was unable to respond. Martha felt the sadness of not possessing a faith that could reassure her that, having served her apportioned span, she would now be ushered to a place of reunion. She looked through the cracked window-pane. Dawn was some hours off, back east, approaching slowly. To be reunited. The town of Denver was mantled in a deep snow, the arms of the trees sheathed in a thin frost, the same thin frost that enveloped Martha's faithless heart.

The evening sky is streaked with red and yellow. I watch as the sun prepares to go down beneath the horizon. To my left, there is panic. Voices begin to climb. A pioneer has broken an ox by driving it too hard. It has to be slaughtered, but at least there will be fresh meat. He ignores this commotion and stands before me with frustration written across his face. I know that I have slowed down their progress. It is this that he wishes to talk with me about. He rolls a cigarette, his fingers clammy and stiff, and then he gestures me to rest upon the hide-bottom chair. He is a man who speaks as much with his hands as his voice. I had noticed this when he first came in with his bundle of flannel shirts and coarse pants. 'Well?' This is his beginning. I know what will follow. I look beyond him. A storm is working its way across the land. My old ears can still hear the dull rumbling of thunder.

Six weeks ago we set out across the open prairie, dust clouds rising, the noonday sun at full strength, a party of seventy colored people walking to the side of our wagons. The wagons were drawn by six oxen trained to work in pairs, animals which have a tendency to skittishness, and as such they initially frightened me. The first and rear wagons were attended to by experienced drivers, but the rest were handled by we pioneers. The idea was that I should cook for all those without family, mainly bullwhackers, all men, and this I tried to do, rustling up bacon and salt pork and any game or beast that the men might happen to shoot along the way. I made sure each wagon had ample amounts of flour, sugar, coffee and rice, and a plentiful supply of ten-gallon water kegs. Other provisions and equipment in my charge included vinegar, soap, matches, cooking utensils and field stoves. But it was never easy. Before dawn, the freezing wind ripped through our clothing and right into the marrow. At noon, and early in the afternoon, the sun often caused us serious discomforts, made worse by the type of clothing that we wore. Heavy pants and flannel shirts for the men, and high-necked, long-sleeved, dark dresses that wouldn't show the dirt for the women. At night, we drew the wagons into a circle, and camp fires were built, meals cooked, and tales told of white expeditions where cruelties were often inflicted upon colored men and women.

The wagon train soon settled into a routine where one

difficult day seemed much like the next, and where there was
no discernible change to the uniform landscape. However, I
felt myself growing weaker, and I tried in vain to diguise my
ailments. Some days we covered ten miles across the dry grass,
some days twelve or fifteen, depending upon repairs or the
weather. We saw Indians, and I felt some sympathy with them,
but the Indian bands kept their distance and watched, choosing
not to make anything of their encounters with the dark white
men. Except on one occasion, when a column of a dozen
warriors, at their head a chief, rode out towards the train.
Behind them came the squaws, some with papooses slung
across their backs, and all around them yapped pitiful-looking
dogs who would in time become food. The chief halted, as
did the wagon train, and he dismounted. By means of facial
expressions and gestures, he made it known that we could pass
in peace. I watched as our leader rewarded him with sugar and
tobacco, and he in turn was rewarded with grunts of approval.
Our only other visitors were the dark, shaggy buffalo who
moved at such a slow pace that it was difficult to make out
their progress. Our leader forbade the men, who were tiring
of my pork, to stalk and hunt these monsters, informing them
that should they be *spooked* and stampede, they would happily
trample all before them. The occasional deer or game bird
was the only alternative to that which we carried aboard the
wagons.

Ten days ago, the river source began to dwindle to a mere
trickle, and water was severely rationed. I watched the oxen
pulling the enormous loads with heroism, and I witnessed the
equally impressive bravery of the pioneers who, dehydrated
as they were, energy flowing back and forth, still managed to
pursue the torture. My own state became perilous, racked as
I was with exhaustion, but still I managed to keep my misery
to myself. Until yesterday. When it became clear that I was
unable to prepare any more meals. I had long since been
relieved of laundry duties, owing to the water rationing, and
I had occasionally begged a ride on a wagon while all others

walked. But then, this final humiliation. Yesterday morning, under the dazzling, intense blue of the Colorado sky, the foothills of the Rockies in the distance, this frustrated man sat before me with a stern face and shared with me his water ration. Suddenly, and without warning, his face softened and he spoke. 'Today and tomorrow you will rest, Martha. Ride in Jacob's wagon on the flour sacks. Tomorrow evening we shall speak again.' He took my hand with what I imagined to be real affection.

'Well?' This is his beginning. I know what will follow. 'You must find some shelter, for you will never survive the journey to California.' I say nothing. The sun finally disappears beneath the horizon. I look across to the large fire where they are preparing the evening meal. Six weeks ago, I was one of them. But times have changed. Still, I cherish these brave people – these colored pioneers – among whom I travel. They took upon themselves this old, colored woman and chose not to put her down like a useless load. Until now. 'Tomorrow, Martha.' I nod, unable to find the words to convince him that he must not feel guilty. None of them should. I am grateful. That is all. I am simply grateful. I smile at this man who is young enough to be my son. 'Thank you,' he says. He turns away before one of us discovers words that are best left undisturbed.

At dawn, they bear me like a slaughtered hog up and into the back of a wagon. But first they have cleared out some supplies to make room for me. Other wagons will bear the burden of carrying these provisions. He approaches and tells me that I will be taken to Denver, which lies some miles off their course. If I leave now, I may reach by sunset, which will give the wagon a chance to rejoin the group within two days. It is still cold. He offers me an extra blanket, which I take. We are to peel off from the main group, myself and two men, and strike out alone. He tells me that I have nothing to be afraid of. God willing, he hopes one day to find me in California. I thank him. All about me the pioneers stir. Sunken-eyed, still tired. I nursed and fed many of them through the first trying days, forcing food and water down their throats, and rallying them to their feet in order that they might trudge ten more miles towards their beloved California. Once there, they all dream of tasting true freedom, of learning important skills, of establishing themselves as a sober and respectable class of people. This is their dream. My weakness will delay them no longer. I hear the snap of a whip, and the driver yelling a sharp, impatient phrase to his oxen. As we move off, the tears begin to course down my old face.

We pass into a town on whose outskirts stand log cabins, some finished, some unfinished, but clearly being attended to. The town is growing. As we journey on, I see stores, rooming houses and saloons. But I see only two people. Indians. I remember the day the colored troops of Leavenworth paraded Indian scalps, fingers with rings attached, and ears that had been pulled clean off. They behaved like the men whose uniforms they wore. And now the Indians disappear from view. Up here in the Rockies, my breath is short and I gasp for air. I lie back down, but cannot rediscover my previous position. And then the wagon shudders to a halt, and one of my fellow pioneers appears before me. 'This is Main Street, Miss Martha.' I look at him as he pulls his collar tight up under his chin. Behind him the wind is rising, and the sky is beginning to darken. 'We're under instructions to set you down right here and high-tail it back to the others.'

In the pre-dawn hours of an icy February morning, Martha opened her eyes. Outside it was still dark, and the snow continued to spin. A dream began to wash through her mind. Martha dreamed that she had traveled on west to California, by herself, and clutching her bundle of clothing. Once there she was met by Eliza Mae, who was now a tall, sturdy colored woman of some social standing. Together, they tip-toed their way through the mire of the streets to Eliza Mae's residence, which stood on a fine, broad avenue. They were greeted by

Eliza Mae's schoolteacher husband and the three children, who were all dressed in their Sunday best, even though this was not Sunday. A dumbstruck Martha touched their faces. Eliza Mae insisted that her mother should stay and live with them, but Martha was reluctant. All was not right. There was still no news of Lucas, and her Eliza Mae now called herself Cleo. Martha refused to call her daughter by this name, and insisted on calling her a name that her children and husband found puzzling. Soon it was time for Martha to leave, but her daughter simply forbade her mother to return east. Martha, feeling old and tired, sat down and wept openly, and in front of her grandchildren. She would not be going any place. She would never again head east. To Kansas. To Virginia. Or to beyond. She had a westward soul which had found its natural-born home in the bosom of her daughter.

Martha Randolph won't be taking any washing today. No tubs, no ironing. No cooking, either. Martha will simply sleep through the day. The woman, her cold body wrapped in her black coat, left the Denver streets which were now clad in thick snow. She opened the door and looked in upon the small colored woman, who stared back at her with wide eyes. The unsuccessful fire in the pot-bellied stove was dead. The woman gently closed in the door. Martha won't be taking any washing today. And the woman wondered who or what this woman was. They would have to choose a name for her if she was going to receive a Christian burial.

III

CROSSING THE RIVER

Journal of a voyage intended (by God's permission) in the *Duke of York*, snow, from Liverpool to the Windward Coast of Africa, etc., commenced the 24th August 1752.

Officers and Seamen belonging to the *Duke of York*.
Commenced pay 24th August 1752.

NAMES	QUALITY	
James Hamilton	Master	
John Pierce	1st Mate	Discharged 21st Dec. 1752 *Fortune*
Henry Allen	Surgeon	
Francis Foster	2nd Mate	Deceased 26th April 1753
William Smith	3rd Mate	
Joseph Griffith	Carpenter	
George Davy	Boatswain	Discharged 15th Jan. 1753
William Barber	Cooper	
Thomas Gallagher	Steward	
Jonathan Swain	Cook	Deceased 14th March 1753
Mark Brown	Gunner	
Edward White	Carpenter's Mate	Deceased 23rd April 1753
Samuel Morgan	Fore the mast	
Matthew Pitts	do.	
John Lawson	do.	
Robert Lewis	do.	
Joseph Cropper	do.	Discharged 20th Nov. 1752
Richard Forrester	do.	
Edmund Fellows	do.	
Jacob Creed	do.	Discharged 20th Nov. 1752
George Robinson	do.	

NAMES	QUALITY	
Thomas Taylor	Fiddler do.	
James Whitaker	do.	
Peter Welsh	do.	
Owen Thompson	Ship's Apprentice	
Edward Gibson	do.	
Matthew Arthur	do.	Deceased 5th March 1753
John Johnson	do.	

Monday 24th August . . . At 3 p.m. cast from the pier head at Liverpool, run against the flood. At 7 p.m. moored with the sheet anchor. A light breeze and some rain . . .

Tuesday 25th August . . . All day cloudy weather, fresh gales. Four of our people, Edmund Fellows, James Whitaker, Edward Gibson and John Johnson, fixed the longboat's sails. Carpenter mended the channel bend. John Lawson fixed stoppers for the cables. Pilot boat came on board with 3 sheep, and 2 quarters of beef . . .

★

Thursday 27th August . . . All day fair weather. A brig informed us of variable winds . . .

★

Saturday 29th August At daylight this morning unmoored. High water, fresh gales about SW. For Windward and Gold Coast . . .

★

Wednesday 9th September Thick and fresh gales. Rain in the night, strong and at times very hard. Looking very dirty to the westward. At 2 p.m. came in with the sheet anchor in 10 fathoms. Saw the land of Dublin to the NW and W. In the road, His Majesty's Ship, the *African*, 3 Dutch, and another English vessel. Continues very bad weather . . .

Thursday 10th September All night northern lights flying about the wild sky. Daylight came on thick and the gale increased about WSW and West. At noon let go the starboard anchor under foot . . .

Friday 11th September . . . Begin to be sensible of a change of climate. Hazy weather. Some small rain. Indifferent smooth water . . .

★

Saturday 19th September On this morning discovered William Barber, Cooper, guilty of broaching a cask of ale reserved for cabin use and filling it with water. Put him in irons and, the facts being fully proved, ordered 12 lashes . . .

★

Tuesday 29th September . . . At 1 p.m. the land ahead proved to be the island Grand Canaries: soon after saw the peak of Tenerife at a great distance. People at work upon the cables. Carpenter began to raise the gratings of the women's room . . .

★

Monday 5th October . . . The water once again a deep sea colour. Sounded but could get no ground with 60 fathoms of line. A great many flying fish about us. Caught a small dolphin . . .

Tuesday 6th October . . . Carpenter fitted up state room to serve as a shop on the coast. Removed most of India cloth from hold into cabin. Got ship's arms chest aft. Marked off the slaves' rooms, and Carpenter and Mate set about building the bulkheads. All hands engaged. Gunner making cartridges, etc., for the carriage and swivel guns . . .

★

Sunday 11th October . . . Very variable winds and weather.

At 9 a.m. sails set with a pretty breeze. Got soundings at about 35 fathoms, white sand and black stones. Caught a small shark. By 2 p.m. a great deal of lightning and thunder. Very strong ripplings . . .

★

Tuesday 13th October . . . Saw land, Sierra Leone eastward about 3 miles. At 3 p.m. passed 4 vessels at anchor off the bar. One, *Mary*, a snow, of Liverpool is known to me. The *Halifax* of Bristol is almost slaved. The 2 others are schooners from New England. Have 14 fathoms of water, red sand. At sunset anchored in Frenchman's Bay. Fired 7 guns. The rest of the day was passed in feasting and firing.

Wednesday 14th October Fair weather. Made a trip with the yawl for water. Visited on board with Captain Williams of the *Mary*. He informed me that the *Devon* of Bristol was recently run on shore by the slaves in an insurrection and totally lost. There was loss of 11 crew. Upon my return the ship's company, to a man, complained that in my absence the Boatswain, Mr Davy, had used them ill. I thought it proper to put him in chains lest he might occasion disturbance when we get slaves on board.

Thursday 15th October . . . Corrected the Carpenter with a dozen stripes of the cat for making a commotion while fetching wood . . .

Friday 16th October In the morning I went on board Mr Sharp's shallop to Whiteman's Bay to view some slaves. Was shown 10, but bought none. Lame, old, or blind. In the afternoon ran up with the flood to the island factory. Got there a handsome dozen, paid the goods for them, and brought them up . . .

★

Wednesday 21st October . . . Came up from the Leeward the

Virtue, Morris, sloop, of Barbados. He has some 40 slaves on board in 2 months. He gives a disturbing account of trade down below. The price of slaves has run to 125 bars and upwards. Bartered with Captain Morris for 4 hogsheads of rum at 4/- per gallon . . .

★

Thursday 29th October . . . When it lies in the desk, the thermometer at 74, but when exposed to the heat of the sun it rose, at noon, to 96. I was much surprised to detect so great a difference . . .

★

Wednesday 4th November . . . Variable weather, mostly a land breeze, and in the night thunder and lightning. Discharged the Boatswain from his confinement, upon his promise of amendment . . .

Thursday 5th November . . . Last night Captain Morris's longboat came in with 10 more slaves having been 2 days gone. He pretends that the trade hereabouts is all engaged to him, but I am not an apprentice . . .

Friday 6th November . . . Dispatched Mr Pierce in the yawl with a letter for Mr Jones at Whiteman's Bay. I wish to know whether he can give me any encouragement to stay longer hereabouts. This evening he returned with a half-dozen fine man-boys, but the bars were excessive dear. According to Mr Pierce's testimony, gleaned from Mr Jones, the resident white men are all exhausted. This parcel of a half-dozen being the last of the present crop . . .

Saturday 7th November Fair weather, faint sea breeze. In the morning had a visit from some Portuguese of Pirates Bay. They brought a woman slave, whom I refused being long-breasted. I shall proceed down the coast once the longboat is repaired . . .

★

Thursday 12th November This morning set the punt on shore with Jacob Creed and George Robinson. Instead of returning on board they visited a French schooner and got drunk. Afterwards they returned to shore to fight, which when they were sufficiently tired of, attempted to come off, but the ebb being strong, and they by now too tired to pull well, they came upon the rocks. I sent Mr Foster to them, and he was obliged to slip the rope. I gave both of these *gentlemen* a good caning, and would carry them both confined in chains to the Americas but for the consideration of our being a slaving ship . . .

★

Saturday 14th November At daylight unmoored. At 10 a.m. came in the *Wanderer*, a French-built cutter in 7 weeks from London. At noon, being high water, weighed and worked down against the sea breeze . . .

★

Monday 16th November . . . Put a fresh cargo into the yawl. Left the ship before noon and rowed into shore. Was shown 11 slaves, of whom I picked 5, viz., 4 men, 1 woman. Paid what goods I had in the boat were suitable and I am to send the rest . . .

Tuesday 17th November . . . Went on shore directly to look at 4 slaves but they were all old. Rowed up the river and at dusk reached the town. No trade here at present, but they promised to immediately send word of my arrival to Mr Lewis . . .

Wednesday 18th November . . . Mr Lewis has promised me 2 dozen of the finest slaves if I will tarry a few more days. To this I agree. I return to discover the Boatswain, Mr Davy, once more very abusive and being blind drunk. I secure him in irons and am determined to deliver him up to the first man-of-war . . .

*

Friday 20th November Between 2 a.m. and 3 a.m., the watch upon deck being either asleep or consenting, 2 of the people, viz. Joseph Cropper and Jacob Creed, ran away with the yawl, though chained. At daylight she was perceived lying on shore, and I dispatched Mr Smith to bring her off before the blacks knew she was in their power, otherwise she would have cost me, I suppose, near to 100 bars. My people I do not expect to again encounter . . .

Saturday 21st November This morning had excessive rain for 2 hours with violent thunder and lightning, but, thank God, no damage ensued. By 3 p.m. Mr Lewis came aboard with the promised slaves, most being remarkably fine and sturdy. I purchased 17, viz., 12 men, 5 women. In future the day must begin with arms and sentinels, there now being above 50 slaves on board . . .

*

Tuesday 8th December . . . Sent Mr Foster in the yawl with goods for 5 slaves, that is to say close to 500 bars which in earlier times might have purchased 20. He returned at sunset in triumph, though it will not do to continue giving nearly what the slaves will fetch in the Americas, exclusive of freight and commissions, and besides the tediousness of trade and the great risk of mortality . . .

*

Thursday 10th December This morning fired 3 guns for trade, but it would appear that everybody is engaged, and the country hereabouts now full of goods. At 4 p.m. the *Fortune*, Jackson, snow, of Liverpool anchored nearby. At 7 p.m. I went aboard and dined with the frail veteran of the coast, Captain Jackson. We agreed to go downwards and take our share of trade, and assist and protect each other, for there is much villainy to the south, and it is judged precarious for a single ship in these times. Captain Jackson confesses that he has recently been obliged to part with 130 bars for a prime slave, one of his people having walked 2 days in the woods to look at him and bid. I am resolved to stop short of such extravagance . . .

★

Sunday 20th December An excessive dismal night, populated by a tornado which proved the most violent I have ever suffered. At the height of the squall the yawl broke the best chain on board, but by some miraculous gesture the two remaining ropes managed to hold her secure. We peered on, the night being so close there was no seeing unless in the glare of the lightning, and at regular intervals sought confirmation that our smaller party was still with us . . .

Monday 21st December . . . The storm having subsided, we anchored at noon in 13 fathoms of clear water and fired 3 guns. Soon after we saw the *Fortune*. As she drew nearer she began to fire minute guns, and we perceived her colours at half-mast, which we understood to be a melancholy signal of Captain Jackson's death. She anchored nearby, and the First Mate came aboard and informed me that in the midst of last night's terrible flurry the Captain had passed away most peacefully. I went on board with Mr Pierce and tendered him the command. He seemed greatly honoured by the charge. Soon after I returned to the *Duke of York* and at sunset fired 6 minute guns.

★

Wednesday 23rd December This morning Mr Pierce came on board and conveyed to me his desire to complete the loading of his cargo on some other part of the coast, his ship's crew reasoning that this part of Africa had brought them only ill-luck. To this I readily agreed. If the weather remained fair, the *Fortune* would, he announced, weigh anchor with the tide . . .

★

Friday 15th January At 8 a.m. set out in the punt to deliver Mr Davy to HMS *Humber*, man-of-war, at Sierra Leone. Hard rain and a great sea, that I was several times afraid that we might be filled. Got safe round the rock by 3 p.m. and aboard the *Humber* by 5 p.m. I discharged my Boatswain. On my return I discovered that the Carpenter had finished strengthening the *barricado*. 1 small girl had been added to the cargo in my absence. Mr Allen, Surgeon, assured me I would regard her a bargain. On a cursory glance I was able to confirm for myself the strength of his judgement. The first part of this night has blown fresh with a short, ugly sea . . .

[At Sea, 10th January.

My Dearest,

I have, these past few days, been discouraged from writing by the mighty apparatus of the seas. But being unable to hold off and tolerate further delay, I now try my eyes by candlelight and attempt to form characters that, I trust, will not try your own. At present, I cannot imagine writing with pleasure to any on land or sea but your own dear self, my head being full of the petty concerns of this valuable vessel, and the lives of the people who dwell hereabouts, whose fortunes are entrusted to my care. These are, indeed, petty concerns when set against my love for you, for I can declare, with honour, that barely an hour of my past life comes to mind with any pleasure, excepting valuable and precious time I have passed in your company, and for that I think the innumerable miseries and pains of my previous unhappy life, not a dear purchase. My affection for you goes beyond any words I can find or use, and I simply wish that it were possible for you to travel with me, and strengthen my purpose in fatigue and difficulty, without actually suffering them. How trifling they would seem to me!

But, I submit, I travel abroad in the comfortable knowledge that my better, precious part is safely at home, and though she understands absence to be painful, she knows it is so for her sake. I am engaged in active business, and have some new scene every day to relieve my mind; besides I have long been used to suffering. On the contrary, you, by marriage to one such as I, have exposed yourself to anxieties to which you were a stranger. I know you have done this willingly, and I love you all the greater for this sacrifice.

My last letter concluded abruptly, for I was ill and disconcerted by an incident in business. I feared it might give rise to bad consequences, and sadly this came to pass. I take a good deal of raillery among the sea-captains, for they *know* I have not a secure knowledge of life, and I *know* they have not. They claim I am melancholy; I tell them they have lost their wits. They say I am a slave to a single woman; I claim they are a slave to hundreds, of all qualities. They wonder at my *lack* of humour, I pity theirs. They declare they can form no idea of my happiness, I counter with knowledge that being pleased with a drunken debauch, or the smile of a prostitute, can never give one such as I pleasure. They pretend, all the while, to appeal to experience against me, but I stand firm. On my own ship such discord recently swelled into near-mutiny, for there is among my officers one in particular who sees me as little more than a *gentleman-passenger*. I had been warned, prior to our departure, that I might expect trouble in abundance from Mr Davy, the Boatswain, and he recently unleased his drunken invective on myself and others of our company, and then in a flight of madness attempted to seize the ship. But no more of this business, except to say that, indeed, all was very nearly lost, but now we are found. It seems that the disparity between my dear late father's great reputation, and my own youthful 26 years, fired some hereabouts, under the skilful guidance of Mr Davy, into a frenzy of hostility, the assumption being that I owed everything to my connections, and nothing to my own experience or abilities. But again, I say, no more of this business.

I confess that, when alone, the recollection of my past with you overpowers me with a tender concern, and such thoughts give me a pleasure, second only to that of being actually with you. I have written myself into tears, yet I feel a serenity I never imagined till I was able to call you mine. To win your love was my principal desire, and without it, all that you possessed, and might have bestowed upon me, would have seemed dull by comparison. I have the confidence that you love me, a confidence which renders me superior to all the little entertainments that might allure me, and all the difficulties which are daily thrown in my way. Whatever dangers and hardships I meet, I declare that no one has heard me complain. Those of my company who pity me because I appear not to be fond of what *they* call pleasure, know not what renders me superior to it. I was once, in earlier times, as eager as they after pleasure, but you have thoroughly refined my state, so that my sole pleasure is to dream of our future children, and our family life together. What I have in view at the end of this voyage, is so fixed in my thoughts, that to be acknowledged and rewarded by you, outweighs any hardship that I might possibly suffer.

I am, etc.
Inviolably yours.
James Hamilton.]

★

Wednesday 20th January . . . Fair weather, the thermometer reading 79 degrees. In the afternoon took the yawl in to see if any trade has come down as yet . . .

★

Friday 22nd January . . . Fresh gales of wind from the N to the NE with some rain. Bought a pair of man-boys from an African *prince*, as they are styled. Dispatched the yawl to the shore with instructions to fill a load of water . . .

CROSSING THE RIVER

★

Thursday 4th February This morning at daybreak I was saluted by the agreeable vision of my longboat, and soon after she came on board with crew well and a dozen slaves, viz., 4 men, 2 women, 1 man-boy, 1 boy (4 feet) and 4 girls (under-size). Mr Smith brought news that in the coming weeks there is likely to be an extraordinary run of trade and no competitors. Prices may fall below 100 bars in these conditions. In the evening I ordered the fiddler to play and strong liquors to be drunk. Hectic days lie ahead . . .

Friday 5th February . . . Put another cargo in the longboat and sent her and the yawl to Mr Johnson's with a charge to trade vigorously. The Carpenter seems to have rid himself of the drinking habit, and is busily extending the bulkhead of the men's room. This afternoon, bartered with a Frenchman for 2 anchors of brandy, 20 cwt of rice, and a man slave of quite unnatural proportions. Hot hazy weather.

Saturday 6th February This morning the yawl returned upon the flood tide with information that the *Robert*, a New England sloop, is down the coast with near 200 slaves on board, and that there has been an insurrection in her, in which the Chief Mate, 2 ordinary seamen, and 27 slaves were killed. The good news is that this portion of shoreline has proved fertile ground, and we can presently expect a brimming longboat. At 4 p.m. I dispatched the yawl laden with more goods . . .

★

Wednesday 17th February . . . An unwholesome land wind. Have the Surgeon and 4 more people ill of a fever. Carpenter purposefully employed in building the bulkheads in the women's room, Gunner cleaning the arms . . .

★

Saturday 27th February . . . A continual calm. At 3 p.m. weighed with the flood tide to drive downwards, but at sunset can hardly perceive we have made any advance. The Carpenter's work is complete, having constructed yet another platform in the men's room. The ship is clear enough to take the remainder of our slaves without inconvenience. This day fixed 6 swivel blunderbusses in the *barricado* which will, I hope, be sufficient to intimidate the slaves from any thoughts of an insurrection . . .

Sunday 28th February Anchored this morning in 15 fathoms. An excessive high surf upon the shore, which prevents the canoes from coming off. I left the ship in the punt and got over the bar, but not without some danger, the sea running high for so small a boat. Reached safely to the town by sunset. My great desire is to complete 50 slaves before I go downwards, and I have great reason to expect to do it here in a matter of days . . .

★

Saturday 6th March A hazy morning with both sea and land breeze. The fever has again taken hold among the crew and sadly dispatched one Matthew Arthur. Was obliged to bury him immediately, being extremely offensive. I sent the punt on shore with 6 casks to be filled with water. In the evening she returned with the water, and brought me a goat as a present from the King. We saluted him with 5 guns. It appears he is eager to go and look for trade for me . . .

Sunday 7th March Began this day with much activity. Cleared the women's room and scraped it. Watched the punt struggle over the bar as she returned for yet more provisions. Begin to be tired of waiting here, yet by all accounts this is the only place I can expect to lie without competition upon the whole coast. This evening the wind rose, and the current being very irregular the ship turns round like a top.

★

Friday 12th March At 3 a.m. unmoored, and at 9 a.m. weighed. Sailed downwards and anchored in 12 fathoms at sunset. Calm sea breeze. Perceived the canoes endeavouring to come off to us, and the blacks making a great fire upon the beach. Fired a carriage gun, and hoisted a light . . .

Saturday 13th March . . . At noon the canoes once again on board, brought 8 slaves, viz., 2 men, 1 woman, 2 boys, 3 girls. All small, the girl slaves all below 4 feet. Mr Wilson informed me that he had met with Mr Pierce's *Fortune*, and that the ship had well in excess of 300 slaves, and had not purchased above 3 in these parts, being concerned with quality. Sadly his yawl was lost here . . .

Sunday 14th March . . . At 1 p.m. the sea-breeze came in and had a fine gale. Steered SE along the shore and anchored at 8 p.m. abreast the town in 13 fathoms, the natives making a great smoke upon the beach. In the road the *Charity*, Donald, a New England rum sloop, almost fully slaved. Received intelligence from Mr Donald that prices in these parts are more extravagant than ever, but I fancy he seeks to deceive me. Just before midnight departed this life the Cook, Jonathan Swain, after a week's illness. He was in a continual delirium.

Monday 15th March . . . Lay until noon in expectation of a canoe, but nobody stirred. Weighed with the evening tide . . .

★

Thursday 25th March At daylight saw a longboat on shore. She came aboard at 9 a.m., brought with her 5 slaves, 2 fine boys, and 3 old women whom I instructed them to dispose of. Had a very discouraging account of the state of affairs to Leeward, all about the river being full of an

113

epidemical sickness that is ravaging amongst the slaves. The *Britannia*, Parsons, of London, was obliged to off before he had finished, having buried 25 on the coast. Discharged, cleaned and reloaded the small arms. At sunset saw a sloop rigged boat, standing up the coast . . .

★

Friday 2nd April . . . By the favour of Divine Providence made a timely discovery today that the slaves were forming a plot for an insurrection. Surprised 4 attempting to get off their irons, and upon further search in their rooms found some knives, stones, shot, etc. Put 2 in irons and delicately in the thumbscrews to encourage them to a full confession of those principally concerned. In the evening put 5 more in neck yokes.

★

Wednesday 7th April Weighed at daylight. Soon after saw a ship to windward come fast up with us. At noon I went on board, proved the *Highlander*, Daniel Wilkes, of London, with materials for a new fort on the Gold Coast. Informed him that I propose to take few more slaves for we are weak-handed through disease. I have in mind to engage no slaves under 4 feet. Returned in a leaking yawl . . .

Thursday 8th April . . . Hoisted the yawl upon the deck for she could hardly keep swimming alongside. Carpenter at work. He informs me he shall be obliged to remove every foot of plank in her bottom, being quite destroyed by the worms. The Surgeon informs me that 5 of our white people and some 11 slaves with the flux, but none without a prospect of recovery . . .

Friday 9th April Fair weather. Sea breeze. At 9 a.m. went on shore, but Mr Ellis not being upon the beach, I determined to follow him to his town. Bought a man from a stranger and sent him aboard. Then set out. Reached Mr Ellis just before dark. He promises if I will stay 21 days he will

114

sell me as many more slaves as I can purchase, with good assortment, after which time I will be fully slaved.

Saturday 10th April Set out from Mr Ellis at sunrise, and got safe on board by 3 p.m. Saw 3 other vessels passing down, and feared that they might hurt my trade. Mercifully, none anchored by us. At 6 p.m. George Robinson seduced a woman slave big with child, and lay with her in view of the whole quarter deck. I put him in irons. I suspect this has not been the first affair of the kind on board. Her number is 72 . . .

★

Thursday 15th April Went on shore, met Mr Ellis, got only 7 men slaves from him. He says I must wait, for he has been as much disappointed as myself . . .

★

Saturday 17th April . . . When we were putting the slaves down this evening, one that was fevered jumped overboard (No. 97). Got him in again but he died immediately between his weakness and the salt water he had swallowed. To remain much longer on the coast may affect my interest and diminish my expected profits. I am yet unable to judge when I shall probably weigh for the Americas.

Sunday 18th April This morning perceived an English snow at anchor, run in and went on board her; the *Dolphin*, Freeman, 10 weeks from Liverpool, has been 6 days on the coast, brought me a letter from the owners which was well-received . . .

Monday 19th April Close weather with much thunder, lightning, and variable winds. At daylight had a canoe on board, with two young traders to offer their services. Matthew Coburn and Peter Ross of the river hereabouts, and I sent them back on shore with goods for rice, etc., and to look out for slaves. I grow impatient with Mr Ellis and am now determined to trade goods with any who can deliver up slaves. This afternoon the weather grew more agreeable. Loosed and aired the sails, discharged and reloaded the small arms . . .

Tuesday 20th April . . . This day buried 2 fine men slaves, Nos 27 and 43, having been ailing for some time, but not thought in danger. Taken suddenly with a lethargic disorder from which they generally recover. Scraped the men's rooms, then smoked the ship thoroughly with tar and tobacco for 3 hours, afterwards washed clean with vinegar . . .

Wednesday 21st April . . . Coburn and Ross came on board. Brought a large canoe-load of wood, but no slaves. I sent back 12 casks for water, and informed them of my desire to be supplied with more rice, and some fowls, etc. Buried a man slave (No. 8) having been about 10 days ill of an obstinate flux. This evening Mr Ellis's shallop crossed the bar and requested that I put goods in her to the amount of 1000 bars. At 1 a.m. observed John Johnson illegally entering into the state-room scuttle and stealing brandy. Clapped him in irons.

Thursday 22nd April . . . Turned Mr Johnson out of irons and gave him a smart dozen. From sunset till midnight very coarse weather, hard rain, strong gusts of wind and a very high swell. In this commotion 2 girl slaves, who have long been ill of a flux, died. Nos 117 and 127.

Friday 23rd April At sunrise, a snow and a sloop, both French, anchored at Leeward. Close dirty weather, and a great sea tumbling in. At 7 p.m. departed this life Edward White, Carpenter's Mate, 7 days ill of a nervous fever. Buried him at once. Put overboard a boy, No. 29, being very bad with a violent body flux. Have now 3 whites not able to help themselves . . .

Saturday 24th April At 8 a.m. calmed. Attended to the spare sails, discovered the rats to have done a great deal of damage. We are over-run with them, those cats we brought from

England having long since departed. Towards noon saw Mr Ellis's shallop with as much surprise as pleasure, for I had quite given her up. At 3 p.m. she came on board, brought 10 slaves, viz., 3 men, 3 women, 1 boy, 2 girls, 1 small boy. Mr Ellis excused his long stay on account of a general sickness which had seized them in the River, but he seems pretty well recovered. It appears his two partners linger at the point of death. Mr Ellis claimed to be in possession of 30 slaves, of superior quality, and he pledged them to me. He demanded 75 bars, which in these times would appear to be a good price. Trusted him with goods to induce him to return with slaves. Sent the punt in with water casks and instructions to come off with rice, yams, palm oil, etc.

Sunday 25th April . . . Mr Coburn and Mr Ross brought two small boys, under 3 feet 10 inches. Sent them in again with positive orders that we have little ones enough, at the price they now bear. Received from them twenty gallons of palm oil, 8 cwt of rice, besides yams and plantains. This afternoon, sent a grapnel to the yawl, gave her a heel each way and scrubbed her bottom. Likewise hoisted the punt in and cleaned her . . .

Monday 26th April At sunrise a stern sea breeze. Instructed the Carpenter to make a new rudder to the longboat. At 8 a.m. a large ship anchored here within us. The *Mermaid*, sloop, of New York. Then came up from to Leeward, His Majesty's Ship, the *Prince Edward*, Captain Henry. Saluted him with 5 guns. This afternoon departed this life my Second Mate, Francis Foster, after sustaining the most violent fever. I am afraid his death will retard our trade, for he is very diligent, and always gained a great influence upon the natives. It stands fortunate that our ship is almost slaved. At sunset buried Mr Foster. Hoisted the colours to half-mast, fired a dozen minute guns. Will send the punt to the *Prince Edward* on the morning tide.

My Dearest,

These last few days have been amongst the most fatiguing I can ever recall. I, therefore, write to you in the hope of making some amends for this misfortune. Those, myself aside, who have experienced pleasant and agreeable evenings in your company, could never imagine the contrast between such sweet times, and the present miserable situation. I am continually assaulted by the combined noises of slaves and traders; suffocated by heat; and subjected to perpetual talking, the greater part of it to no serious purpose. Last night I managed some two hours of sleep, and I dreamed of you. I *saw* us walking together, and discoursing on the many things which have occurred since our parting. We took our repose beneath a heavily branched tree, and rehearsed that most happy of scenes, when you first gave to me your hand. I sat stupid for some time, and embarrassed you by my awkwardness. But my heart was so full, its beat heavy and irregular, that I knew not how to utter a word out. Your kindness and patience soon restored to me the use of my tongue, and we both concurred that the greater intimacies that have followed are the source of our supreme happiness. But then my dream was invaded by daylight, and the noise of people above my head broke the pleasing illusion. I submitted, most unwillingly, to a very different scene.

The principal cause of my sleeplessness, indeed, my distress, has been the unfeeling intransigence displayed by a certain Mr Ellis. At every opportunity, I ask after my dear late father, but he parries my enquiries. I have constantly demanded of him that he transport me to the very place where my late father, only two years past, lost his life, but he refuses to aid me. He can see plainly enough that I need to vent my grief, but he responds to my entreaties with the curious suggestion that my father traded not wisely, and with too much vigour. He goes on, and hints that Father cultivated a passionate hatred, instead of a

118

commercial detachment, towards the poor creatures in his care, and he urges me to not err in this direction. But more than this he will not say, no matter how fervently I plead my case. I intimated that it was his Christian duty to let me set my eyes upon my father's resting place, but Mr Ellis scorned the idea of any of my name claiming kinship with the Christian faith. I confess that I was unable to respond to this charge, for indeed my father held dear to the belief that the teachings of the Lord were incompatible with his chosen occupation, and that it was folly to try and yoke together these opposites in one breast. Yet Father made no mention to me of this *hatred* that Mr Ellis claims sealed his fate. My dear, I too must confess to deep feelings of revulsion, but hatred is a word altogether too fierce to describe my natural passions, for in the same manner that a continued indulgence in this trade and a keen faith cannot reside in one breast, one heart can surely not contain the warring passions of both love and hatred. This being true, then my father's heart must surely have hardened on his final fateful voyage, either this or it was broken clean in half. It would appear that Mr Ellis seems determined to keep from me the more intimate details of this mystery, and it distresses me that his replies are so framed as to imply that my lack of years are the sole impediment to a fuller confession.

I believe my poor Second Mate, Mr Foster, will soon be gone to the sea. Besides my personal regard, I shall miss him on your account, for I have often aired my mind by talking to him about you. I judged him alone to be worthy of the subject, but beyond this person there is none with whom I would degrade your name. I will, henceforth, be forced to keep my pleasures and pains to myself, and am now likely to perform what remains of the journey alone. But I shall want no company, being contented to recall how happy I have been in yours. I went, only this morning, on deck, where the weather was perfectly still, the moon bright, and passed an hour thinking deeply of you. I indulged the hope that you were in a pleasant slumber, and free from the calamitous thoughts which plague your loved one upon the seas. As long as you are favoured with health, and a moderate share of the good things of life, then I will bear all the changes of this world. You cautioned me to be watchful of my own life, for your sake, which is a most engaging argument. I know not which of us must depart first, but it is probable that one must survive the knowledge of the other's death. If it should be my lot, I cannot tell how I might bear it, for being too young to fully grieve for my dear mother, the departure of my father was the first blow, and a mighty severe one. That I loved him, is beyond doubt, although he remained strange to me in many ways, as often befits a great man. But my love for you is of an altogether different amplitude, and I fear that should you depart first, I would soon join. In the meantime, I do not expect to glide through life without meeting rubs, but I have a confidence that you love me, which I would not exchange for any consideration the world could offer. I will try Mr Ellis again, but I expect to be rebuffed, and to leave this coast with the compensatory knowledge that, despite Mr Ellis's suggestion, the reputation of my late father is secure and growing, although that of his son – the youthful *gentleman passenger* – continues to be mocked by the *salty dogs* who, I fear, will always believe my position due only to preferment. No matter. Let it suffice that I eat, drink, and sometimes sleep. I am in health, and some spirits, and shall do everything necessary to procure a future happy reconciliation, for beyond this trading community lies family life. My dear, I long to dwell safely in your arms, and revel in the imagined joys that our projected children will bless us with.

Yours, etc.
James Hamilton.]

Tuesday 27th April . . . Employed most of the day in fitting out the longboat, put goods in her for 10 slaves, and dispatched her to shore. In the afternoon loosed and aired the sails, smoked the ship with tobacco and brimstone. Sent the punt in shore to induce a large canoe to fetch more of our water casks.

Wednesday 28th April This morning buried a fine woman-girl (No. 123) of a fever which destroyed her in a single day, with much vomiting and clamour. The doctor, who is now himself recovered, grows anxious. A high swell makes the vessel labour very much. We wait upon Mr Ellis. At work mending the sails, but the rats out-do us. They forcefully bite the people if they catch them asleep. This evening, found 3 knives and similar tools in the men's room.

Thursday 29th April At 8 a.m. a stiff sea breeze. This morning put more goods and provisions in the shallop and sent her away for the river. Soon after buried a man slave (No. 39), his severe flux having baffled all our medicines. At 2 p.m. sent the yawl in over the bar. Instructions to clean and fill more water-casks, and to bring off Mr Ellis if he could be located. This evening the yawl returned with information that Mr Ellis will be here soon. Mr Coburn and Mr Ross appear to be making trade with a French sloop that stands downwards.

Friday 30th April At dawn the brig *Wanderer*, Jones, of Rhode Island, anchored within us. At 10 a.m. he came on board and informed me that downwards there were several ships and no slaves. Bought a hogshead of rum of Captain Jones. This evening a ship passed us steering downwards, showed no colours. Cleaned and reloaded the small arms. Towards midnight a great deal of lightning, and threatening clouds all around.

Saturday 1st May . . . The canoes made a single trip with water, saved a butt and a half. The frequent showers of rain deter them from making more than one trip. Cannot send the yawl on account of the current which runs stronger than she can row ahead. The Cooper has finished all the casks, we simply wait. Buried a girl slave (No. 20), ill of the flux. Should I not get my capacity of slaves before the next slant of wind and current offers to go up, believe it will be best to suffer the loss, and Mr Ellis's gain, rather than spend more time to no purpose.

Sunday 2nd May . . . The season advancing fast and, I am afraid, sickness too. Almost every day one or two more taken with the flux, of which a man-boy (No. 59) died tonight. I imputed it to the English provisions, and have begun to feed them rice. Brought off 24 casks of water and 3 loads of wood, no word from Mr Ellis. A William Givens brought about 290 lbs of rice and 2 women slaves. I gave him goods, and encouraged him to procure me others if he does so in haste.

Monday 3rd May Mr Ellis chose this morning to bless us with his presence. Shortly after 9 a.m. the heavy canoes crossed the bar, and before noon all were aboard. 32 slaves, viz., 19 men, 3 man-boys, 4 women, and 6 girls, and none to be rejected. Delivered up the longboat to Mr Ellis's people, and put the remainder of his bars in her. Her bottom is much eaten with the worm, and I have been much inconvenienced . . .

*

Thursday 6th May . . . Made two trips with the yawl for water and rice. Canoes brought 6 loads of wood. Got on board 4000 lbs of rice, dry and in good order, all hands filled more than 5 butts. Have near 7 tons of rice in good order. One more turn of water and wood in the afternoon finished this troublesome job. Buried a boy slave (No. 189) of a flux. Have a promise, from Mr Ellis, of more trade in the morning if the wind does not suit to sail. Towards midnight wind came off the land with rain.

Friday 7th May Weighed at dawn with the land wind, steered downwards, anchored at 2 p.m. abreast of the trees in 15 fathoms. I think our *Duke of York* has found new heels. All night bad weather; filled 4 casks with rainwater. Passed us in the offing the *Wanderer*.

Saturday 8th May Very unsettled weather with a great deal of rain; could not weigh all day, until 6 p.m. when backed in a hard squall to West. Took the advantage of it and weighed immediately. Turned the yawl off with 3 hands, she being very heavy to tow. We begin to be short of supplies . . .

★

Tuesday 11th May A continual thick fog. At 8 a.m. weighed, run into 11 fathoms which was as near as I dared venture, but could make nothing of the land, though we saw the breakers very high. By noon the wind faint and fog increased. Could not see the land, but by the noise of the surf determined it must be very close. Stood out to 12 fathoms and anchored, for it would not be safe to attempt to steer. Hoisted in the punt and coated her with pitch, tar and brimstone . . .

★

Thursday 13th May . . . We begin to be very short of firewood and water. At noon weighed with the land wind, the fog as thick as ever. Steered upwards by the lead in 13 fathoms. At 3 p.m. anchored, being afraid to keep under sail with us so near in. Propose to try with the boat tomorrow if it does not clear up. Steadfast in my belief that we are close by the factory.

Friday 14th May . . . Mr Smith returned in the afternoon, informed me that we were but a league below the factory. He brought with him fresh water, and the information that they will happily let us purchase 3 tons of rice, of which I am in absolute necessity. Other articles are to be got here without much difficulty. Fired 5 guns while he was away.

★

Wednesday 19th May . . . This morning witnessed the final delivery of 3 canoes of firewood. Have little now to wait here for. Paid with the last of the cloth according to promise. Returned across the bar with the yawl, and prayed a while in the factory chapel. Stood beneath the white-washed walls of the factory, waiting for the yawl to return and carry me back over the bar. Approached by a quiet fellow. Bought 2 strong man-boys, and a proud girl. I believe my trade for this voyage has reached its conclusion.

Thursday 20th May At 2 a.m. weighed with a light breeze at West. Made but little headway because of the great swell. Sounded several times. At dawn buried a man slave (No. 62) who had died of a pleurisy. At noon discovered myself indisposed of a small fever, and my eyes grown very weak. Mr Allen assures me that I am (by God's blessing) sure to recover. The purchase of a relatively modest 210 slaves may yet ensure my continued mortality. In the evening, by the favour of Providence, discovered a conspiracy among the men slaves to rise upon us. Near 30 of them had broke their irons. Secured the men's irons again and punished the ringleaders. Should they have made their attempts upon the coast, when we had a half-dozen out of the ship, I cannot imagine the consequences. They appeared gloomy and sullen, their heads full of mischief. Before midnight buried 3 more women slaves (Nos 71, 104, 109). Know not what they died of, for they have not been properly alive since they first came on board . . .

Friday 21st May . . . During the night a hard wind came on so quick, with heavy rain. Occasioned a lofty sea, of which I was much afraid, for I do not remember ever meeting anything equal to it since using the sea. At dawn brought the ill-humoured slaves upon deck, but the air is so sharp they cannot endure, neither to wash nor to dance. They huddle together, and sing their melancholy lamentations. We have lost sight of Africa . . .

IV

SOMEWHERE IN ENGLAND

1

JUNE 1942

They arrived today. First I heard the distant rumbling of their trucks, and then the roaring of engines as they laboured up the hill. I stepped out of the shop and stared. The trucks were lined up by the gate. A few had already squeezed through and chipped the gate-posts as they did so. Those that waited kept their engines running, wasting petrol. Then men began to tumble from the trucks. They stretched and looked around. Then, one by one, they began to saunter down the drive. They looked sad, like little lost boys. Some of the villagers couldn't contain themselves. They began to whisper to each other, and they pointed. I suppose we were all shocked, for we had nothing to prepare us for this. Soon all the trucks were empty and the last of the men were vanishing down the drive, nervously smoking their cigarettes, holding them between finger and thumb. I wanted to warn them, but in no time at all they were gone. It was too late. We prepared to drift back to our daily occupations. Mid-afternoon. Summer. The weather was glorious, and everybody's garden was a riot of bluebells and daisies. Once the men had vanished, eyes turned upon me. I was now the object of curiosity. The uninvited outsider. There was nobody with whom I might whisper. I stared back at their accusing eyes and then stepped back into the shop.

JUNE 1939

Every fortnight he came down to town to buy for his shop. I was the clerk in the warehouse office, charged with keeping the books right and putting a smile on my face when anyone came in. And then he came in, but this time with words that had hitherto been stuck at the back of his throat. He dealt them carefully. I've been coming in here for some time now. Yes, I know. You're not wed are you? I shook my head. I was wondering if you'd care to come out for a drink with me? If I'd care to? He wasn't much to look at. But he didn't look like he would hurt. Me, at least. And so I said yes, and found myself in the snug of the Brown Fox with him and his words. Craftily dealt, asking me all about myself, interested only – at this stage – in steering me towards subjects which he no doubt imagined would make him appear to be a fascinating chap. It made him a listener and me a talker, but it did not make for fascination. At some point I told him. I live with my mother, I said. In 1926 she fled to the bosom of Christ. She'd lost her husband, then she lost her job in the General Strike. Luckily, God took her up. What I mean is, God took her up to do good works for Him. On this earth. She hasn't done much since, except God's work. He nodded and threw me a smile. This man who in all likelihood had seldom seen the inside of a church. Perhaps this was what I liked about him. The fact that I could see his ignorance. Read him like a book. Another drink? Why not? If he's buying. I thought of my mother. She'll be pretending she's missing me now. I know her. She'll be looking at the clock and shaking her head. Wanting to know what I think

I'm playing at stopping out past eight o'clock. Mother, I'm twenty-one years old. She'd perfected a look of such contempt. I got it that night, and for weeks afterwards, whenever I came back from the pub. But she never asked any questions. It was as if she didn't want to ask in case that meant that she cared. That much I understood about her. That she did care, but she didn't want me to know this. She was angry with me. Always angry. He started coming down twice a week. One night, in the Brown Fox, I said yes. But I let him know that I'd rather do it in an office than in a church. I told him that I thought we were both wrong for a church. All that ceremony. What do you think? He agreed, and so I finished my half-pint and made ready to leave. I noticed that these days he didn't spend much time asking me about myself. It was always him now. He told me there were not many lasses up in his village. And being thirty now he'd have to hurry up. He laughed too loudly. As he waited with me by the bus stop, we tried the first experiment of a kiss. I should have known then.

AUGUST 1939

When she realized that I was serious about getting wed to Len she stopped talking to me. I stood before her, but she wouldn't look up. She toyed with her embroidery, passing the antimacassar between her clammy hands, pulling it first one way and then the next. I told her that she would stretch it out of shape, but she wasn't listening to me. She sat impassively, and digested the information that I would soon be gone. She was trying to comprehend the fact that somebody actually wanted me. That in spite of my history I might actually be interesting, if not exactly exciting, to somebody. She'd told me many times that she didn't trust men. They'll just abandon you in the most callous fashion. And hadn't she been right? They're here, and then they're gone. Jesus. Now there was somebody you could trust. When the Lord said come unto me, He didn't mean until the pubs were open, or until He found some other woman. The Lord accepted you with open arms and embraced you. She beckoned me to sit. This house, I thought. I wanted to scream. At least I can get out of this two-up, two-down dump. She put aside her embroidery. Are you sure about this man? Of course I wasn't sure. I'd only known him seven weeks. She looked at me, as though trying to warn me about something. But then, having lost a husband in the Great War, she probably had the right to warn me. I assured her, if there's a war, he'll not be going away. He's got a black lung from being down the pit. If there's a war he's going nowhere. She stared at me. I looked across at my father's picture, which sat on top of the wooden mantelpiece.

I had no memory of him, being just a baby when he died. She had never explained anything to me about this man in a silly felt hat, standing beneath a chestnut tree and staring directly into the lens of the camera. A confident, happy man. A man I feel sure would never have tolerated a woman such as my mother. But perhaps she was different then. Occasionally I've found my dad on a bronze plaque, near the Town Hall, but his name is scattered among the names of hundreds of others. This is merely a place to find him, but not to discover him. When she dies, I'll take it. The photograph might help me to discover him. This is what I think. And then I hear her voice. If you must leave, then do so. I assume that this is her blessing. But she goes on. At least you're not getting wed to a soldier. You should never do that. You'll be left on your own. Then again she's quiet. Just when I'm thinking, that wasn't too bad, she nettles me. Men are at their best in pursuit. I thought I should tell you. But I expect you've found that out already.

JUNE 1942

Apparently we were unlucky to get them in our village. It's all over the papers. We're having an invasion all right, but it's not Jerry. We've been invaded by bloody Yanks. Nobody wants them, but the Hall is large and has plenty of grounds for their tents and things. Everybody expects trouble. People keep talking about their Yank arrogance. Saying that they think that all they have to do is to blow their own trumpets and the walls of Germany will fall down. But our lot are quiet. They keep themselves to themselves, and when they meet us they seem polite. I see them going about their business. And a lot of them like to go to church. They dress so smartly it puts us to shame. The military police are easy to spot with their white helmets and gloves. The truth is, they don't have to mix much with us for they have their own newspapers, films, radio, everything. To most folks' relief, they appear willing to keep themselves to themselves. I met one of them this morning. He was whistling and chewing gum at the same time, which made him look like a fish. When he saw me he lowered his eyes. I could see he was slightly frightened. I said good morning as I passed by, but he shrank a little and pretended not to hear. And then, almost as an afterthought, I heard him whisper, morning ma'am.

JULY 1942

They stand in the shop and talk. Usually two of them. Sometimes there are three. There is no room for any more. They tear out their coupons and drop them on to the counter. I don't care. I've got to ask for them. It's the law. I'm not playing games. If I go too, who'll look after the shop? They stand in the shop and talk about the Yanks. They're still shocked. Upset, even. And then they realize that I'm present, and that I can hear what they're saying. And so they leave. But not before they bestow their cigarette-tar smiles upon me. I heard one of them say, she's missing Len, and I know that I was meant to hear it.

AUGUST 1942

I'm enjoying the long summer days. I like to watch the sunset
through the pub window. I have my own corner. Well, it's
not my corner, it's just a corner that nobody else seems to
sit in. Maybe nobody else sits in it because they know that
I sit in it. They probably think they might catch something
off a commoner like me. They should be so lucky. Cheeky
monkeys. I don't trouble anybody. I just sit in my corner
and drink my half of bitter and watch the sun set. I didn't
used to do this when he was around. The pub was his place.
Mine was above the shop, waiting for him to come back.
The braggart. I don't think they ever expected to see me
lower myself and come into the pub. I expect they think
I'm lonely or something. Well, they can think what they
like. I'm not looking for anybody. I'm just having a drink.
His best mate is at the bar. He's a crafty bugger. Always
quick to come over, touch his cap, and ask me if I'm all
right. Hardly gives me time to get the words out of my
mouth (I'm all right, Stan, thanks) and he's back at the
bar, foot up, head occasionally swivelling around to look
at me (smile, nod, wink) before he turns back around and
starts talking about me with the rest. I could bloody crown
him. The hypocrite. It's Home Guard this evening. In their
bloody silly uniforms. One gun between them. Whose turn is
it tonight to carry the gun? God help us if this is the best they
can muster up to defeat the Hun. A butcher, a baker, a bleeding
candlestick-maker. Half a dozen farmers and labourers, a
couple of toffs, and a bobby who thinks he's better than the

rest because he's got a proper uniform. He calls the meeting
to order. They look at me as though I'm in the way. I stare
back at them. We've got to prevent anything from landing in
the fields hereabouts. The same conversation as last week.
Planes, gliders, airships, 'owt. Airships? I said Airships,
all right. Hazards. We've got to put hazards out. Timber,
bedsteads, old cars, ranges, anything you can lay your hands
on. But that doesn't include the cricket pitch, does it? We
don't have to put 'owt on the cricket pitch, do we? It includes
the bloody cricket pitch an' all. But that's not right. Bugger
what's right, it's what's got to be done. I get up, walk to
the bar, and order another glass of beer. Some of them stop
listening to the bobby and watch me. The bobby pretends
nothing is happening. He continues to talk. It doesn't make
any difference that we've got Yanks here now. We've still
got our job of work to do, is that clear? They nod. Dogs.
He pulls out a piece of paper from his breast pocket. Latest
orders for this branch of the Local Defence Volunteers. A
chorus of dissent. Home Guard. We've been Home Guard
for two bloody years now. Tank traps. We've got to prepare
barricades on all roads leading into the village. Broken-down
carts, tyres, junk of all kind is to be stationed by the side of
the road, ready to be shifted into place. We'll have ditches to
dig and we're to stuff them with barbed wire. I'm to carry a
gun in case of parachutists. Also, those of you who own motor
vehicles, you're to immobilize them when parked. Remove the
rotor arm or pull out the ignition leads. There's no chances
to be taken, understand? He pauses for a moment, and then
scratches his head as though puzzled. I hand the barman
elevenpence. Doesn't seem any point to me, says the bobby.
Pleasure motoring's forbidden anyhow. Nobody's going anywhere. This is all stuff that they've been doing in the south
and other parts for a while now. Seems like they forgot about
us. He blinks, takes a swig of beer, and then continues in a
more formal voice. But now we've been told, we'll act upon
it. Any questions? I laugh as I walk back to my seat, but I

manage to get a hand to my mouth. I catch it. Any questions? Sensible questions from this bunch I couldn't imagine. One by one they troop out of the pub. Defeated by their own lack of imagination. I watch the sun go down. And think about Len. Sitting all alone in his cell. I wonder if he's thinking about me. Then I realize that I don't really care. Soon there is only myself, the barman, and two of the men in the pub. I close my eyes. Later, I realize that I must have fallen asleep, but they'd chosen to ignore me. I hear one of them whisper, She can't take her drink. If I had twenty-three shillings I'd buy a bottle of whisky. Just to show them. But I don't have it. And then I hear their joke. About the new utility knickers. One Yank and they're off. Their language goes right through me. I pull myself to my feet. Goodnight. Goodnight, I call back.

SEPTEMBER 1939

Our wedding day. Into the Registrar's office. One of the war brides. Get married quickly for now nobody's any idea what's likely to happen. Nobody has. He's got her up the aisle. Nudge, nudge. On my side, my mother. That's all. And on his side, Stan. A couple more mates from the village came down to the big town, but I was barely introduced and they didn't stay. Pathetic, I thought. But then he's got no parents so I shouldn't be so snooty. They'd long since gone. He's only got his mates. I should have been so lucky. I hadn't even got mates. A wedding. My wedding. It was the only wedding I was likely to have, so I thought I'd better do it right. Len was surprised that I didn't have anything in my bottom drawer. Not even a tin of pineapple chunks, or a jar of marmalade. I told him, you're the shopkeeper. My mother, well, she found a way not to cry. Set her face like a mask and just stared straight ahead as if she couldn't see what all the fuss was about. Maybe this reminded her of her day. Maybe she didn't want me to see that she cared. Maybe. Earlier in the month, I'd been with her when the war started. Eleven a.m., Sunday morning. When the National Anthem came on the wireless she stood up. When it finished she sat down and was quiet for a few moments. Then she said that they'd already begun recruiting for Air Raid Wardens. She informed me that this was going to be a civvies' war. I said nothing. She sighed, and then announced that she'd have to start stocking up. She calculated twenty fags at two shillings, tea at two and six, matches a penny ha'penny. She reckoned up how much she could afford to buy with her savings, and I listened. And then I told her that the date was set. A fortnight hence. I'd be wed. But she didn't say anything. She just continued doing her sums in the margin of the previous day's newspaper, using a little stump of pencil that was blunt at one end and chewed at the other.

SEPTEMBER 1939

And then the wedding was over, and we were off to Wales for a week in a small hotel on Anglesey that seemed populated with rich ladies who were already hiding from the war. They always dressed properly, with earrings and lined skirts. They even dressed for breakfast. Then came their morning walk, then lunch, gin and tonic, and an afternoon nap. Then cards. Dinner. Sherry. Bridge. They always stood for the National Anthem on the wireless come evening. I'm sure they all harboured a secret desire to salute. The anchor of their lives had prematurely dropped. I watched them watching me and Len. All right, so he might not be up to much in your eyes, but he's decent and honest. Or so I thought. They didn't talk to me. Sometimes they forgot themselves and nodded as they spread some jam on their crustless toast. I looked closely. The backs of their hands were mottled with purple veins. I think they knew that I was jealous of them. How could they not know? Why shouldn't I be jealous of them? They had money. They'd found a way to hide from the world. They had each other. And there I was. I had Len. I had to train him not to sleep with his socks on. To undo his shoelaces before he took off his shoes. To do up his cuffs instead of just rolling them back. He was thirty going on seven. I liked it when they forgot themselves and sometimes nodded. But when they saw Len I noticed that they simply turned away. I wondered what they knew that they weren't telling me. But I couldn't ask. Len and I were supposed to be together. A team against the rest of the world. Man and wife. Him and me. I couldn't side with them.

SEPTEMBER 1939

We got lost on the way back up. Len had borrowed a motor car from one of his farmer friends, but there was only enough petrol to drive us there and back. Petrol had already gone on coupons. We couldn't even go for a spin around Anglesey. So we parked the car up by the hotel and left it. Until we were ready to come back, that is. It was like dusting off an old friend and readying yourself to make an escape. We left early in the afternoon. It's not enough time, Len. Shouldn't we have left earlier? He looked at me. That 'woman, you're talking daft' look of his. Very endearing, I must say. Enough to make you feel like you'd no right to be on this earth. Two hours later, he got lost. Just like I knew he would. It had been a bit touch and go getting down to Wales, but somehow we'd got lucky and made it. Len had pointed out (in his defence) that all the street and road signs had been taken down. In case of invasion. It'll help the Hun. But coming back up our luck ran out. I thought you said you knew the way. I do know the way, I've just got a little mixed up, that's all. A little mixed up seemed to me to be putting it mildly. But there was no point in arguing. No point whatsoever. As the day set around us, we had no idea of where we were. There were slogans in all the papers about saving petrol. They read: Is your journey really necessary? I'd begun to wonder this myself, honeymoon or no honeymoon. Next village, I'll stop and ask somebody, he said. And then I noticed a light on in a small cottage, and Len pulled over. He got out and left me in the car. I saw a woman open the door. They spoke, Len pointed, she looked, I smiled

politely. I hated him for doing this to me. Making me feel
helpless and at somebody's mercy. Me, I didn't want to be
anybody's charity case. Especially not when I was supposed to
be with my husband. The man who said that he would protect
and honour me. Some joke. Well, Len came back and said we
weren't far wrong but we couldn't go anywhere because of the
blackout. I said nothing. I just looked at him. I let him know
what I thought. And I reckon he understood all right. But he
didn't say anything except, come on, let's get our stuff. She's
got a spare room and she says that we can have it for the night.
Len laughed. Then he went on. I think she's relieved I wasn't
the warden. I looked at Len but still said nothing. Reduced to
being a bloody beggar. Her husband was already away. Left
her and a three-year-old daughter behind. The girl's in bed, she
said as she buttered us some bread and asked us if we wanted
our eggs turned over. No, mine's fine as it is, said Len, his
feet under the table. It's easy to get lost, she assured me. Don't
bother, I thought. I already know he's a bloody fool. And then
Len did it. He fished into his inside pocket like some bloody
spiv. Here, he said. I'd like you to have these. No, we'd like
you to have these, he said. We appreciate what you've done
for us. And he gave her some coupons like she was a common
tart. The look on the woman's face. Well, I nearly died of
embarrassment, but I was learning. This was Len. His way
of dealing with people. That night I couldn't so much look at
him, let alone let him touch me. No, Len. What's the matter?
Nothing. Is it because we're in a strange house? Goodnight,
Len. I hope this isn't going to become regular. Goodnight,
Len. Goodnight, but I'm not right pleased. Goodnight, Len.

SEPTEMBER 1939

When we got back the evacuees had arrived. A dozen boys and girls of a sensible age standing in the church hall. Gas masks in a cardboard box, an identification tag around their necks, and carrying a bundle of personal belongings. They huddled together, their feet swimming in big shoes that were clearly badly scuffed hand-me-downs. Some of them looked as if they had never had a decent meal in their lives. Most of them had already wolfed their emergency rations. A block of chocolate, a tin of corned beef, and a tin of condensed milk. Amongst the grown-ups, confusion and resentment reigned in equal proportion. Why us? None of the other villages had been designated as reception areas. Before us stood a dozen frightened children, the farmers eyeing the husky lads, the girls and scrawny boys close to tears. And then a decision was reached that while it was still light we should send them back. Somebody whispered that all these children wet the bed. That half the mattresses in England were awash, and that at eight and six per child it wasn't really worth it. I looked across at Len, who firmly shook his head. Not even one of them, he said. They can bloody well go back to where they come from. We're not in the charity business. At four o'clock I noticed that the church bells didn't ring. It was a decree. No more church bells because of the war. The children stood in silence.

SEPTEMBER 1942

Today an officer came into the shop wearing dark glasses. He seemed a bit surprised that a bell rang when he opened the door. Excuse me, ma'am. He took his hat off. He should have taken his glasses off as well. I wanted to say to him, it's not sunny out, you know. So you can take them off, you know. Unless you've got something to hide, that is. I've come to talk to you a little about the service men we've got stationed in your village. Oh yes, I thought. It took you nearly three months to get here, did it? Well get on with it then. I'm all ears. A lot of these boys are not used to us treating them as equals, so don't be alarmed by their response. What are they going to do, I thought, throw themselves on the floor before us if we smile? They're not very educated boys and they'll need some time to adjust to your customs and your ways, so I'm just here to request your patience. I see. He relaxes now. Would you like a smoke? No, I don't. Mind if I do? No, go ahead. So he does. Husband out? Yes, he's out, I say. What business is it of yours? I think. Smug bugger. That's what I think of him, standing there in his uniform, telling tales on his fellow soldiers behind their backs. Behind his glasses. Why did you send them to us then? I ask. Why not to some other place? No, no, he says. There's no problem. We're not sending you a problem or anything. It's just that they're different. We want you to know that you'll have to be a little patient, that's all. I smile at him and he smiles back. His white teeth, his confident pose, pulling at his cigarette, lazily blowing out smoke. He really thinks he's something.

NOVEMBER 1942

I stood outside the church today and stared up at the trees. They've worn their leaves shabby. Hardly a breath of wind and they start falling. Ahead of us is winter. And it's not exactly warm up here on this ledge. The wind gets a good go at us and gives us a pounding. Just thinking about it makes me shiver. I turned up my collar and got ready to carry on with my walk. And then I heard their voices starting up. I knew it was them for nobody else in this village sings that way. Like they mean it. I forgot all about the trees and winter. I found myself just staring at the church and listening to the sound of their voices and their clapping hands. Across the road I saw old man Williams. He was out with his dog. He stood and listened as though, like me, he too hadn't heard anything like this before. Just the two of us listening.

DECEMBER 1942

According to today's copy of the *Star*, all over Britain standards of behaviour are breaking down. A young woman Air Raid Warden recently said that if gas spattered her clothes she'd have no hesitation in taking them off and walking starkers. According to this woman, every right-minded person in Britain should be ready to do the same. The *Star* thinks she's barmy. But they don't stop there. It is to be regretted, says the *Star*, that one of the more popular jokes on the factory floor is one which is made at the expense of our boys in the sky. What does an RAF man do when his parachute doesn't open? He brings it back and gets a new one. The *Star* wonders if we're not all the victims of German propaganda that's designed to undermine our confidence. Apparently, some *Star* journalist was outraged because when he was in London he was charged 6*d.* for an apple and a guinea for a pound of grapes. The man who sold them to him then added salt to his wounds by asking him if he'd not heard that there was a war on. I've been getting some choice comments, about tinned sardines and baked beans, for instance. We've had a directive to put up their points value because they've been proving too popular. It's hardly my fault, is it? And as for the National loaf. Well, it's definitely got a khaki tint to it, and it feels to me like paper that's been repulped once too often. Full of straw-like bits. But if you don't like it, nobody's forcing you to eat it. I don't know why they're always complaining to me.

JANUARY 1943

I got a letter from Len. I knew it was him before I opened it. Mean handwriting. And addressed to a Mrs Len somebody. My name isn't bloody Len anybody. Happy 1943! it says at the top. And bits of it are censored. He says that when he comes out he wants us to move away. Further north. Anywhere. But he says that we have to get away from here and start afresh. I see. He claims that he can't stand the shame and he doesn't see why I should have to put up with it too. Well, I'm doing all right. They still talk about me when they think I'm not listening, but I'm doing all right. I don't see why I should have to leave. He'll have to go by himself, I reckon. He can't expect me to follow him around like some silly puppy. No, if he wants to go, then he can go. Good luck to him, I say. I'll have to write to him and tell him this, in a nice way, of course. No need for him to suffer any more than he has to. I've got nothing against Len personally. No reason to hurt him. He just needs to grow up a little bit. A lot. And he'd be better off growing up with somebody else. When I get a minute I'll let him know this. Better he gets it straight. Nothing to be gained by kidding each other. Not now. The best years of our lives and all that. If he wants to sling his hook and go off somewhere, then good luck to him. Good luck to you, Len.

FEBRUARY 1943

Two of them came into the shop this morning. One tall one. One not so tall one, but he wasn't short either. Far from it. They were both quite stocky, and both of them were polite. After all this time, they still seem surprised at how cheap things are. One woman told me I ought to put up the prices for them. She said Len would have. I said I know. But look where Len is now. I didn't tell her this last bit, though. They both took their caps off. And then they asked me to a dance they're having on Saturday. Asked me politely. Well, I can't dance, I told them. You'll learn, said the tall one. He smiled. We've got our own band, ma'am, said the other one. You hear us play, you can't help but dance. He laughed. So I laughed too. Then we were all laughing. A dance, I said. On Saturday, said the tall one.

OCTOBER 1939

Last night I woke up in the middle of the night and thought to myself, bloody hell. What have I done? I've come back to this village with Len, after marriage, after Wales, after being lost. And I'm married now. For nearly a month. A wife. In this bleak and silly little village that's filled with its own self-importance. The only relief I have from this place is when I travel down to see my mother, whose sole occupation in life seems to be to make me feel guilty. A guilt I'm determined to resist. I stare at her as she lies in bed. She's taken to her bed as a permanent place of refuge. I stare at her and listen as she talks incessantly about the phony war. You've been listening to the wireless, haven't you, Mother. She ignores me and continues in her own vein. About how she'll not be digging for victory and growing cabbage and onions. About how, although nothing has happened as yet, they'll soon be coming home in boxes like in the last war. It'll happen, she keeps saying. She pauses, then starts up again. She can't be bothered with her gas mask, she says. All that spitting on the mica window to stop it from steaming up. And it smells, of rubber and disinfectant. I don't tell her that most people have stopped carrying them around. That the novelty has worn off. If you'd have stayed down here you'd have been in Air Raid Precautions, I suppose. WVS, for you. Do you have it up by you? I shake my head. I expect that's why you went, isn't it. Nothing much to do up there except knit socks for the troops. I don't rise to her. Whenever I do she just snaps and tells me not to use Latin in front of her. So I don't bother.

She goes on. But meanwhile, they make us live in the dark like bloody bats. It's ridiculous. Anderson shelter? Two bits of bent steel stuck in the mud, not fit for a pig to wallow in. And nobody'll be hanging out any washing on the Siegfried Line, you mark my words. She knows I'm not really listening to her but she doesn't care. She just likes to have somebody to talk to. Somebody whom she feels it will be all right to bore. She feels she has a right to bore me. I'm her daughter. And then she falls asleep and I have to make my way up the hill on that long, slow bus journey back to the village. It is pretty. I have to give it that. The view from the road, just outside the village, carries all the way across the moors. Well, you'd have to be blind or stupid not to notice that in its own way it's grand. Nothing but green fields and small villages for miles. But then entering our village is like coming into a tunnel. You can't see anything except small houses dotted on either side of the road. And then a big church. A small pub. A nob's hall. Our shop. Some more houses. And so this is my home now. God help me. Maybe I was better off in the warehouse. If I've thought this once I've thought it a million times. But then again, I always say to myself, it's probably just the war. Nothing can look good to anyone in the war. Let's be honest. It's not a great time for anybody. They say that eventually there'll be serious shortages. We'll see.

DECEMBER 1939

I've made a friend. Sandra. She's just had a kid. A boy, Tommy. I don't know if she thought calling him Tommy was funny or something. I've never mentioned it. Her husband has already been called up and gone off. He lives in a photograph on the mantelpiece. There are two leaves to the frame. In the other leaf is a poem:

> To My Dear Husband
>
> Where'er you are my Husband true,
> In these war-troubled days,
> My loving thoughts go out to you
> In countless kinds of ways.
> God keep you, Dear, where'er you roam,
> And bring you, one day, safely home.

That's all that's left of him at present. This picture and when she talks about him. Which she doesn't do all that much. She invited me over for tea. I can see you're a bit lost around here. And Len. Well, he's not the type to go out of his way to introduce you around, now is he. She used to work for Len in the shop. But then she fell pregnant and got wed. I think it was in that order. She offered me a treat. Two Rich Tea biscuits. I expect you have plenty of these in the shop whenever you want them, but for me it's a treat. It's a big thing. Don't get much sweet stuff these days. She sat me down. They say people are queuing in town, trying to beat the system. And that doctors and dentists are hard to come by. Not just panel ones, private too. And that some people are getting mail a week late. I looked at her and wondered if Len had only come after me because he needed somebody to replace her in the shop. Maybe I'm being a bit silly, I thought. Maybe I'm reading too much into everything. I don't know. At least I've made a friend. Sod Len and his pencil-thin moustache. He's happy now that he's got some mug to work for him in the shop. He's happy now that he's able to leave me in the shop and go to the pub with his mates. Are you listening to me, love? Sandra stared at me. You do tend to dream a little, don't you. I've been wondering if I should grow my hair like Veronica Lake. Or if I should just stick to the normal two and sixpenny shampoo and set. I smiled at her. They censor my husband's letters, can you believe that? The kid started to cry. Tommy. Tommy started to play up. She picked it up and held it in her arms. Then she rocked it back and forth until it began to gurgle like it was choking. Tommy's laughing, she said. Here, do you want to hold him? I held up the Rich Tea biscuit. I'd love to, but I've got my hands full at the moment. Got any of your own, have you? Sandra's not much past twenty or so. About my age. I could see that now. Don't look like that, she said. I had to get married and get started. Women in my family go off early. But you've plenty of time yet. Nice of her to say it. Polite of her. She looked sad now. You don't know what it's like when the postman passes the door. The day is ruined. Absolutely ruined. She's the only person I know in the village apart from Len. Long, thin, blonde hair. At first I thought I saw blackened roots, then I realized she was just in some shadow. Why do I have to be so bloody critical? So what if she bleaches her hair? What business is it of mine? I think I'm jealous of her looks. But I do want to be generous to her. Len is a quiet bloke, she says. In his own way he's kind, but it'll take you a while to get to know him properly. Now I resent her. I don't like being told about my own husband. But she feels as though she's helping me. Len hasn't bothered to introduce me to anybody. After all, Sandra has taken it upon herself to come into the shop and find me. A lot of the other girls have gone, she says. There are not many of us left. ATS, munitions work, they've nearly all gone. But some Land Army Girls are due to come here. And then there's us. Mothers. I'm not a mother, I say. Sandra smiles. But I suppose working in the shop is vital work, isn't it? They won't put you in the factories, will they? No, I say. I've been classified. Len's disabled. He can't manage by himself, so I'll not be going in the factories. Well, we'll have plenty of time to get to know each other better, then. I'm glad there's somebody around like you. I thought it'd only be me and a few others. And to be honest, most of them are just interested in your business. They're not interested in you, just in what you're up to. I don't have much time for that. Neither do I, I said. Neither do I. She looked at me funny. My mind started to race. I'd been looking right at her. Perhaps she thought I meant her. I couldn't think of anything to say which would convince her that I wasn't talking about her. So I just smiled back. I looked at her with a stupid grin painted on my face. I'm sorry, I said to myself. I don't know how to behave. I like you. I've never been much good with people. She handed Tommy to me. Then she went to fill the kettle again. I knew she was watching me from the kitchen, watching me holding her child, worried that I might do something daft with him. I held him awkwardly. And then I heard the water splashing against the enamel as she started to fill the kettle. But I knew that she was still watching me. I turned around and she beamed at me. Had enough of Tommy? she asked. No. I held Tommy close to me. I'll be all right.

NEW YEAR'S DAY 1940

Len and his mate Stan borrowed a car so they could drive into town. On business, they said. Drinking business more like, but I went with them so I could see my mother. I told them that I'd meet them outside the bank at six. Len didn't want to see her, but it didn't matter. There was no need for either of them to pretend. They'd passed that stage. At about five-thirty, I began to walk back into town, and I noticed that all the iron railings had been ripped out. By the park. Front gardens, everywhere. Together with the pots and pans, that they punctured as soon as you handed them over, the railings would be used for Spitfires. Things were changing. We'd been told that in a week or so we'd have to start rationing bacon, ham, sugar and butter. Customers would only be able to get them with a ration book. I stood by myself in the cold and shivered. The moon was full and the sky was bright with stars. There didn't seem much point to the blackout. I looked up and wondered if Hitler had found a way to turn out the stars over his country at night. It was after seven. Len was late. Bladdered, I imagined. Not for the first time in my life I felt the humiliation of being abandoned.

MARCH 1940

The cold of winter has insisted on hanging on a few weeks past its time. Sandra has been looking increasingly lost and unhappy. These days I go around to visit her two or three times a week. She can't breast-feed Tommy any more because she says her milk's all dried up due to worry. He won't take the bottle, so she has to spoon-feed him, which can take hours. Tommy has become an increasingly noisy problem, but I've grown to like him, and to even want to hold him. I never thought that I would want to hold a baby. Sandra seems to like this. The fact that I literally take him off her hands. Today she sat me down and gave me a cup of tea. And then she told me that she was pregnant. I looked at her but said nothing. She was expecting me to say something. That much was clear. She was expecting a reaction of some kind. Horror. Laughter. Something. But I said nothing. Did you hear me? I said I think I'm pregnant. No, in fact I know I'm pregnant. I'm nearly three months gone. She didn't have to tell me how far gone she was, for I knew that it wasn't him. I had no idea who it was, but it was clear that she was hoping that I might ask. But I said nothing. I just sipped at my tea. A small mouthful at a time. Don't you want to know who? I was looking out of the window now. As usual, nothing and nobody in the streets. A perverse part of me longed for her to tell me that it was Len. But it wasn't. It's Len's mate, Joyce. Terry. The farmer. She didn't have to say who Terry was. I wasn't so stupid that I couldn't figure that out for myself. Sandra's voice began to break.

He gives me extra things for Tommy. Like a baby sister or brother, I said. I couldn't help myself. Do you think it's funny? whispered an incredulous Sandra. She sounded hurt. I was sorry I'd spoken. I apologized. Sandra paused. I don't know what I'm going to do, she said. I'm not going backstreet. I don't want to get rid of it. I'm too frightened to. And I don't want to marry him. Does he want to marry you? I don't know. I don't think so. I hope not, I said. Doesn't seem to me a good enough reason to commit marriage. A bun in the oven. God, she looked pathetic. Helpless. Child in her belly. Tommy in my arms. Cup of tea in her hands. Why didn't she just keep her legs shut? It's easy enough to do. Not exactly difficult, is it? I suppose I was lonely. She answers the question without me having to ask it. I suppose I was lonely and stupid. I should have used something. Yes, I said. Like self-control. Now she was hurt. I could see it on her face. I was sorry I said that. There was a pause and then I continued. I think you'd better write to him. Let him know before he gets back. What do you think? I think so, she says. But what if he doesn't want to come back? What's Tommy going to do for a father? I pointed out the obvious. That this is a war. That if Tommy ends up without a father, he won't be the first and he won't be the last. That's the truth, Sandra. And then she started to cry. I made some enquiries, she said. Her voice quivered. But you can't put it up for adoption without your husband's permission. I'm done for. Dusk approached. The sky got darker. I could see it was freezing out. I would soon have to go and help Len close up the shop. Always a last-minute rush with those coming in from the town. And we've just started to ration meat. I didn't want to leave her on her own in such a state, but what could I do? I touched her arm. Sandra, I said. Write to him. Tell him. It will make you feel better to know that he knows. And they can get leave. Compassionate leave. Then he can come home and the two of you can sort out whatever it is that you've got to sort out. It'll be better that way. I've not told anybody else, she says. So I'm the only one who knows? And the doctor. At the clinic in town. It was getting darker. The shadows were lengthening. I think you should tell him, I said.

MARCH 1940

Last night Len beat me. After he came back from the pub.
Drunk. Once he's got a mood on, that's it. He'll find a reason.
It didn't hurt all that much. It happened so quickly. And I
understood why he was doing it. Maybe that's why it didn't
hurt all that much. He was just working off the embarrassment
of not having a uniform. Not even one of the silly bugger
Home Guard uniforms. Civvy Street guilt. He was playing at
being a man. Secretly drumming on me behind closed doors.
But I told him. The next time he raises his hand to me it'll be
the last time. Drunk or sober. It'll be the last time.

MAY 1940

France has gone. It looks like we'll have to fight to the bitter end by ourselves. Everyone's talking of invasion. And what to do. They say you've got to stay at home. If you're out when they come, you mustn't run or you'll be machine-gunned from the air like they did in Holland and Belgium. It says, in the *Star*, that you're not to supply the Germans with food, petrol or maps. And if you see anything at all suspicious you're to go straight to the police. They sometimes talk to you like you're mental.

FEBRUARY 1943

I've been thinking about it all week, but trying to pretend that it wasn't a problem. However, this morning I had to face up to the truth. I didn't have anything to wear to the dance. And I simply didn't have the money to go out and buy anything new. A plain dress, some flat shoes and a coat would have to do just nicely, thank you very much. This evening I stood in front of the mirror. When I smiled it took the lines a few moments less to set, and a few moments longer to disappear once I put my face right again. It wasn't my imagination. I didn't have to be told. I pulled on my coat and picked up my handbag, then I walked through the village towards the hall. As I approached, I saw a soldier standing by the chipped gate. Come for the dance, ma'am? I hid my ring. Yes, I've come for the dance. I panicked. Am I the only one? Have I got the time right? He offered me gum. No thank you, I said. I recognized him, I recognized them all from the shop. And they all knew me. I don't suppose they knew my name, but they knew my face. I went inside. There were a few more soldiers in the grounds. Walking around in pairs. Laughing. They seemed odd in this grand place. But then I realized that I probably seemed odd here too. The toffs have moved on for the war. Big of them, I thought. Hey, ma'am. Looking for the dance? I nodded. Over there. He was a military policeman. He pointed with his rifle. I hesitated. Hell, just go straight in. So I did. I walked across the lawn – like a real madam – then up the stairs and into a big room. The first thing that I saw was the food. They had stuff on the table that even I hadn't seen in years. Lemons and grapefruits. Tins of chocolate. Life Savers. Beef steaks. Salami. Sliced tinned peaches. One of them took my coat. May I, he said. Thank you, I said. So polite, I thought. I looked up and saw a few ATS girls from the next village, and some Land Army girls, and a few married ones, all sitting in a line looking frightened. I decided that I'd better go and sit with them. So I went over and sat next to a Land Army girl who was in uniform. She smiled at me but made a point of not saying anything. Then they began to play gramophone records, which didn't make that much sense to me because they were all standing and we were all sitting. What were we supposed to do? In the corner I saw the officer who'd come into the shop and talked to me about them. He looked over and waved. Hello, Duchess. I stared back through him. I was rather proud of this stare. I could see that it upset him somewhat, but he wasn't sure what to do. I kept staring through him. The Land Army girl next to me came to life and wanted to know if everything was all right. I told her, yes, that everything was all right. Why shouldn't it be? I see, said the girl. And still nobody would dance to the gramophone records. And then I noticed that the band were climbing up on to the small stage. They'd pushed some boxes up tight and tacked a cloth drape around the edges, but it looked proper. It looked like a real job, not just something they'd slung together. And then they began to play. It sounded great, but it made everybody feel uneasy. A sitting line of us facing a standing crowd of them. And then I found myself on my feet and walking towards the two who asked me, the tall one and the shorter one. I asked the tall one if he'd like to dance. He smiled at me nervously. I could see the gap in his teeth in the middle of the bottom row. It's usually at the top, I thought. Where people have a gap in their teeth. It's unusual to see somebody with a gap in their teeth at the bottom. But that was all right, it was different and I liked that. He put one hand on my shoulder and held out the other. I stretched my arm out to meet it, and he steered me backwards and into the space that was the dance floor. A foxtrot. Over his shoulder I could see everyone looking on. I could see it on their faces. They were shocked. And maybe a bit jealous, but I didn't care. And then, one by one, the soldiers found the courage to go over to the girls and soon they were all dancing. My partner leant forward and whispered into my ear. Looks like you've started the party. You oughta be proud of yourself. I didn't say anything. You don't seem shy and uneasy like the rest of them. I still didn't say anything. I just listened. Listened to him and listened to the music. You from round here? Why? I asked. Well, I was just wondering. I don't know. I guess you don't act like them in some ways. Can't say how exactly, but just different. Inside I was smiling. That was just what I wanted to hear.

JUNE 1940

Their faces were drawn and defeated. They looked like they'd
seen hell. I couldn't believe that these were our boys, in
shirtsleeves and with no uniforms. Boys is right. That's what
they looked like perched up there on their jeeps and in the
back of the trucks. They were starving. Len and I offered
some of them tea, but they waved their hands and politely
refused. I thought to myself, well, Hitler might as well
just come marching through now. We better start learning
German. Most of them were too ashamed to even look you
in the eye. Our heroes returning from Dunkirk. And yet,
all over the papers, they're still trying to tell us that one
Englishman is worth two Germans, four French, twenty
Arabs, forty Italians, and any number of Indians. I thought,
that fat bastard Churchill will no doubt turn it into some kind
of victory. He'll be on the wireless again tonight, huffing and
puffing, and Len will be lapping it all up like a bloody silly
little spaniel. If Churchill tells me one more time that this war
is being fought for freedom and true principles of democracy
I'll scream. But, as I looked on at them, I thought to myself
that this war can't go on for much longer if this is the state
we're in. That much was clear for anybody to see. It might
as well be the white flag now. We're going to lose England.
We've legally placed ourselves, our property and our services
at the disposal of His Majesty, and I for one don't expect to
get anything back. And sure enough this evening he was on
the wireless, the stuck-up pig. I wanted to turn it off, but Len
likes to listen. So I went out for a walk. One of the LDVs

flashed a torch in my face and asked me who goes there. I wanted to say to the stupid sod, it's me, Hitler. I was hoping you wouldn't catch me because I was planning on invading tonight, starting right here in this village. But now you've buggered up my plans, you crafty devil. Oh, it's just you, Mrs Kitson. I wandered back and sat with Len, who told me that we always start badly. That we English lose every battle but the last. He'd believed the official story behind the looks on those lads' faces. I was getting good at learning the difference between the official stories and the evidence before my eyes. And even when there was no evidence, I was learning what to disbelieve. And so I sat with Len and began to swear out loud. What's the matter with you? Nothing, Len. Nothing. I'm just fine.

MARCH 1943

I've been wondering about him ever since the dance. I didn't
think he was letting me down by not showing up at the shop.
I'm not that presumptuous. After all, we only danced a few
times and then I was passed around. It was only fair. There
wasn't enough of us so we had to be shared. It turned into a
'Ladies, excuse me' dance, which meant anyone could cut in.
At the end of the dance we all left together, so there was no
question of anyone walking out with anyone. They brought
us our coats, and gave us presents. An orange, a pack of
cigarettes, and some candy, as they call it. Chocolate is what
we call it, and for most of us it was like being given lumps
of gold. The Yanks really have no idea of what it means. I
think we were maybe a bit rude, like kids, for once they'd
given us the chocolate we all muttered a hasty goodnight.
Everyone just wanted to escape with the chocolate in case
the Yanks changed their minds. The next morning I woke
up and thought about him. I wondered if they'd be having
another dance for us, or if they'd decided that one was enough.
I decided that all dances should start that way, with me and him
gliding across the floor and breaking the atmosphere. That was
three weeks ago. I have a feeling that they thought me a bit
above myself. But still, I have nice, if awkward, memories.
But today everything is fine again, for he came into the shop
with a big smile upon his face and a bunch of daffodils. He
told me that he didn't know what we called these things. He'd
never seen them before, for they didn't have them where he
came from. But he thought he'd like me to have them. He

dresses so smartly, and he doesn't chew gum when he talks. Not like the officers and the others. I don't know why they think it's so clever to do this. It's vulgar. Anybody could tell them that. His hair is well combed, with a sort of razor parting on the left. It's short, like thin black wool, but he puts some oil or something on it because it shines in the light. Quite bright, actually. Here, take them. He handed the flowers to me and I thanked him. I looked for a jam jar to put them into and he lit a cigarette. Excuse me, do you mind? he asked. Of course I don't mind. I don't say this, but I hope he understands. I just shook my head a few times. I'll be back in a sec, I said. You don't mind watching the shop, do you? I went out the back and found a jar. I wondered if I should ask him. I didn't know why I was even going through this for it seemed obvious to me that if I didn't ask him then nothing was going to happen. I took a peek back through into the shop and saw him just standing there like a spare part, not knowing what to do. And then I came back in with the daffodils standing proudly in a jar. I just asked him outright. Would you like to go for a walk? He looked confused. As though I was trying to trick him into something. A walk? Or perhaps you're not allowed to do this. To go off limits, or whatever you call it. Is that it? If so, I'm sorry for asking, but it's just that I thought a walk would be nice. Still, it doesn't matter if you're not able to do it. No, he says. But maybe Sunday. I don't think we get any recreation again until Sunday. Would that be all right? We get most of the day. I looked at him and realized that Sunday it would have to be. We sometimes go to your pub. It seems a nice place. Most of the guys like the English pub, although your beer still tastes a little strange to us. But you do like it? I asked quickly. Yeah sure, we like it. We drink it. There's nothing else to drink. He laughed as he said this. I don't mean to be rude, he assured me. Look. I've got to get back. I've got duties to take care of. Sunday, I said. Sunday, he said. And that was him gone, leaving me with the daffodils.

JUNE 1940

I can't figure out if Len is trying to impress me by joining the Local Defence Volunteers (or Look, Duck, Vanish, as people call them – they even call themselves this). Or maybe Dunkirk has secretly shaken him up. An army instructor came to one of their meetings in the pub. Taught them the German for 'Hands up!' Showed them how to spot different types of aircraft, how to handle a rifle and bayonet. Last Sunday, he took them out into the woods and they used grass sods as grenades. They're planning campaigns. Making decisions. Do we march east to protect Sam Smith's brewery, or north to guard Joshua Tetley's brewery? But Len is getting bored. He's younger than most of them. I think it's making him feel guilty. Reminding him that he should be in the real army. He'll soon stop going. LDV service is compulsory, but nobody really bothers that much by us. There isn't really anyone to check up. We're off the beaten track. They're more bothered by those dodging proper military service. Len's black lung is an embarrassment to him, but it's a genuine handicap. He's better than some of his mates, who are skiving off with all kinds of made-up illnesses and ailments. Now they've got something to be embarrassed about, not Len.

JUNE 1940

I was serving two Land Army girls. We all heard the shot. I ran straight from the shop up the street, hair flying this way, legs that. I knew she wouldn't tell him. Straight into the house and there she was, lying on the floor, blood spreading. And Tommy screaming. And that bullying bastard sitting there as bold as brass with the rifle in his hands and tears running down his cheeks. He kept repeating himself. Get the police, I've just done in my missus. The dirty bitch. Sandra had her eyes open and was staring into mid-air as if nothing was the matter. I've just done in my missus. The dirty bitch. As if she couldn't quite understand what all the fuss was about. The thing I noticed about him, though, was his uniform. It seemed odd that he should be sitting there in his uniform. Back from the war to kill. His wife. I told her to write the bloody letter, but she would have to do it her way, wouldn't she. And look where it landed her. Somebody must have already called for the coppers, because it didn't take them long to arrive. When they did, he just got up and went with them. One of the coppers put a blanket over Sandra, like she was asleep. Then he told me that there was no point in my sticking around. I might as well get along, hadn't I. He offered to escort me (his words) out of the house. Somebody had already taken Tommy.

JUNE 1940

Tonight I saw Len, sitting in the pub with his mate, Terry the Farmer. Len was always lecturing me. You don't mix with anybody. It's all right, you know. You can come into the pub for a drink with us. We won't harm you. How do you expect anyone to get to know you if you won't show your face out? I'd generally look at him, but say nothing. And off he would go to the pub and leave me sitting by myself, listening to ITMA on the wireless. But tonight I went to the pub. I put on my coat and walked up the road. He was sitting in the corner with the man Sandra's husband should have shot. Mr bloody Farmer perched there like Lord Muck, everybody knowing it was him who'd done it to her, sipping a pint like nothing was the matter. What'll you have? asked Len. I'll be having nothing, I said back to him. Nothing as long as you're sitting here with this slack bastard. I could see it in Len's eyes that he was ready to belt me one there and then, in front of everybody. If he wasn't so vain, he'd have done it. I think you'd better go home, was the best he could come up with. Why? I asked. Because I said you'd better. So I turned and left. I didn't have any desire to argue with him. And I didn't want to sit in the same place as him as long as he was with that bastard. So I turned and walked back out and into the night. It was so quiet. It was like the whole world had stopped because of this bloody stupid war. And what about Tommy? I supposed they'd find a good home for him. I walked back to the shop, went upstairs, took off my clothes, and climbed into bed. I didn't want Len near me. Not now, not ever. And I didn't want him to see me crying.

JULY 1940

All I could think of this morning was that a whole month has passed since Sandra died. And then the inspector showed up. I was standing in the shop with Len, going through the books for the week, when suddenly we heard a van pull up. Len went to the window and fingered the curtains. Then he turned to me and shouted in a whisper that I'd got to go out the back with the eggs and get rid of them. I didn't need telling twice. He doesn't tell me much, doesn't Len, but I wasn't born yesterday. I work in the shop with him. I'm married to him. I know his game. I dashed into the back of the shop and started to push everything into a flour sack. Hurry up, you silly cow. Why should I hurry up if this is the best he can call me? I heard the doorbell ring, and then there were voices. Me, I took the sack and went out the back. Then I was away through the woods and down the hill, laughing all the way like a crazy bugger. When I got to the stream, I opened the sack up wide. There was nobody around. I was standing by myself. That bastard Len. I knew it was a crime. It was madness. It was the sort of thing that somebody who was plain bloody daft would do. I knew all of this. But I did it anyway. I just threw everything into the stream. Egg after egg. Let the fish or whatever have them. Len said to get rid, so I was getting rid. I'd just pretend that I didn't understand what he meant. I thought, it's a hell of an expensive way to spite somebody, but he bleeding well deserves to be treated with spite. When I'd finished, I sat on the bank and laughed. I didn't know what the bloody hell I was doing in this place. With him. I couldn't be any worse off in a factory or in the WAAF. I must have been mad. It was mad. To have come to this place at all. I picked up the empty flour sack. Then I looked at the stream. I threw the sack in after the eggs. I didn't want any of it. What did I need with an empty sack? I didn't want any of it. By the time I got back from the stream he was in the pub. It was night. I was asleep when he came in. Or at least I was pretending to be. He asked me, so I told him that I'd done what he wanted me to do. I'd got rid of them. He laughed. Then he reminded me that tea and margarine were now on coupons. Then he went to the bathroom. When he found out that it was the truth that I'd told him, I knew he'd want to take a strap to me. But until then he laughed. I think he liked me for a minute or so. He thought I was funny.

SEPTEMBER 1940

Apparently, London is still getting it bad. It's their turn every night. I've been reading about it. It's all in the papers. ARPs can get no sleep. They're working hand in hand with the police force around the clock. UXB means unexploded bomb. They say if a bomb's got your name on it, you hear a whine, then a silence before the explosion. This is because it's travelling faster than sound. Those who've dug in their shelters stand a better chance. There's those that will take your bolts, spanners and sheets, and put your Anderson into the ground for you. But it will cost you a few bob. There's money to be made out of misery. Torches, batteries, firemen's axes, chemical fire extinguishers, whistles, you name it. You can even buy ARP-approved bomb removers. Top of the line is 'The Gripper' – 'grips bombs from any position only 10/6'. If it got a bit lively outside, I'm not sure if I'd want to get into a shelter. They say you've to take food, warm clothing and blankets to make yourself as comfortable as possible, and sing songs like 'Me and My Girl' and 'Swanee River'. It doesn't sound like me. Today Len caught me reading the papers. He asked me why I'm always reading, reading, reading. I didn't say anything. Then he said we might lose the war. He reckons being up here, we don't really understand how bad it is. We get a rosier picture. The war's still a bit of a joke to us. I thought, he's changed his tune. But I said nothing. The *Star* has started to run a competition called Hitler-Hits. They give you the first line and whoever sends in the best second line gets £10.

SOMEWHERE IN ENGLAND

If you listen in Hamburg you may hear Lord Haw-Haw say,
We've killed 10,000 Englishmen – one less than yesterday.

I wish I'd have thought of that one. Today's first line is a
hard one,

On every hand in Germany it's very plain to see . . .

NOVEMBER 1940

That silly brummie bugger Chamberlain's dead. Almost exactly six months after stepping down. Common opinion is that the strain of holding the highest office killed him. Our blackout curtains need to be fixed. The bobby told Len that last night he saw light. I went into my sewing box to find a needle and thread. I thought, they're a blessed nuisance. The curtains, that is. Then I saw a rag doll I'd been making for Tommy out of old stockings. I'd only to sew on the buttons for eyes. That was all I had left to do.

DECEMBER 1940

Thursday was always a popular going-out night in town. I wonder if Hitler knew this. Maybe it was simpler than this, maybe he just knew it was going to be a full moon. It was the clearest night I'd ever seen. I could hear the town sirens in the far distance, wailing their warning, and then I heard the queer engines of German bombers, all out of tune. They sounded different from ours, uglier. And then, away on the horizon, our boys; the ripping sound of anti-aircraft batteries. Everybody knew they were after the steelworks. Firth Brown and Co., J. Arthur Balfour and Co., Vickers. All of them. But there were too many Jerry planes and I knew we were going to get a pasting. It was a real bomber's moon, and from up there in the sky our roads must have looked like frosty white ribbons pointing the way to the target. First flares, then incendiaries, then the heavy bombs. We all stood shivering on the hillside and looked down. The town soon looked like a thousand camp fires had been lit on it, beautiful little fairy lights, everywhere blazing. You couldn't look anywhere without seeing fire. Len slipped a blanket around my shoulders, and the vicar started singing 'Nearer my God to Thee'. I gave him a dirty look, but he didn't stop. In between the verses, I heard somebody whisper, The town's on fire. There was a huge celestial glow, as though the sun were about to rise out of the heart of the town. And then the vicar stopped. He pulled a piece of paper from his frock pocket and announced, 'Repose.' There were maybe two dozen of us. We all turned from the town and looked at him.

God is our Refuge – don't be afraid,
He will be with you, all through the raid;
When bombs are falling and danger is near,
He will be with you until the 'All Clear'.
When the danger is over, and ev'rything calm,
Thank you Redeemer for courage and balm;
He'll never forsake you, He'll banish your fear,
Just trust and accept Him, and feel He is near.

When he finished, there was silence. We all turned and looked back at the town. Fires were still blazing, but we couldn't hear any more planes. Maybe it was over? Len whispered in my ear, I'm off to the pub. I'll see you back later. I watched him and his mates walk off. I even heard them laughing. I imagined that I could hear the sound of the 'All Clear' in the distance. But, of course, I heard nothing. And then I looked around at the vicar who was praying, stifling his fear between two folded hands.

DECEMBER 1940

Today I took a bus down to the town to find my mother. I hadn't slept much. In fact, I hadn't really slept at all, but I felt wide awake. The countryside looked much the same, but when I saw the town, I wanted to cry. Tram lines were twisted like liquorice. Iron girders were discarded across the street, jutting up into the air and pointing towards the now empty grey sky. I couldn't believe that this was my town. The bus couldn't go any further, so we all got off and began to walk. I stared at buildings that were now reduced to one or maybe two walls. Neat rectangular holes that used to be windows provided useless ventilation. Everywhere I looked I could see mountains of rubble, crushed cars, and battered trams. Up above me, the loose, swinging arms of cranes picked their way over the carcass of the town. And in the streets, men with flatcaps and women with head-scarves scavenged at the ruins of their houses, avoiding any hot debris, trying to find bits of furniture, photographs, anything that remained of their lives. As they did so, others – maybe family members – stared on, dumbstruck. I stepped gingerly around a sea of broken glass, and then saw a formal queue of parents taking turns to lift their children into the cockpit of a crashed Jerry bomber. I wondered about the pilot, and then realized that I should be wondering about my mother. I increased my pace. Down a side street, I saw charred bodies covered in soot and glass. Then I realized that they were just Burton's dummies. It occurred to me that I was lost. That all the familiar landmarks had gone and that I was no better than the sad woman I saw wandering with a bird cage in one hand and some photographs in the other, singing 'It's a long way to Tipperary'. The bashing had obviously sent her beyond. I asked for directions from an ARP who looked half-asleep underneath his tin helmet. He said nothing, but simply pointed me towards a junction that I recognized. I wanted to ask him about the football rattle in his hand, but he looked too tired to answer, so I just said thank you. He nodded a quick acknowledgement. I walked on knowing that there was no longer any such thing as a familiar route. Fire hoses like long, endless snakes were strewn across the roads. Fires still spat, but down here the odd girder was all that remained of most buildings. I saw groups of patient employees standing outside shops and offices with no idea of what to do, their work places wrecked. The whole town was in a state of shock. Everybody seemed to be suffering their own private war tragedy. The odd car rolled by at a funereal pace, but heads didn't turn. People simply gawked at the destruction. I turned off the main street and continued to pick my way through the back streets. I looked on at the ATS girls, who seemed to be working non-stop, helping the police, driving, standing side by side with the ARPs. They made me feel useless.

DECEMBER 1940

I suppose I knew that she'd be dead before I got there. It didn't seem possible that others should have died, but not her. I saw the house, or what was left of it. A gap in the street, like a broken tooth. There were no windows, the front door hung off its hinges, and I could see that the ceiling plaster was down and that soot and dirt were everywhere. Nothing looked burned, so I knew that it wasn't an incendiary. These could be put out with earth and water. That much I'd managed to understand from the papers, not that she would have bothered to do anything about it. It looked like the blast had come from a nearby bomb. And then I saw that the houses across the road had been hit. The ARPs were still cordoning off the road. I saw old Mr Miles. On his back he had a leather coat so mangled it looked like someone had thrown a dead cow over him. When he saw me, he handed his roll of string to another warden. I ducked under the barrier. He put his hand on my shoulder. I'm sorry, love. He took off his tin helmet. You know what she was like. She wouldn't go in the shelter. She made us laugh, though. She said, I've never had a front seat in a war, and I'm not missing my chance now. Where is she? I asked. They've taken her off in a corporation bus with the others. It were not good around here as a lot of folk took their chances. They weren't banking on a direct hit. If you're a bit squirmish, you'd best make yourself scarce. We're not finished yet, and there's more trapped under that lot. I looked behind him as his fellow men, cigarettes dangling from their lower lips, feet stamping to keep themselves warm, shovels in hand, prepared to dig again in the rubble. You'll get a chance to see her later, love. They'll not be burying anyone for a while. Can't do nothing for them. I expect they'll want you to give identification. And don't worry about your household salvage. There'll be no looting while we're about. So don't worry. You can come back later today, or tomorrow. Sort out your stuff. I looked into Mr Miles's tired and crease-lined face, and I knew that this kind old man was near the end of his tether. I wondered how many others he'd had to talk to like this.

DECEMBER 1940

By mid-afternoon it had started to snow. I was sitting in the park watching the endless flow of people filling tin baths from the lake. There was no water. After Mr Miles had sent me on my way, I spent a couple of hours wandering around the town in a daze. I'd noticed the long queues at standpipes. In some lucky streets, the water cart arrived with its large round cylinders. People with buckets and jugs and saucepans, whatever they had, pushed and shoved. The water, flecked with charcoal and lime, spluttered out of large taps, but at least you could drink it. And then the water-cart man shut off the taps and there was no more. That's it until tomorrow, loves. And off he went to another lucky street. Some went back to the standpipes. I continued to walk and saw folk rummaging like paupers among the rubble of their houses. I spied on people's lives. The fronts of their houses were often blown clean off, leaving the furniture still arranged, books and crockery in place. In one house, a hole in the back of a cabinet, that must have been previously hidden against a wall, was now revealed for all to see. Nearly everybody's roofing slates had slid down and into the street, exposing sad, gaping lattice work. Some had been really unlucky. The insides of their houses had collapsed, mixing brick, wood and glass with papers, curtains and clothes. Ladders were up against what walls remained, and broken furniture was stacked neatly on the pavement. I couldn't stand it any more. The Church Army Mobile Canteens, the WVS Mobile Canteens, the Salvation Army Mobile Canteens, all bringing food and drink to the workers and the homeless. In one street, Jerry had dropped a thousand-pounder bang in the middle of the tram track. The overhead wires were all down. A little girl was bawling as she looked at the burned-out shell of the tram. And outside a barber's shop, a sign: 'We've had a close shave. Come and get one yourself.' I walked on in my dazed state, trying not to think of her lying wherever she was. And then I went into the park where I must have fallen asleep. The snow woke me up, cold flakes slapping against my cheeks. I opened my eyes and peered through the pale, watery light of afternoon. It was then that I saw people filling tin baths from the lake. I decided to go back to the village. There was no point in going back to the house and sorting through her things. They'd be wet and useless. And no point in going to find her. She didn't need me at this moment. I decided to get back to Len. To get back to the village.

DECEMBER 1940

The corporation buried them today. Christmas Eve. Some had private services, but most went at the same time. They were all there, the dignitaries. The Lord Mayor, representatives of the Civil Defence Services, clergy from all denominations. I stood in the snow. It had snowed for nearly two weeks now. I thought of her standing looking up at the skies as Jerry dropped his bombs. The best cinema show in the world. I imagined that's how it must have looked to her. Standing out there in the cold night air, with all that noise, and the red glow of the fires lighting up her neighbourhood. I could picture the child-like pleasure on her face. And then the service was over and we began to leave the cemetery. I remember thinking that it didn't feel like Christmas. And that it was so cold that I would have to ask the fuel controller for extra coal.

JANUARY 1941

I read in the *Star* that the King and Queen visited the town yesterday. They stayed three hours and visited bombed-out houses and talked to folk. All I could think about was the smell of the chemical lavatories and cesspools in people's back gardens. I hope the corporation did something about them. There's nothing anybody can do about the snow. It's not stopped for weeks.

FEBRUARY 1941

Len, of course, had refused to come to the funeral. She never did like me, he said. But that wasn't the point. As far as I was concerned, it was a matter of respect. Who said that she had to like you? She tolerated you. That was a lot for her. Believe me. But Len still wouldn't come to the funeral. When I got back from the funeral he laughed at me. He lowered his newspaper. She died because you left her down there on her own and went off with me, he said. I walked out of the room. I decided that on the first Sunday of every month I would take the bus into town. I would play daughter. This morning was Sunday. Despite the cold I had no choice. There's one bus in the morning and one that comes back at night. They've cut to a skeleton schedule, having decided to commandeer the buses to serve as emergency ambulances. This being the case, I knew right off that I would have to spend the whole day there. It didn't take long at the graveside. It was very much a matter of Hello, Mother, how are you? Hope you've found Dad again. And if you've found him I hope you're happy. Happier than I am, at any rate. I can't rightly see how you couldn't be. You'd have to be a miserable bugger to be unhappier than I am. Now that she was with her maker I had the feeling that she was listening to me. Which is more than she ever did when she had some breath in her body. I left, then decided that I should buy her some flowers. I bought them at the hospital next door. Handy that, having a hospital right next door. I suppose some might look upon it as being a bit creepy, but I didn't think so. After I'd bought the flowers I walked back into the cemetery and laid them on the grave. I stood back. I wondered if it was possible to place them in such a way that people would understand that they were meant for my mother and not for the other two people who shared this communal grave with her. An infant. Didn't last a day. Its mother had no money. Probably no bloke either. And an old man. Truly old. Lived sadly past his time until there was nobody left. Probably wore out his memories like a gramophone record that's been played too often. I tried to place the flowers so that Mother would know. But did it really matter? After all, nobody had brought flowers for the other two. Let them all share them, I thought. And then I went for a walk in the park. I sat by the lake and stared unashamedly into space for the rest of the afternoon. People used to come and feed the ducks. But nobody's got bread to spare any more. The ducks have to eat whatever it is they used to eat before people were generous. Then the weather turned bad again. It began to snow. The branches of the trees were already bowed under a thick crust of ice. So I went to the pictures to get out of the cold. I found it difficult to find a cinema without a House Full sign. Other people must have had the same idea before me. Lonely people. Single people have no shame about going to the cinema. Why should they? It's dark. Nobody can see them. Nobody cares. But these days, I hate the films. Short government instructional films on how to win the war. They treat you like a fool. What to do. How to do it. How to save. What to save. And then a feature about how classless England is now that we're all pulling together to win the war. Classless my arse. A toffee-nosed bugger's still a toffee-nosed bugger to me. And then the lights came on and we all filed out. Outside it was getting a bit dark. I waited at the bus stop. There were a few people I recognized in the queue. They nodded, then wrapped up warm and kept themselves to themselves. Like me, they're likely to have been visiting family or friends. Except in their case I imagined their lot were still alive. The bus takes about an hour or so to reach the village. Longer these days. As we laboured up the hill, the tyres spat gravel and ice behind them. We're its last but one stop. We clambered off and tried to avoid giving each other a final nod. And we succeeded quite well. Very well, in fact.

JULY 1936

Everyone at the factory's going off for the summer. Most of them are going to Scarborough, but some are travelling across the way to Blackpool. They've all got a real beano in mind. But me, well, I'll not be going anywhere. I know that she won't let me. She'll just tell me it's a waste of money and that will be the end of it. There won't be any discussion, that will be it. Like when she made me leave school four years ago. I told her that Dad would have wanted me to get my school certificate, and maybe even one day go to college. She just stared at me and said, How do you know? She spoke to me as if he were nothing to do with me. I didn't say anything else. As a child, I soon learned that it was best to say as little as possible to her. But whenever I picked up a book to read she would finger her Bible and look askance at me. She once hit me because she said I read too much. Apparently, there was no need to read so much. It was wilful disobedience on my part. She didn't seem to understand that this was my way of hiding from her. Everything was seen as some kind of betrayal of her. I was always a disappointment. So I had to leave school and go to work. After all, I couldn't expect her to support me any longer. How did I imagine she'd managed up until now? And so I left school. I've learned, over the last four years, to ignore her. To try not to hear her bleating, self-important voice. And I've continued to lock myself up in books. And now everyone's talking about going off for the summer. But they haven't asked me to go with them. They haven't even asked me if I'm going somewhere else. They're not interested.

I expect they imagine they'll get the same frightened answer that they got when they once asked me to a dance. I'm sorry, I stuttered. I expect they think I'm coy because I'm not much to look at. She doesn't go anywhere because she's ugly. Well, it's true, but it's not the whole story. It's not even the half of it. I'm just happier with books. They don't shout at me, or accuse me of anything. They don't even know that I'm not much to look at.

CHRISTMAS 1936

I've got an extra job tearing tickets at the Lyceum Theatre ('Yorkshire shows for Yorkshire folk'). Something to keep me out of her house for a bit longer each day. Once people are in, I get to see the show. But it's not much of a show. In fact, it's the pantomime, Mother Goose, but at least I'm getting to know a new world, and meeting people from a different background. That's how I met Herbert. He's an actor. He talks to me about Shakespeare. He seemed surprised that I'd read some of Shakespeare's plays, and some poets like Wordsworth and Coleridge and so on. Herbert has begun explaining to me about the difference between comedy and tragedy. We talk a lot about these things. He laughed when I told him I hated my name because there were no Shakespearean characters called Joyce. We usually have a drink before the show. He's trying to get me to like gin. I'm always trying to get the glass back on to its wet spot on the bar. And then, last night, Christmas Eve, I agreed to go out with him and the rest of the cast after the play had finished. There's always places that will stay open for actors. Everybody seems to love actors. We all toasted Christmas as the clock struck twelve. Then later, having walked me home, Herbert kissed me goodnight outside the house and said how much he loved me. All I could think of to say was, I'm eighteen. He just smiled and kissed me again.

APRIL 1937

She didn't even knock. She just came straight into my room and stood waiting for me to say something to her. I couldn't say anything because I couldn't stop crying. It annoyed me that she refused to see this. That she wouldn't even acknowledge the fact that I was really upset. He wasn't replying to any of my letters. None of them. And there was nobody at the factory that I could tell. She took a long look at me, but all she could say was, It's the first time in ages I've seen you without a book. And I thought about it. She was right. But she didn't even ask me why I was crying. If she had have done, I would have told her. But it was as if she just wanted to see what the noise was all about. And once she'd found out, she left and closed the door behind her.

MAY 1937

After the abortion, I went to church with her. Or, as she put it, I came to Christ. I still worked at the factory, but I said even less than before. I didn't talk to anybody at all, even if they spoke to me. It was part of my performance. I didn't speak. But I thought that Christ might be prepared to speak with me. At least He might express some interest in me. But He didn't. So I left the church. Or I left Christ. I could never figure out which. And then she left me. My abandonment of Christ was the last straw. I'd chosen to leave He who had made her life possible. This was, for her, the unkindest cut of all.

CHRISTMAS 1937

On the train down, I stared out of the window. I would be
spending every penny I'd ever managed to save in my life.
When I got to London, I moved into a bed and breakfast
near King's Cross station. It occurred to me that I could
last – with some luck – perhaps a lot of luck – four days.
And then I didn't know what. I found Herbert on the second
day. He was at the Lyric Theatre playing in Mother Goose. A
different production. Even though it was London, it seemed
a worse production somehow. Even the posters were shabby.
The whole thing was disappointing. But not as disappointing
as Herbert, who got me a seat in the stalls and said we could
talk afterwards. In a pub in Hammersmith that was thick with
tobacco smoke. The Dog and Pheasant. He bought me a gin,
and a pint for himself. And then he said he couldn't reply to
my letters. He told me about his wife and his two children, and
I listened with my mouth open. And then I spilt my drink. It
toppled over and I watched as it pooled on the table. He bought
me another gin, then said he had to get some Woodbines from
the bar. I never saw him again. I sat there by myself, an idle
finger spinning the ice. I'd been jilted. I realized that Herbert
had no idea of what it was like to be anyone but himself. But
this didn't make any sense, because he was supposed to be an
actor. And then it was ten o'clock and I heard the landlord
shouting. Time, ladies and gentlemen, please. Let's be having
you. Time. Outside the pub, a man asked me if I had a light.
Then, before I could answer, he winked at me and smiled. He
had yellow teeth. My stomach turned a slow somersault.

FEBRUARY 1938

This morning I started a new job. In a warehouse which imports foodstuffs from all over the country and abroad. My job is to serve the people who come in. Shopkeepers, mainly, from all over. I'm supposed to look cheerful. And talk. The factory. Well, they'd had enough of me not saying anything. But I hate this new talking job. I hate this town. I'm trying to start reading again, but it's not easy. Every night I hear the dull beat of her feet as she drags herself up the creaking stairs. Then I realize that I'm no longer sure of why I'm reading, let alone what it is that I'm reading. I just want to cry, but I've promised myself that I'll never let her see me cry again. Never.

SEPTEMBER 1941

It's autumn. I've been here two years now. I've resigned myself to the fact that I won't ever like it. But at least I don't pretend. Len knows how I feel. He also knows how I feel about the war. I hate the 'Wings for Victory' and 'Salute the Soldiers' weeks. I'm just waiting for it all to end and then I'll be off. Today I asked Len about his parents. He's usually reluctant to talk about them, but for some reason he rested down his cup on the kitchen table and began to speak. But he didn't look me in the eyes as he did so. He talked for a good while, in fact until I thought he might cry. But he didn't. He was quiet for a while, and then he simply stood up and went out. I knew then that we'd never really been married. We didn't know each other. We didn't trust each other. Later on, he came in drunk and talking nonsense. He told me that he thought Hitler looked like a hysterical lavatory brush. And that because Russia was the only country to stand up to Hitler, maybe their system was right. I expect he heard this rubbish in the pub. He slumped against me as I helped him up the stairs to bed.

DECEMBER 1941

Len's in prison for doing what hundreds of others, the length and breadth of this country, are still doing. Namely, trading in the so-called 'black market'. They took him away the day after the Americans were gracious enough to join us in the war. The fact that they chose to stand by and watch as we lost Norway, Belgium, France, Denmark and Holland only served to stir up plenty of negative passions towards them. I sat with Len and listened to the announcement on the wireless. When it was over he snapped the *Star* shut and dropped it by the side of the armchair. Then he stood up. I heard the door slam, and his boots register on the cobbles. And the next morning the inspectors arrived. Representatives of the Price Regulation Committee of the North East Region, based in Leeds. To pinch him. But Len had gone to town. He had been warned three times, but he wouldn't listen. Eggs could be bought only for the purposes of hatching, but farmers, shopkeepers and customers formed a partnership that made a nonsense of such decrees. Only Len would have to pursue his subversive activities on a grand scale. One thousand eggs. Possibly more. Officially, you could only charge $3^3/4d.$ for an egg. But there were plenty who'd pay up to 15 shillings for a dozen. Len was well aware of this. They waited outside in the motor car until Len came back up from town. When he did, he knew straight away that something was up. They followed him in the door. The two of them. Len looked at me, and then back at them. He spoke to them like he was talking to a pair of hounds. You two. What do you want in my shop? It's you we want, lad, they said. We've found what we're looking for. And we've got your mate. Now you'll be coming with us. Len spun around and stared at me. What have you told them? I shrugged my shoulders. You didn't tell them 'owt, did you? The inspectors looked at him. Is there something she shouldn't have told us, is that it? Course not, snapped Len. You're a lying bastard, aren't you. Len moved towards me. One of the inspectors put his hand on Len's arm. All right. You're coming with us, and the door's this way. Your wife can bring your things along later. No need for you to get alarmed now. It's all pretty straightforward. You arresting me? We're taking you in, lad. I told you. We've already got your farmer mate. The two of you will have plenty of time to get your story straight. What about her? Are you suggesting we take your wife as well? Len glared at me as though I were somehow responsible. But he couldn't say anything, otherwise it would look as though he was guilty of something. Which, of course, he was. So he allowed himself to be marched off in silence. And I slept well that night. I stretched out in the bed. I knew that whatever happened, I wouldn't have to share my bed with him again. That if he came back now, I'd stand up all night in the corner of the room before I'd ever condescend to join him in bed. Something was lifted from me the moment they took him away. My chest unknotted. I could breathe again. He expected and received little sympathy from the Magistrate, who terminated his speech with the observation that for shopkeepers and prostitutes these lean years were proving to be years of plenty. Len was encouraged to view himself as a vulture picking at the carcass of his wounded country. I returned to the village alone. To face their accusing eyes. I had not 'stuck by him'. It was now important for me to abandon any vanity. To learn to ignore whatever they might be saying about me. I've been training myself. In the evenings I attend to the blackout curtains, then sit by myself and listen to the wireless. I follow the war, listen to ITMA, and read. I often think of my mother. But I never ask her for help.

I don't ask for anybody's help. And in the shop, no matter how they look at me, I always ask them for their coupons. I wonder if they realize that if the inspectors hadn't have taken Len, then the services were about ready to take me. I was about to be classified 'mobile', as they're getting desperate. My invalid husband would have just had to learn how to look after himself. As he will have to when he gets out.

APRIL 1943

He came on the Sunday morning that I go down to visit my mother. The first Sunday morning of each month. He was dressed smartly in his uniform and he was carrying yet more daffodils. I've brought you some more of these yellow flowers. I like how they look. I smiled. Once again, I left him in the front of the shop while I went around the back to find a jar. I saw the ring that I'd taken off and put by the kitchen tap. My God, what was I doing? There was something brassy about having taken it off and not having replaced it. But I didn't care. I left the ring there, jammed the flowers into a jar, and came back through into the shop. I didn't know if I should bring you some candy, he said. But it doesn't matter. I can let you have some whenever you want. All you have to do is say when. He seemed nervous, so I touched him on the arm. That's all right, I said. Don't worry. Let's go. I smiled at him and he seemed to relax a little. For a walk? Not exactly, I said. I thought we could go and see my mother. His face dropped. It's all right, I said. She's dead. He didn't know what to do. I tell you what. I'll take the flowers, if that's all right with you. We can put them on the grave. Then he started to laugh, and I realized that it would be all right. My mother used to like flowers, I said. I took them out of the jar. We waited at the bus stop. People passed by on their way to church. It was nothing to do with him. They didn't talk to me anyhow. I wondered if there was some way of letting him know this. That it wasn't anything to do with him why they weren't talking. But I decided that it was too early to tell him this. I might as well let him work some things out for himself. We talked on the bus. Most of the time I just listened, for he talked more than I did. He told me a bit about himself, and why he joined the army. Me, I didn't like to ask too much because I don't know much about Americans. Or Coloureds. I was sure that I was going to make a mistake. Bound to. So I said nothing. I just kept my mouth shut and listened to him talking to me in that sing-song accent of his. I like it. It makes me laugh, although I'm not sure that it's supposed to. The way he stretches out words. When we got to town we went straight to the cemetery and he was very proper. I let him put the flowers on my mother. He asked me if I wanted to say a prayer. I looked at him, unsure as to what to do. I thought I'd better just tell the truth. I don't know any prayers, I said. This wasn't really true. I do know some, but I'm not very good at such things. Like prayers. He said that was all right, but would I mind if he said one. I said, course not. So he did. When it was over, I thought that I'd better tell him that there's not really that much to see and do in the town. That's the honest truth. I don't care what anybody says. It's not really any place to show a visitor. He suggested that we could talk as we walked the streets, so we did. And again we talked about him, and I tried to avoid the way people were looking. They were looking at me. Not him. They just nodded at him. Some people asked him for a Lucky Strike. He always gave away two, and a smile. I thought that was nice. It made me think nice things about him. But nobody would say anything to me. I knew what they were thinking. That he was just using me for fun. There was no ring on my finger, but I didn't think that they had the right to look at me in that way. Just who the hell did they think they were? I told my friend that I thought we should sit down in the park for a minute. I didn't feel all that well. In fact, I told him, I felt a bit dizzy. He wrapped his finger and thumb around my wrist. You sure you're getting enough to eat? Yes, thank you. You sure you don't want me to fix you up with some Hershey bars? I smiled. We sat awkwardly and in silence, he

with his thoughts, I with mine. I just kept thinking, I can't
see what they're getting out of it. Being so cruel. But I was
just making myself more and more angry, and I could sense
that it was getting difficult for him. I slipped my arm inside his
and asked him if he fancied going to the pictures. He smiled.
Sure, why not? And so there we were, in the dark in the
Elektra Palace, watching the first house, but I wasn't really
watching, and I sensed that he could tell. I felt such a fool, but
I didn't know how to tell him that it wasn't his fault. That it
was nothing to do with him. Honestly. When we came out it
was dark and I knew we'd missed the bus. I didn't know what
to do. We walked aimlessly towards the bus stop and then I
realized that I'd better own up. He looked at his watch.
I've got to be back in an hour. Surely there's some other way?
What about a taxi? I told him that I'd never taken a taxi. I didn't
know if they still ran, what with the blackout and everything.
Then I told him that I was sorry. That I didn't want to get him
into trouble. He looked at me. Don't worry. It's not your fault.
I knew he wasn't telling me the truth. He was trying to spare
my feelings. We stood and waited for an imaginary taxi. Small
'starlight' bulbs have now replaced all the standard ones. These
bulbs cast faintly illuminated circles down on to the pavement,
which is supposed to make it easier for us to see. I explained to
him that apparently you can't see these lights from above. He
touched my arm. I could see that he was worried. After half
an hour, he flagged down a military jeep. MPs, he whispered.
We both climbed into the back of the jeep. He told them I'd
been kind enough to introduce him to my mother. Then she
got sick and we had to wait on her. I wanted to laugh, but
I was frightened. The two men in the front of the jeep said
nothing. And I knew now that I had got him into big trouble. I
wanted the earth to swallow me up. He laced his hands around
his knees and we rode back in silence.

APRIL 1943

Last night I dreamed about the matinée we saw last Sunday afternoon. Not the actual film, because I hardly watched that. But a different film. In fact, it was like a different day altogether. The film was about a soldier on leave who meets a squire's daughter. Her toffee-nosed father is a veteran of the 1914–18 war. He's not sure about this young whipper-snapper walking out with his daughter, but slowly he comes to realize that he's not a bad lad. And the young soldier is won over when he realizes that the old boy goes firewatching with the local yokels. In other words, he does his bit. I hated the film because it didn't tell the truth, but my friend quite liked it. He told me that this was his first English film. Afterwards, I took him for fish and chips, then we got the bus home. When I woke up, I thought I was going to cry.

MAY 1943

I hadn't seen him in nearly three weeks now, so I decided
that the next time one of the soldiers came into the shop,
I'd gather up my courage and ask him about my friend. And
then this morning the officer with the dark glasses, Mr Hello,
Duchess, he popped in to ask the way to some place or other.
After I'd told him what he wanted to know, I asked him if
my friend was being punished. At first he looked surprised,
then he just said, yes. I told him that this was unfair, and
that what had happened was no fault of my friend's. But the
officer pretended that he didn't hear me. He smiled, saluted,
and then turned on his heels and left. I closed the shop early
and began the short walk down to the camp. I went up to the
soldiers on the gate. They asked me what I wanted, but I just
told them that I wanted to see the man in charge and they did
nothing after that. They just stood to one side and I walked
right through. I went up to the main office and was shown
into a room where a man was sitting behind a desk. Yes,
he snapped. Then, after he looked up and saw who it was
standing in front of him, he stood up and extended a hand.
I'm sorry. Please take a seat. I looked at him but continued
to stand. He sat down. My friend, I said. He's being punished
for something that's not his fault. He furrowed his brow as if
he didn't quite know whom it was I was referring to. Your
friend? I wasn't about to play this game. I stared right back at
him. He knew who my friend was. I went on and explained
how it was my fault that we missed the bus. How I was the
one, if anybody, who should be blamed. He then started to

tell me about discipline. And how important it was in the army that orders were obeyed. And that if you made an exception for one, you soon found that you had to make an exception for everybody. I listened. And then I explained again that it was my fault that we missed the bus. He looked at me. What would you like me to do about it? Believe me, I said. The bloody little squirt looked back down at his desk. I'll see what I can do, he said. Which really meant nothing, for we both knew he could do whatever he wanted to do. I turned and started to leave. But it's not that we don't want our men to mix with you village girls, it's not that at all. It's just that we don't want any incidents. It hasn't been easy for any of us. I turned and walked out of the door. Walking back across the camp, I had the feeling that everybody knew who I was, and that they knew why I'd been to see the commanding officer. I wandered back up towards the shop. Some villagers stopped and stared at me. They pointed by simply nodding their heads in my direction. Both inside the camp, and outside, I was attracting attention. But for the wrong reasons.

JUNE 1943

Today he came into the shop. I couldn't help myself, I let out a little scream of delight. He didn't want to buy anything. He just wanted to talk. He told me how embarrassed he'd been in the back of the jeep. I said that he had no reason to be embarrassed. After all, I was the one who should be embarrassed. I was the one who'd got us into the mess to start with. I said, If I'd been keeping a check on the time then it would never have happened in the first place. We fought over this and then fell silent when an old woman came in for her fags. She looked in the direction of my friend, but said nothing beyond 'ta' as she left. For a while the noise of the doorbell echoed in the silence. It registered a change of tone for the whole conversation. My friend lowered his voice and said how grateful he was that I had taken the trouble to come and help him out. I decided to close up the shop. Well, it was almost time anyway. I turned the sign around and drew the latch. Once I'd done this he relaxed. He told me that the military police hadn't taken him back to the camp. After they dropped me off, they'd driven him down the road to a clearing and told him to get out of the jeep. And then they beat him with their sticks. He said they beat him so hard that he thought his kidneys were going to burst. I closed my mouth, which I now realized had been hanging open. When they took him back to the camp, they'd made a report that said that he'd been drunk and difficult. As a result, the commanding officer had decided that he was to be confined to the camp until further notice. I was horrified when he told me this, but he seemed to take it as a matter of course. He told me that the army only liked to use them for cleaning and the like. I asked him if he'd like to come to the pub with me for a drink. I wanted him to continue talking to me. I wanted him to try to understand that I needed to know more about him, otherwise I would keep getting upset and just make more mistakes. I was bound to if I didn't get any help. He asked me if I thought it was proper that he should go into the pub with me. I looked at him and told him that there was nothing wrong with his going into the pub with me. Why should there be? Fine, then we'll go to the pub, he said. I locked the door behind us. I noticed that there was nobody on the streets. I expected everybody was having their tea. It was that time of the day. And in the pub, there was just the odd old boy. Nobody, really. He ordered a pint and a half of bitter. The landlord liked them. The Americans. I think he had a soft spot for them, wanted them to feel at home. And once they realized that the beer was always going to taste flat and warm, and that sometimes you would have to drink out of a jar if he ran out of glasses, then they were all right about everything. He even laughed when one of them handed him back a pint and told him to pour it back into the horse that it came from. And I liked the landlord. I'd noticed that after he'd been in the cellar to tap a new cask, he had a habit of taking a quiet smoke in the back parlour, as opposed to the public bar. It was as though he needed time to himself to collect his thoughts. I liked that about him. And then he'd come through into the public and knock out his empty pipe. Travis brought the pint and a half over to the seat in the corner. I told him that from here we'd soon be able to watch the sun go down.

JUNE 1943

Once back at the shop, he sat with me upstairs. And I offered him tea. Hot tea, as he insisted on calling it. And he said very little. It had already been said. I asked him if he was hungry, but he just shook his head. I'm not much of a cook, so that solved that. I realized that he probably didn't want to listen to the wireless, and I couldn't blame him. So we were happy with the silence, and the occasional comment. It wasn't too difficult or too awkward. If we had something to say, it was said. And that was the end of it. It grew dark outside. There was no noise, as ever. Across the room I saw the framed photograph of Len and me on our wedding day. Turned down. Its face buried in a thin layer of dust on top of the chest of drawers. And then Travis got to his feet. I have to go now. I have to get back. I'm sorry if I've taken up too much of your time. I just wanted to say thank you. Did I ever – he changes tack now – did I ever show you pictures of my home town? Or pictures of my folks? He must know that he never did. It's not the type of thing that a man would do for a virtual stranger and then forget about. And certainly not this man. I was already sure of that. No, I said. But I would love to see them. Okay, he said. I'll bring them along. Next time. He saluted. I laughed. And then he reached out his hand for me to shake. I'll walk back with you, I said. He gave a little laugh, as though nervous. Now don't you worry, he said. Little danger of my getting lost. Although, never know who you're gonna run into on the roads. Military Police. Anyone. His hand was beginning to look foolish, so I took it and held it between both of mine. And I surprised myself, for I squeezed it. Gently. Then he leaned forward and kissed my hand. Thank you, I said. Thank you, he said. The lights were out. I could see his eyes gleaming. He wrestled his hand out from between mine. I wanted to catch it like a slippery fish, but he was too nimble for me. I have to go now, he said. I'll be fine by myself. I'm sorry. I smiled. I knew he meant it. I knew he did. He was sorry that he had to go. After I closed the door behind him, I went back upstairs. I picked up the cup and saucer that he had been drinking out of, and I ran my finger around the rim of the cup. A little tea stain. And then I saw the mark in the settee where he'd been sitting. The room smelt of him. A good smell. I could smell him on me. I wasn't going to be alone again. As long as I didn't open any windows or doors. As long as I didn't wash anything. Then I could make the smell last a little longer.

JULY 1943

Yesterday they arrested Mussolini. The BBC announcer said that Hitler's 'utensil' had fallen off the Axis shelf. I was sitting in the pub by myself when the news came through. The landlord got out the monthly ration of whisky to celebrate what he said looked like the end. He offered me some, but I said no. Then he said that the Yanks would probably have to go over to Italy to clean up. He said he'd miss them. I felt a door closing inside of me. I looked up at him. He asked me again if I wanted a whisky. I nodded. He knew what he'd said. At least I have to give him that. It was still bright out, so I walked home the long way round to give myself some time to think. As I passed the church hall it occurred to me just how difficult it is to come by cosmetics, nail files, hair grips and the like. I'd never had much reason to fret over them before. Such things had never mattered. But now I found myself thinking that I could kill for a bar of scented soap.

JULY 1943

There are some girls from the town who seem to have no shame. Some factory girls, some plain common tarts, mainly bottle-blondes, all of them with legs like Grecian columns. They've started to frequent the camp. Apparently, some of them even spend the night there, and they go far beyond furtive clutching. He told me that nylons, nail varnish, perfume and the like, all these things that they can get from the PX, this stuff is known to them as 'shack-up' material. He said this is why he'd never offered me any, but clearly his mates weren't so fussy. It appears that some girls will do anything for goods or provisions. Since soap and sweets went on coupons, things must have got worse. I heard a woman in the shop today saying that there are some of them up there at the camp who'll let loose for a fresh orange. She went on. After all, you can only eat so much Spam. She said, These days sex is about the only thing that isn't rationed. She reckoned that this went some way towards accounting for the diseases that they say are going around.

DECEMBER 1943

Len came back today. He told me that he still loves me. He'd
had time to think things over. I might not realize it yet, but
the truth was that in spite of everything, he couldn't help
himself, he loved me. I liked that. In spite of everything.
Bloody charming. That made me feel really wanted. But I
didn't say anything. I just looked at him standing in front
of me, looking around his kingdom. He didn't have to say
anything. I knew what he was thinking. I knew what he felt
about me being in his place. But I wasn't going anywhere. He
could look all he wanted to, but this was also my place now.
He wanted to say something. I wanted him to say it. But he
said nothing. So I spoke. Len, I said. I don't want to live with
you as man and wife. What do you mean? His look said that.
Nothing else. Just, what do you mean? I mean, one of us will
be sleeping on the settee in future. I don't really mind who. I
don't care. Len sat down. In fact, he half sat, half collapsed.
Then he began. I hear there's talk about you and an American.
I knew there would be talk. In fact – I shouldn't say this – I had
been hoping that Len might find out. I knew it was cruel. But
what could I do? It's how I felt. I was hoping that I wouldn't
have to find some awkward way of telling him. Yes, I've got
a friend, I said. Now it was my turn to sit. I faced him, and
passed him the torch of conversation. He could say whatever
he wanted to say. And so he did. I don't think you should
have friends like that. It makes a bloody fool out of me. I
laughed. And getting put inside. Getting yourself carted off
to jail doesn't make me look like a bloody fool, is that it? Len

stood up. He pushed his finger into my face. He jabbed at me to punctuate his sentences. You won't see him, or any of 'em. You won't go to town, to the pub, have them in here, talk to them, nothing, as long as I'm here. I'd never have married you, or taken you out of that bloody slum, if I'd known you were going to behave like a slut. Now am I making myself clear? Yes, Len, I say. You're making yourself perfectly clear. But I won't have any of it. It's not for me to say what you do, any more than it is for you to talk to me in this way. His poor jaw dropped. I'm your bloody husband. Yes, I said. You're my bloody husband. In name only. His fist caught me across the left side of my face. I could feel the swelling right away. As though somebody was puffing up my face like a balloon. And then he kicked me in the stomach and I doubled up. I'm your bloody husband whether you like it or not. Not in name, you slut. In fact. In law and in fact. Now, like I told you. We're leaving. I've got work north of here. We're selling the shop. It's half mine, I gasped. And we're not selling. I didn't see why I should have to bother with this conversation. So I said nothing further. We're leaving, said Len. I remained silent. Do you hear? A piece of coal fell, and for a few seconds the fire blazed as the unburned coal caught. It made a crackling, definite noise. We both stared at the fire. For a moment we were caught by its performance. Then we looked at each other. I knew he wouldn't touch me again. He'd made his point. And then there was the shame. I suspect there's always a certain amount of shame involved for all men. After they've thrown the punch. They look and see you cowering. And the thought crosses their mind that perhaps they ought not to have done this. That perhaps this is not a proper way to hold a conversation. They're sorry. It's pitiful. I looked at him and dared him to continue to talk to me. I dared him to hit me again. But he wouldn't. I knew this, but I taunted him with my silence until he left for the pub.

DECEMBER 1943

Half an hour after he left, it became clear to me what I should do. I pulled on my coat. I was in a hurry. I closed in the door behind me and began to walk briskly towards the pub. I looked up. The moon was wrapped in a thick and heavy fog, and I was cold so I started to run. It was Friday night and I was sure that they would all be there. I was sure of it. I opened the door to the pub and all eyes were on me. I walked in and stopped. The place was full. My heart was pounding away and I couldn't catch my breath. Len saw me. He frowned. He might as well just look on, I thought, because I'm in the pub and I'm not going anywhere. He was sitting in the corner with his friends. So I went over and sat next to him. I think he must have already realized that the strange man in the pub was my husband. But he didn't do anything. Except reach up and touch my face. What happened? I didn't say anything. I just looked across at Len. Why? Now I looked back at Travis. His friends fired questions. Her old man beat her up? Because of you, man? They tried to ask without making things uncomfortable for me. Then they remembered. One of them asked me if I'd like a drink. Like a drink, Joyce? I don't think I do. This is what I said. That I didn't think I did, thank you. And so I waited for a while. But I could see that I was making them uneasy. I got up and decided to go. Travis stood and said that he would walk with me. No, I said. Again I glanced purposefully at the husband. Then I left. Before I did so, I touched his hand. I just wanted you to know. These were my parting words. But know what? I thought.

FEBRUARY 1944

Len was drunk. That's not something I have to remember. Len was usually drunk. His arms and legs were moving at the same time. Like a machine. He made big circles and small circles. And like a machine Len struck every time. And then suddenly he was there, pulling Len away. He knocked him down with a punch. I watched Len's mouth open and close, and these words. These ugly words coming from my husband. Len climbed to his feet, but again he was knocked to the ground. And then two more soldiers. His friends. They were trying to hold back the man who had rescued me. They were saying, no. Enough. Travis was holding Len by the throat. Len had fear in his eyes. Travis told him that if he ever laid a finger on me again, then he would be found somewhere in a ditch with an American bullet in him. Len had to be brave, so he continued to spit out his ugly words. But it was not really bravery. He just wanted to look brave. That was Len. But he wouldn't say anything to me. He didn't care enough about me to actually say anything to me. My friend. He is my friend. Maybe he cares too much. I didn't feel I deserved this. To be rescued like this. Truly. To me it seemed strange.

MARCH 1944

Len has gone to his new job in the north. He's said I can have the divorce. No point in squabbling about it. He reckons we should be able to get a special quick one, what with him having a record and everything. In the meantime, I'm to run the shop. He asked me if I would. I said yes. After the war he says he'll come back. If I decide to leave before the war's over, I'm to let him know. He'll sell the shop. But meanwhile he gets a share of the profits. That's Len's way. There's always something in it for him. Before he left he told me that I'm a traitor to my own kind. That as far as he's concerned I'm no better than a common slut. And everybody in the village agrees with him.

JULY 1944

Today I checked to make sure. I was right. Pregnant women get extra concentrated orange juice. An extra pint of milk a day. An extra half-ration of meat a week. An extra egg (up to three a week). Free cod-liver oil. Free chocolate-covered vitamin tablets. And a baby.

8 MAY 1945

Today's the day that everyone's been waiting for, but it's all confused. It's over, but it's not official. We know now that there will be no more sirens, searchlights, or blackouts. But somebody has to make it official. I spent the whole evening looking out of the window. At about ten o'clock, people began to give up and drift back inside. The street party will have to wait. Greer slept through all the excitement. Up above, the light, damp clouds have now begun to swell. It will bucket down all night.

9 MAY 1945

Churchill spoke at three p.m. He called it the people's victory, but we all knew it was his. Churchill's. At the end of his speech, there was loud cheering. Everybody spilled out into the street to enjoy the two days of holiday. The bunting meant something now, as did the Union Jacks and the portraits of Winnie. We had won the war. I put my hair up in a wrap and stepped out to join them. I held Greer and watched as they put on hats and sang. Then they danced the hokey-cokey and swilled down dandelion and burdock and ginger beer. I'd done my bit. I'd supplied them with their food. Some went off to church. The bells were ringing again. I hoped that at least one of them might remember Sandra. Others lit a bonfire, and on to it went army forms, and ration books; anything to do with the war. And there was a crude effigy of Hitler. That burned quickly. At nine p.m., the King made a speech in his usual stammer. I'd never had much time for these people, but it was moving. Some of them even spoke to me and smiled at Greer. Just before midnight, I took him inside, out of the evening chill.

1963

It was nearly four o'clock. I stared at Greer and longed for him
to stay as dearly as I longed for him to leave. I'd explained that
I thought he should go before the children came back. He said
he understood. The silences had become more awkward, but
at least they remained free of accusation. A handsome man.
Yes, a man. No longer a baby. Or a boy. He got to his feet.
I knew he would never call me mother. He could go, but
would he come back? It wasn't for me to ask him. I hadn't
asked him here in the first place. For eighteen years I hadn't
invited him to do anything. Not since the lady with the blue
coat and maroon scarf. With her tiny dog named Monty. She
was so wet you could pour her into a jug. My GI baby. No
father, no mother, no Uncle Sam. It must go into the care
of the County Council as an orphan, love. If you're lucky, it
might be legally adopted into a well-to-do family. Some are,
you know. For weeks afterwards I wandered around the park
looking at women pushing their prams. Their awkward babies
screamed as though they'd tumbled straight from the womb
and into these contraptions. For eighteen years I hadn't invited
Greer to do anything. Your father and I, Greer. We couldn't
show off. We had to be careful. And bold. We started a dance
once. My God, I remember that. And for weeks afterwards,
every time I thought of him I was sure my knees were going
to give way. Then, later, they took him away from me, to
Italy. I'd go to the cinema in the hope of seeing him. But they
just showed the Tommies. Never the Yanks. And if they did,
never the Coloureds. I once got two letters from him on the

same day, and I didn't know which one to open first. And then he came back on New Year's Day, 1945. For the wedding. And now, I don't even have a picture of him. I'm sorry, love. I destroyed everything. Letters, pictures, everything. When I met Alan. It seemed the right thing to do, but I was stupid. He spoke again. I'd better go now, he said. My God, I wanted to hug him. I wanted him to know that I did have feelings for him. Both then and now. He was my son. Our son.

NEW YEAR'S DAY, 1945

He came back on compassionate leave. The doctor had said I was having a breakdown and a baby. Just seventy-two hours, that's all they'd given him, then he'd have to go back. I went down to town to meet him, but I nearly wept when I saw him getting off the train. He looked as thin as a door, and so tired. He didn't have that bounce in his step. He didn't have any joy in his face. Everybody stared at him. I think they must have felt sorry for him, bending under the weight of that bag on his back. He looked like the saddest man in the world. Even before I'd fallen pregnant, he'd asked me if we could get wed. At first I thought it was only the war talking, but eventually I told him yes, as soon as I was rid of Len. Maybe I was a bit worried that he'd leave me behind after the war. He'd already told me that we couldn't live together in America. It wouldn't be allowed. I thought getting wed would be a way of keeping him here. In England. As he walked towards me along the black length of the platform, with that slow stride and those hunched shoulders, I could see just how shattered he was. He had huge bags under his eyes, and he hadn't shaved for days. And then he saw me, and the child pushing at my coat. He stopped and stared. I could feel myself colouring over. And then he came right up to me, and I started to cry. The doctor was right, my nerves wanted building up. He let his bag fall to the platform. Joyce. That was all he said. Just, Joyce. I could see now, the gap in the middle of his teeth. At the bottom. And then he reached out and pulled me towards him. I couldn't believe it. He'd come back to me. He really wanted me. That day, crying on the platform, safe in Travis's arms.

1945

I stood there in that freezing room, the eyes of the two unknown witnesses staring at my back, Travis at my side, my belly out in front of me, wishing the Registrar would just hurry it up a bit. He had this thin smile painted across his mouth, and there was something about him that I truly disliked. When I came to make the appointment, he told me that he'd done one other GI bride's wedding. I didn't tell him that he'd not have done one like this, though. After the divorce came through, I'd written to Travis in Italy and told him. He wrote back and told me that he'd got his commanding officer's permission, as long as he didn't try and take me back to America with him. They weren't having any of that. Me, I wasn't right over there. After I got his letter, I went to the Registrar and made an appointment. He told me that he'd done one other GI bride's wedding.

1945

Nobody said anything, but when they lifted him clear of my body and began to towel him down, I knew what they were thinking. I stared at him. My beautiful son. The nurse placed him in my arms. He's like coffee, isn't he, love. I had no idea then that his father would never see him. Later, after I'd got the telegram, after the war was over, the lady with the blue coat came to visit. I could see her looking at me and thinking, poor disillusioned cow. You'll be better off, love, with somebody else looking after him. Trust me. I know what I'm on about. I mean, how are you going to cope? You won't know what to do now, will you. Let's be sensible. You're going to have to start a new life on your own. And so we were sensible, my son and I. My son who hadn't asked me to turn him over to the lady with the blue coat and maroon scarf.

1945

The Red Cross man knocked once. Then again, impatiently. Hardly gave me time to set Greer right and get down the stairs. I opened the door and he handed me the telegram. I didn't have a chance to say much of anything. He just smiled slightly and began to back away. I closed in the door. The telegram didn't say much. I had to try to imagine it. To die at first light on the Italian coast. Fear. Mud. Shivering cold. Noise. Silence louder than any noise. Mortar fire. A bullet. A young man screaming in pain, shouting out for mercy to a God he no longer believed existed. His flesh ripped open by hot, flying metal. A man with blood flowing like red wine from his open veins. In a strange country. Among people he hardly knew. I remembered what my mother had said to me when I told her that I was getting married. At least you're not getting wed to a soldier, she'd said. You should never do that, for you'll just be left on your own. I closed the shop. I didn't open up for three days. On the second day, two of them came to see me. They'd heard. They asked me if there was anything they could do. No, I said. Thank you, but no. After the telegram, I tried not to be angry. I knew everything was going on around me like normal. People were still having their usual at the pub. They were still going off to work the next morning. I was the only one who'd lost anything. They'd lost nothing. Just been inconvenienced a bit by this war. We hadn't even been bombed in this bloody stupid village. I wanted to break something. I really wanted to smash something to bits. The following month it was all over. I put my hair up in a wrap and stepped out to join them. I held Greer and watched as they put on hats and sang. Then they danced the hokey-cokey. I'd done my bit. I'd supplied them with their food. Some went off to church. The bells were ringing again. I hoped that at least one of them might remember Sandra. Others lit a bonfire, and on to it went army forms and ration books; anything to do with the war. And there was a crude effigy of Hitler. That burned quickly. At nine p.m. the King made a speech in his usual stammer. I'd never had much time for these people, but it was moving. Some of them even spoke to me and smiled at Greer. Just before midnight, I took him inside, out of the evening chill. A week later she turned up. The lady with the blue coat. With her dog, Monty. And Len was back. He wanted his shop. I had no money. Nothing. Only Greer. She said, You're going to have to start a new life on your own. And so we were sensible, my son and I. Into the care of the County Council as an orphan, love. It hadn't really dawned on me, but it was true. His father would never see him. Never. I left the village, the shop, my ex-husband, and went to live back in the town. On my own. For weeks afterwards, I wandered around the park looking at women pushing their prams.

1963

I was in the kitchen, wringing out clothes in the sink. I happened to glance up. I saw him, standing at the front gate. I knew that it was him. I knew that one day he would come looking. That he would find me. I could hear myself breathing. But apart from this, I was calm. I surprised myself. He had a piece of paper in his hand that he kept glancing at. Then he'd look back up at the house, then back down at the paper. Then he pushed the paper into his pocket. Alan was at work, and the kids wouldn't be back from school until four o'clock. The first thing that occurred to me was that he'd chosen his time well. That maybe he'd planned it all right down to the last detail. I looked at his hair. It was too short to be styled into that greasy Teddy Boy look. I hated that look. He unlatched the gate and began to walk up the path. I wasn't going to be able to pretend that I wasn't in. I waited until he'd knocked once. Then when he knocked a second time I went to the door and opened it. We stood and looked at each other, me drying my hands on a tea towel. My God, he was handsome. Come in. He seemed shy. Come in, come in. He stepped by me, dipping a shoulder as he did so in order that we didn't have to touch. I closed in the door but for a moment I didn't turn around. I was ashamed. I wasn't ready. Standing there in a plain dress, with my lank hair, and my bare legs, and my slippers looking like the left-over scraps from somebody's fluffy rug. Forty-five years old, and I knew I looked awful, but there wasn't any time to fret over appearances. Not now. I took a deep breath and turned to face him. I almost said make yourself at home, but I didn't. At least I avoided that. Sit down. Please, sit down.

I hear a drum beating on the far bank of the river. A breeze stirs and catches it. The resonant pounding is borne on the wind, carried high above the roof-tops, across the water, above the hinterland, high above the tree-tops, before its beat plunges down and into the interior. I wait. And then listen as the many-tongued chorus of the common memory begins again to swell, and insist that I acknowledge greetings from those who lever pints of ale in the pubs of London. Receive salutations from those who submit to (what the French call) neurotic inter-racial urges in the boulevards of Paris. ('No first-class nation can afford to produce a race of mongrels.') But my Joyce, and my other children, their voices hurt but determined, they will survive the hardships of the far bank. Only if they panic will they break their wrists and ankles against Captain Hamilton's instruments. *Put 2 in irons and delicately in the thumbscrews to encourage them to a full confession of those principally involved. In the evening put 5 more in neck-yokes.* Survivors all. In Brooklyn a helplessly addicted mother waits for the mist to clear from her eyes. They have stopped her benefit. She lives now without the comfort of religion, electricity, or money. A barefoot boy in São Paulo is rooted to his piece of the earth, which he knows will never swell up, pregnant, and become a vantage point from which he will be able to see beyond his dying *favela*. In Santo Domingo, a child suffers the hateful hot comb, the dark half-moons of history heavy beneath each eye. A mother watches. Her eleven-year-old daughter is preparing herself for yet another night of premature prostitution. Survivors. In their diasporan souls a dream like steel. *I praise His holy name that I was fortunate enough to be born in a Christian country, amongst Christian parents and friends, and that you were kind enough to take me, a foolish child, from my parents and bring me up in your own dwelling as something more akin to son than servant. Truth and honesty is great capital, and you instilled such values in my person at an early age, for which I am eternally grateful to you and my Creator.* Enduring cities which whisper falsehoods through perfectly shaped wooden lips. *A dream began to wash through her mind. Martha dreamed that she had traveled on west to California, by herself, and clutching her bundle of clothing. Once there she was met by Eliza Mae, who was now a tall, sturdy colored woman of some social standing. Together, they tip-toed their way through the mire of the streets to Eliza Mae's residence, which stood on a fine, broad avenue.* For two hundred and fifty years I have listened. To voices in the streets of Charleston. (The slave who mounted this block is now dying young from copping a fix on some rusty needle in an Oakland project.) I have listened. To reggae rhythms of rebellion and revolution dipping through the hills and valleys of the Caribbean. I have listened. To the saxophone player on a wintry night in Stockholm. A long way from home. For two hundred and fifty years I have listened. To my Nash. My Martha. My Travis. *Joyce. That was all he said. Just, Joyce. I could see now the gap in the middle of his teeth. At the bottom. And then he reached out and pulled me towards him. I couldn't believe it. He'd come back to me. He really wanted me. That day, crying on the platform, safe in Travis's arms.* For two hundred and fifty years I have listened. To the haunting voices. Singing: Mercy, Mercy Me. (The Ecology.) Insisting: Man, I ain't got no quarrel with them Vietcong. Declaring: Brothers and Friends. I am Toussaint L'Ouverture, my name is perhaps known to you. Listened to: Papa Doc. Baby Doc. Listened to voices hoping for: Freedom. Democracy. Singing: Baby, baby. Where did our love go? Samba. Calypso. Jazz. Jazz. Sketches of Spain in Harlem. In a Parisian bookstore a voice murmurs the words.

Nobody Knows My Name. I have listened to the voice that cried: I have a dream that one day on the red hills of Georgia, the sons of former slaves and the sons of former slave-owners will be able to sit down together at the table of brotherhood. I have listened to the sounds of an African carnival in Trinidad. In Rio. In New Orleans. On the far bank of the river, a drum continues to be beaten. A many-tongued chorus continues to swell. And I hope that amongst these survivors' voices I might occasionally hear those of my own children. My Nash. My Martha. My Travis. My daughter. Joyce. All. Hurt but determined. Only if they panic will they break their wrists and ankles against Captain Hamilton's instruments. A guilty father. Always listening. There are no paths in water. No signposts. There is no return. A desperate foolishness. The crops failed. I sold my beloved children. *Bought 2 strong man-boys, and a proud girl.* But they arrived on the far bank of the river, loved.

A NOTE ON THE AUTHOR

Caryl Phillips was born in St Kitts, West Indies, in 1958. Brought up in England, he has written for television, radio, theatre and the screen. He is the author of one book of non-fiction, *The European Tribe*, and four previous novels, *The Final Passage*, *A State of Independence*, *Higher Ground* and *Cambridge*. His awards include the Martin Luther King Memorial Prize, and a Guggenheim Fellowship. He is Writer-in-Residence at Amherst College, Massachusetts.

About the Author

Kieran has been passionate about stories and storytelling ever since reading *The Hobbit* at age six. He graduated from Southampton University with a degree in English Literature and works as a Reception teacher in a primary school. He lives on the Isle of Wight with his family, and between work, fatherhood and writing doesn't get nearly enough sleep.

About the Illustrator

David Wyatt lives in Devon. He has illustrated many novels but is also much admired for his concept and character work. He has illustrated tales by a number of high profile fantasy authors such as Diana Wynne Jones, Terry Pratchett, Philip Pullman, and J. R. R. Tolkien.

THE FIVE RE:

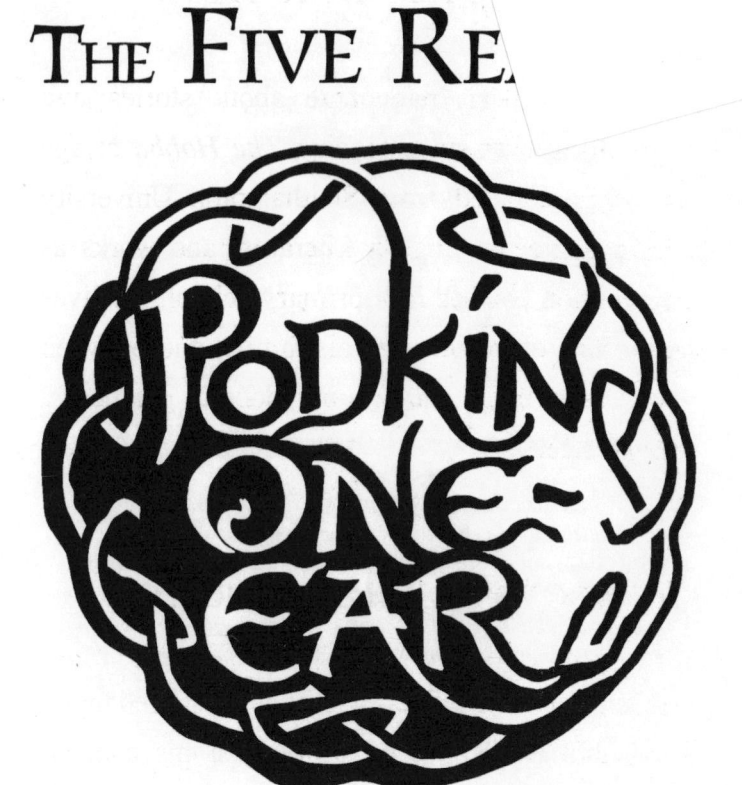

KIERAN LARWOOD
ILLUSTRATED BY DAVID WYATT

ff

FABER & FABER

First published in 2016
by Faber & Faber Limited
Bloomsbury House,
74–77 Great Russell Street,
London WC1B 3DA

Typeset by M Rules

Printed by CPI Group (UK) Ltd, Croydon CR0 4YY
All rights reserved
© Kieran Larwood, 2016

The right of Kieran Larwood to be identified as
author of this work has been asserted in accordance with
Section 77 of the Copyright, Designs and Patents Act 1988

*This book is sold subject to the condition
that it shall not, by way of trade or otherwise, be lent,
resold, hired out or otherwise circulated without the publisher's
prior consent in any form of binding or cover other than that in
which it is published and without a similar condition including
this condition being imposed on the subsequent purchaser*

A CIP record for this book
is available from the British Library

ISBN 978–0–571–32840–6

FSC
www.fsc.org
MIX
Paper from
responsible sources
FSC® C101712

2 4 6 8 10 9 7 5 3 1

For Amelie

CHAPTER ONE

A Bard for Bramblemas

Crunch, crunch. Crunch, crunch. The sound of heavy footsteps, trudging through knee-deep snow, echoes through the night's silence.

A thick white blanket covers the wide slopes of the band of hills known as the Razorback downs. Moonlight dances over it, glinting here and there in drifts of sparkles, as if someone has sprinkled the whole scene with diamond dust.

It is perfect – untouched except for one spidery line of tracks leading down from the hills towards the frosted woodland beneath.

Crunch, crunch. Crunch, crunch go the footsteps of the track-maker. He is hunched and weary, using a tall staff to help him through the snow. He might have been an old man, if it hadn't been many hundreds of moons since men trod these lands. Move closer and instead you will see he is a rabbit, walking upright in the way men once did, his ears hidden beneath the hood of a heavy leather cloak, fierce eyes peering out at the wintry midnight world.

The thick fur on his face and arms is dyed with blue swirls and patterns, which marks him out as a bard. A travelling, storytelling rabbit. A wanderer with nothing on his back but a set of travel-worn clothes and a head stuffed full of tales and yarns: old, new, broken and mended. Just about every story you ever heard, and many more yet to be told.

Don't worry about him being out in the cold on such a wintry night. His trade will see him welcomed in any warren. That is the tradition and the law throughout all of the Five Realms of Lanica, and woe betide anyone who doesn't keep it.

Crunch, crunch. Crunch, crunch. His breath steams out behind him as he forces his way

through the snow. Listen closer and you can hear him mumbling curses with each hard-fought step. Closer still and you can hear the strings of wooden beads around his neck clicking and clacking. The bone trinkets and pouches around his belt knocking and niggling.

He marches with a purpose, as if he has someplace to be and he is already late. But where is there for him to go? There is nothing but snow and trees from here all the way to the horizon. Until, of course, you remember that he's a rabbit. Rabbits live underground, in warrens and burrows: warm and safe, out of the winter ice and frost.

And that is indeed where he is heading. Into the woods and through the trees until he stops before a pair of huge entrance doors, set into the side of a little hill. Behind them is Thornwood Warren, and there had better be a warm welcome for him, or there will be serious trouble.

Boom, boom, boom! He smacks the end of his staff against the oak and waits for an answer.

Back when rabbits were small, twitchy, terrified things, warrens were little more than a collection of

holes and tunnels in the ground. Now, in this new age, they are something different altogether: there are entire villages and cities built under the earth, completely out of sight.

The bard knew that behind those wooden doors would be nest-burrows and market-burrows, workshops, temples, libraries, larders, pantries and a dozen kitchens to feed them all. There would be soldiers and healers, servants, cooks, smiths, weavers, tailors, potters and painters. Old rabbits, young rabbits, poor rabbits and noble rabbits. All walks of life hidden away in cosy, torch-lit, underground houses; all arranged around every warren's hub: the longburrow, a great feasting hall with a huge fireplace, rows of tables and nearly always music. Music, noise and merriness – that is what rabbits love. Especially tonight, for this was Bramblemas Eve: the night on which the winter solstice was celebrated with a special feast, and the promise of presents in the morning, left behind by the mysterious Midwinter Rabbit.

And stories of course. Special stories, told by a visiting bard – that is, if he ever got inside the place.

Boom, boom, boom! He smacks the doors again and is about to do so a third time when he hears a muffled voice on the other side.

'All right, all right, keep your ears on, I'm coming!' There are more words about stupid people being outside on this kind of night, but luckily the heavy wood absorbs most of those. Finally, the doors creak open, spilling golden torchlight on to the snow, and the face of a burly soldier-rabbit pokes out.

'Who in the Goddess's name are you?' he says, glaring at the stranger. Underneath the hood, the pale green eyes glare back.

'Is that any way to treat a bard, come to tell tales on the Eve of Bramblemas? Is that how the old ways are kept here at Thornwood?'

Even though the soldier-rabbit is the size of a small armour-clad mountain, something about the bard makes him tremble a little. 'Sorry, sir,' he says, and pushes the door open further with his shoulder. 'Come in and share our hearth on this Middlewinter night . . .'

'*Mid*winter, turnip-head,' corrects the bard, stepping into the torchlight and the warmth. The

warren doors close behind him, and he shakes the snow from his cloak with a shudder. 'Now. Which way to the fireside?' And he strides off down the paved entrance hall as if he has been here a hundred times before.

'What's a Midwinter Turnip-head then?' mumbles the puzzled guard, before turning to trot after him.

*

Just as every warren is carefully built around the longburrow at its centre, the rabbits inside are organised around their chieftain. He is the leader of the tribe, just as his father was before him, and his son will be after. Between him and his wife, all the warren decisions are made, all the arguments settled and all the feasts and festivals organised.

In Thornwood, the chieftain is Hubert the Broad. A great big-bellied lop rabbit, with brown and white patched fur, ears down to his knees and a stomach you could build a house on. He is currently sitting on his throne at the head of the feasting table, a bramble crown on his head and his great piebald stomach bursting the seams of his tunic. He is singing a merry song about the Midwinter Rabbit getting stuck in his

6

burrow, while all the little rabbits sit laughing at his feet. When he sees the bard enter, he stops, stands and raises his drinking horn in salute.

'Welcome, bard!' he shouts, in a voice that shakes earth from the ceiling. 'Welcome, on Bramblemas Eve!'

'That's more like it,' mutters the bard, shrugging off his leather cloak. He keeps his hood on, but the light from the fire still shows off the swirls and whorls of blue patterns dyed into the fur on his bare arms.

'We thought you weren't coming,' says Hubert. 'But Bramblemas Eve is full of surprises. Will you sing for your supper?'

The bard chuckles. 'My voice is too old and cracked for singing.' He takes a seat by the fireside and warms his hands. 'But I might be persuaded to tell a tale or two.'

'Bring this man some food! Quick, sharp,' Hubert shouts, flicking his ears at his cupbearers. They scurry off and return moments later with a bowl of buttery turnip soup and a platter of cornbread. The bard tucks into it like a rabbit starved and, finishing it, wipes his mouth with the back of his paw.

'I suppose that deserves a tale,' he says. 'What would you like to hear?'

The little rabbits swarm to his feet, all crying out at once. 'Beobunny!' 'The Fisher Rabbit!' 'Podkin One-Ear!'

'Did I hear someone mention Podkin One-Ear?' says the bard, settling further into his chair. 'Podkin the Horned King? The Moonstrider? Podkin of the magic knife?' When the little ones nod their heads and shriek with excitement, he folds his painted arms and tugs at his beard.

'I do know some tales of that one, but they will be different from those *you* have heard. Nothing about shooting fire from his eyes or wrestling giant rabbits with bare hands. Nothing like that at all.'

'What kind of tales, bard?' 'Why are they different?' 'Why won't there be fiery eyes and giants?'

'They're different,' he says, 'because they are *true*. And because fiery eyes don't exist anywhere except in fairy tales and the heads of silly young rabbits.' The bard waves a hand for silence, and then he begins.

Chapter Two

The Worst Bramblemas Ever

The Gorm. First, you need to know about *them*.
Nowadays, thank the Goddess, they are
nothing but a bad memory. Something to scare
the little ones with at night. But back when your
grandparents were young, rabbits lived in constant
fear of their strange riders, of the screeching of
metal in the night and the echoing of their terrifying
war-horns.

The Gorm.

Nobody knows exactly how they came to exist,
only that they were first seen in a little warren called

Sandywell, up in northern Enderby, where the Red River meets the sea.

A meek little tribe of rabbits lived there. Grey-furred sable bunnies that liked fishing, sailing and building boats. They never caused any trouble, and nobody paid them much attention. Until, one day – everything changed.

Some say there was something in the river that got into their veins. Some say they tunnelled too far down and came across something cursed and poisonous. Others say it was the work of witches. Whatever the reason, they stopped being the Sandywell greys overnight, and turned into something else. Something evil and unnatural.

First the warren changed – just a little at first – until eventually great spikes of jutting metal burst out of it, sticking up into the air like poison porcupine quills, and the land around became blackened and scorched. The waters of the Red River turned black and noxious as they ran past. Animals that lived in the woods and waters either died or became warped and ruined. Folk started calling the warren Splinterholm and stayed well away. But that didn't help them.

Next, the old Sandywell rabbits reappeared, except now you wouldn't have recognised them. They were clad head to foot in iron armour. Iron – that metal that rabbits find impossible to work with, and poisonous to the Goddess herself.

The Sandywell rabbits had not only shaped and moulded it; they had bonded with it somehow. It seemed as though the metal had fused and pierced their very skin. It ran through their veins and bled into their eyes, turning them blank and rusty red. The rabbits used the metal to bend and shape the creatures around them as well: the dumb giant rats that all rabbits use as beasts of burden, and the black crows of the nearby woods. They changed *them* into shrieking flocks of rusted metal harpies.

When they rode out of Splinterholm, they came to devour and destroy, and they were called the Gorm by all who feared them.

If they called at your warren, then that was the end of you – they would kill your chieftain and his sons. They would rip your warriors into shreds. Then they would carry half of you off to be *changed* into Goddess-knows what. The rest would spend their

miserable lives making food and supplies to feed their new masters, never knowing when they too would be dragged away, wailing in the night.

It was a dark time for all rabbitkind, is what I'm saying.

It was in those days that Podkin One-Ear lived. He wasn't a hero back then: he hadn't slain any giant rabbits, or formed any robber bands, and he hadn't even begun to think about rescuing maidens. In fact, he was only a youngling; eight summers' old. Oh, and he still had both his ears.

Podkin was the son of Lopkin, chieftain of the Munbury warren, which meant that someday he himself would be chieftain, just like his father's father had been, and *his* father ... all the way back to when the Goddess first made the twelve tribes. For now, that all seemed a long way off, and that was the way he liked it.

He had an older sister called Paz, who liked to boss him around as much as possible, and a young kitten of a brother called Pook, who didn't do much except chew things and ask for soup.

You might think as a young rabbit that Podkin

was already showing signs of heroism: great skill with a sword, maybe. Bravery, courage, wisdom, determination.

You would be wrong.

If anything, he was perhaps the laziest, most spoilt son of a chieftain in the whole Five Realms! At least he was, up until the start of this story. His father tried his best to prepare him for leadership with lessons in history, rabbit-lore and soldiering, but Podkin took great delight in avoiding them all. Daydreaming and snoozing were the only things he practised and, to be fair, he was very good at them. He was the despair of all his tutors, especially poor Melfry, the weaponmaster, who resigned three times or more from the task of teaching Podkin. The young rabbit simply had no interest in doing what was expected of him.

So it came to pass, that on a Bramblemas Eve – much like this one – Podkin One-Ear (although technically Two-Ears at this point) was sitting upstairs in the wooden gallery that ran around the edge of Munbury longburrow. He was lazily pushing around a toy wagon, munching on a stolen piece of

cornbread and daydreaming about the Midwinter Rabbit, who would be visiting that night (hopefully with a sackful of presents). Would he get the wooden soldiers he'd asked for? Or the toy sword and shield? Or would it be the disappointment of a badly knitted woollen tunic, like last year?

'What are you doing up here, Pod?' His sister had tiptoed up the stairs and was now glaring at him. Podkin's little brother Pook was nestled in the crook of her arm, chewing away at a carrot. 'Mother sent me to get you. They're about to have turnip soup and dance the Bramble Reel. You should be there, seeing as you're next in line to be *chief.*'

Paz took it hard that she was never going to lead the warren, even though she was the eldest. But it was tradition, fair or not, that the first son took over.

Podkin yawned deliberately. 'The Bramble Reel. How exciting.' He took Pook from her and tickled his tummy. He could hear all the festivities in the hall below, and had absolutely no desire to join in with them. 'Please stand aside, so I can rush down the stairs and prance about like a prize pudding.'

'If you don't come down, you're going to be in trouble,' said Paz. 'Do you have any idea what it takes to be chieftain? Nobody will want to follow a lord who spends all his time tickling his baby brother, playing with toys and hiding away in corners daydreaming.'

Podkin huffed and flicked his ears at his sister. 'You're just jealous because you think you would make a better chieftain than me.'

'Well, I would, wouldn't I? Anyone can see that.' Paz started ticking off a list on her fingers. 'I'm the eldest. I do what Father and Mother tell me. I go to all my lessons, instead of hiding in the meadow and picking daisies like a rat-brained, fairy flump. If there was any justice, girls would be allowed to become a Chief, instead of brats like you who don't deserve it!'

Podkin was about to leap on Paz and pull her ears, when the warren horn began to sound. The three young rabbits rushed to the edge of the gallery and looked down on to the hall. Soldiers were grabbing spears and shields, children were being herded into the corners and their father, Chief Lopkin, was

striding towards the burrow entrance, drawing his sword. His great silver broadsword that everyone thought was magical.

'Mi'winter wabbit! Mi'winter wabbit!' Pook shouted, trying to wriggle free.

'It's not the Midwinter Rabbit, Pook,' said Podkin, the argument with Paz forgotten. 'It looks like trouble. And trouble doesn't leave presents outside your burrow at night.'

Frightened murmurs were drifting up from the crowd below. 'A rider', 'a lone rider coming', and then 'a rider wearing armour ... *iron* armour', and finally 'it's the Gorm! The Gorm are here!'

This last shout caused mass panic. Podkin could see his father shouting, but his voice was swallowed up by the hubbub. The warren was terrified, losing its head. This was the time it really needed its chieftain: somebody to *lead* them all. Pod watched Lopkin breathe deep, then bellow in his great commanding voice: '*Silence!*'

The whole longburrow instantly froze, hundreds of scared eyes turning to Lopkin who stood amongst them, his magic silver sword flashing. He let the

silence stand for a moment before speaking in as calm a voice as he could.

'A rider approaches, true. A Gorm, true. But it is a lone rider, and he carries the white flag of peace. We will let him enter and see what he has to say.'

The sound of the heavy oak entrance doors opening echoed down the warren. The rabbits in the longburrow pressed back against the walls. Spears were raised, breath was held. Something was making its way along the entrance hall.

'Will it be okay, Paz?' whispered Podkin. He had always been in awe of his tall, powerful father. He had always seemed invincible – at least until now.

'I don't know, Pod,' Paz replied. 'Father has his sword ...'

The look in her eyes was enough to make Podkin truly afraid for the first time in his short life.

Chief Lopkin called out the traditional greeting to the darkness of the tunnel. 'Enter, stranger, and be welcome on this Bramblemas Eve.'

Clank.

Screeeeeech.

Grinding metal, followed by the clump of heavy leather boots. It seemed the rider had dismounted whatever had been carrying him and was now coming down the entrance tunnel on foot. One hundred and fifty terrified rabbits all held their breath.

Clank.

Screeeeeech.

Pook began whimpering. They could now see something moving in the darkness of the tunnel. Torchlight from the great hall caught on metal and bounced back in orange glints.

'Enter!' Lopkin called out again. 'We mean you no harm!'

With a final grinding squeal, the figure emerged and leapt from the tunnel to land in the centre of the warrior's circle.

The rabbits had all heard terrifying tales of the Gorm, but none had done the real thing justice.

This wasn't a rabbit any more. If it ever had been, it was now something else entirely. A walking slab of metal and meat, pierced through with rusty thorns and nails. Its armour overlapped in sheets of jagged, dented iron; mottled with rust and splashes of dried

crimson that looked very much like old blood.

Its head was completely covered by a helm, dotted all over with cruel shard-like spikes and curved metal horns that almost scraped the ceiling. From the shadowy eye slits, two dim scarlet pupils glowed: blank and mottled with rusty red veins.

Podkin was so scared, he wanted to cry. Worst of all was the thing's jagged black iron sword. That and the skulls that hung from its belt. Rabbit skulls, painted all over with evil-looking runes. Skulls of all sizes, including ones that looked like children's.

The Gorm rabbit turned his head to and fro, taking in the warren's inhabitants, before resting his gaze on Lopkin himself.

'I don't want your welcome.' The deep voice echoed inside its iron shell. A cold, iron, killer's voice. 'I came to tell you I am taking your warren. That, and your magic weapon.'

Instantly, every spear was raised and pointed at the armoured intruder. The Gorm tilted his head slightly, as if curious, and leant over to thump his sword three times on the floor.

There was a rumbling, deep below the ground.

The whole floor of the longburrow began to shake, and then parts of it started to crack and crumble. The Munbury rabbits backed against the walls, as piles of mud burst upwards, shattering the tiled floors and overturning benches and tables. From beneath the ground, armoured Gorm began to clamber out into their midst. Pushing their way up through the soil, spilling torrents of mud from their spiked iron shoulders, as the Munbury rabbits stared on in mute horror. Five, ten, fifteen of them and more, each one clad head to foot in jagged rusty armour and wielding an axe or sword.

'This warren is ours now,' said the first Gorm, his voice like the metallic screeching of his armour. 'And we will kill anyone who thinks otherwise. So says the chief of all the Gorm.'

'Scramashank,' said Chief Lopkin. The Gorm Lord's name was well known amongst rabbits, and well feared.

Lopkin raised his silver sword and stepped into a battle stance. 'Scramashank – leave my people out of this. We will settle this between the two of us.'

'They aren't your people any more.' Scramashank

laughed, as if this were all some elaborate Bramblemas joke. 'They are the Gorm now. Or they will be. Once you are dead.'

In a flash of iron, Scramashank swung his sword over his head and down, trying to cleave Lopkin in half. The chieftain raised his silver sword just in time, and there was an almighty *clang* as the blades clashed, showering sparks about the hall.

'Father!' Podkin and Paz both screamed out at the same time. Pook began to bawl and wail.

They had a brief glimpse of Lopkin gazing up at them, Scramashank drawing back for another blow, and then they were pulled back, away from the gallery rail.

All three young rabbits shrieked, expecting to see a Gorm standing behind them, but instead it was their Auntie Olwyn. Tears had dampened the fur around her eyes, but her jaw was set and fierce.

'Come with me, you three.' She pulled them back towards the stairs.

'But, Father . . .' Podkin began.

'Don't think about him. He has to fend for himself.' She was dragging them down the stairway.

'You have to leave with me *now*. Before the Gorm come for you too.'

She was too strong to resist, and even as the sound of shouts and clashing metal began to echo up from the longburrow, the little rabbits ran with their aunt through the Munbury tunnels. Twisting this way and that, they soon ended up at their parents' bedchamber.

'In here,' whispered Auntie Olwyn, shoving them inside and barring the door behind them. She ran straight to the bed and began rummaging around underneath it.

'What are you *doing*, Auntie? We have to go back! We have to help Father!'

'There's no helping him now. He'll soon be in the Land Beyond, Goddess save him,' she said, under her breath. She stood up, holding something long and thin, wrapped in cloth. She thrust it into Podkin's hands.

'Your father told me to give you this, should anything ever happen to him. And your mother told me to bring you here, if the warren should ever fall.'

'To the bedroom?' Paz looked at her aunt as if she had gone suddenly mad. Podkin was peeking under the cloth bindings. They hid a battered old copper dagger, dull and blunt with a crude face carved on the pommel.

'There's a secret tunnel here.' Olwyn pulled on the bedpost and a little door slowly opened in the wall. She gave each of the children a quick kiss on the forehead. 'Go now,' she said. 'Get out of the tunnel and run as fast as you can. Get to Redwater warren and ask for help there. Don't even *think* of coming back here. Not ever.'

'But what about you? What about Mother?' Podkin asked.

'Don't worry about us. We'll be all right. And if not, we'll see you in the Land Beyond. Remember, children: your parents love you. They love you so very much.'

With that, she bundled them into the tunnel and then, before they could do anything about it, she shut the door behind them and locked it tight.

CHAPTER THREE

Starclaw

I don't need to go into detail about that awful flight out of the dark tunnel, about how the three of them sobbed and wailed their way to the surface, and out into the snowy woods. Or about how they ran through the rest of that dark, blizzard-choked night, terrified that every shadow hid an enemy, that every second could be their last on this miserable earth.

You don't need to know how many times they thought about going back, of trying somehow to save their mother or their aunt or their friends. Or how often each one of them stumbled to the ground,

overcome with grief, until the other pulled them up and onwards again.

That terrible night can only really be remembered by those two poor little rabbits (Pook was thankfully too young to know what was going on beyond being cold, hungry and away from his mother) and neither of them will ever speak of it again – not even to each other.

All you need to know is that, as the sky began to lighten in the east, the young rabbits staggered into a clearing and finally rested against the trunk of an old frost-covered oak.

'W-where do you think we are?' stammered Podkin. 'Are we anywhere near Redwater?'

'How am I supposed to know?' said Paz. Pook was nestled inside her tunic, the only one of them feeling slightly warm. 'I was lost five minutes after we came out of the tunnel. Maybe if you'd paid attention in our geography lessons ...'

'*You* were paying attention for me! And you don't know where we are either, so the lessons were a fat waste of both our time, weren't they?'

Neither of them spoke for several minutes. They

knew how serious it was to be lost in the woods in this weather. The cold was deadly, and there were hungry wolves and bears around, not to mention the Gorm.

'I think we should . . .' began Paz, but she was interrupted by an explosion of fluttering overhead. A large bird flapped its way up through the falling snow and away over the trees. 'Just a crow,' she said, relieved. 'I thought it might be . . . you know . . .'

'Not just a crow,' whispered Podkin. 'It was one of them. Didn't you see? It had metal spikes bursting through its skin. And its eyes . . . its eyes were like theirs . . .'

'You're imagining things, Pod. After what happened . . . your mind isn't working properly.'

'It is! I *saw* it!'

'A crow? How can a crow be like them?'

'Don't you remember Father saying?' Podkin was crying again now: big fat tears that splashed down to melt holes in the snow. 'They change things. Things like crows and rats. They turn them into their servants. That crow spotted us, and it'll tell them where we are.'

Paz still wasn't convinced, but they had to keep moving. Hoping all the time that they would see something to give them a clue as to where they were. If only everything wasn't covered in so much cursed snow.

Paz shifted the sleeping lump inside her tunic that was Pook, and started to move off again, only to notice Podkin wasn't following. He had his nose stuck in the cloth-wrapped bundle that Auntie Olwyn had given him. 'Come *on*, Podkin! We have to get moving!'

But Podkin wasn't budging. 'Wait a minute, Paz. There's something here.'

Podkin hadn't paid much attention to the dagger all night. In fact, he had been using it as a walking stick to help pull himself through the snow, and had half forgotten he had it at all. But now that there was some dawn light, he was curious as to why it was so special, and a quick peek had revealed a piece of parchment wrapped around the blade. He pulled it out.

'It's a message.' He handed it to Paz. 'Here, you look. I can't read Ogham.'

29

As I'm sure you will all know, Ogham is an ancient written language and was designed for simple marking of posts, trees and standing stones. Podkin had always been too lazy to learn it, much like everything else, although now he was sorely regretting it.

The Ogham Alphabet.

Paz stared at the parchment for a few seconds, her breath steaming around her head in a cloud as she gasped. 'It's a letter from Mother.'

My darlings. If you are reading this, then our worst nightmares have come true, and the Gorm have come to Munbury. Thank the

Goddess that you have escaped. This dagger
you are holding is our warren's greatest
treasure: the magical dagger known as
Starclaw. Your father lets everyone think that
his silver broadsword is the magic weapon,
but it has always been this simple copper
knife. It is one of the Twelve Gifts given to
the first tribes back at the start of time. It
may not look special, but it has the power
to cut through anything. Anything, that is,
except iron.

We know the Gorm are hunting the Twelve
Gifts for some evil reason, so this dagger
must be kept from them at all costs. That is
now your job.

Run fast, my darlings, and run far. Your
father and I love you more than you will ever
know. Mother.

If Paz hadn't already cried out every last tear in her body, she would have started sobbing again. Instead she stood, numb both inside and out, staring at the copper dagger in Podkin's hands.

All Podkin could think to say was, 'What use is a magic dagger that doesn't cut iron against a load of iron-armoured warriors?'

'What were you thinking of doing with it, genius? Storming back and chopping the Gorm to bits?'

Podkin shrugged. 'It is a *magic* weapon.'

'But we're not heroes out of some story. We're just children.'

Podkin stared at the dagger again. A useless hunk of metal, and yet so precious to the Gorm that his father had to die for it. He was so upset and confused he felt like flinging it away into the snow.

Only his mother's plea stopped him. Would he ever see her again? He tried to think of the last words she had said to him, the last time he had hugged her, but he couldn't remember. It suddenly seemed so important, but his mind was frozen blank.

'Run fast, my darlings, run far.' That would have to do instead. He would keep hold of the dagger for her sake. He rolled it and the parchment back into the blanket and looked up at his sister.

'Well, what shall we do then? We don't even know where we are!'

'Redwater is north-east. The sun is rising in the east. We head that way.'

Podkin didn't feel as if he could go another step, let alone run all the way to Redwater. He was about to argue some more when he thought he heard a noise in the distant woods.

The rabbits pricked their ears, listening for something in the heavy silence of the falling snow. In amongst the muffled forest sounds and Pook's wheezy little snores, they heard it again: a sound that made their blood run cold (well, cold*er* – it was already almost frozen).

Somewhere far behind them, but growing louder very quickly, was the echoing wail of a strange horn. And behind that was another, quieter sound. The clanking, scraping of iron against iron.

CHAPTER FOUR

Timber!

If there's one thing rabbits are good at, it's running away. It goes back to the days when we were tiny tasty bundles of fluff: top of everyone's menu, and afraid of our own shadows. The slightest hint of danger, and we'd be scurrying for shelter before we became breakfast for something with sharp teeth and an appetite.

But Podkin and Paz had already done their fair share of running that long cold night. Their muscles were torn and aching, their fur matted with clods of frozen snow. Paz's arms were weary from

carrying Pook, even though he was only a little bundle. The best they could manage was a kind of panicky stumble, on through the trees and away from the sounds of the oncoming Gorm. Those terrible wrenching sounds that were getting closer by the heartbeat.

Paz hoisted Pook further up with a grunt, ignoring his little squeal of protest. 'We need to run faster, Podkin!'

'I'm going as fast as I can,' Podkin managed to gasp.

If Podkin had had the energy, he would have grumbled some more, but it was all he could do to keep moving. They struggled on, wading through the snow, until they found themselves faced by a wall of earth and tree roots. There were banks on either side of them too. In their panic they had dashed into a cranny: a scooped-out section of the forest floor, hidden beneath the swathes of drifted snow.

From the trees behind them came the screeching of jagged metal armour. The Gorm were close now – minutes away, seconds even.

Podkin stared around, eyes wide with terror.

'We're dead,' he whispered, his voice harsh and strangled. 'There's no way out. They're going to kill us, just like they did Father.'

'Shut up! You're scaring Pook.' Paz pulled her tunic tighter around the baby rabbit, who was starting to squeak with fear.

'Well, what else is going to happen? How can we get away?'

Paz stood still for a moment. Her brain was whizzing, trying to come up with an idea that would save them. She was good under pressure, but there had never been pressure quite like this before. 'It did say that dagger could cut through anything except iron, didn't it?' she said. Podkin nodded.

'Right then.' It wasn't much of an idea, but it would have to do. She grabbed Podkin and whispered into his ear.

*

Half a minute later, after a desperate scramble up the cranny side, Podkin stood hidden behind a tree. With shivering paws, he unwrapped the cloth bundle and drew out the copper dagger.

It should have been cold metal, as icy as the snow

around him, but instead the hilt was hot – tingling almost. Could that be the magic? Would it really cut through anything? It certainly *felt* powerful. Not like the wooden practice swords he used to use in his boring weapons lessons.

Podkin swished it through the air a few times. Just a dagger, but to him it was more like a short sword, although he didn't feel much of a soldier. Certainly nothing like his father: facing down the Gorm Lord all on his own. *Father.* Was he looking down on them now, from the Land Beyond, or wherever he might be? Would he try and help them somehow, or would he only be able to watch them die? *Now is not the time for this*, Podkin told himself. They had a plan. He had a job to do.

Below him cowered Paz, out in plain sight, backed up against the bank of tree roots. She was clutching Pook to her chest and looking suitably terrified. Bait for their hastily assembled trap.

From his hiding place, Podkin could hear the Gorm, riding through the forest on their mounts. They were heavy, lumbering things, smashing against saplings and branches and ploughing the

snow aside with brute force. He could hear the tortured creatures breathing and growling; he could hear the slow grinding of armoured plates sliding against one another.

Pod held the dagger hilt close to his face and gave a small prayer to the Goddess. Should he do it now? *No*, he told himself. *Better to have a peek first. The timing must be right.*

Podkin never wanted to see another Gorm in his life, but he forced himself to peer around the tree trunk. There were two of them: riders sitting on top of things that might once have been giant rats.

Rats were normally docile, fluffy, stupid creatures that spent most of their time eating and squeaking. These looked as though they had been forged from shards of rusted iron, pounded together in the blacksmith's of hell.

They were covered all over with plates of jagged metal, studded with spikes and hooks, and scrawled on in blood-red runes. At the front, where their heads should have been, were fanged, drooling mouths, and glaring out from holes in the armour were blank rust-red eyes. They weren't rats any more. Every

part of them, down to their bones, had been changed and twisted. These things were now beasts. Iron beasts. Monsters.

They clanked and shrieked their way along the little track of footprints that Paz had left, their riders leaning forward on their backs, gnashing their teeth with hunger. They looked as if they had grown out of their mounts' spines, or been fused together into some new horrid form of life.

A voice came then. Sharp and loud, it sounded like sheets of tin being ripped into shreds. 'You! Girl! Where is your brother? Where is the chieftain's son?'

Podkin heard Paz say something, but it was too weak and stuttering to make out. Could it be she was terrified speechless, or was she just luring the Gorm riders in? That was the sort of clever trick she would try. Podkin remembered all the wily things she would do to taunt and tease him back in the warren. Nasty names and embarrassing pranks. He used to hate her sneaky cleverness then, but now he silently thanked the Goddess for it.

'Speak up, you little runt!'

The rider's voice sounded very close to Podkin. With small, silent steps, he edged around the tree trunk.

The two riders were right below him now. He could see the little pits and scratches on the surface of their armour. He could smell the hot iron stink of their steaming breath.

Now. Do it now!

He remembered being shown how to chop down a tree, back when his father was trying to teach him to do chores. He hadn't really listened because why should a chieftain's son have to do hard work? Now he really wished he had paid more attention. *Something about cutting out a wedge...*

He almost had to shout at his frozen, terrified body to make it respond. Tearing his eyes away from the Gorm, he set the edge of the dagger against the tree trunk. The blade was blunt tarnished copper, marked with notches and dents. It made him doubt the magic. There was no way it would even make a mark on the wood, let alone cut through it. Why had he listened to Paz's stupid idea?

Podkin held his breath, teeth gritted. If the riders

looked up and saw him now, it was all over. He had to get this done – and quick. He moved the blade up the trunk and angled it downwards. Holding his breath, he pushed it into the bark.

He half expected nothing to happen, so when it did, he was shocked dumb. The dagger slid through the hundred-year-old oak like it was butter. Podkin only just managed to stop it before it came out the other side.

Now the upwards cut. Quick!

Podkin pulled the dagger out and made another cut from the bottom up. A thick triangle of wood dropped out and thudded into the snowy ground. Down below, the riders were slinking forward; Paz was still stammering something about losing her brother in the snow. And then came a low, groaning sound that made Podkin's ears judder. It took a moment for him to realise it was coming from the oak tree as it began to topple forward. Slowly at first, but picking up speed, cracking and snapping branches as it fell. Pod saw the Gorm riders look up, surprised clouds of breath gushing from behind their iron masks, and then the tree hit them with an

explosion of snow crystals and a roar that echoed through the forest.

It took several moments for the snow clouds to settle, for the echoes to bounce away into silence. When all was quiet again, Pod peered down into the cranny and saw the great oak trunk snapped in half, blocking the whole thing. Snow crust lay crumbled and piled around it. Of the riders, nothing could be seen except a twisted shard of armour and a splash of rusty crimson blood on the snow.

INTERLUDE

The bard stops talking and gazes in Chief Hubert's direction, smacking his lips and generally trying his best to look thirsty. Hubert takes the hint and flicks an ear at his dozing cupbearer, so hard it nearly knocks him backwards. The startled rabbit grabs a wooden flagon, filled to the brim with frothy honey mead and dashes over to the storyteller. Amongst protesting cries from the little rabbits sitting around his feet, the bard drains the whole flagon in three long gulps, and then wipes the froth from his beard with the back of his hand.

'Don't stop! Don't stop!' the rabbits cry. 'Tell us what happened next!'

The bard lets out a belch, frowns, then lets out another. 'Give me a minute,' he says. 'My pipes don't

work as well as they used to. Bless my turnips, that was good mead.'

'Were the Gorm really real?' one little rabbit asks. 'My brother said they were just made up to frighten baby bunnies at night.'

'They were ... *burp* ... really real,' replies the bard. 'Excuse me.' He eyes a plate of fresh steaming cornbread, next to a huge bowl of turnip soup, a knob of creamy butter slowly melting in its centre. But his audience have no intention of letting him stop for much longer.

'What do you think it was that changed them then? Did anyone ever find out? Was it the witch's curse, or was it something else?' The fear in the little rabbit's eyes makes it all too clear she is worrying that the same thing might happen in Thornwood.

'Could've been a curse,' says the bard. 'Could've been something much more horrible. As far as *this* part of the story goes ... Ooh dear. I *really* shouldn't gulp my drink like that ... As far as this part of the story goes, nobody had any idea. That's all you need to know for now.'

The bard is about to carry on, but something in the little rabbit's eyes makes him stop. Wide, white and terrified, with tears glistening in the corners. He likes to scare his audience a little, but this is Bramblemas Eve. She should be going to bed with dreams of sugared carrots and carved wooden dollies, not lying awake, scared witless.

He tugs his beard a few times, then reaches into one of the pouches on his belt, bringing out an ancient, much-folded piece of leather.

'Listen,' he says. 'I don't normally do this, but . . .'

'What?' the rabbits all squeal. 'What have you got there?'

'This?' says the bard, unfolding the stained leather. 'This is something I found on my travels. Something I don't usually read out to children. Especially not when I'm in the middle of a tale.'

'Oh please read it! *Please.*' The little rabbits are desperate for something secret, something forbidden.

'It's an account, you see. A tale of its own, copied down word for word from this old rabbit I met, far to the east of here, in Hulstland.' The bard holds up the leather to show rows and rows of tiny runes, burnt

or inked into it. The rabbits all kneel up to squint at it, even though most of them can't yet read.

'A tale of what? The Gorm? How they were made?'

'Rhubarb and radishes, but you are nosy ones! Yes. How the Gorm came to be, in the words of one that was there. Now, I'll read it to you, but only if you promise to remember where we got to in the story. Do we have a deal?'

The rabbits all shout about how well they can remember, and that the deal has definitely been made. Nodding and waving at them to shush, the bard spreads the leather out on his knee and begins to read.

My name is Auna. I am old now – a longtooth as they say here in Hulstland – but once I was a young rabbit, born in a little warren on the northern coast of Enderby called Sandywell. A simple place, full of simple grey-furred fisher-rabbits.

That warren has another name now, and the rabbits don't fish any more. Now they are called the Gorm, and they do things that set

your fur shivering and your ears shaking.
But it wasn't always that way. That's why I
want my story written down: so that others
can learn from it. So that the same thing
doesn't happen to any other warren like it
did ours.

When I was a little doe, we had a happy,
carefree life. We lived right on the edge of the
sandiest beach you ever saw, and we used to
spend hours running around the dunes and
splashing in the rock pools.

When I think back, all I remember is the
sun in my eyes, sand between my toes and
salt spray on my fur. Happy days.

Our chief was a funny little rabbit named
Crama. Crama the Cautious, he was known
as, for he never made a decision without
going over it a hundred times or more. He was
known for changing his mind, getting muddled
and generally putting everything in a pickle.

I remember hearing my father and his
friends moaning about him many an evening
in the longburrow, but nobody dared do

*anything about it. He had the magic helmet
of the Goddess, you see. A great metal thing
with copper horns. On him it looked like an
upside-down cauldron, but it protected him
from any spear or blade, and he never took
it off. It did have a special name, but we just
called it 'the Copperpot'.*

*Sandywell wasn't the most exciting
warren to live in, but it was safe and warm
and we were happy. At least until that
terrible day.*

*I don't like to speak of it, but I know
I must.*

*Crama, our chief, had finally decided that
we needed to dig a new longburrow. The
sandy soil of the warren tended to crumble,
and the older parts were wearing away. It
was a big job, and all the rabbits had to help.
Even us young kittens: we carried baskets
of soil out for the diggers and brought them
drinks and food.*

*The soil was soft and loamy, and the new
burrow fast appeared. Then, after a few days*

*of digging, a cry went out that something
had been found. I remember dashing down
there with my friends, expecting to find pots
of gold or fairy treasure. Instead there was
something . . . something else.*

*It makes my fur crawl to think of it, even
now, after all this time.*

*The thing. It was there, jutting up out of
the ground like a great rotten fang. It was
dark metal: iron of some sort, perhaps. We
had seen lumps of iron before. We knew it
was metal the Goddess hated, and that no
rabbit could work it. But they had been tiny
lumps – the size of your paw or so. This thing
was huge. As tall as the biggest rabbit in the
warren, and then some.*

*And there was something about it. It didn't
feel right. You could sense it pulsing and
grinding inside itself – as if it were angry or
full of something nasty.*

*It was jagged and rough, but under the
surface you could see things. Things that
seemed to twitch and move. Spikes and horns*

here, a tentacle there. Even an eye or a mouth.

We all knew it was evil. That was very clear. Nobody wanted to go near the new longburrow after that. Our priestess sealed off the tunnel with magic charms, and we all tried to pretend it hadn't happened, but none of us slept easy after that night.

And then the noises started.

Deep in the dead of night, you could hear them. Voices mostly. Some belonging to rabbits, some belonging to something else. Sometimes there was laughing and chanting too, although not in any language we had heard before. And then the hammering started.

From that day Crama, our chieftain, was almost never seen in daylight.

Every night, when the warren was asleep, he went down there with his soldiers to be near that thing. It changed them. Told them how to take the iron and hammer it and shape it. Whispered dark secrets and forbidden promises in their ears. That evil

shard of metal took our chief, it did. What
could it have offered him? Power, strength,
riches? Maybe it took away all his caution
and gave him something else instead?

I know this for sure, though: all the time
he was forging it into something else, it was
forging him as well.

The bard stopped a moment – he could see the
little rabbits enraptured. The older rabbits too. The
entire longburrow was now hanging on his every
word. He cleared his throat and continued.

A week or so later, the night hammering
stopped.

The next day, Crama showed himself. It
was a Mer's Day feast, as I remember – the
day we honoured our goddess of the sea.
We were all sat in the longburrow, about to
start a dinner of grilled mackerel and crab
cakes. The last fish I ever ate.

Crama walked into the longburrow with his
soldiers, and every rabbit almost screamed.

*The oversized Copperpot wasn't on his head
any more. In its place was a different helmet.
An iron one, all twisted and spiked. It had two
horns, like a mockery of the Goddess's helm,
but they were mismatched and jagged things.
He walked taller and broader than before.
This was not Crama the Cautious any more.
This was a part of that evil iron thing, walking
around in rabbit form.*

*He spoke to us then, in a grating, scraping
voice that none of us recognised. In the years
since, I've tried to remember what he said,
but the truth is I wasn't really listening. All I
could do at the time was stare. Stare at that
iron war-helm of his, but mostly at his eyes –
his and all his soldiers'. They weren't rabbit
eyes any more, you see. They were red like
rusted iron or dried blood.*

*Some rabbits stood up and protested. Our
priestess was one, my uncle another. The
soldiers grabbed them and took them away,
deep into the warren. We never saw them again.*

That night, my family and I (and a lot of

*others besides) all crept out of Sandywell
and ran. We ran for our lives, and we
didn't stop until we had forests, rivers and
mountains in between that place and us. If
you're listening to this, and you want to stay
safe and free, you'll do the same.*

*And wherever you end up, take this one
piece of advice from an old rabbit who's kept
her skin long enough to know: keep your
warren safe, keep your warren warm but . . .*
don't dig too deep.

The bard folds up the old leather parchment and
tucks it back inside his belt pouch. There is silence
for a little while afterwards, as the little rabbits
imagine horrid things buried in the earth beneath
their bottoms. But buried is perhaps better than a
wandering witch putting curses on you and turning
you into a monster. The bard looks at the little girl
rabbit and sees she is slightly less terrified, which
will have to do.

The silence doesn't last for long, of course.

'Was the Copperpot a magic weapon like Starclaw

then? Did the chief turn into Scramashank?' A little speckled rabbit looks up at the bard with huge saucer eyes glinting in the firelight. Her friends all nod, wanting to find out too.

'Even more questions? You are an inquisitive one indeed, aren't you?' The bard reaches down and tweaks one of her floppy ears. 'Way back, before memories even began, the Goddess herself gave each of the twelve rabbit tribes a magic treasure. Sandywell had the Copperpot, and Starclaw was the prize of Munbury warren, who were once the greatest tribe of all.'

'Did we get a gift? Where's our magic weapon?'

The bard laughs at this and winks over at Chief Hubert, who is rolling his eyes as he sips at a bowl of buttery turnip soup. 'Thornwood warren is too new for that. It hasn't been here much more than sixty years. In fact, at the time of my story, it was little more than a scrape in the ground – which is why the Gorm never bothered with it.'

'Where are the magic gifts now then? Who's got the dagger? Did the Gorm destroy the helmet? What other magic things were there?'

'Yes, yes!' call the other rabbits. 'Where is the dagger now? What happened to it? What happened?'

Bang! The bard brings his wooden flagon down on the tabletop, making all the little rabbits jump.

They squeak and shiver for a bit, until he fixes them all with his best glare. Then they are completely silent. When all that can be heard is the crackle of the fire and the slurping of Chief Hubert's soup, he speaks again.

'I do believe we had a deal, didn't we?'

'They were running from the Gorm!' one rabbit calls out.

'Podkin had just toppled a tree on to the riders!' yells another.

'They were squished like raspberry jam! There was blood everywhere! And eyeballs and things!'

'All right, all right,' says the bard. 'That's quite enough gory detail. Now. Let me carry on where I left off . . .'

CHAPTER FIVE

Redwater

Well. As you so beautifully described, the fleeing rabbits had just toppled a tree on to two Gorm riders. Very impressive too.

After they had stood for a few moments, taking in what had happened, slowly realising they were still alive, they headed off into the woods again.

The sun was well risen now, and they followed it eastward, crunching through the snow as drips from melting icicles pattered on their heads and ran down their necks, making them shiver even more.

Before long they stumbled down another bank

and on to a narrow, frozen river. Paz, who actually *had* been paying attention in those geography lessons, recognised it as the Red River.

'This is the river that runs past Redwater warren! Don't you remember it?'

Podkin was too cold to remember anything, even if he had been listening, about river names and types of trees. The terror of nearly being caught, and the amazement at the power of Starclaw was gone. All he really wanted to do now was lay down in the soft white snow and fall asleep forever. But there was a dim little thought tugging away at the corner of his mind. Hadn't they used to come here at Midsummer, every other year? There had been other little rabbits, hadn't there? And dandelion salad, with carrot juice dressing. He was sure he remembered that.

'W-was it different then? Not w-w-white everywhere?'

Paz gave him a worried look and grabbed him by the arm. They half-ran, half-fell all the way along the riverbank until they came to an arched wooden bridge, and from there they followed a snowy track, cut into the forest floor. It led them to a pair of oak

doors, set into the hillside. Notched Ogham writing, carved into the gateposts, declared it to be Redwater.

'Thank the Goddess,' said Paz, tears in her eyes as she used the last of her strength to bang on the door. Podkin could do nothing but stand and shiver at her side, and little Pook was too cold even for that.

After a few moments, the warren door creaked open, and a ginger-furred guard-rabbit poked out his head.

Now, Paz and Podkin might have been half-frozen, but they had been here several times before, and they remembered the famous hospitality of the Redwater rabbits. Everyone for miles around knew how excitable and fun-loving they were. Any rabbit who stopped here was practically dragged inside and made to eat, sing and dance until they dropped.

Which is why they were shocked by this gloomy-faced, dreary soldier who peered at them now. His ears drooped, his eyes were shadowed and bloodshot. His leather armour was unlaced, unpolished, battered and torn. It barely fitted, hanging off him like old clothes on a scarecrow. If they hadn't been so frozen, they might have wondered why such a

skinny, undersized rabbit was doing the job of a hardened warrior.

'What d'you want?' he said, not looking like he cared in the slightest.

Paz could sense something was wrong but was too desperate to listen to her gut. She cleared her throat and spoke. 'We need help. Please.'

'The G-g-gorm are after us,' Pod added.

'S-soop?' whispered Pook, poking a shivering nose out of Paz's tunic.

'We're from Munbury warren,' said Paz. 'We're Chief Lopkin's children.'

The guard's eyes widened at this, and he slammed the door on them. For an awful moment, Podkin and Paz thought they were being shut out, but then they heard the guard shouting for help through the doors.

'Are they g-g-going to let us in?' Podkin asked, through chattering teeth.

'I think so,' said Paz. 'But something's up. We'd better hide the dagger.'

Podkin just looked at it dumbly, as if he was wondering how the thing had appeared in his hand. Quickly, Paz snatched it off him, wrapped it around

with the cloth and shoved it inside her tunic, next to Pook, who gave a weak little squeak of protest. She had just hidden it away when the door creaked open again, this time revealing a familiar face: Lady Russet, the Redwater chieftain's wife.

Even though Podkin's brain was practically an ice cube, he could see the terrible difference in the Lady. Before, she had been a plump, bristling bundle of life, with zinging fur, a bubbling giggle and eyes that sparked like glimmers of summer sunlight.

Now, her skin hung off her face in folds. Lines of worry creased her brow; her eyes were hollow, haunted and red-rimmed, as if she'd been crying. Crying for a long, long time. When she spoke, her voice was light and happy, but it sounded forced, as if she was trying to hide some great sadness.

'Why, if it isn't little Paz and Podkin! How you've grown since the summer. And is that tiny Pook nestled there? You poor things – you look frozen half to death! Is it true what my guard says about the Gorm? In Munbury warren? Come in, come in at once! You'll be safe here, I promise.'

Podkin knew this wasn't right: that he should

probably turn and run back into the icy woods, but he could hear the crackle of a fire somewhere down inside the warren; and he could smell roasting parsnips and freshly baked bread. At that moment, getting warm and eating were more important to him than anything else, even his safety. That might sound silly to *you*, sitting by a toasty hearthside with a belly full of turnip soup, but try spending the night running for your life through a Midwinter forest. You'd chew the legs off a rabid badger for a snack and somewhere cosy to sleep.

In fact, warmth and food *were* more important than anything else right then. Although the little rabbits didn't know it, they were actually very close to freezing to death. If Podkin had lain down in that snowdrift like he'd wanted to, the sleep he drifted off in would have been his last. He would have woken up in the Land Beyond, and there is no coming back from that place.

So that was how they came to enter Redwater warren, even though it was a mistake Podkin would regret for the rest of his life ...

They were led through to the longburrow and sat down on benches next to the fire. Lady Redwater went

off 'to see that rooms were made ready for them', and some silent, shuffling serving rabbits brought out hot buttered parsnips and a few small loaves of bread.

As soon as the blood started moving round his body again, Podkin's hands began to shake so badly he could hardly hold his plate. He managed a bite of parsnip eventually, and it burnt and tingled as it slipped down his throat. It was the best feeling he had ever had.

After a little while, the shaking stopped, and he found himself gulping down mouthfuls and tearing through the bread like a starved rabbit. Paz was doing the same, and little Pook even began to move around a bit. His nose wrinkled and his big eyes peered out from Paz's tunic. 'Neeps! Neeps!' he called, opening his mouth like a baby bird, as Paz spooned hot parsnips inside.

As his body thawed out, so did Podkin's wits. He noticed the longburrow was dark and damp. Thick cobwebs filled the corners, and the fire before them was a tiny one, nestled amongst huge banks of ash. The fireplace hadn't been swept for months.

He looked around at the tables and benches,

remembering the feast days of Midsummer, when the hall had been packed to the rafters with cheery rabbits. There was hardly any furniture left now. And those chairs – had they been patched up? Was the back of that bench splintered?

The food wasn't quite right, either. The parsnips were stringy, the bread gritty and burnt on the outside. The last feast day they had eaten a huge glorious meal here. There had been a giant carrot, hollowed out so that when it was cut, a cascade of roasted turnips and swedes tumbled over the table. Now *that* was proper Redwater food. Not this hastily cobbled-together meal in front of them.

Once he'd started noticing one or two little things, his eyes picked out more. Were those gouge-marks on the earth wall there? What were those dried red stains, spattered on the floor?

And also, come to think of it: where were the children? The chieftain's children they had played hide-and-seek and blind bunny's bluff with every year since he could walk? They were as noisy, loud and bubbly as any Redwater rabbit ever was. If they weren't in the longburrow itself, they should at least

be able to hear them shouting and chasing each other somewhere in the warren. This was Bramblemas morning, after all. There should have been a cluster of little rabbits in the longburrow, all showing off what the Midwinter Rabbit had brought them in the night. At least, that was always what happened in Munbury warren.

I had been hoping for a set of wooden soldiers, Podkin thought. He wondered if they had been delivered anyway and were sitting next to his empty bed, or whether the Midwinter Rabbit knew about the Gorm and had kept away. It didn't seem important any more, even though it had been all he'd thought about for weeks. *How quickly your life can turn upside down.*

'Paz,' he whispered. 'Where d'you think Rufus and Rusty are? Wouldn't they have come out to see us if they knew we were here?'

Paz nodded. Her eyes had been zipping everywhere, noticing the same things as Podkin. Mostly, she had been staring at a metal sculpture that she hadn't seen before. A tall iron pedestal that jutted up from the longburrow floor. It wasn't

a model of anything in particular, just a mass of twists and coils, all jagged, uneven and unfinished. *Why do they have an iron statue in their warren?* she wondered. Everyone knew that kind of metal was hated by the Goddess. And what was it about the thing that set her fur on edge? It reminded her of something, but her poor, frozen, terrified mind couldn't quite place it.

And then it came to her.

The Gorm.

She wanted to tell Podkin but didn't speak because two serving rabbits had just entered the room. They were carrying some kind of large box between them, covered over with a thick blanket. They kept to the shadows as they edged their way around the longburrow. They had their heads down, but Paz could see them darting nervous, scared glances at them as they passed. Out through the hallway to the main doors they went. When they were gone, she hissed at Pod. 'What was that they were carrying?'

Pod was about to shrug when he heard a muffled cawing sound coming from the hallway. Some kind of animal? A bird? That sound – they had heard it

before, just a few short hours ago. Podkin and Paz looked at each other, both thinking the same thought at the same time.

It's not a box, but a cage. And inside must be one of the Gorm's spy birds. A warped, tortured crow with dead eyes and rusted metal feathers. The bird, the statue, the dead, empty warren. Suddenly it all made terrible sense.

'They're working for the Gorm!' Podkin hissed. 'They're letting them know we're here!'

The Gorm must have taken Redwater, just like they had Munbury. Chief Russet must have been killed, his guards murdered, and the rest of the warren turned into slaves. And as for the children ... Podkin didn't like to think. Without its heart and soul, the warren was slowly dying. They had chosen the worst possible place to run to.

'We have to get out!' Paz started to say, but Podkin was already up and running. She grabbed Pook and went to follow when, from the corner of her eye, she caught sight of the iron pillar. Something inside it had squirmed, juddered, like a fat eel stuck in a shallow puddle of mud. Could that even be

possible? And then it made a sound: a grinding, screeching wail that grew louder and louder.

She didn't stop to hear any more. Clutching Pook, she dashed after her brother as fast as her quick rabbit legs would carry her. They sprinted out of the longburrow, in the opposite direction of the main entrance, just as a shout went up from the gallery above. Someone had been up there watching them, and from the voice it sounded a lot like Lady Russet herself.

'Stop them! Don't let them escape!'

Into the tunnels of the warren they ran, the screams echoing behind them. Heading away from the main doors may have seemed a daft thing to do, but Podkin knew there would be guards there. He also knew warrens had many little back entrances and bolt-holes. He could hear his father's voice reciting one of his favourite phrases: *'a warren with only one entrance is basically a trap.'* A trap – like the one they had just walked into.

They dashed through dark winding corridors, changing direction every time they heard footsteps nearby. The Redwater rabbits were closing in on

them, hounding them through the tunnels like ferrets used to chase their small fluffy ancestors.

Shouting voices echoed behind them, and little Pook began to wail as he was bounced around inside Paz's tunic. 'Neeps! Neeps!' He could sense his sister's fear but was also very concerned that his meal had been interrupted.

'There!' Paz shouted. 'Up ahead!'

The tunnel had become lighter, and as they rounded a corner, they saw a small open gateway and the snowy forest beyond. They sprinted for it, as fast as terrified rabbits can, as Lady Russet's voice called out behind them: 'Seal the warren! Close all the gates!'

Slams and bangs began to echo through the passageways and, with numb horror, Podkin saw a metal portcullis begin to grind downwards over the doorway ahead. Their escape was being blocked. They were going to be trapped inside.

Sometimes, when your life is in real danger, when everything seems lost, there is a well of energy deep within you that can give you a final, desperate surge of power. It isn't always much: but often it's just enough to scrape through trouble by a whisker.

Podkin and Paz reached for theirs now, and doubled their speed down the tunnel, as the heavy grille clanked further and further down.

Paz reached it first, and dropped to her knees, sliding underneath the portcullis's prongs and out into the snow. Podkin was a split second behind. He copied his sister, kicking his legs out and falling backwards to skid underneath. Looking up, he saw the roof of the tunnel pass by: the gateway, the falling portcullis, and then the grey sky of the open air above.

I did it! he thought. *I'm free!* But then there came a sharp searing pain in his ear. He tried to get up, but something was holding his head down. Something very painful. He heard Paz scream, and he twisted around to see what had happened.

The portcullis was down, and they were on the outside: or at least most of them was. One of his long silky brown ears was still inside, and speared through it – holding him in place – was a prong of the portcullis.

He had been pinned to the ground.

He was trapped.

CHAPTER SIX

One-Ear

Paz heard the clang of the portcullis behind her and turned to see Podkin lying safely outside the warren. She felt a surge of relief, which quickly disappeared when she saw the look of agony on his face.

Why isn't he getting up? she thought. *Has he sprained an ankle? Hurt his back?* And then she saw the portcullis prong, spearing his ear to the ground. That was when she screamed.

She dashed to his side and took his hand. 'Oh, Pod! Your ear!'

Her brother's eyes were bulging and his teeth were gnashing in pain. She realised he must be trying his hardest not to scream, so that the Redwater rabbits wouldn't discover where they'd gone. The poor thing could hardly move his head. There was no way they could escape into the woods now.

A voice came from back in the tunnel, somewhere in the dark. 'If only you hadn't run. Then none of this would have happened.'

As Paz watched, she saw a figure step towards the portcullis, closer to the light. It was Lady Russet. The gaunt, haunted Lady Russet, with cold dead eyes.

'Let us go, milady,' Paz looked up at her and pleaded. 'You were always our friend. Don't let the Gorm take us!'

'The living statue they left here has sensed you. We have already sent the crow,' said Lady Russet. 'By now it has reached its masters and is calling them to us. It is too late.'

'How can you do this? Why would you help them? They're evil, Lady Russet. They killed our father!'

For a moment, there was something like pity in the Lady's eyes. Paz thought she even saw a tear

form there, before it trickled away into her fur. 'They killed my husband too,' she said, her voice little more than a whisper. 'And all our guards and warriors. But they have my children ... Rufus and Rusty. If I give you to them, I might get them back.'

Paz's fury at this cowardly, spineless thing the chieftain's wife had become suddenly overflowed. She jumped up and grabbed the bars of the portcullis, shouting down the tunnel at her. 'What would my father say if he saw you now? What would your *husband* say? Call yourself a rabbit? You're no better than a weasel, you ... you ... *traitor*!'

Lady Russet jumped backwards, eyes wide, vanishing into the shadows. It was a good few moments before she spoke again, and when she did her voice was shaky and broken, as if she were holding back from sobbing.

'It won't be long until they are here. Your brother is stuck, and I won't free him, but if you are gone when they arrive, I will say he came here on his own. You and the little one can escape. That's the best I can do.'

With that, she was gone, back into the warren,

leaving the little rabbits cold and frightened in the snow.

*

'You heard her, Paz,' said Podkin eventually. 'You have a chance to get away. Leave me here, and take Pook somewhere safe.'

Paz gritted her teeth and shook the portcullis bars. 'I am *not* leaving you behind,' she said. 'There must be some way to get you free.'

'Caw! Caw!' Pook was wiggling around inside her tunic, shouting at the top of his voice.

'What?' Paz snapped at him. 'The crow's gone, Pook.'

'Caw! Caw!'

'It's gone, Pook! No bird! Gone! Now stop shouting at me so I can think of what to do!'

The baby rabbit gave a frustrated yell, then started wriggling about like mad, pushing the cloth-wrapped dagger out of Paz's robes where she had stowed it. It took a moment for her to realise what he was doing.

'Of course! Not *caw*, but *claw*! Starclaw! You're a genius, Pook.' Paz gave him a quick nuzzle, then

dragged Starclaw out, ripping off the cloth covering as fast as she could.

Clang! She swung it hard against the portcullis. She tried again and again, but nothing happened. *Clang! Clang!*

'Aaargh ...' Podkin moaned. The vibrations were like tiny explosions in his wounded ear. 'Stop doing that!'

'Oh, whiskers! The gate's iron. The stupid dagger won't cut through it. How did they even get an iron gate? Unless the Gorm gave it to them ...' Paz cursed again and shoved the dagger into the snow. What was the point of having a magic weapon if you couldn't use it half the time?

Podkin whimpered, his hands reaching up to his pinned ear. There must be some way to free him. Could she cut away the stone of the gateway floor? Or the lintel above, perhaps? She wondered how much time they had.

Her question was answered by a horn blast, somewhere on the other side of the warren. They had hardly any time at all.

'Go,' Podkin said again. 'Just go.'

No. Paz shook her head. There had to be some other way around it. Her quick little mind whirred, ticking through all the possibilities. In the end there was only one option.

'Pod.' She gripped him by the hand and squeezed. 'The dagger can't cut through iron, but it can cut through . . . your ear.'

Paz gulped. Podkin gulped.

The portcullis had speared his ear over halfway down. He would have to lose nearly the whole thing.

'Please don't,' he said. 'Just leave me for the Gorm. They probably won't kill me. Will they?'

'You're officially the chieftain of Munbury warren now,' said Paz. 'They'll do to you what they did to Father. Scramashank will wear your skull on his belt.'

'But my *ear*.'

'I have to do it now, Pod. There isn't much time.'

Podkin and Paz looked at each other. Finally Podkin nodded.

Paz pulled the dagger out of the snow. Inside her tunic, Pook squeaked and hid his eyes.

'Hang on,' said Paz. She remembered a lesson on

wood lore about how spider webs could help stop a wound bleeding. She stood on tiptoe and pulled a good handful of matted cobwebs from around the door, ignoring the fat spiders that scuttled over her fingers, angry at having their winter sleep broken. Then she lowered the dagger tip to rest against Pod's ear.

'Will it hurt?' he said.

'It might.' Paz remembered the way the dagger had chopped through the tree trunk like it was butter. 'But it'll be quick.'

'Then do it,' said Podkin, closing his eyes.

It was funny how he didn't feel anything at first. Not the slice, not the cobwebs being pressed over the wound, nor the handfuls of snow after that. It was funny to be running off into the woods, leaving a part of his body behind. But the funniest thing of all was that, even after his ear had been sliced off, he could still feel the burning pain of the portcullis piercing it. A burning pain in an ear that was no longer there.

INTERLUDE

'Hey! That wasn't how he lost his ear!'
    'It was clawed off by a wildcat!'
'No! A vampire rabbit ate it in one bite!'
'It was pulled off by a giant lop!'
'I heard he chopped it off himself, and made it into a boat to escape an island full of monsters!'

The bard folds his arms and gives the little rabbits his best glare. Eventually their squeaking subsides, and they sit frowning up at him in silence.

'Roasted radishes, you are a noisy bunch! I don't really care what you've heard about how Podkin became the One-Eared,' he says. 'This is *my* story. It belongs to me. And in my story, he had to cut it off to escape the Gorm.'

'That's daft,' says the inquisitive rabbit. 'How can

anyone own a story? It isn't a real thing. It's just words.'

'Stories belong to the teller,' says the bard. 'At least half of them do. The other part belongs to the listeners. When a good story is told to a good listener, the pair of them own it together.'

'So the story is ours now?' asks another rabbit.

'It will be,' says the bard, 'if I ever get to finish the blooming thing.'

'I think it makes sense,' says a quiet piebald rabbit at the front. 'There's no such thing as vampire rabbits anyway. I always thought he lost his ear in a battle, but this version sounds like something that would have happened.'

'Thank you,' says the bard. 'You're obviously a very sensible little rabbit. The chieftain's son, also, might I guess?'

Behind him, Chief Hubert swells with pride (or he would do, if he wasn't already as swollen as any rabbit could get without exploding all over the longburrow). The inquisitive rabbit makes the most of the interruption to pipe up once more.

'But *how* do you know what happened? If you weren't really there, I mean.'

The bard sighs and rolls his eyes. 'I'm a storyteller. I tell stories. That's my job.'

'So this *is* just made up then.' The inquisitive rabbit doesn't look very impressed. 'Well, if you're going to make up a story anyway, you might as well put vampire rabbits in. Vampire rabbits are exciting.'

'By the Goddess's sacred celery ...' The bard puts his head in his hands and makes a quiet sobbing sound.

The sensible rabbit digs his friend in the ribs with an elbow. 'Vampire rabbits aren't *real*,' he says. 'If the story has things in it that don't seem real, then we won't want to believe it. If we don't want to believe it, the story falls apart. Then there really is no point in listening to it.'

The bard peeps out between his fingers and gives the sensible rabbit a wink.

'There is a god,' he says, 'of bards and storytellers. His name is Clarion, and he has been known to whisper the art of stories into the ears of a chosen few rabbits while they sleep. I believe he must have paid you a visit or two, my wise little friend.'

It is the sensible rabbit's turn to puff up with pride, making him look like a tiny replica of his father. A hint of what will he become when it is his turn to become chieftain.

'Very well.' The bard clears his throat and gives his audience another glare. 'If you've quite finished interrupting, might I be allowed to continue the story?'

CHAPTER SEVEN

The Witch in the Woods

I t was very hard for the little rabbits to go back out
into the winter forest. What little warmth they
had gained from Redwater warren soon vanished,
and this time they had no idea where to run. As far
as they knew, the whole world was against them and
nowhere was safe.

They knew they didn't have much of a head start,
either. The Gorm would be arriving at Redwater
soon, and in five short minutes they would discover
Podkin's severed ear. After that, they simply had to
stroll along the trail of footprints in the snow, and

then it would all be over in the flash of a twisted iron blade.

Podkin wasn't too worried by it all. He had lost quite a lot of blood, which tended to make you dizzy and dozy. He was currently dreaming that he was walking on top of a fluffy white cloud. His sister was there, carrying a talking carrot that looked a lot like his brother, Pook; and for some reason, his ear was very sore. He thought he'd probably wake up soon, then go out and see if he could find a nice spot by the river for a snooze.

Paz dragged him along by the arm, casting worried glances at his missing ear. The wound was still oozing blood, and the fur on his head was thickly matted with it. She needed to stop and bind it, but there wasn't time.

Pook had also started shivering again. He was making quiet, miserable little whines, and she wasn't sure how much more of the cold he could take. She was trying her hardest to move quickly, not to leave such obvious tracks, to keep to the deeper parts of the wood ...

All in all, she had begun to think it might be

better if the Gorm did get them. At least it would all be over quickly.

Which is why she wasn't too surprised when they stepped into a clearing and saw a hunched, twisted crow sitting on a tree stump and staring at them with blank red eyes.

'Oh no,' she moaned. 'Oh no.'

The crow blinked and tilted its spiked metal head. Its beak opened slightly, dripping some oily, coppery fluid. Its feathers rattled and scraped against each other, giving off a cloud of powdery orange rust. Paz tried to think of some way to stop it before it flew off and betrayed their whereabouts. Throw the dagger at it? Jump on top of the thing and squash it? There was really nothing she could do.

'Caaa!' it squawked, and began to spread its wings for take-off, when suddenly it exploded with a clang and a puff of iron feathers. Paz shrieked and stared at the drifting cloud of jagged plumage. The crow itself had been knocked to the floor, stone dead.

'I hate those pesky birds,' said someone on the other side of the clearing. Paz raised the dagger, ready to defend herself, as a stooped old she-rabbit

in a patched cloak crunched towards them through the snow. Her hand clutched a leather sling, empty now of its pebble bullet. 'They should learn to mind their own beeswax.'

'Um ... hello?' said Paz.

'Is it morning yet, Mummy?' said Podkin.

'Soop?' said Pook.

'It's about time you three showed up,' the she-rabbit said. 'I've been waiting about in the snow for ages. Blooming cold, my poor feet are.'

'You've ... you've been expecting us?' Now Paz wasn't sure if *she* was dreaming. Or was this another agent of the Gorm? She didn't have any metal shards poking out of her face, but still ...

'Expecting you, dear? I should say so. Saw it in the bones, years ago. And now we'd better hurry and see to that ear. We'll lose him if we don't, and then we'll lose everything else.'

Paz looked at her poor suffering brother and then stared at the old rabbit, trying to work out whether to trust her or not. She was clearly mad, but was she a safer bet than trying to escape the Gorm on their own? The she-rabbit stared back, with piercing blue

eyes that looked much younger than her face. Her nose wrinkled and twitched as she waited for Paz to make her decision. Finally, she nodded.

'All right. We'll come with you.' *But if you try to trick us ...* Paz had Starclaw clutched in one hand. It would cut through the rabbit's flesh just like it had Podkin's ear.

The she-rabbit nodded, as if satisfied that things were going to plan. 'Good, good. Just what you're supposed to say, dear.' She walked to the edge of the clearing, and then paused to draw a bronze sickle from her belt. Bending down, she started cutting a slender pine sapling with it. While she was busy, a thousand thoughts raced through Paz's mind. *What if she's a traitor like Lady Russet? What if she's a witch? Don't you remember what happens to little rabbits that go off with witches in the forest?*

The she-rabbit finished cutting off the sapling and used it like a broom to swish away their footprints in the snow. When she had finished, she looked up, an impatient frown on her face.

'Well? Are you coming or not?' she said. 'Hop along, my little bunnies.'

Then she turned and vanished into the undergrowth.

*

Witch or not, there wasn't much else Paz could do but follow. They wound their way through the bushes and trees, Podkin moaning softly and stopping every now and then for the she-rabbit to hide their tracks, until they came to the biggest oak tree that Paz had ever seen. It had a cascade of gnarled, squirming roots that spilled down from a sloped bank of earth. The towering trunk was thick enough to be four or five centuries old, and its branches – weighed down with snow – dipped to the forest floor, making a kind of latticework cave. A cage of wood and snow that, in a happier time, would have made an amazing play den.

However, it wouldn't be much good at keeping out the Gorm. Paz watched as the she-rabbit ducked through the branches, hoping she had a better plan than just hiding amongst the tangles of roots.

Instead, she pushed at a spot on the packed earth of the bank. It looked like a bare patch of mud, covered in moss, lichen and dead leaves but – to Paz's surprise – it swung open to reveal a hidden

door. She hurried inside, helping the bleary Podkin along. As soon as they were in, the old rabbit shut the door and bolted it.

This is it, thought Paz. *This is when the witch makes us into a pie, or maybe some kind of casserole.*

But no such thing happened. Instead, the she-rabbit hung up her cloak and busied herself by stoking the fire inside a little clay stove. She put a pot on top and poured in water from a clay pitcher, before taking Podkin's hand and leading him to sit on a little stool by the hearth.

Paz couldn't help worrying that the warming stove might be intended for them but, seeing as they weren't being eaten *just* yet, she took the chance to look around. They were in a tidy little house, burrowed beneath the huge roots of the oak. The earth between them had been whitewashed, and reed mats covered the floor. Pots, pans and utensils hung from the ceiling, and there was a small fireplace, complete with mantelpiece, where the stove nestled.

Shelves had been carved into the earth of the walls, and more had been added, made from old warped planks of wood. Every inch of these were

packed with a strange collection of items, too many for Paz to really take in.

She saw lots of clay pots and jars, all labelled with neat Ogham writing, some overflowing with dried herbs and bulbs: wild garlic, rosemary, foxglove, rosehip and lots of mushrooms, like ink cap, blusher, penny bun, brittlegill and angel's bonnet.

Paz saw many other, stranger things that she could only wonder about. A glass jar filled with bird skulls; a painted wooden mask with fangs and huge eyes; a clay model of a peaceful rabbit, sitting cross-legged, from whose head a spiral of scented smoke slowly uncurled.

So this is what a witch has in her house, she thought. But there were other, more homely things too: a bed in the corner, a spinning wheel, loom and some cupboards. There was even a leaded-glass window, framed by tree roots. Paz went over and peered outside. What she saw made her clap her hands over her mouth to stop her from screaming.

A pack of Gorm riders were a few metres away, grinding their way through the snow. Their hunched iron beasts were ploughing up the ground, spattering

it with black oil, while their riders sat atop, slowly turning their heads this way and that. Their jagged, serrated swords twitched, hungry for rabbit flesh. She could hear the screeching and grating of metal; she could smell the hot oil and burnt-blood stink. Any moment now, they would spot the secret door in the bank and come crashing through ...

'Don't you worry about them,' said the she-rabbit, as she took the water from the stove and set it down beside Podkin. 'They won't find us here. There's enough glamours and 'chantments about this place that Hern himself couldn't find it, if I didn't want him to.'

And true enough, now the Gorm were turning their mounts and seemed to be heading off towards the far end of the bank and away.

Proper magic. A little voice in Paz's head said. *Not only a witch, but a good one.* She smiled to herself and went over to where Podkin was sitting.

'This is nasty,' said the she-rabbit. 'Going to need stitches.' She had a blunt, matter-of-fact way about her that Paz found reassuring somehow. She clearly knew what she was doing.

'Will he be all right?' Paz asked.

'As right as a one-eared rabbit can be. Still, it'll do him a favour in the long run. Nobody'd be as interested in telling stories about a normal rabbit.'

Stories? The long run? What was she talking about?

As Paz watched, the old rabbit gave Podkin something to drink that sent him to sleep. They moved him over to the bed, and then cleaned the wound with warm water. The she-rabbit stitched it with a bone needle and thread, before putting on a poultice and binding it tight. She spoke as she worked, and Paz discovered her name was Brigid, and that she lived in the woods alone, foraging for food, herbs and anything else she needed. She didn't say, but Paz guessed she had been living under the oak tree for a long time. Long enough to lose the knack of talking to others. Social skills were very important for warren rabbits, but Paz guessed you didn't need them when the only person you had to worry about pleasing was yourself.

As soon as Podkin was quietly sleeping, Brigid made some stinging-nettle broth, which Pook gulped down. They sat by the fire, listening to the sounds

of the crackling wood. It felt wonderful to be warm, fed and safe, even though their enemies were still not so very far away.

Paz found herself drifting off to sleep. Pook was already snoring on the hearthrug, and at some point Paz joined him, dimly aware of Brigid covering them both with a patchwork blanket. She tried to say 'thank you', or to ask one of the many questions that were whizzing about her head, but the sleepiness was too strong. She let herself fall into it.

*

When she awoke, she saw Brigid sitting on a chair by the stove, holding the magic dagger Starclaw in her hands. She was turning it over, thoughtfully, pausing every now and then to peer at the copper face on the hilt.

Paz watched her, wondering what to say. She didn't want to appear rude, but seeing Brigid with the dagger made her uneasy: partly because she didn't think she should be touching it, and also because there was a good chance it might slice off her fingers.

The old rabbit didn't even look at Paz, but somehow still knew she was awake. 'Powerful magic

in this here dagger,' she said. 'One of the Twelve Gifts of the Goddess, if I'm not mistaken.'

'How ...' Paz began, not knowing whether to admit what Starclaw was. 'How d'you know that?'

'Got one myself.' Brigid smiled and pulled the little copper sickle from her belt. When she brought it near the dagger, it flashed blue for an instant. Paz thought she saw Starclaw give an answering twinkle.

'How did you get one?' Paz asked. 'I thought they were only given to chieftains of the twelve tribes?'

'They were.' Brigid tucked the sickle away again and looked into the flickering flames of the stove. 'I was a princess once. Not that you'd know it now, of course. I reckon you must be too. My father was the chief of Redwater warren, a long time back now. One of his Guard double-crossed him and forced him out. All our family had to leave, cast out of our home like wandering tinkers. I knew about the sickle and decided *that* lot didn't deserve to have it, so I took it with me. It glows red whenever it's near poison. Blue when it's near something good. Taught me all I know about herb-craft and healing, it did.'

Paz found it hard to imagine the bent old

she-rabbit as a princess, sitting at the head table in the longburrow, or dressed in her finest for the Carrotmas feast at harvest time. 'Was it Chief Russet who did that to your family? He always seemed such a friendly rabbit . . .'

'Not him, but his father before, the evil two-faced son of a weasel. He was the captain of the Honour Guard as well. Always too trusting, my old father. And look where it got him. My folks moved on afterwards, but I stayed here in the woods. I watched them turn the warren inside out, looking for my sickle. And it was here with me the whole time.' She gave a dry chuckle that sounded like a pile of leaves rustling. When she laughed, Paz could see the little girl still inside her, and she found herself smiling too.

*

The three little rabbits stayed with Brigid for more than two weeks. Podkin slowly began to build up strength while his ear healed. He was very bad-tempered about the whole thing (he used to secretly think his ears were his best feature), but when Brigid told him he had to get as much rest as possible, he was quite pleased. It was the first time in his life

that anyone had actually *ordered* him to have lots of snoozes.

Pook enjoyed rolling around on Brigid's floor, playing with the rattling bones and pebbles she used for scrying the future. He just used to toss them about the hearth, making patterns and piles, but Brigid said he had a gift for soothsaying, all the same. Every now and then, she would walk over and examine the bones he had thrown and mumble some comments like 'yes, he will come in handy' and 'must stock up on that sleep potion then'. Pook would look up at her with big, loving eyes and nod in agreement.

Paz went out foraging with the old rabbit several times, and was beginning to learn a fair bit of forest lore. She learnt which mushrooms were good to eat, and which would make you cough up your innards; how to find a squirrel's stash of winter nuts and which trees had bark that you could chew to stop a fever. She learnt the names of plants like Candlewick, Maypops and Love-in-idleness, and how to prepare and use them as medicine.

Podkin watched all this, and couldn't help but

feel a little jealous. After all, *he* was the one with the magic dagger, wasn't he? Shouldn't he be the one learning about spells and poisons? It all sounded quite exciting, even if it did involve having to listen and remember things.

One day he built up enough courage to ask Brigid if she could tell him about magic. 'What kind?' was all the old rabbit said. Paz looked up from where she was crushing dried seeds with a mortar and pestle and pricked her ears with interest.

'There are different kinds?'

'The good kind. And the bad.'

'What's the bad kind?'

'You've seen that, well enough.'

Podkin knew she was talking about the Gorm. To confirm it, Brigid took down one of the strange tapestries from her wall and handed it to him. It showed a circle made up of two snakes, each one eating the body of the other. One was a scaled sea monster with fins and spines: brutal but impressive. The other was a twisted metal thing, all jagged and sharp.

'The two types of magic,' Brigid said. 'Natural magic and dark, iron magic. The world is made

of the two, but they balance each other out like this –
always eating at each other, neither one ever winning.
Least, that's how it's supposed to be.'

'Why the two?' Podkin asked. 'Why can't
there just be natural magic that doesn't want to
hurt anyone?'

In answer, Brigid went to one of her teetering
shelves and took down a carving. It was of two doe
rabbits, standing arm in arm. Podkin recognised one
from the garland of flowers around her neck, and the
little chicks and birds that peeped out from the folds
of her dress: the Goddess Estra, bringer of all life.

The other rabbit looked much more stern. She clutched a fearsome bow, and her robe was cinched around the middle by a belt made of tiny skulls.

'The twin sisters,' Brigid said, making a strange gesture in the air with her paw. 'Estra and Nixha. Goddesses of life and death.'

Podkin stared at the carving, running his fingers over the worked, polished wood. 'I've heard of the Goddess, of course,' he said. 'And I think I remember learning there was someone who took you to the Land Beyond when you died. But we didn't talk about that much, back at home.'

'Most rabbits in these parts don't.' Brigid shook her head. 'But dying is as much a part of life as living. Down south, in the other lands, there's them that worship only Nixha. Funny bunch they are, my dear. I would tell you to stay clear of them, but ...'

Podkin sensed that the old rabbit was about to go off on one of her strange ramblings again, so he interrupted with another question. 'What do the goddesses have to do with the Gorm then?'

'Well,' said Brigid, taking the statue back and

setting it carefully on her shelf. 'That there is the story at the beginning of everything.'

'Will you tell it to me? Please?'

Brigid huffed and puffed for a bit – there was nettle soup to make and a pile of acorns to shell for bread – but finally she took Podkin over to the hearth where Pook was busy playing with a heap of bones and pebbles. Paz followed too, and the pair of them sat down at Brigid's feet, as though she was a bard telling a bedtime story.

'Right then, dearies,' said Brigid, when she was comfortable. 'The story of the goddesses at the beginning of things, just how the old priestess at Redwater told it to me when I was a fluffy-eared kit.

'It is said by some that back then the world was a dark and evil place. The whole of it: all lands, all seas, was covered by poisonous, seething metal. An evil, wicked mass of horridness that was all part of one being. Gormalech, he was named, and he had eaten whatever was here before, in his never-ending greed and gluttony.

'So, there hangs our world – floating in space, all

covered with nasty, living iron. And it would have stayed there too, cold and alone for all time, if it hadn't been for the goddesses.

'Sometime, goodness only knows how long ago, the goddesses stumbled upon our world and decided it was the place for them. Perhaps they could see through the swirling poison of Gormalech to what was beneath, perhaps they had known the place as it was before he got control of it. Who knows?

'Anyway, they wanted to stop here, and a good job for us that they did. The only problem was: how to get rid of him that was globbing up the place with his stink and poison and nasty iron evilness?

'First of all, they called to him and asked if he wouldn't mind jiggering off somewhere else. Of course, he says "no, not for all the carrots in my back garden", or something like that.

'The next plan, then, was to challenge him to a contest. Winner takes all, sort of thing.

'Estra, the Goddess, chose a game of dice. Fox Paw, she called it, and she trounced old Gormalech.

'Nixha went next, and challenged the evil creature to a contest of archery and needless to say,

he lost. Nobody can fire an arrow like Nixha. She never misses, as we will all find out when she comes for us, at the end of our time.

'Finally, it was Gormalech's turn. He simply wanted a fight and, being several thousand times bigger and meaner than those two dainty does, he bashed and beat them to bits.

'Well, the end result of all the competing was that nobody had really won. None of them was best pleased, but they realised they had reached a stalemate. So they came to an agreement. The goddesses would rule the surface of the world, bringing life (and death) back to it, as it was before. Gormalech would go deep underground, where iron and all the other metals come from anyway, and between them they would share the place.

'They called their agreement "the Balance", and promised each other that they would abide by it. From then until the end of time.

'And that is how the story goes.' Brigid dipped a clay cup into the water bowl that sat by the fire and took a long drink. 'Bless my ears, that's the most I've spoken in decades.'

'So Gormalech is the one creating the Gorm?' Podkin said, his voice almost a whisper. 'Because he wants the world back again, do you think? But that means the Balance is broken, because the Gorm are winning now, aren't they?'

'They are. The Balance is indeed broken, my dear. They've found some way to wriggle out of it. They're growing in power. The old magic of the goddesses is under threat.'

Podkin looked over to where Starclaw and Brigid's sickle lay together on the kitchen bench. 'They wanted our dagger. That's what Scramashank was after when he killed Father. But why?'

Brigid shrugged. 'Spite, maybe. Or something worse. I've heard they want the Twelve Gifts destroyed, so that all knowledge of the gods and goddesses fades forever.' She looked down and noticed Podkin was trembling with fear at the thought. 'Don't worry, little one. Magic is a balance, like I said. If it swings too much one way, just means that sometime soon it's going to swing back the other. That's the rules of the deal, don't forget, and that was a deal that can never be broken.'

Podkin thought on that for a moment, and realised it meant that the Gorm were due some revenge. Even though he was still trembling a bit, he managed a hard little smile. Looking up at his sister, he saw she was smiling too.

*

The children missed their parents terribly, and wished more than anything that they could just go home to find everything back the way it was. But even so, the little house in the woods had started to seem like a safe, happy place.

It was only one day, when Paz noticed Brigid scraping the last of her dried nettle leaves from a pot to make soup, that they realised they had to move on. It wasn't fair for the old rabbit to suddenly have to provide for three hungry mouths.

'But she can find more food,' Podkin said, when Paz mentioned it to him. 'She's got you to help her forage now.'

'Yes, but it's winter. And a hard one too. Have you seen how much soup Pook gets through in a day?'

'But where will we go? Redwater was the only safe place we knew, and look how that turned out.'

Podkin ran his fingers over the stump where his left ear had once been.

Paz gave his arm a squeeze. 'Brigid will know of somewhere,' she said.

*

So they asked the old rabbit that night. As it often was with her, it seemed as though she had been expecting the question.

'There is a place, my dears,' she said, with a sigh. 'Not a nice place, or a safe one, but a place where the Gorm won't think to look for you.'

She told them of a town of runaways and refugees that had sprung up amongst the crumbling tombs of an ancient graveyard. An underground warren at the forest's edge, amongst the bones and teeth of creatures long gone from the world.

'Boneroot, it's called. You'll have to be careful there and keep your wits about you, but I promise you, there won't be anyone turned by the Gorm. Every rabbit in the place has run away from them. All their warrens have been taken or enslaved, or just plain burnt to ash. They hate the Gorm as much as I do, and that's a whole lot of hating.'

There were mercenaries there, she said: soldiers you could hire to work for you. She pointed to the silver bracelet Paz wore, and the gold buckle on Podkin's belt. 'If you trade those precious things, you might get someone to fight on your side. Someone to protect you – maybe take you somewhere safe, off across the Eiskalt mountains, where the Gorm have never been. That's what I'd do, if I was you.'

Podkin listened to all this with a sad dread. The last thing he wanted was to go out into the cold, cruel outside world where bits of you got cut off and lost forever. He kept thinking Brigid would change her mind and ask them to stay ... Maybe if he looked especially scared and miserable? But of course, she didn't. She always seemed to know what was going to happen. If *she* thought they were leaving, that meant there was no getting out of it.

Paz, who had spent more time with the old witch, knew a little of how Brigid could unpick and unravel threads of knowledge from the future. Was going to Boneroot something they had to do? Was it part of Podkin's story that she kept mentioning? But if it was a good thing, then why did she sound so sad? What

was going to happen to them there? The worries buzzed around her head, making it spin.

Pook didn't want to leave, either. He clutched a few of Brigid's bone pieces in his paw and tried to catch hold of her cloak whenever she moved near him. Paz could see her keeping away on purpose, but reluctantly, as if it was something she had to do. How hard it must be, to know the events that had to happen for the future to unfurl just the way it should. Especially if some of those events were hard or unhappy ones. Would she be able to let them happen, no matter how much it hurt, just because they had to? Paz didn't think she had that kind of strength. It made her admire the old rabbit even more.

Brigid gave them directions for Boneroot, sketched in charcoal on a piece of bark. As a parting gift, she produced some winter cloaks with hoods, knitted hats and scarfs. They were all exactly the right sizes for each of them, but had been folded and put away for so long, they had to have the dust shaken off. Podkin couldn't work out how she had done it.

She had also made him a cloth scabbard in which he could carry Starclaw, strapped to his back and hidden away. She warned him to guard the dagger well, as it was valuable beyond any treasure, and made him promise that he would never let the Gorm touch it.

Finally, they stood in the snow beneath the old oak tree and said their goodbyes. The little rabbits all hugged Brigid and kissed her wrinkled nose. She had tears in her eyes as she waved them off.

As she glanced back through the trees, Paz thought that she saw the sickle on Brigid's belt give a silver glimmer of goodbye, and Podkin, although he had no idea why, felt his magic dagger grow heavier at his side.

CHAPTER EIGHT

Boneroot

Following Brigid's map, the young rabbits found the Red River again and walked along to where it forked. There was a little bridge made of fallen logs lashed together, which they slipped and slid across, and then they followed the smaller branch south again. Before them lay Grimheart forest, a huge mass of trees that filled the entire horizon. The silver-grey, frosted branches were like an ocean of icy wood; the whole Gorm army could be hidden in there, or a thousand packs of hungry wolves, thirsty for blood. Robbers, bandits, murderers – Podkin's

imagination ran through them all, until he found it hard to force his feet towards it.

Luckily, they were only going to skirt the forest itself, heading to the east and keeping to the edge of the woods where the trees were thinnest.

Their breath steamed out in misty halos around their heads, but their cloaks and hats kept them warm. Every crunching step, every twig that snapped under their feet, they expected to see a Gorm crow burst from the trees to call its masters down on them. Their ears (or ear, in Podkin's case) were constantly twitching as they listened for the clank of iron armour or the harsh, jagged sound of Gorm-speak.

But either the Gorm had exhausted their search of the forest or Brigid had laid some special charm on their new cloaks. They passed undisturbed and unseen through the frozen winter trees.

Brigid said the journey would take them at least two days and, following her advice, they stopped for the night, found a big snowdrift and scooped out a little cave inside. Pook thought it was great fun, as they all packed the snow hard to make the

walls of their little burrow. He had been too small to enjoy the snow last year, and there had been so little time this winter, what with preparing for Bramblemas, and then ... everything that happened after. Paz and Podkin watched him roll in the powdery snow, tasting ice crystals on his tongue and remembering snowball fights and snow burrows they had made in the winters past. How simple everything was then, and how little they had appreciated it.

Their shelter was finished before darkness drew in. They were quite proud of their work: Podkin even built a little wooden shelf for a beeswax candle. He had great fun chopping a whole tree to pieces in the process, delighting in the way Starclaw swished through the trunk as if it was an over-boiled carrot. He might have reduced half the forest to matchwood if Paz hadn't stopped him.

Supper was a small meal of oatcakes and dried beetroot slices, washed down with melted snow-water. When they curled up to sleep for the night, their den was actually very snug and cosy.

Podkin lay awake, looking out through the tunnel

at the stars in the night sky. He could see the Big Radish, the Rat and the Snake: all constellations his mother had taught him as he sat on her knee, looking up at the night sky. She had been on his mind a lot lately, ever since his ear had begun to heal. Rushing to Redwater and the pain of what happened there had been so awful – only now had he started to realise that they'd no idea of what had happened to her.

He nudged Paz awake with his foot.

'What?' she whispered. 'Is something outside?'

'No. Just the stars.'

'What is it then? I'm trying to sleep.'

'It's Mother,' said Podkin. 'We ran off so fast, we don't know whether she's alive or . . .' He was about to say 'killed by the Gorm', but it reminded him too much of that last sight of his father, facing down Scramashank with his sword drawn. He couldn't bring himself to speak the words.

'I don't know,' said Paz. 'I hope she's all right, but it's not like we can go back and check. If we do, the Gorm will take us, just like they did the Redwater children.'

'If she *is* back there,' Podkin continued. 'D'you think she'll be like Lady Russet? D'you think she'll start working for the Gorm?'

Paz started to laugh, but it made Pook stir from where he was snuggled against her, so she put a hand over her mouth. 'Can you imagine Mother doing that?'

At first Podkin was shocked. How could she laugh about it, after everything that had happened? But then he imagined his mother, the mighty Lady of Munbury, bowing down and scraping like a humble servant. It just wouldn't be right. Podkin smiled too, then felt tears suddenly spring to his eyes. His fierce, proud mother. She had once chased the chieftain of Deepdell warren out of the longburrow for being rude to his father. Even the toughest warriors in the Munbury Guard were terrified of her and her steely glare. He gave a silent prayer to the Goddess that she was out there, somewhere, looking up at the stars, just like him.

'What's the point in loving people, Paz, if they only get taken away from you? I know we'll never see Father again. Or Mother, probably. It hurts

so much to think of it ... I almost wish I'd never had parents.'

Paz was silent for a moment before rolling closer and putting an arm around him. 'It does hurt, Pod. It hurts more than anything in the world. I think it always will. That's just part of our life now. But we have to be strong. That's what Father would have wanted.'

Podkin sighed and snuggled into his big sister. 'I know. I was just saying.'

'Besides. They aren't really gone. They'll always be with us. No matter what the Gorm do, we will remember them. They can't take our memories away, can they?'

'Do you still hear Father's voice sometimes? In your head?' Podkin asked. But Paz had fallen asleep, her quiet snores blending with Pook's in their tiny scooped-out snow burrow.

'I do,' Podkin whispered to himself. And then he buried his head in his arms and cried himself silently to sleep.

*

It was late afternoon on the next day when they arrived at Boneroot. Brigid had told them to look out

for carved symbols on the tree trunks. A circle, like the snake picture she had shown them, marked with the Ogham symbols for *b* and *r*.

Pook had been the first to spot one, even though he shouldn't have had any idea what they were talking about. He had pointed to a gnarled willow trunk, shouting and cooing so much that Podkin was worried he would bring the Gorm down on them. When they finally got him to be quiet, they noticed the symbol, chopped into the bark and smeared with mud to make it look old.

Once they'd found one, they became easier to spot, and more frequent. It was like following a treasure trail, or hunting for the little painted wooden carrots that used to be hidden in the meadow every Lupen's Day at the start of spring.

Next they had to look out for the stone tree that Brigid had described. Podkin thought this might be just a riddle, until he almost walked into it.

Jutting up from a clutch of bramble bushes, the carved stone was as broad as an ancient oak. It curved at the top, and was spattered all over in crusty patches of overlapping lichen. Stepping back to look

at it, Podkin realised it was actually the remains of an arched doorway.

The rabbits stared at it for a while. It was a wonder to them why anyone would build something like this above ground, and how they had even managed to do it. The thing towered over them, sculpted so cleanly. There had been a stone fireplace in the Munbury warren, but everything else had been built out of wood, carved all over with patterns of twining leaves and the daisy that had been their tribal symbol. To make something this big out of stone would have taken such effort; and it was only *part* of a doorway. What had the rest of the building been like?

A voice suddenly echoed out of nowhere, making them all jump. 'Who goes there?' They looked around the darkening woods, trying to spot its owner, but couldn't see anything. Surely it hadn't come from the stone pillar itself?

'Erm . . . hello?' Podkin called.

'I said, *who goes there*?' The voice repeated. This time it clearly came from somewhere near the ground. They peered at the roots of the bramble bush

and were surprised to see a hole hidden there. A pair of eyes peeked out, staring at them suspiciously.

'Just some children,' said Podkin, remembering what Brigid had told them to say. 'We've come to buy herbs for our master. He gave us a map to follow.' He demonstrated this by waving the piece of bark in the air.

'You won't find many herbs left at this time of year,' said the voice. 'And this is no place for children.'

'Please,' said Paz. 'If you don't let us in, we'll freeze. And if we don't come back with herbs, we'll get beaten.'

'Hmpf,' said the voice. 'Let me see your eyes then.'

At first Podkin thought this was a strange request, but then he realised what the guard was checking for: signs of the red rust of the Gorm. Proof that the evil iron poison hadn't possessed them.

One by one they knelt and stared at the guard-rabbit, pulling their eyelids down so he could see them better. He must have been satisfied, as there was a grunt and the sound of a door being unbolted. All of a sudden, the ground around the hole fell away

to reveal a tunnel, lit inside by flickering candles. The owner of the eyes was standing there: a scarred old warrior rabbit with a long braided beard and patched leather armour. He looked like the veteran of several fierce battles, ones in which his enemies ended up with several missing body parts. Podkin wouldn't want to be someone trying to sneak past *him* into Boneroot.

He beckoned them in, all the while keeping one hand on his sword hilt and a frown on his face. 'You can go down, but if you want my advice, buy your herbs and get out quick. There's rabbits down there that'll eat you lot for breakfast. While you're still squeaking too.'

They walked past the guard very quickly, careful to nod him a polite thank you, and emerged into a long tunnel, which sloped steeply downwards. Every warren that Podkin had ever been in had had a grand entrance burrow, paved or tiled, hung with tapestries or plastered and painted. This was just a muddy tunnel, roots poking out the sides, lit by a few smoky candles. What had they just walked into?

Behind them, they heard the door thumping

closed, shutting them inside Boneroot. There was nothing else to do but keep going on down the tunnel and into whatever lay beyond.

*

The first thing Podkin noticed was the smell.

He had grown up in a warren, and no matter how clean and hygienic the rabbits, a large amount of furry bodies in a small enclosed space always gave a certain spice to the air. Especially if there had been turnips for dinner. Or, Goddess have mercy, beetroot curry.

This smell was something completely different. It was more than just an aroma; it was a solid, living wall, and walking down the tunnel was like doing a running leap headfirst into it. It nearly knocked the little rabbits over. Every smell in the world was there, all blended into one musty, meaty, fruity, furry pong.

'Takes yer breath away, don't it?' came the voice of the guard-rabbit behind them, who must have heard their disgusted gasps. They couldn't even reply. Squinting against the stench, they carried on down the tunnel to find just what it was that smelt so bad.

It was rabbits. Hundreds of rabbits.

There were hordes of them, in every shade and colour of fur. Brown rabbits, white rabbits; piebald, skewbald, spotted and brindled. Giant rabbits, towering over the crowds; tiny Elfin dwarves, smaller than children; fluffy-maned Lionheads, spotted Harlequins, velvety Rexs, woolly Angoras. And then many more breeds and tribes that Podkin had never seen or heard of. All these creatures, scared out of their homes by the Gorm. How many of these rabbits felt as lost and alone as he did?

The noise was almost as loud as the smell: a babbling surge of chatter, music and shouting that washed over them as soon as they stepped out of the tunnel and into a huge chamber, in which the swarms of rabbits rattled like beans in a jar.

The stone archway was nothing compared to what Podkin saw now. More pillars of carved and fluted stone stretched down from the chamber ceiling to the floor, holding everything together and allowing this enormous space to exist. It was a colossal cavern: big enough to fit ten longburrows with room to spare.

Up above, the roof was a mass of roots and vines

that twisted down the ancient stone and ran across the chamber floor. The pillars, the roots, the walls – every spare inch of them were draped with lanterns or studded with thick candles that had spilt rivers of melted wax over everything.

In between the stone columns, the rabbits had created the craziest, most bustling market Podkin had ever seen. The place was blurred with stalls and kiosks selling all sorts of goods. There were grand painted booths, tables draped with cloth, and in some places just tatty blankets spread on the floor.

Trader rabbits stood amongst them, behind them, on top of them – haggling and arguing with customers, shouting out their wares and filling the chamber with so much noise it made Podkin's head spin. There was mead for sale; roasted, stewed, fried and boiled vegetables of every description; clay pots, candles, lamps, weapons, clothes, armour, musical instruments, potions, charms, books and scrolls, wooden toys and dolls ... too much to even begin to take in.

Who was in charge here? Who was keeping the order in this crazy mess? He could see no guards or

soldiers anywhere. The whole place was free to do just what it liked, and yet somehow it was working.

The little rabbits stood for several minutes, blinking with wide eyes and trying to take it all in. They suddenly realised that Munbury warren – the place they had thought of as the centre of the world – had actually been a tiny scrap of a home compared to this.

'Wow,' Podkin finally managed to say.

'Yes,' agreed Paz. 'Wow.'

'Soop,' added Pook.

The whole thing reminded Podkin of the Tinker Fair that used to come to Munbury just after Summertide each year. A mismatched collection of wagons and tents, with goods from all over the Five Realms spread out for sale. There were always jugglers too, and acrobats, fire-breathers, stilt-walkers.

'Looks like the Fair, doesn't it?' Paz said, thinking the same thing.

'Do you remember the year Father tried to swallow fire?'

'And he singed his beard right off?'

Podkin started to chuckle, but then he remembered that his father was gone. Instead of laughing, he felt like something was broken. His eyes met Paz's. He knew she felt it too. The world itself was wrong now: incomplete. How could it go on like it always had, with people buying and selling knick-knacks and trinkets, when his father was no longer a part of it?

These rabbits hadn't even known Lopkin of Munbury had existed. The three children stood in silence, letting the sounds and smells of the market wash over them.

'Well,' said Paz, a few moments later. 'Where d'you think we should start looking? For the mercenaries?'

It took Podkin a moment to remember that was why they were here. He forced himself to return to the present and its problems. A mercenary. A guardian. But how were you supposed to find anything in such a nameless jumble of rabbits?

'We could try asking someone?'

'What an amazing idea. You must be some kind of genius.'

'You don't have to be so sarcastic,' said Podkin, scowling. 'Have you got any better ideas?'

'Ideas? What would I have ideas for? I'm not the chieftain, am I? Girls aren't allowed to be chiefs, remember?' Paz tucked Pook under her shoulder and trotted over to speak to the nearest stallholder, a black-furred rabbit selling jars of pickled beetroot, forcing Podkin to scurry after her. 'Excuse me – do you know where we can hire soldiers? Is there a shop or a booth or something?'

'Soldiers? You mean sellswords?' The rabbit looked the children up and down, suspicious. Her eyes seemed to linger on Paz's silver bracelet and Podkin's belt buckle. 'What do you little 'uns need hired thugs for?'

'We're just curious, that's all.' Podkin couldn't think of a convincing lie quickly enough. The rabbit raised an eyebrow and pointed across the hall to a fenced-off area next to one of the pillars.

'Over there. But you won't find much worth hiring. All the fighters I know have been scared off by the Gorm. Fled, they have – less dangerous over the mountains. Can I interest you in a jar of beetroot?'

After politely declining, they edged their way through the crush of bodies until they reached the

sellsword stall. They could see a few ragged rabbits lounging around inside the fenced-off area: a broad, muscular buck with long snow-white fur that he wore spiked into porcupine points all over his head, whose left arm and leg were splinted and bandaged. A black-furred giant with torn ears and a missing arm. A brown, spotted Harlequin rabbit with a wooden leg and a crutch.

Podkin's gaze was caught by one grey-furred rabbit with blank white eyes who sat silent and still in a corner. Was that all Boneroot had to offer? Some ragged, worn-out scrappers, one of whom was blind? They would be better off facing the Gorm on their own.

'I don't think much of that lot,' said Podkin.

Paz nodded. 'Me neither. Although I suppose they won't cost much to hire. My bracelet will pay for the lot of them twice over.'

Podkin was about to walk into the enclosure to find out, but he never got the chance. A strong-fingered hand gripped his arm so tightly that it hurt, and he felt the sharp sting of a knife tip pressed against his ribs.

He saw Paz's eyes go wide with fear, and looked up to see an evil-faced rabbit with patchy brown fur and mean orange eyes. He leant over them and whispered with breath that stank of rotten vegetables and stale mead.

'You three little nippers are mine now. And your pretty jewellery too. Come along with me, nice and quiet, or I'll chop this one's other ear off. Snickety snip.'

He grinned, showing yellow broken teeth, and pushed his knife harder into Podkin's chest so that Podkin yelped. There was nothing Paz could do but follow as her brother was dragged off, out of the hall and into the maze of endless side tunnels.

CHAPTER NINE

Shape and Quince

P odkin was dragged deeper and deeper into the Boneroot tunnels, the stinking rabbit's hand tight around his arm, his knife jabbing in his ribs. He could hear Paz following behind, and Pook quietly crying. Every now and then the rabbit looked over his shoulder and made a comment. 'That's it, little girl. You just keep following nicely and I won't have to slice up your brother.'

The further they got from the marketplace, the quieter it was. The noise of the market was still there,

131

but muffled and distant, as if the whole thing had been a dream.

At first there had been some signs of life and light – shop fronts and houses – along the tunnel sides: a pickled-radish vendor; a line of washing hung up to dry; a tavern. But now there was just the odd empty burrow-mouth – dark lonely voids in the tunnel, which was already being slowly choked and filled up with spidery roots. Podkin wondered, in between sharp prickles of the knife in his side, whether the whole world would one day look like that, once rabbitkind had crumbled into dust. The roots, moss and earth would slowly crawl over everything, hiding it away like they had never existed at all.

Every so often they came across a piece of rib, or a jawbone, jutting down from the roof or sticking up out of the floor. People had propped candles on top of some, and they were now decorated with stalactites of dribbled wax. Who did they once belong to? Who buried them? If he wasn't in fear for his life, Podkin might have stopped to ponder it all.

It was damp here: mildewy and rotten. There were piles of mouldering rubbish all over the floor,

adding to the stink of decay. Mushrooms grew out of the tunnel sides, glowing pale in the murk, like strange little ghosts or the eyes of lurking monsters. Every now and then, something wriggled on the floor. Fat, pale earthworms or grubs of some kind. Podkin heard Paz step on one. There was a soft *pop*, followed by a muffled squeal. She always had hated creepy crawlies. That's what made it so much fun to hide them in her bed, back in Munbury.

Oh, if only they were back in Munbury.

Podkin thought about trying to draw the dagger and fight the big rabbit off, but it was too tricky to get to. By the time he'd untangled it from its cloth scabbard, the smelly oaf would probably have chopped him into pieces. Then the rabbit would have Starclaw as well. There was absolutely nothing Podkin could do.

Finally they came to a burrow entrance, out at the furthest reaches of the tunnel. There were mounds of rotting scraps piled outside. Half-chewed radishes, shards of broken pottery, sticky pools of mush that might once have been food. The entire floor of the tunnel was heaving and pulsing with maggots.

A dim glow seeped out from the doorway. Podkin had a few seconds to wonder what terrors might lie within, and then the smelly rabbit pulled back the tattered blanket that covered the entrance and shoved him through. Paz and Pook were pushed after, crashing into his back and knocking them both to the floor.

'Well, well, what have you caught, Quince?'

Podkin looked up to find himself in a small burrow. A typical living area for most warren rabbits, but one that seemed tiny to him. The walls were bare earth, a patch of old whitewash here and there, but more patches of black mould and bubbling fungus.

There was a large wooden chest by one wall, and two cages made of crudely lashed-together hazel branches against the other. The rest of the floor space was covered with piles of empty and broken clay bottles, gnawed carrot tops and layers of dust and cobwebs. This was a neglected and half-derelict place. It smelt stale and putrid, almost as bad as the tunnel outside.

A small fireplace was hidden amongst the junk, and a few sputtering, smoky logs were burning there,

giving the place a hazy orange glow. Sitting beside it, warming his belly, was another rabbit: a huge fat lop, his ears held back by a stained bandana. He had a long braided beard with a silver bell tied at the end, and was watching them with small eyes. By his side was a huge wooden club, studded at one end with rusty spikes and nails.

'I have hit the jackpot, Mister Shape,' said the smelly rabbit, Quince. 'Two posh little bunnies and one little sprogling. Found them peering at the sellswords like they was at a zoo or something.'

'Sellswords, eh? Well, if they wanted to see the best fighter in Boneroot, they only had to come here for a peek.' The fat rabbit stood up, his stomach rolling off his lap to hang about his knees. He wore shoulder pads and leather greaves, but his great scarred belly was bare and as broad as an oak trunk. 'Get them up so I can look at them.'

Podkin felt his good ear being pulled, bringing him to his feet. Paz was yanked up too, squealing in pain. Pook whined and tried to hide in his big sister's tunic.

'Hern's whiskers! Look at that belt buckle!

And that bracelet. They look awful heavy for such little kittens. Perhaps you should lighten their load, Quince.'

The smelly rabbit laughed and roughly pulled off Paz's bracelet. He grabbed Podkin's belt and sawed through the leather with his knife. Podkin wanted to shout about how it had been a Midwinter present from his father, but the look on Mister Shape's face made him keep his mouth shut.

'They got anything else, Quince?'

Podkin felt the weasely rabbit's hand close over Starclaw's scabbard, and the knife was yanked free. He closed his eyes in despair. *The one thing you were told to keep safe, and you couldn't even do that.*

'Just this crummy old butter knife, Mister Shape. Doesn't look fit to trim me toenails with.'

Shape gave it a glance, but he was more interested in the buckle and bracelet that Quince had just tossed him. 'We'll consider that your first night's rent paid,' said Shape. 'You can keep that toy knife for now. You couldn't do any harm with it anyway. And it might come in handy for cutting purses. After all, you'll be earning your room and board in future.' Both

the nasty rabbits laughed hard at this joke, although Podkin had no idea what it meant. 'Show them their room, Quince.'

The smelly rabbit went over to the wooden cages. He pulled open the door to one, and the three little rabbits were kicked inside.

'Just in case you are thinking of sneaking out in the night,' said Mister Shape, 'you should know one of us is always awake, watching you very closely.'

Quince cackled and waved his knife in the candlelight so it sparkled, leaving the rabbits in no doubt as to what would happen to them if they tried to escape. As the evil rabbits laughed some more, Podkin and Paz looked at each other, wide-eyed and terrified.

*

The rest of that night felt endless, uncomfortable and frightening. Podkin and Paz sat in their little cage, staring out at the burrow where Quince and Shape sat, while Pook snuggled between them, whining for food. Once or twice they tried to whisper to each other, but the two villains always heard them. Quince had a long stick he used to poke and prod

them through the bars, trying his best to crack them on the heads or shins where it really hurt. In the end they gave up trying to speak, and just sat in miserable silence.

Podkin noticed the huddled shape of two other rabbits in the second cage. Small ones. Children like him, probably. They had obviously learnt not to make any sound. Once he thought that he glimpsed an eye peeking at him before blinking shut again. He wondered how long they had been there, trapped without anyone to rescue them. The thought made him shudder.

After Goddess knows how long, Pook whimpered himself to sleep, Paz too seemed to have drifted off, and snores started to come from the two big rabbits guarding them on the other side of the bars. *This is my chance*, Podkin thought. *But what can I do?*

Podkin's scared little mind whirred, trying to think of a plan, but came up with nothing. *What would Father have done?* He tried to listen for the reassuring voice inside his head, but there was only silence. *Would he have sat here and waited for what misery morning would bring?* Never. By now, he

would probably have sliced through the bars and run charging at the villains, ready to chop them into rabbit hotpot.

Well *that* wasn't going to happen. He had missed every single one of his weapons lessons. He barely knew the handle of a sword from the pointy end. But maybe he could cut a small hole in the bars for them to sneak out? It sounded like a much better plan, with a lot less slicing.

He thought he might be able to slide Starclaw out from under his cloak and chop through the cage bars, and was just inching his hand across to do it when a voice from the shadows outside made him freeze.

'I'm still awake, you little rat-weasel,' came Shape's deep, rumbling tones. 'And I'll be awake for the next two hours, until it's Quince's turn to watch you. You'll not get away that easy.'

The fat rabbit chuckled to himself, and settled back to sipping mead, or whatever he was doing. Sure enough, ages later, he nudged Quince awake, and lay down to sleep on a scrap of blanket.

Quince is smaller, Podkin thought. *Maybe I could get out and lop off his head before he could wake*

up Shape? But he knew he wouldn't do it. Toppling a tree on someone is one thing; chopping a rabbit's head off would be unbearable.

Waiting 'til morning it is then. Podkin couldn't help but feel he'd failed some kind of test. But then he was well used to failing tests. In fact, he was probably an expert at it.

Sorry, Father. I'm just not a hero like you. He rubbed the bare spot where his belt buckle had been and dreamt memories of the Bramblemas day he had unwrapped it, with his proud father smiling on.

*

Come morning, a bleary-eyed, exhausted Podkin sat in a corner of the cage. Paz and Pook had both had a pretty good night's sleep, all things considered. But Podkin had barely managed to catch a wink. Noises from outside the cage had stirred them, and the three rabbits gave each other nervous glances, wondering what horrible thing was going to happen next.

Both Shape and Quince were up now. They opened the cage door and dragged Podkin out by his collar. The little rabbit stood in the dingy burrow, swaying on his feet, while they pulled another rabbit

out of the second cage. It was a tiny brown rabbit with a fuzzy cotton ball of a face and pointy little ears. Another, just like it, peered sadly through the cage bars.

'Listen up, new boy,' said Mister Shape, bending down over his fat belly to peer in Podkin's face. 'You're going to go back to the market to spend the rest of this lovely day begging, scrounging and stealing everything you can get your little paws on.'

'Food, we want,' said Quince. 'And drink. And money. And anything we can sell to make money.'

'Basically,' Shape continued, 'we want you to fill your pockets with as much stuff as you can, and then bring it back here to us.'

'And if I don't?' Podkin asked. He didn't like the sound of stealing, much less coming back to this stinking ferret-hole of a burrow.

'Why, if you don't, then we might get hungry and decide to eat your big sister,' said Quince.

'A nice little snack she'd make, eh, Quincey?' said Shape, his broad belly rippling with laughter. Podkin gulped. Shape, suddenly serious again, grabbed him by the collar and pulled him close.

'She's our insurance.' He growled in Podkin's face. 'Keeping her safe is what makes you come back here every day.'

'Every day?'

'Oh yes.' Shape gave an evil grin. 'You work for us now. And you're going to be working for us for a *very* long time.'

In the cage, Pook started crying. And crying. And crying. It got louder and louder, until it became a piercing wail. Paz tried to quieten him, afraid of Quince's jabbing stick, but he wouldn't shush, not even when Paz mentioned soup. She looked out at Podkin, scared.

'Shut that brat up!' Shape yelled. 'Or by Hern's hairy kneecaps, I'll do it for you!' Quince made to grab for his stick, so Podkin quickly spoke.

'He won't be quiet, not as long as he's in that cage,' he said. 'I'll have to take him with me. You won't hear him then, and you've still got my sister to make sure I come back.'

He wasn't sure what he was going to do with Pook, exactly; he just knew he had to get him away from Quince and Shape. Perhaps the pair of them

could escape somehow? Come back with help for Paz? But there was nobody who would help them, now that they had no money to bargain with.

'Take him then,' Shape shouted. 'Just stop that flaming screeching!'

Quince opened the cage door and pulled Pook out of Paz's arms, then swung him at Podkin. Podkin just about managed to catch his little brother and at least the shock had stopped him crying for a moment.

'Right. Enough of this chin-wagging,' said Shape. 'Get out there and get us some loot.'

With several nudges from his bony foot, Quince shoved Podkin and the other rabbit out of the burrow and into the tunnel, then pulled the blanket shut. Podkin managed to catch Paz's eyes for a moment as he left. She looked lonely, sad, frightened – but she had enough time to motion to him. A small, flicking movement with her fingers. *Run*, she meant. *Go. Leave.*

She was telling him to take Pook and not come back.

Chapter Ten

Fox Paw

Outside in the gloomy tunnel, Podkin stood and stared at the other little rabbit. She stared back for a moment, then shrugged her shoulders and hurried off down the tunnel, towards the market.

'Hey, wait up!' Podkin scampered after as best he could, struggling not to drop Pook in the process. He caught up with the rabbit by a flickering candle, which was balanced on the crumbling tip of some creature's leg bone, jutting out of the tunnel wall. The light threw wavering patterns over the dangling roots and piles of rubbish on the floor, making it seem like they were at the bottom of a particularly filthy lake.

The small rabbit gave him another impatient look, as if Podkin was keeping her from something important. 'Yes?'

Podkin stood, huffing and puffing, thinking of something to say. 'Um . . . hello. My name's Podkin. And this is Pook. I just . . . I was just wondering . . .'

'Look,' said the rabbit. 'I don't mean to be rude, but we really should get to the market as quickly as we can. If we don't come back at dusk with plenty of food and some coins . . . well, let's just say it won't be very pleasant.'

'Do you do this every day?' Podkin asked. 'Stealing and begging from the market? Haven't you tried to escape?'

'Escape?' The little rabbit looked at Podkin as if he was crazy. 'They've got my brother. How could I escape without him?'

'But your parents,' said Pod. 'Can't you find them? Can't you tell the guards or the chieftain or someone?'

'My parents are fifty years old and living in a warren on the other side of the Eiskalt mountains.' When Podkin looked at her as if she was talking Thriantan, she sighed and shook her head. 'I'm not

145

a *child*, Popkin – or whatever your name is. My brother and I are dwarf rabbits. I might be as small as you, but I'm actually fully grown. Those stupid ferret-brained lumps back there think we're children too. That's why they grabbed us.'

'Have you been there long?'

The dwarf rabbit shrugged. 'Six months, I think. Although it seems like longer. They had another rabbit caged up when we got there, but he got sick and died. They buried him further up the tunnel.'

Podkin gulped. He really didn't want to end up shovelled into a shallow grave in this dingy, miserable place.

'So, you see, it's best to try and keep them happy. That way they don't hit you. Try and find as much food as you can, but don't get caught stealing anything. There aren't any guards in this place, and definitely no chieftain, but the stallholders do horrible things to thieves.'

The dwarf rabbit patted Podkin on the shoulder, and then turned and headed up the tunnel. Podkin watched her go, calling out before she disappeared from sight: 'It's *Podkin*, not Popkin!'

'Sorry!' The rabbit called back. 'I'm Mishka. But you can call me Mish. My brother is Mashka.' And then she was gone.

Mish and Mash, Podkin thought. Well, at least they weren't in this mess completely on their own.

'Mish!' said Pook.

*

Some time later, Podkin and Pook stepped out of the side tunnel and into the market hall once more. Again, he was hit by the wall of stink and noise, although this time his nose was a little more used to it. He could actually pick out some smells: spices, frying vegetables, roasted coffee, tanned leather, burning incense; each one fought with the other, trying not to be overpowered, and making his head spin.

He stared out at the heaving mass of rabbits, all bustling about their business. From somewhere out there, he had to find enough food and coins to keep Shape and Quince happy, and avoid getting caught and strung up by the ears (or ear) in the process. He felt sick with fear. To top it all, his arms were already weak and burning from carrying and dragging Pook down the tunnel, and he had never stolen anything

in his life. His mother always used to say that the Goddess thought very poorly of thieves and robbers. Would she understand if a little rabbit was doing it to save his sister's life?

His eyes drifted across the seething marketplace to the entrance tunnel, which was little more than a dark hole across the crowded cavern. Did Paz really want them to leave without her? Could he even do such a thing? She was his big sister. Annoying, yes. Bossy, definitely. But she was near enough the only family he had left. And he did love her very much (even though he would never admit it).

Besides, she was the one with all the ideas – the quick thinker, always coming up with a plan in an instant. He was just the lazy, spoilt chieftain's son, daydreaming and snoozing around until he became head of the tribe and could daydream and snooze even more. He wouldn't last ten minutes looking after Pook by himself.

Paz would never leave me behind, he thought. *So I'm not going to leave her.* He took a deep breath and began to look around for something to steal.

So, where should he start? Cutting some rabbit's

purse? That was obviously what Shape expected him to do, leaving him Starclaw. He had no idea how to go about it, though. And what if you got caught? *The stallholders do horrible things to thieves*, Mish had said. He wondered what that could be. Throwing them in a dungeon? Sticking red-hot pokers into their squidgy bits? Chopping off their hands? He'd already lost an ear so he really should start being more careful about holding on to his body parts.

How about grabbing something from a stall? There were hot pies over there, and next to it a rabbit selling clay jugs of mead. Was he fast enough to snatch something and run for it? Not with having to carry Pook as well. Maybe he should have left him crying in the cage. Perhaps if Shape had got sick enough of the noise, he might have let them all go.

'Soop!' Pook said. 'Soop! Soop!'

'You're not having any soup,' Podkin told him, but there was a soup-seller nearby, and the delicious smell was everywhere.

'Soop!' Pook screamed. Podkin started to pull his little brother away from the tempting odours, round behind a stone pillar where the air was

more dank and musty. But it didn't have any effect on Pook's howling, which was getting louder, if anything. What did his mother use to do when this happened? Smack his bottom? Shove a rotten turnip in his mouth?

No, she used to distract him with something. Take his mind off his stomach for a moment until he forgot what he was screaming about.

'Look, Pook. Over there! A really fat rabbit selling carrots . . .'

'Ca-ot! Ca-ot!'

'No, no . . . bad example. Look over there! A big lop rabbit! Look at his long ears, and on his stall he's got . . . oh.'

'Hu-ny! Hu-ny!'

Podkin felt like crying. He sank to the floor, amongst all the muck and rubbish from the market, and let Pook's shouts merge with the noise of the stalls into one big thunderous racket. There was no way he could find enough loot to keep Quince happy. There was no way he could escape Boneroot along with his brother and sister, and even if he did, the Gorm were looking for him everywhere. What was

the point? He might as well just lay here in the dirt until he starved to death and . . .

Something hard was under his leg. Something round and hard. Something round and hard and coin-shaped.

Holding his breath, he dug his paw into the grime and muck beneath him and fished it out. It looked like a lump of sticky old mud, but when he rubbed it against his cloak, the unmistakeable glint of metal shone through.

'Oooh!' Pook said. 'Shiny!'

Quickly, Podkin polished off the rest of the dirt. It was a large coin, marked with a rabbit's head and made of an orangey-brown metal. Copper, he thought, or bronze. Having never worried about money before, he wasn't sure what it was worth. Not as much as gold or silver, definitely, but might it be enough to satisfy Quince and Shape?

'This is good, Pook,' he said. 'But we need more, I think. Can you help me find some more?'

'Shiny!' Pook squealed, and started rummaging around in the dirt and rotten food of the market floor. Surely there had to be more coins hidden in all this

litter, and scavenging for it was much safer than stealing. Podkin got on his hands and knees and joined him.

*

An hour later, they had covered half of the market, scrabbling about in the dirt between the stalls. Podkin had been kicked in the ribs by two stallholders and chased off by several more. And they had nothing to show for it except an old apple core, which Pook was now sucking on. That and the original copper coin. So much for his get-rich-quick idea.

'This is not good, Pook,' he said.

The little rabbit wasn't listening. Something had caught his attention on the other side of the market. 'Bone! Bone!'

Pook had dropped his soggy apple core and was pointing excitedly at a dingy corner. Three or four scruffy-looking rabbits were crouched in a circle, taking turns to roll dice. Some kind of game, Podkin supposed.

'Bone!' Pook started crawling over. The dice must have reminded him of the casting bones he'd played with at Brigid's place. He was drawn to them in the same way.

Podkin didn't think the scruffy rabbits would take

kindly to a strange baby ruining their game. He jumped up and ran after Pook, grabbing him just before he managed to snatch up the dice in his chubby little paw.

'Oi, nibbler! Keep your brat out of our game!' A black and white rabbit with torn ears and brown teeth tried to slap at Pook as Podkin pulled him back.

'Yeah,' said another scrawny brown buck. 'Unless he wants to join in!'

Three of the rabbits roared with laughter, while the fourth looked miserable. He threw a handful of copper coins on to the floor and the others snatched them up. Podkin stared. A whole *handful* of coins.

'Are you playing for money?' he asked. He remembered seeing guards back at the warren doing something like this. His mother never allowed him to watch too closely.

'Fox Paw. Winner takes all,' said the brown rabbit. 'Care to chance your luck?'

Fox Paw. The name rang a bell. Wasn't it from that story Brigid had told them? The dice game the Goddess herself had played when she beat Gormaduke, or whatever he had been called. Surely that must be a sign?

A foolish rabbit and his radishes are easily

parted. That was what Auntie Olwyn always used to say. Or was it his mother? Someone much more sensible than him, anyway. It meant that gambling was for ferret-brains. They'd only managed to find one single coin all morning, and here he was thinking of throwing it away.

But... Pook had been so good at rolling the bones on Brigid's hearth. *A natural gift*, she'd said. And the little tinker was itching to do it again. What if it *was* a sign from the Goddess? He looked at the piles of coins lined up in front of the rabbits. *It is a stupid thing to do*, he thought, *but there's nobody around to tell me otherwise.* Just for once, he could be as stupid as he liked, and what if it worked?

'We're in,' he said, holding out his copper coin. 'But my brother gets to roll for me.'

The scruffy rabbits hooted and roared at this, so much that others wandered over to see what was going on. Soon there was a little crowd around the game, with Pook in the middle trying to grab at the dice.

'Let's play then,' said the brown rabbit. 'D'you know the rules?' When Podkin shook his head, he laughed even harder. 'There's three dice, see? Bone

ones, with six sides apiece. They're marked with a one, a two, a three, four, five and a fox's paw. Each time you roll, you add the numbers up. You can roll as many times as you like, but if you get one single fox paw, you're out. The one with the highest score at the end wins the money. Understand?'

Podkin nodded. Basically, you didn't want to roll a fox paw. Simple.

The black and white rabbit sneered at him. 'Seeing as it's your first game, you can start.'

'Roll, Pook,' Podkin said. The crowd behind him gave a little cheer. Pook grabbed the dice with glee and threw them down.

A whoop went up from the crowd, and Podkin realised he had been scrunching his eyes shut. He looked down to see two threes and a one.

'Beginner's luck,' said the brown rabbit. 'Roll again?'

Perhaps they should stop and keep the score, Podkin thought. He had no idea of what a good total was. If they rolled again, they risked losing everything. But that was what games of chance were all about, weren't they?

'Go on, Pook. Roll again.'

The little rabbit snatched the dice up and flung them. For one horrible moment, Podkin was sure there would be fox paws showing, but the crowd cheered again. A pair of twos and a three.

'Eleven,' said the brown rabbit. He was starting to look less amused. 'Roll again, why don't you? It's easy to get higher than that.'

'Stop there!' someone from the crowd called out. Other voices joined in: 'They'll never beat that!' 'Eleven's amazing!' 'The Goddess herself only rolled 9!' Podkin began to pull Pook back, but he had grabbed the dice again. He threw them in the air, chortling with joy.

'Pook!' Podkin yelled. He watched the dice spinning in slow motion, tumbling to the muddy floor and bouncing up and down again. Surely, this time, there would be a fox's paw showing. Instead, there were three fives.

'Cheat!' The black and white rabbit yelled. 'You must be cheating!'

The crowd behind Podkin booed and shouted at the black and white rabbit, and he quickly backed

down. He folded his arms and shot evil looks at Podkin across the circle.

'Have another go, little one,' the brown rabbit cooed at Pook, trying to make him lose his score. 'One more roll. It's such fun, isn't it?'

Podkin tightened his grip on Pook, but the little rabbit didn't even move to touch the dice. Instead, he wrapped his arms about his podgy legs and stared at the scruffy rabbits, as if daring them to go next.

The child's a born gambler, Podkin thought, amazed.

Seeing Pook's turn was over, the other rabbits tried their luck. The brown rabbit rolled a fox paw first time, as did the black and white. The third scruffy rabbit managed a second roll before he threw three fox paws together. There were cheers and whoops from all the onlookers. 'Pay up!' they called. 'Pay them their due!'

With sulky faces, the scruffy rabbits each handed over a copper coin. The money chinked heavily in Podkin's outstretched paws. By some miracle, he had turned one coin into five, when by rights he should be walking away with nothing.

'Shiny!' Pook said.

INTERLUDE

The bard stops talking and pauses for a moment to tug his beard. He gives his audience a thoughtful look. 'I suppose I should say a few words to you about gambling, and how it's a very stupid thing to do.'

'Podkin the Great did it,' says the inquisitive rabbit. 'And he was a hero.'

'And the Goddess herself,' added the sensible rabbit. 'And *she* is a goddess. Obviously.'

'My Uncle Colm does it all the time,' says another rabbit. 'He won a whole keg of mead once.'

'My daddy won a spear and a shield and a cloak and some trousers. In fact, everything the other rabbit was wearing.'

'Yes, yes, yes.' The bard waves his hands to stop the chattering. 'I'm sure lots of people have won

lots of things, including the Goddess herself. But for everything they won, I bet ... I mean, I'm *sure* ... they lost even more. Pook won because he had a touch of magic about him when it came to casting bones. Not many other rabbits have that blessing. Whatever tales of glory you've heard, gambling is for idiots.'

A cheer comes from the corner of the room where the guards are playing dice. The doorman has come off duty and seems to be winning.

The bard shrugs. 'I rest my case.'

'We get the picture,' says the sensible rabbit. 'Don't gamble. Now what did Podkin do with the money?'

The bard smiles and continues.

CHAPTER ELEVEN

Sellswords

If you recall me saying, Podkin didn't know much about money and what it was worth. He was a chieftain's son, and everything he'd ever wanted had been his without having to pay for it. A spoilt brat, some might say. But now that he'd had a sour taste of real life, those five copper coins clutched in his paw seemed like all the treasure in the world.

He tucked them inside his cloak and swiftly pulled Pook away from the dingy corner, back into the market throng. The last thing he wanted was those scruffy rabbits trying to steal their money

back, so he spent a while dodging to and fro, hiding behind stalls, roots and crumbling pillars. Once they were good and lost he stopped to think.

What should he do with his winnings? Give it all to Quince and Shape? The thought made him sick. Maybe he could give them a few coins and keep the rest hidden? But then they might search him . . .

He could buy Pook and himself something to eat, then take them the rest? Then he thought of poor Paz, shut up in that cage on her own, cold and scared and lonely. Spending money on themselves would just be selfish.

Looking around for inspiration, he saw that they were standing near the sellsword enclosure. The group of mercenaries were identical to the ones on show the last time they were here, and the agent was still sprawled by the gate, calling out his business with as much enthusiasm as a bored snail.

'Hired swords. Hired swords,' he mumbled. 'The fiercest fighters in the whole of the Five Realms. The greatest warriors in . . . whatever. Some of them fought somebody else once upon a time, and apparently they were quite good. Better than average, at least . . .'

Business must be slow with that kind of patter, Podkin thought. They'd be glad of any coin. With his five coppers, he might be able to hire the lot. Then he could take them back to Mister Shape's burrow and watch them make matching fur coats out of him and Quince.

Before he really knew what he was doing, he had marched up to the agent and prodded him in the belly.

'Excuse me,' Podkin said, in his best regal voice. 'Would you be the rabbit to see about hiring some mercenaries?'

The agent looked him up and down for a moment, and then roared with laughter. He didn't stop until tears were running down his face.

'That's very funny, kid, but go and play your games somewhere else. I'm trying to do business here.'

'It doesn't look like it,' said Podkin, with a sniff. 'I want to hire your men. All of them.' He pulled the coins from his cloak and held them out to the agent.

'Five coins? Five *whole* copper coins?'

'That's right,' said Podkin. 'Consider this your lucky day.'

'Ha!' The agent was about to laugh again, then

began to look irritated instead. 'Five poxy coppers? Do you know what that's worth? It'd get you half a mouldy carrot and a jug of ditchwater if you were lucky. It's not enough for a single one of my men! Goddess above, I don't know whether to laugh at you or clip your ears. Sorry . . . ear.'

'Not a single one?' Podkin's lovely visions of rescuing Paz and watching Shape and Quince get flattened vanished in a puff of smoke.

'Well, I say that . . .' the agent scratched his head. 'It'd get you *him*.' He pointed to the corner where the grey-furred, blank-eyed rabbit sat on his tattered blanket. 'For an afternoon.'

Podkin stared. A blind soldier rabbit for an afternoon. It was hardly the help and protection that Brigid promised they'd find. Could it even be enough to free Paz and give them the chance to escape Boneroot? Probably not, but what other choice did he have?

'I'll take him,' he said, handing over the money.

*

'Crom,' the grey rabbit said. 'My name is Crom.'

'And have you been a soldier long?' They were

standing just outside the sellsword enclosure, with Podkin craning his neck to look up at his new employee. Pook was trying to climb one of his legs. The grey rabbit, Crom, just stared straight ahead with those blank white eyes.

'Yes. Very long.'

His fur was criss-crossed with old scars, and his armour was dented and scratched. He looked like he'd seen a good deal of fighting, for sure, although Podkin wasn't sure how you could fight when you couldn't even see. 'But what about . . . your eyes?'

'I fought for a long time before this happened,' said Crom. 'And I can fight now. Just . . . differently.' Podkin nodded, still not convinced. The grey rabbit didn't seem bothered. He cleared his throat. 'May I ask you a question?'

'Um, yes?' Podkin said.

'Why is it you want to hire a sellsword, anyway? I can tell you're only a child. You shouldn't even be in a lowdown place like this.'

'Some rabbits have my sister,' Podkin said. 'They've got her shut in a cage, so that I'd come out

here and steal stuff for them. I need you to set her free, so that we can get out of this place.'

'Shape and Quince?' Crom said.

'Yes! Do you know them?'

'I've heard of them,' said the grey rabbit. He shrugged. 'I hear a lot of things.'

'Do you think you can beat them?' Podkin asked. 'I mean – Mister Shape is pretty big.'

'I can take care of myself,' said Crom, patting the sword at his side. It looked well-used and sharp. Bigger and scarier than Starclaw, although it didn't look as if it was magic.

'We'd better go then,' said Podkin, peeling Pook off Crom's leg. 'Before my time runs out.'

*

Somehow, they found the tunnel that Pod had emerged from earlier, and started walking back into the damp, musty darkness. Podkin led the way, glancing back now and then to see Crom walking with his arms outstretched, fingers tracing lightly along the earthen walls.

Halfway down, Podkin started struggling with Pook, and the little rabbit began to whimper with hunger.

'Give him here,' said Crom, and he hoisted him on to his broad back. Pook clung there, nuzzled against the scarred fur and gradually nodded off to sleep. Podkin thought it was worth the five coppers not to have to carry the little rabbit any more.

They had only gone a bit further when Crom suddenly stopped and looked behind them, his hand on his sword hilt.

'What is it?' Podkin asked.

'Someone's coming up the tunnel,' Crom whispered.

Podkin squinted back down towards the market. He could just about make out the silhouette of something hopping and scuttling back there. It grew closer as he watched, until he could see it was the dwarf rabbit – his fellow captive – scurrying after them as fast as he could run.

'Popkin,' she managed to gasp when she reached them. 'What ... what's going on? Who are you taking back to the burrow?'

'*Pod*kin,' corrected Pod. 'And this is Crom. He's a soldier I've hired to give Shape and Quince a good kicking.'

'To fight *Shape*?' said Mish. 'But your sellsword is . . . I mean he can't—'

'It doesn't matter that he can't see,' Podkin interrupted. 'He's still going to beat them. Aren't you, Crom?' There was a grunt from the darkness behind and above him. Podkin thought it sounded confident, although it didn't really matter. He'd thought of a way to give Crom an edge – quite literally.

'Are you sure about this?' Mish said. 'If it goes wrong, there's no telling what Shape and Quince will do. My brother . . .'

'It won't go wrong,' said Podkin. 'I promise. And we'll make sure both our siblings are freed.'

'If you can do that,' said Mish, 'I'll be in your debt forever.'

*

For the rest of the walk to the burrow, Podkin silently prayed to the Goddess that his plan would work. For the second time today he was about to gamble everything on a hunch. Either the Goddess herself was guiding him, or the stress of the past few days had driven him round the twist. He hoped it was the first option.

The tunnel grew darker and damper. Just as the stink of mildew and mushrooms became almost overpowering, they arrived at the blanket-covered entrance.

The three of them (four, if you included Pook) stood silently outside for a few moments, listening. Someone was snoring, and there was the crackle of a small fire. Every now and then there was a rustle of movement, and once or twice Podkin thought he heard a soft, sad sigh that might belong to Paz.

Just as Crom was reaching out to push through the blanket, Podkin stopped him – his little hand tiny against the big warrior's arm.

'Wait,' he whispered, as quietly as he could. 'I want you to use this.'

Struggling with his cloak, Podkin managed to uncover the hilt of Starclaw and pull it out of its scabbard. He felt the familiar warm tingle of the metal, and was suddenly reluctant to let a strange person touch it. It was *his*. His only. What if the big rabbit never gave it back?

It's all right, Podkin. You can trust him. It was

almost as if his father was there, whispering in his ear, telling him what to do. Podkin swallowed hard and gave up the blade, knowing it was for the best. He pressed it into Crom's calloused hand.

The sellsword weighed it, twisted it and ran his fingers over the hilt. In his grip it looked too small and puny to do any damage. He knelt to whisper back to Podkin. 'I have my own sword, boy. This is just a little dagger.'

'Yes,' Podkin replied. 'But I want you to use that one. It's very special. And besides, I'm still your boss, aren't I? At least until the end of the afternoon.'

Crom shrugged. He scooped Pook off his back and handed him to Podkin, then swept aside the blanket and stepped through.

*

There was a grunt of surprise from the burrow beyond. Podkin and Mish dashed through in time to see Quince standing in the centre of the room, his mouth hanging open. The scrawny rabbit was clutching his prodding-stick; he looked like he was just about to give Paz a jab or two through the bars of her cage.

'Hern's bristly britches,' he cursed. 'What's going—'

He never got to finish the sentence, as Crom strode right up and cracked him between the ears with Starclaw's hilt. There was a hollow clonking sound, and Quince folded up into a senseless heap on the floor.

'Podkin!' Paz jumped up and grabbed the bars of her cage. Pod had time to flash her a grin, and then there was a roaring from the far side of the burrow. Shape had been sleeping there, clutching a half-drunk bottle of mead. Now he was up, staring at Crom and roaring at the top of his voice.

'You! You're that blind rabbit nobody wants to hire! What in Hern's name are you doing here? And why'd you knock out my partner?'

'I'm acting on behalf of my client,' said Crom. 'And if you know what's good for you, you'll let all these little rabbits go.'

'Your *client*?' Shape gave Podkin an astonished look. For a moment, Pod thought he might give in, but instead he reached for his giant club and flexed his shoulders.

'I'm going to kill you, blind rabbit. Then I'm

going to take your client, turn him inside out and wear him as a hat.'

Podkin gulped. In his head, on the way here, Crom had seemed so huge and strong. Now, standing a few paces away from the hulking Mister Shape, he didn't look half as impressive.

'What have you done, Pod?' Paz hissed from her cage.

He cringed. 'I think I've just turned myself into some very unpleasant headgear.'

Shape charged then, roaring as he came. His spiked club, Beatrice, whistled through the air towards Crom's head. Crom just stood there, motionless. Podkin had a vision of the club knocking off his block, as if he were a particularly realistic snow rabbit, but at the last minute he stepped to one side and raised Starclaw to parry the blow. Of course, as the club was made of wood, the magic dagger sliced through it like it was a giant cucumber.

The severed part of the club flew off and embedded itself in the top of Paz's cage. Suddenly off balance, Shape stumbled – a look of pure surprise on his

face. He managed to keep himself upright, staring at the severed piece of club in his hands. His pause gave Crom the chance to twist himself around in a spinning movement, bringing one of his powerful legs up at the same time to kick Shape in the chest. The huge rabbit went flying backwards, crashing into the earthen wall of the burrow, smashing a hole right through and bringing half the ceiling cascading down to bury him.

In less than a few seconds, the fight was over.

There was a stunned silence, and then Podkin, Mish, Paz – and even the caged Mash – started cheering and whooping. Podkin took Starclaw back from Crom and used it to cut open both the cages. Paz rushed out and hugged him hard, tears in her eyes, and then Mash hugged him as well. There was so much hugging going on, Podkin almost turned to hug Crom, but the grey rabbit was standing so silently and solemnly that he thought better of it.

'I can't believe it! I can't believe it!' Mash shouted. 'We're free! We're free!'

'As I promised, I am forever in your debt,'

said Mish to Podkin, bowing so low, her little ears brushed the floor. Mash did the same, and Pod noticed they were almost identical, the only difference being the delicate black tips on the end of Mish's ears.

'It wasn't me,' said Podkin. 'I mean, *I* didn't do anything. It was all Crom.'

Mish and Mash bowed at the warrior rabbit as well, but he appeared not to notice. Instead, he knelt to speak to Podkin.

'That dagger,' he said. 'It wouldn't happen to be magic, would it?'

'Magic?' Podkin stammered for a moment, realising he might have made a mistake in revealing the sacred weapon to someone five times the size of him who was able to knock out two violent criminals in the time it took to peel a carrot. 'Whatever do you mean?'

'Your dagger cut through that club like it was made of air. I've only seen one weapon that could do that, and it was one of the sacred Twelve.' Crom reached out a hand and gripped Podkin by the shoulder. Not a firm grip yet, but one which could

squish him like a grape should it be required. 'Tell me how you came by it, boy. Tell me the *truth*.'

Podkin looked into those blank eyes, wondering what kind of story he could come up with that would explain Starclaw. In the end, he realised there was no story. He had had enough of gambling and bluffing for one day, anyway. He would tell the truth, and if he ended up getting kicked through a wall too, so be it.

'It's my father's,' he said, in a quiet voice. 'He is . . . *was* . . . a chieftain. Of Munbury warren, to the west of here. And you're right. It *is* magic. It can cut through anything in the world. Except iron.'

'Your father then. Is he . . .?'

'Dead.' Podkin felt hot tears run from his eyes into his fur. 'The Gorm killed him, at least, we think so. Now it's my dagger, and they're trying to kill me too.'

The room was silent for a moment. Podkin stared at Crom, wondering what was going on in his head. Was he planning to kill them himself and take Starclaw? Or turn them over to the Gorm and collect a fat reward? He was a mercenary, after all.

Finally, Crom spoke. His voice was soft, almost gentle. Not gruff and harsh like it had been before.

'I knew your father, Podkin. I knew him well. We fought together many times, right up until he became chieftain of his warren. He was a good rabbit and a good friend.'

'He . . . he was?'

'Yes. And he would not have wanted to see his children lost in a place like this, running for their lives.'

Still kneeling, Crom drew his own sword. Podkin wondered what the blind warrior was going to do with it. There was nothing left to fight, surely? But Crom simply turned it over, holding the hilt out to Podkin and bowing his head.

'I offer you my service, Podkin, son of Lopkin. My life and my sword are yours to command.'

Not sure what to do, Podkin touched the sword lightly and muttered a thank you. Crom nodded, stood and sheathed his weapon. He still looked fierce, but a little friendlier somehow.

Podkin gave him a smile, even though he knew he couldn't see it. 'Does this mean I get a refund?'

Crom surprised them all by throwing back his head and laughing. 'It means I don't have to sell my skills any more, thank the Goddess.'

'This is all very nice,' said Mash, still holding his sister in a tight hug. 'But can we leave now? We want to get as far away from this stinking place as we can and never come back.'

'That makes six of us,' said Paz. 'I don't know what Brigid was doing, sending us here. I thought she was so wise and clever . . .'

Podkin looked up at the serious, deadly face of Crom. 'Maybe she still is, sis,' he said. *Maybe there's been a reason behind everything that's happened today.*

From the ruined corner of the room, Shape gave a groan and his fat belly jiggled, sending more chunks of earth tumbling down on to his head. The rabbits looked at each other and nodded. Time to be somewhere else.

They were just heading out of the door, when the booming sound of a horn blast echoed down the tunnel. It was followed by another, then another.

'What's that?' Podkin asked.

'The Boneroot alarm,' Crom replied. 'Someone has forced their way past the entrance.'

'Who could it be?' Podkin thought he knew the answer even as the words left his mouth. By the terrified look on everyone's faces, they all did too.

'We have to get out of here,' said Paz. 'Right now.'

CHAPTER TWELVE

The Burning

Crom headed straight for the doorway, throwing the curtain aside. From the tunnel came the alarm again. Could Podkin hear the sound of clanking armour as well, or was that his imagination? He felt his heart begin to pound against the flimsy bones of his chest.

'Wait!' Mish shouted. 'Our weapons!'

The two dwarf rabbits ran to a battered wooden box that leant against the crumbling wall of Shape and Quince's hovel. They threw open the lid and began to rummage inside, flinging copper coins,

cut purses and empty mead jugs everywhere.

Finally, they pulled out an odd selection of items and began putting them on. Both had two bandoliers made of soft leather and covered in tiny buttoned pouches. Mash also had a long piece of wooden pipe, and Mish grabbed a wooden catapult. She tested the rubber on it and grinned.

'There's more weapons,' she said. 'You should arm yourselves.'

Podkin waved Starclaw in answer, but Paz ran to the box and dragged out a bronze short sword. She swished it through the air a couple of times.

'What've you got that for?' Podkin asked. 'You don't even know how to use it!'

'I do.'

'How? Mother would never let you loose with a deadly weapon! She wanted you to learn weaving and embroidery.'

'I got Melfry the weaponmaster to teach me,' said Paz. 'Whenever he couldn't find *you*, because you were off snoozing somewhere.'

Toasted turnips! Podkin thought. *That would have amounted to quite a few lessons. She's probably*

pretty good. He nodded at his sister with a grudging admiration as she turned to follow Crom out of the burrow. Now was not the time for a squabble.

Before leaving, he had a quick rummage in the box and pulled out Paz's silver bracelet and his belt buckle. Goddess-be-damned if he was going to leave them behind for Shape and Quince. He tucked them into his cloak pocket and hurried after the others.

The small group stepped out of the doorway, weapons at the ready. Crom scooped Pook on to his back and ran a paw along the mildewy earthen wall. 'Does this tunnel lead anywhere? An exit? Somewhere to hide?' He sounded like a soldier now – a captain about to lead his troops into battle.

Mish and Mash both shook their heads. 'It's a dead end down that way,' said Mash. 'Just a load of rubbish and slops.'

'Then we have to go back into the main chamber. Everyone stay behind me and don't get separated,' Crom ordered. It was the last thing they wanted to hear, but they fell in line all the same.

The tunnel seemed longer and scarier than ever.

Noises floated towards them that were nothing to do with the market. Snatches of shouting, shrieks of fear. Podkin dreaded what would meet them when they stepped out into the main chamber. He thought of the Gorm, bursting up from the ground, pouring out into the Munbury longburrow to rip away everything he loved. To see that again, to feel that much terror ... every muscle in his body tried to make him turn and run the other way.

In his hand, Starclaw fizzed and juddered. It was like the dagger knew his fear, and was angry about it. Podkin stared down at it in the gloom. Could it really read his mind? Was it trying to help him?

Anger was good. Anger was powerful. It gave him the courage to keep moving forward down the tunnel, and when he got to the end – well, it might not be enough to make him want to actually *fight* the Gorm, but it would help him find the strength to get past them, if he could. Out into the forest, where he actually stood a chance.

'Quietly now! Keep low!' Crom's commands snapped Podkin from his dreaming, and he realised they were almost at the tunnel mouth.

The other rabbits were all crouched low, keeping to the shadows. Mish jumped on Mash's shoulders to put out a candle that was lighting the tunnel, and it became even darker. They crept forwards, so that they could see into the huge chamber of Boneroot market.

The place was in chaos, but not of the mad, busy, bustling kind. The stalls at the closest end of the market were all overturned and trampled. Goods were crushed and smashed, banners and bunting strewn everywhere. Crowds of jostling rabbits were scrambling away, towards the far end of the chamber, throwing things out of their path as they went. It was a stampede of crazed terror, and Podkin could see what was causing it.

Directly opposite the tunnel mouth they were crouching in was the Boneroot entrance, now crammed full of hunched, armoured shapes. It *was* the Gorm, just as he had known it would be when the alarm sounded.

There were twenty of them at least, standing between the crumbling pillars and winding roots, with more stomping into the chamber behind them.

Torchlight glinted off their cruel armour as they stood in formation, looking around at the place they had just destroyed with their blank red eyes.

'They're just standing there,' whispered Paz. 'Why aren't they chasing the market rabbits?'

Podkin saw she was right. Surely they should be attacking, or at least smashing the rest of the market into pieces? It was almost as if they were waiting for something.

There was a commotion in the tunnel, and Pod realised they were about to find out what. The Gorm parted, making space for someone to enter. Someone taller and fiercer than the rest, with a pair of lopsided iron horns curling upwards from his helmet.

Scramashank.

He was here. He had caught them.

Or had he? Did he know they were hiding, just a few metres away? Maybe the Gorm had just stumbled upon Boneroot by accident? Did that mean they would be able to sneak past and escape somehow?

All these thoughts raced through Podkin's head in a few seconds. He didn't feel brave or angry any more. Even the thrumming dagger he was holding

couldn't stop him trembling. He looked up at Crom with white-rimmed, terrified eyes, waiting for the signal to run, run for their lives.

'Hold,' the big rabbit whispered, sensing the fear of the others. 'Not yet. Not yet.'

Podkin grabbed Paz's hand and squeezed tight, looking across at the Gorm and their evil, father-killing lord. There was no sign that he'd seen them. Scramashank was beckoning his troops, two of whom were dragging something down from the entrance.

Was it a rabbit? Yes. A half-dead, beaten scrap of one. By his long beard and patched armour, Podkin recognised him as the guard who had let them in through the hidden door. His face was bruised and bloodied now. He had clearly put up a good fight, for all the good it had done him.

'Lift him up.' Just hearing Scramashank's voice again made Podkin want to cry. Oh, if only he were some kind of legendary warrior, like in the stories, who could storm out there and smash the Gorm to pieces, instead of hiding in a tunnel, trying not to wet himself.

'Can you hear me?' The guard-rabbit had been hoisted upright, and Scramashank was face-to-face with him, staring right into the poor creature's eyes. He made some kind of noise, halfway between a grunt and a whimper.

'Thought you'd hidden yourself away, didn't you? Thought you were all safe from the Gorm, down here in your stinking little pit.'

The rabbit grunted again.

'It was only a matter of time, of course,' Scramashank continued. 'We were bound to find you. Just as we'll find every rabbit in all the Five Realms. There is nowhere you can hide from the Gorm.'

His men cheered at this, and banged their swords against their armour, making a hideous, clanging din that echoed around the chamber. When it had died down, Scramashank grabbed the guard-rabbit's beard and jerked his head up, hard. 'Enough talk. I'm in a good mood today, so I'll give you one chance to spare your miserable life.'

'I'm looking for some rabbits. Little rabbits. A boy, a girl and a baby.'

Podkin and Paz both held their breath, clinging on to each other as hard as they could.

'They have something I want. A dagger or a sword – I'm not sure what it looks like, only that it *isn't* a silver broadsword.' Scramashank paused to snarl, angry that he'd been tricked by Lopkin's decoy. 'If they've been through this festering fleapit, you must have seen them.'

What would the rabbit say? Would he betray them? *Please, please, please*, Podkin thought, not sure who he was even praying to.

The guard-rabbit lifted his head higher with the last of his strength. He opened his mouth to speak, and Scramashank leaned in closer to listen.

Then the brave, wonderful guard spat into the Gorm Lord's face.

There was a moment of total silence that seemed to stretch on forever. Scramashank was like an iron statue, motionless as the gob of spittle ran slowly down the faceplate of his helmet. Then, with a speed and strength that shocked even Podkin, the Gorm Lord grabbed the guard-rabbit and threw him across the chamber.

He sailed through the air like a broken doll, crashing into a candle stall, sending sparks and hot wax showering everywhere. Flames began to spring up amongst the market wreckage and tinder-dry roots, and with nobody to put them out they quickly spread.

Was this the diversion they had been waiting for? Just as Podkin looked up at Crom for a signal, he caught sight of movement from the corner of his eye. The Boneroot rabbits had regrouped themselves into a ragtag army of a kind, and had used the guard's questioning as a diversion. Sneaking up amongst the abandoned stalls, they had crept into position and, even as flames began to leap up around them, they let fly a hail of spears, arrows and stones at the Gorm invaders.

The Battle of Boneroot had started.

Podkin stared on in horror. Besides the attack on Munbury, he had never witnessed any *real* violence, and that had been nothing compared to this. Missiles pinged and zipped through the air, most of them clanging harmlessly off the Gorm armour. A few seconds later, the Gorm responded, sending long,

iron-tipped spears whooshing towards the Boneroot rabbits. Around them all, the fire grew, filling the air with stinging smoke.

Still Crom waited.

It wasn't until the flames had spread almost up to the mouth of their tunnel that he finally made a move. Clouds of smoke billowed everywhere. Podkin couldn't even see the Boneroot entrance any more, so he was sure the Gorm couldn't see him.

'*Now*, everybody!' Crom shouted. 'With me, and as fast as you can!'

They stood and ran, down from the tunnel and on to the cavern floor. The entire marketplace had become a bonfire, sending sheets of flame shooting up to the root-covered ceiling above. Showers of sparks whirled amongst the black smoke, and burning streamers of bunting flapped this way and that like huge snakes made of fire. Boneroot rabbits danced in and out of the inferno, shooting arrows then dodging away again before Gorm spears could find them.

'I know a way out,' Crom called back to the group. 'But you must guide me.'

He put out his hand and Podkin grabbed it, thinking to lead him along, but the warrior rabbit hauled him up and on to his back, next to the mewling, shaking Pook.

'Be my eyes, Podkin. We need to find the sellsword stall. Quickly now.'

Podkin had a vague idea where it was, but it was difficult to see in the smoke. He put an arm around Pook to comfort him, then shouted into Crom's ear. 'Forward! Keep going along this side of the cavern!'

With Crom leading the way, and Podkin steering him like a rider on a giant rat, they made their way as quickly as they could along the edge of the market floor. They had to dodge pieces of burning canvas and step through the shattered remains of stalls as they went, which slowed them down dangerously. Podkin snuck a quick glance across the cavern to see the Gorm steadily advancing, stepping through flames that licked off their armour. *I hope they boil inside*, he thought, but they just kept striding on as though they couldn't even feel the heat.

'Nearly there!' he shouted in Crom's ear. He thought he could see the bodies of some rabbits

amongst the debris. Was that one of the gambling rabbits, lying curled beneath that broken stall? And there – was that the rabbit with the pickled beetroots that had given them directions when they first arrived? Podkin felt like they should do something, but there was no time to stop and help. It was every rabbit for himself.

'The sellsword market!' Paz yelled. 'There it is!'

Just a few steps further, behind a wall of roiling black smoke; there it was – the fenced enclosure where Podkin had first spotted Crom. He remembered wondering how a blind rabbit could possibly fight. Now his very life depended on him.

'Quick, everyone. Into the enclosure. Head for the stone pillar at the far side. There's a passage behind.'

They all dashed across the now-empty space, past the tattered blanket where Crom had sat for Goddess knows how long. Sure enough, there was a tunnel entrance, just the right size for a small rabbit, hidden amongst the shadows.

Paz was just about to dart in, when something struck the stone pillar by her head with a loud crash. Sharp chips of stone exploded off it, hitting her in

the face and knocking her to the floor. It was a spear, Podkin saw, and it had missed spiking her through the head by only a few inches.

Crom spun around, making Pod and Pook cling on for dear life. There, stomping out of the smoke clouds, was a Gorm warrior. His iron armour was blackened by soot, the fur on his ears seared away and the flesh beneath scorched pink. Not that he seemed to care: his jagged broadsword was already swinging towards them, those dead red eyes staring at them as if they were nothing but walking meat.

'Jump back!' Podkin yelled, making Crom leap. Just in time, as the sword *whooshed* past his nose and thudded into the stone floor of the cavern. 'Didn't you hear it coming?'

'The noise,' Crom shouted. 'It's too much. I can't hear where he's coming from. Be my eyes again, Podkin!'

The cacophonic screaming in the cavern, the roar of burning timber, the wash of red-hot air and stink of smoke: all of these things had dulled the senses Crom relied on to make up for his useless eyes.

The Gorm had raised his sword high and was coming at them again.

'Duck!' Podkin screamed. 'Jump right!'

The broadsword swished past them both times, missing them by a few whiskers. How could Crom attack if he couldn't sense the enemy? What if another Gorm came to join in?

'Let's even the field a bit, shall we?' said a voice at Crom's feet.

Podkin looked down to see Mish, her catapult stretched back as far as it would go, pointing at the Gorm's face. Beside her, Mash had the pipe held to his mouth. They both fired at once, little black balls of *something* shooting up at the armoured head of their attacker and hitting both of his helmet's eyeholes at once. The balls exploded, filling the Gorm's eyes with black sticky goo that smoked and burned. The warrior roared, dropping its sword, clawing at its face.

Now was the chance to hit him, but would a blow from Crom be enough to knock him off his feet? There needed to be something behind the warrior's feet – something to make him stumble . . .

A memory popped into Podkin's head from nowhere: playing in the meadows at Midsummer with Rusty and Rufus from Redwater. Pod would creep up behind one and crouch down, and then Paz would push them over, sending them tumbling into the soft, sweet grass. Then they would all roar with laughter, like it was the funniest thing in the world.

A burning underground market was a million miles away from Munbury meadow, but it could still work, couldn't it?

Podkin slipped from Crom's back and dashed around behind the Gorm, crouching into a ball. Paz saw what he was doing, and joined in too, the pair of them making a decent-sized stumbling block.

'Hit him now, Crom!' Podkin shouted. 'Kick out straight ahead of you!'

The warrior rabbit threw himself backwards, dropping to take his weight on his hands and bringing up both feet for a mighty kick. It caught the Gorm in the chest and he toppled, spilling over Podkin and Paz and crashing into one of the stone pillars like a clap of thunder. It was like being rolled over by an iron oak tree, and the two little rabbits were flattened

to the hot flagstones, the wind knocked out of them.

Looking up to where the Gorm lay wedged in the pillar, Podkin saw cracks appear in the ancient masonry, and up above there was an ominous groaning sound.

But there wasn't time to worry about that now. Mish and Mash dragged him and Paz up from the floor and the whole group dashed into the tiny burrow, coughing and choking as they went.

*

The tunnel zigged and zagged in all directions and was choked with webs of root and dust. After ten metres or so, it climbed sharply – almost vertically – upwards. There were wooden rungs hammered into the hard earth walls, but many were as old as time, and simply shattered in their grasping hands. Instead, they had to grab fistfuls of roots to haul themselves up.

It was like climbing the inside of a chimney. Cramped, lightless, full of suffocating smoke. They scrabbled as fast as they could, away from the flames and the roaring behind them.

At some point, Pook was knocked from Crom's

back. The big rabbit was on his hands and knees, his shoulders brushing against the tunnel roof. Podkin grabbed him, and with Paz's help, they heaved him up the tunnel between them. Mish and Mash led the way. All of them coughing and choking from the smoke.

Finally, *finally*, they burst out of the darkness and through a mat of overgrown brambles, into the evening light. One by one, they collapsed into the snow at the edge of the forest and lay there, panting and gasping. It was like being born into a new world.

Podkin grabbed great handfuls of snow and mashed it into his face. The smoke had turned his eyes into two throbbing balls of pain, and his nose and throat stung like they had been rubbed with sandpaper and vinegar.

After a few moments, his vision began to return, blurred and watery.

They were well inside the treeline, looking out at the wasteland of shrubs and bushes that hid Boneroot. In the distance, he could make out a shape that might be the stone arch where they had entered. Here and there amongst the trees he could

see lines of moving shapes. Streams of rabbits were pouring out of other hidden exits, fleeing their home like ants from a nest that had just been doused with boiling water.

Podkin felt very sorry for them all. They had run from the Gorm to get here, and now they were running again.

'Did you feel that?' Paz said. She was lying beside him, covered head to foot in black soot.

'What?' he croaked.

'The ground. It moved.'

Podkin looked at the forest floor around them, and then he felt it as well. A deep shudder in the bones of the earth.

'The chamber's collapsing,' said Crom. 'We'd better move.'

Even though Crom was right, and their lives were in danger, none of the rabbits had the energy to lift a paw. They sat, coughing and staring, as cracks began to appear in the snow, not ten metres away from them.

With a painful, groaning, ripping sound, the cracks spread. Trees began to lean inwards, and

spouts of smoke started seeping from the open wounds in the soil.

'Back!' Crom shouted, and this time they somehow found a last shred of energy – enough to scrabble and drag each other further into the trees where the ground was more solid.

Podkin turned round in time to see a circle the size of the entire Boneroot marketplace tear itself out of the earth, and then everything inside – trees, bushes, mud, snow – all folded downwards into the pit with a crashing roar that shook them off their feet.

Where a messy scrubland had once stood, there was now a gaping hole, oozing black smoke into the darkening sky. On the far side, where the ruined arch still jutted upwards, Podkin could see figures staggering out of the wreck of Boneroot. Armoured, hunched figures, steaming with smoke and burnt blood.

He counted ten, maybe fifteen of them before they stopped coming. Most of the attackers must be buried beneath several tonnes of earth, stone and root below.

Good, he thought, and would have even done a

little dance of joy, had he not spotted the last Gorm soldier to step free of the tunnel.

He was bigger than the rest by a good head, and the spikes on his armour were terrible and huge. White bony things hung from his belt, and he was leaning on a massive two-handed broadsword for support. As Podkin stared, he turned to look across the chasm that Boneroot had left, and Pod was sure he could see two glowing red spots of light in the slits of his helmet.

Podkin felt his lips form the name.

Scramashank. He had survived, Goddess curse him.

'What is it, Pod?' Paz had him by the shoulder and was shaking him, a look of grave worry on her face.

He wanted to answer, but all he could do was point. Paz followed his stare and, when she saw what he had seen, she snatched Pook up into her arms and ran. They all ran, as far and fast into the forest as they could – just as if the devil himself were behind them.

Which, in a way, he was.

CHAPTER THIRTEEN

Tales Within Tales

On and on they ran, until it was dark, and the moon was shining down on them like a cold, watchful eye. Eventually they stopped, leaning against tree trunks to rest, and straining to hear above their own rasping and panting – listening for any sounds of clanking armour or cawing of Gorm crows.

'It's freezing out here,' Podkin finally managed to speak. 'But we can't light a fire in case they're following us.'

'And we won't make it through the night if we don't,' said Paz.

'There must be somewhere we can hide,' said Mish.

Mash nodded. 'We could build a shelter from some branches? Or dig a hole in the snow?'

'I know of somewhere we can stay,' said Crom. He heaved himself away from his tree trunk, sniffed the air and started staggering south, deeper into the forest. Pook was snuggled against his chest, having fallen asleep with exhausted terror.

The other rabbits watched him go, half tempted to stay where they were and simply freeze to death until, one by one, they forced themselves to walk after him, into the forest's heart, where the trees were ancient, dark and foreboding.

*

The forest became dense, choked with branches. Thorns and spidery twigs tore at their clothes and sliced their faces. Every now and then, Crom would ask a question about where they were. He was looking for a huge dead oak tree first, then a narrow stream, then a clearing with a ruined log cabin in the centre.

'I don't mean to be rude,' said Podkin, as they

stumbled out of the clearing, still heading southwards, 'but where exactly are we going? We've been walking for hours now. We can't go on much further.' By which he meant that *he* couldn't go on much further, but judging by the gasps and groans the others were making, they were all in a similar state.

As an answer, Crom simply pointed to a large mound they could see rising up amongst the thick trees.

'There,' was all he said, and the rabbits hurried along, not caring what they were rushing to as long as it meant a chance to lie down somewhere dry, warm and safe.

*

The mound was actually a small hill, topped off by a towering scots pine with branches as wide as most other trees' trunks. The great tree sheltered most of the hill from the snow and frosted strands of moss and plants covered everything; ridges and mountains of cracked bark, twining with vines and ivy. The spaghetti-mess of tendrils hung down, trailing over what Podkin first thought was a cave mouth. Looking closer, he saw it was a warren doorway,

set back into the hill and almost swallowed by the growing forest.

'Darkhollow,' Paz said, reading the Ogham runes carved into the stonework. 'I've never heard of it.'

Podkin could make out some time-worn shapes carved into the lichen-covered stone. Some kind of fruit? Pine cones? The wind and rain had smoothed them featureless over many years. This was an old, old warren. Maybe even as ancient as Munbury.

'Nobody's lived here in a long time,' said Mash, thinking the same thing. Mish went up and kicked at the door, making it boom like a drum.

'How are we supposed to get in then?' Podkin asked, through chattering teeth. They all looked at Crom, who silently reached into his jerkin and brought out a long iron key that had been hanging around his neck on a leather thong. The expression on his face was hard to read. Nobody dared speak as he walked up and felt over the surface of the ancient oak door. Finally he found the keyhole and slotted in the key. The lock shrieked, groaned, and then finally clunked. Crom took a deep breath, shoving with his shoulder to open up the entrance.

Cold, musty air hissed out, washing over them in a wave. It smelt of dust and age. They could see nothing inside except a lonely, inky blackness. It was a ghost warren. An empty, lifeless shell of a place.

Crom turned round to face them, spreading his arms wide. 'Welcome to my warren,' he said.

*

The entrance tunnel still had torches sitting in brackets on the wall, as if waiting for someone to return. As the rabbits gingerly stepped over the threshold, Mash took down a torch and lit it with a pair of flints that he kept in a pouch on his belt. When he held the flame high, light filled the burrow, shooting down into the dark depths of the warren, as if the place was hungrily drinking it up.

It looked like it had been deserted for ten, maybe twenty years. Despite the dark, the cold and the shrouds of dust and cobwebs, it had been made well and hadn't leaked or crumbled.

The walls and ceiling were held up by stout wooden beams, all carved with rabbits leaping and twirling through the trunks and roots of the forest.

Pine cones were everywhere, obviously the warren symbol, and in several places Podkin spotted a tall horned rabbit, peering out from a thicket of trees or leaping after a startled weasel. *Hern*, he realised. *The god of the forest.* It made sense that the Darkhollow rabbits would worship him, living in the deepest part of Grimheart itself.

Mash lit more torches from the one in his hand, and other details of the warren appeared. The floor was tiled with patterns and mosaics of coloured clay. There were bare patches on the whitewashed walls, where tapestries had once hung. Wooden doors opened off the main tunnel, on to guards' rooms and weapon stores. In one, they found a stack of torches, lanterns and firewood, all neatly piled, ready for whoever might need it.

They moved into the warren, spreading light as they went. Every now and then someone gasped or made a noise of admiration. It really was a fine place to be hiding out.

Podkin looked behind to see Crom, walking slowly with one hand gently brushing the wall. Was he imagining it, or did the torchlight sparkle on tears

in the big rabbit's eyes? Podkin quickly turned away and joined the others in their exploration.

The tunnel led down to the longburrow. Paz and the others dashed about, lighting lanterns and torches, and carrying firewood to stack in the hearth and set alight. It wasn't long before they had a good blaze going, bathing them all in delicious heat and the sweet scent of burning pine. One by one, they collapsed on the tiled floor and stretched out, letting the warmth ease their aches and pains. Podkin couldn't describe how good it felt to be in a proper warren again, safe and warm in the bones of the earth.

They all sat in silence for a while, looking round at their new home.

It had clearly been a wealthy warren. The fireplace was carved stone, and there were long feasting tables and hundreds of wooden chairs, all with a little pine cone carved into the back, all sitting quietly in the dark, waiting for the next feast to begin.

The warren tapestries were rolled and stacked in a corner. Mash unfurled one and held it up to show the tall horned rabbit again, this time standing

next to a stag whose neck was garlanded with pine cones.

It reminded Podkin of Munbury: an orderly, tidy, pretty little warren that had once seemed like the centre of the world. Except Darkhollow was so empty and lost. It was lonely – a sad, hidden thing, sleeping and dreaming away the years until life and light returned.

It took a while for them all to finish warming up and calming down. Smoke still stung eyes and chests, and everyone was smudged black with soot and mud. Only their feet, which had crunched through miles of snow on their way here, were clean. Brown, white and grey toes wiggled by the fire, slowly coming back to life.

'Are we safe here?' Podkin had to ask. 'Will the Gorm find us?'

Crom rubbed at his tired eyes for a moment before answering. 'I don't think they will. The pine trees are too thick for their crows and their armour. And if they follow anyone from Boneroot, it'll be all the other rabbits. They left much more of a trail than we did.'

Podkin wondered if it was right to feel so relieved that rabbits other than him would be hunted down in his place. But it was difficult not to.

The others must have been thinking the same uncomfortable thoughts. As a distraction, they started giving each other looks, seeing who would be brave enough to ask Crom his story. In the end, it was Mish who spoke up, her little voice echoing about the empty hall.

'Why is this place so empty, Crom?' she asked.

The blind rabbit sat still and silent for so long, Podkin wondered whether he had heard the question. When he spoke, his words were heavy and tired, as if it was a story he didn't want to tell.

*

'I don't suppose you can imagine me as a young rabbit – maybe a few years older than yourselves – but I was once. That was when I first met your father, Podkin.

'The custom in those days was for the sons of chieftains to be sent to live with other clans. Ones where there was a chance of fighting going on, so as to teach them a bit about being a leader and a

warrior. Otherwise it was easy for rabbits to become spoilt and lazy. And spoilt, lazy rabbits make bad rulers.' Paz gave Podkin a *very* pointed look. He stuck his tongue out at her.

'Well,' Crom continued. 'Your father was son of a chief, and so was I. This was my father's warren, and I was due to take over from him.

'As it was, Lopkin and I were sent to a warren called Flintchip, up north in the shadow of the Arukh mountains. They were having problems with long-haired Arukh rabbits and needed men to fight them.

'So fighting was what Lopkin and I did.

'At first I didn't know what I was doing. I had spent all my life lying around in meadows, nibbling clover and snoozing. I hid away from my weapon teachers and couldn't even read or write. I only just about knew one end of a sword from the other.'

That doesn't sound so bad, Podkin thought. He made sure he ignored Paz, who was sniggering and pointing at him.

'So when it came to my first actual battle, I very nearly died.

'I don't know if you've seen the Arukh rabbits.

They are fierce, screaming warriors, with long manes of hair that they braid and hang with beads and paint bright blue. They fight with stone weapons, but they are deadly and well-trained warriors.

'Your father and I were arrow-boys when our army marched on them. All we had to do was keep the archers supplied with fresh arrows and stay well out of the fighting.

'But things didn't go to plan, and a bunch of Arukhs broke through the line. They managed to get as far as the archers, and knocked several of them down. One big Arukh buck smashed right through to where I was positioned, and was about to bring his stone axe down on my head. I just stood there, staring up at him in surprise.

'Then your father, who was no bigger than you are now, leapt up at him, grabbed hold of his braids and smashed him over the head with a clay bottle. Knocked him out cold. Eight summers' old, and able to take down an Arukh warrior. That was your father.'

Podkin and Paz looked at each other. Both had tears in their eyes, but they managed to share a smile.

'After that, I vowed to make a soldier of myself.

Lopkin and I trained every day, and a year or two later we were on the front lines with the rest of the warriors. Proper little scrappers we were, and the life of a soldier started to suit us.

'So much so, that once the Arukhs had been tamed, we carried on looking for adventure. The two of us travelled over most of the Five Realms, helping out wherever there was trouble. We were together every day for five or six years, and we saved each others' lives so many times that I lost count.

'Then one day, word came to Lopkin that his father, your grandfather, had died, and that it was time for him to return home and rule the warren. He was pleased to go, even though it was hard for us to say goodbye. I think, in his heart, he had finally grown tired of the warrior life.

'I hadn't, though. Far from it. I kept on travelling and fighting. I stopped by Munbury once, just after Lopkin was married. Your mother was a fine rabbit, and he was happy. That was when he showed me the dagger, and told me about how it was one of the Twelve.

'I didn't stop for long, as there was more action to

be had. Fighting the giant rabbits in Orestad, pushing back the cult of Cruach, the war god in Thrianta. Then, one day, word came to me that *my* father had passed away, and it was time to come back to Darkhollow and rule as he had.

'I thought long and hard about it, but in the end I refused. I knew what it would mean for the rabbits living here, but I just couldn't give up the life of a soldier. Being a chieftain – it just wasn't in me. I thought the Darkhollow rabbits would choose someone else, but instead they just moved on. Some to Inkcap Dell in the north, some to Stumphaven down south. Others headed off to Orestad. Formed a warren of their own in the forest there, last I heard. They always were a stubborn, superstitious lot. They'd rather start afresh somewhere new than carry on in a place they thought had run out of luck. And the warren has sat here empty ever since.'

The rabbits sat for a while, thinking about Crom's story, listening to the crackle of the fire. They had heard about warrens being taken over by the Gorm, or being wiped out in some tribal war or other, but

they had never imagined a whole tribe giving up and moving on.

Maybe they had never been happy at Darkhollow in the first place. Or, more likely, losing their chieftain had been seen as some kind of sign from the gods. Religion made rabbits do some very strange things, sometimes.

Finally, Podkin spoke up with another question. 'What about your eyes, Crom? How did you go blind? If you don't mind me asking, that is.'

Crom made a noise that was part sigh, part growl. Podkin thought he wasn't going to tell them, but then he spoke again.

'That was five years or more ago. When the Gorm appeared, up north. Some warrens put together a party to go and scare them off, but we weren't prepared for them. Our spears just bounced off their armour, off those twisted monsters they ride . . .

'And there was something else – a witch-rabbit. She rode a black rat and called down lightning from the sky. We charged on her, but she caught me full in the face with a bolt of thunder. Her magic took my sight, and I lay under a pile of bodies for days in

216

some kind of trance. When I woke up, the Gorm were gone, marching on another poor warren somewhere. I crawled away, helpless as a baby. I could tell the land all around was burnt and blackened – it was poisoned and stank of iron and blood. Luckily some rabbits fleeing the Gorm army found me. They took me with them and healed my wounds, but they couldn't do anything about my eyes.

'In the years since then, I've taught myself to fight again, how to use my other senses to get by. But I'll never be the warrior I once was. I used to wish that the Gorm witch had killed me, but now I'm glad to be alive. When you lose something as precious as your sight, you learn to appreciate everything else more.'

With the stories finished, and Pook already snoring his little head off, the rest of the rabbits began to curl up in their cloaks to fall asleep. There were probably beds and blankets somewhere in the darkness of the empty warren, but rooting around to find them was too much effort.

Podkin snuggled up with his back to Paz, enjoying the heat of the fire on his face and the scar

of his missing ear. It was like being stroked softly to sleep by an old friend.

His last sight, before his eyes closed, was of Crom, sitting silently in the firelight.

Podkin imagined him as a young rabbit, standing next to his father, laughing and joking together, all those years ago. Then, with his dreams as warm as his toes, he fell fast asleep.

*

The first few weeks in the empty warren were a peaceful time. They spent their days exploring the tunnels, lighting and airing the dusty old rooms and foraging in the forest above for nuts and berries to eat.

Evenings were spent huddled by the great hearth in the longburrow, and what had started with Crom's tale became a kind of storytelling tradition, for firesides and stories share a special kind of magic together.

They heard all about the life of Mish and Mash and their acrobat troupe. They had joined it when the travelling caravan visited their little village in the Eiskalt mountains.

The dwarf rabbits there lived in warrens carved into the cliffs and were expert rock and tree climbers before they could walk. But Mish and Mash had longed to see the world, and the troupe was a perfect place for them to show off their acrobatic skills. (This part of the story was embellished with exhibitions of several backflips, headstands and feats of balancing that had the little rabbits whooping with applause.)

The dwarf rabbits travelled all over Thrianta and Hulstland in the south, with their band of jugglers, fire-breathers and puppeteers. Life was pleasant and easy then, until they came over the Razorback downs into Enderby.

That was when they first came across the Gorm. The warren where they were performing was raided, and some of their troupe were taken as slaves.

After that, they became something more than just acrobats. They found ways to use their skills to bring down the armoured Gorm giants, and if they met a patrol on their travels, then they made sure there were two or three Gorm who didn't return home to base.

Mish and Mash paused to show the others the contents of their bandoliers. They were full of little packets: mixtures they had made to fire at the cracks and gaps in Gorm armour. There was blinding goo (which everyone had already seen), poison, glue, itching powder, stink bombs and something called 'bang dust'. Everyone was suitably impressed.

So, returning to the story, Mish and Mash and their troupe of guerrilla Gorm fighters still travelled from warren to warren, staying ahead of the Gorm and helping where they could.

Boneroot was a natural place for them to end up, full as it was of refugees and runaways. They had paused there to resupply and to make a few copper coins from performing when the two dwarf rabbits had been snatched from their lodgings by the evil Quince and Shape, and hidden away until their troupe gave up looking for them. When Mish was finally let out on a stealing expedition, they were nowhere to be found.

And the rest of the story, everyone knew very well.

Paz and Podkin took turns telling the tale of their epic escape from the Gorm, and how Podkin lost his ear. After that, there were more stories about life in Munbury warren before everything went so horribly wrong. They talked about Midsummer parties at the standing stones, the time Paz pushed Podkin into the river; Bramblemas Eves, waiting for the Midwinter Rabbit, games of hide-and-seek in the forest . . .

At first, Podkin almost couldn't bear talking about happier times, knowing they were gone forever. But once he began to share his previous life with his new friends, it gave him a kind of comfort. Those memories were like precious, perfect jewels that he would treasure and keep with him forever.

Darkhollow warren was bleak and empty and buried in the forest, but it was also safe and secret and, by night, full of laughter and the crackle of firewood. Little by little, the rabbits began to think of it as home.

INTERLUDE

The bard pauses, takes a swig from his cup.

'Is that it?' says the inquisitive rabbit, folding her arms and pouting. 'What about when Podkin becomes the Horned King? What about all the battles and fighting and chopping things into pieces with his magic dagger?'

'This must be when he starts to be the Horned King,' says the sensible rabbit. 'The warren in the forest is where his army lives in the stories. They have a secret home where nobody can find them, don't they?'

'That's just stupid,' replies the inquisitive rabbit. 'Why would a whole warren full of rabbits just up and leave? If your dad vanished, we'd just pick another chieftain, and carry on like before.'

There is a grunt from the fireside, where Chief Hubert has been listening along. The inquisitive rabbit has the decency to squirm and look embarrassed.

'The way rabbits feel about their chieftains is complicated,' says the bard. 'They believe they are chosen by the Goddess herself to lead them. If a warren loses its chief, and he has no sons to take over, it is seen as a bad omen. So they would often rather pack up and find homes elsewhere, in happy, lucky warrens.'

'So Darkhollow is cursed?' the sensible rabbit asks.

'Perhaps,' says the bard. 'But then, its chief did come back, in a way. And besides, not everyone believes in all that rubbish.'

'Never mind that,' says the inquisitive rabbit. 'What about the fighting? When does Podkin One-Ear get revenge against the Gorm?'

'Stories aren't all about fighting and revenge,' says the bard. 'You have to have a bit of character development in there as well. Some suspense, some atmosphere. A little bit of romance.'

'Yuck!' All the listening rabbits make retching,

spewing noises and pull their ears over their eyes. The bard sighs.

'By Clarion's sacred harp strings, you lot are a hard crowd to please,' he says. 'Very well. Revenge against the Gorm it is then.'

CHAPTER FOURTEEN

The Wagon in the Woods

A month or so passed in the warren of Darkhollow, and everyone had fallen into a comfortable routine.

The warren had been thoroughly swept and aired – dust sheets removed, cobwebs brushed away. The place looked more like a home and less of a haunted shell. The rabbits had found their own rooms amongst the empty burrows, beaten and plumped the mattresses and settled themselves in. Mish and Mash were bunked next door to Podkin, Paz and Pook, and Crom had chosen a room on the other side of the

longburrow. Podkin had thought Crom might take the old chieftain's chambers, but he had opted for a simple cell with a cot and a rack for his armour and weapons. Nobody questioned him about his choice.

The short winter days were spent keeping busy. Mornings saw Podkin, Paz and Pook foraging the forest floor for winter caches of nuts and seeds hidden away by squirrels. Mish and Mash took to the trees, gathering whatever they could find, while Crom chopped firewood.

In the afternoon, the rabbits trained. Mish and Mash taught the little ones acrobatics – backflips, headstands and somersaults – and Crom gave Podkin sword lessons. The little rabbit was a bit reluctant at first, but Crom insisted that a chieftain's son *must* know how to fight. And there was no sneaking off to a hidden cupboard or secret cubbyhole this time. Crom was nothing like old Melfry, the weaponmaster from Munbury. Every time he got even slightly cross with Podkin, the image of Shape and Quince getting pummelled flashed through the little rabbit's mind. Crom was not someone you wanted to annoy.

They used wooden practice swords, which,

Podkin quickly discovered, tended to leave nasty welts and bruises wherever they hit you (which was pretty much everywhere). Paz usually joined the classes as well, much to Podkin's annoyance. She stood nearby, mirroring his movements with her own sword. From the corner of his eye, Podkin could see she was naturally much better than him, which only made him angry. *That* made him lose his focus and make mistakes, leading to another clonk on the head.

Sometimes Crom asked her to join in, and that was even more embarrassing. Paz was bigger, quicker and faster than Pod, and it was all he could do to keep dodging and rolling out of the way. He wished she'd go and play with Pook or hunt berries for tea.

One afternoon in particular was really difficult for Podkin. He had been working on blocking and parrying with Crom, and for once felt like he was getting somewhere. After he had managed to turn aside Crom's wooden blade for the third time, they paused for a breather. As Pod leant on his sword, panting for breath and rubbing the latest lump on his head, Crom cleared his throat.

Thinking that he was due some praise for his effort, Podkin's little chest puffed up and a smile twitched the corners of his mouth. A good word from Crom had come to mean so much to the little rabbit, especially as it didn't happen very often.

But instead, the old warrior waved a hand at where Paz was standing, swishing her sword about and generally showing off. 'Come on, Paz. Let's see if he can block you as well.'

Oh, badgers' bottoms, thought Podkin, as his sister came skipping over, cocky as anything and grinning from ear to ear. Before he could protest, she swung her wooden sword at him, just missing his whiskers.

'Don't dodge, Podkin. Block!'

Jab, jab, swing. Paz came at him relentlessly. He tried to remember the parrying technique he'd just mastered, but in his panic not to let his sister beat him, it all went out of his head.

Clonk! She caught him on the shoulder. *Whack!* She smacked him on his nose. She was winding up for another swing, when Pod's temper got the better of him.

'Stop it!' he screamed, and flung his practice

sword at Paz. 'This is stupid! I'm never going to learn to fight! I don't *want* to learn to fight! Paz can be the chieftain, and she can stick her poxy wooden swords in her earholes!'

Crom's brow was furrowed; Paz's face was surprised and worse, amused. He'd made a complete idiot of himself in front of his father's old friend, just like the old, spoilt Podkin would have done. It was too much. He turned and ran off into the woods.

An hour or so later, when he couldn't feel his toes any more, he slunk back into the warren. Crom was waiting for him by the fire. Podkin went and stood before him, shivering. He expected a telling-off – deserved it, even. He knew that.

But Crom just put one of his big scarred hands on Podkin's shoulder and gently squeezed.

'I'm sorry,' Podkin said, his voice small and almost lost amongst the crackling of the fire.

'Don't be,' said Crom. 'You did well today. I shouldn't have pushed you so hard. I forget how young you are, sometimes. Goddess knows, you should have seen me when I was your age. I didn't know a spear from a carrot.'

'But Paz . . .'

'She's older and bigger than you. Her reach is longer, and she's fast. But keep trying like you did today and you'll be the one whacking her on the head soon enough.'

That will make a nice change, thought Podkin, but didn't say it aloud. Instead he promised himself he wouldn't lose his cool again. He wanted to make Crom proud, maybe because it was the closest he could get to making his father proud. And from then on he doubled his effort, swallowed his pride and tried to learn something from each new bruise.

In the evenings they prepared whatever they had scavenged from the forest and sat down to eat by the fire. There was never very much, and their stomachs always seemed empty, but at least they didn't starve. The Darkhollow well was still good and, with a supply of fresh water, Crom thought they would be fine until the spring when there would be more food around. (Podkin was very glad, because the warrior rabbit had told them several stories about being stranded with no food and having to eat worms and beetles. Pook seemed quite excited by the idea, but

the only crunchy things Podkin liked to eat were carrots and turnips.)

And that was how life went on: pleasantly boring and quiet. Up until, that is, the day that Mish and Mash saw the wagon.

*

They had been in the top branches of a pine tree, Mash told them later, when they heard the squeaking of wagon wheels. Having grown up travelling the Five Realms by wagon, they would have known the sound anywhere.

Seeing as they hadn't met a soul since stepping into the forest nearly two months ago, they were very curious about whom it could be. Clambering and flipping from tree to tree, they followed the sound until they were looking down at a rough, narrow track that wound between the trees.

Wobbling along the rutted road was an old wagon, pulled by a mangy, exhausted creature with matted fur. It might have been a giant rat, but it looked more like a walking skeleton with a broken, stumpy tail and torn, flea-bitten ears.

There were two rabbits sitting on the driving

board, one with a hooked spear, which he used to jab the rat every now and then. The creature was too exhausted even to squeal. It just plodded slightly faster for a few seconds, until the next spiking came its way.

The wagon itself was filled with supplies. They spotted sacks of grain and oats, reed baskets of potatoes and beetroot and kegs marked with the sign of Silverock warren. That could mean only one thing: that gallons of famous Silverock mead would be sloshing around inside.

This instantly got the two dwarf rabbits' stomachs rumbling, and they whispered about whether to try and hook a barrel off the wagon. They also thought about following it, but weren't sure they could find their way back again. Not wanting to end up lost and alone in the deep dark forest, they set off to Darkhollow to report back.

That night, they all sat by the fire and wondered about the wagon and where it might have been going.

'It can't be Boneroot,' said Podkin. 'The warren has completely collapsed. Wasn't it the only place north of here for miles and miles?'

Crom shook his head. 'There's Applecross

warren, up by the river. But trade for them won't come through this part of the forest. It goes upriver on narrow boats.'

'What's wrong with this part of the forest?' Paz asked.

'It's haunted, of course,' Crom smiled. 'There's a cursed warren of ghost rabbits here, didn't you know? That and the Beast of Grimheart.'

'The Beast of what?' Podkin said. 'You never told us there was a beast running around here! We've been walking around the forest every day for ages now!'

'Relax,' said Crom. 'I lived here for years and never saw it. It's just an old legend. In fact, I'm pretty sure we made it up ourselves, just to keep visitors away. The Darkhollow rabbits always were an antisocial bunch.'

'So where can the wagon be going then?' Mish asked. 'Do you think we could rob it?'

'Robbing is theft, and that is wrong,' said Crom. 'But let us keep an ear out for it. If it comes again, we will follow and find out where it's headed.'

*

It snowed harder than ever for the next two weeks: hard enough for drifts to break through the dense branches of the tree canopy and to cover the forest floor. It made foraging nearly impossible, and the rabbits were hungrier than ever. Tracking the cart was the last thing on their minds but, once the snow had eased off and the forest road thawed a bit, Mish and Mash started keeping an ear out again.

One morning they came rushing into the clearing outside Darkhollow, where Crom was busy chopping wood.

'We heard it!' they cried. 'The cart is back! It's just gone past us, heading north again.'

Moments later, Podkin, Paz and the two dwarf rabbits were at the roadside, following the fresh tracks of the cart and rat. (Pook was too small for this adventure and had been left safely behind with Crom, who insisted he was too clumsy to be crashing his way around the woods by touch, when stealth and creeping was called for.)

The rabbits hung back far enough to be hidden from the cartsmen, but close enough to hear the

wagon squeaking and the snow crunching under the giant rat's paws. To find their way back again, they carved crosses into tree trunks here and there, for it was a long cold walk out of the forest.

At last they reached the edge and could spy the cart in the distance. Keeping far back and low to the ground, they followed its marks through the pristine snow. For an hour or more they trudged along, thinking it might never stop, when the track disappeared over the brow of a small hill.

When the rabbits caught up, they lay on the ground and peered down into the valley. If their blood hadn't already been close to ice, what they saw would have made it run cold.

Down below was a cluster of tents, dusted with snow and ringed by a palisade of wooden stakes. The cart was rolling towards it, and coming out to meet it were several rabbits. Large rabbits. Large *armoured* rabbits.

'It's a Gorm camp!' Podkin hissed. Every rabbit instinct in his body told him to turn and run and not stop until he was deep in the forest, locked away inside his new warren. Instead he bit back the fear,

like he had in Boneroot, letting burning anger take its place.

'What are they doing here?' Paz whispered. 'I thought they lived in Splinterholm, far up in the north?'

'They do,' Mash agreed. 'But there must be lots of warrens around here to control. Maybe this is the base they do it from.'

Podkin thought about all the places nearby that had fallen under Gorm control. There was Redwater, and Munbury of course. Further north, by the lakeside, were Applecross and Cherrywood, and probably more that he hadn't heard of. They would need somewhere nearby for all that conquering and pillaging.

He peered closer at the camp, trying to count how many Gorm there might be. At least twenty, he thought – maybe more in those tents. And lots of other rabbits besides. Servants and slaves, probably. But what about those ones in the corner of the camp? Were they shut in some kind of enclosure or something?

'Prisoners,' he said, under his breath. The others looked at him.

'What was that, Pod?' Paz asked.

'Prisoners,' he said. 'Down in the corner there. It looks like they've got people cooped up. Paz, what if . . . ?'

He didn't need to say it. Both of them had kept a secret hope, ever since leaving Munbury, that their mother and aunt might still be alive. Neither of them had mentioned it, in case speaking it aloud might break it or make it vanish, but now, with what lay down in the valley below them . . .

'Can you see her?' Paz asked, craning her neck.

'Not yet, but maybe . . . if we could get closer . . .'

'Keep down!' Mash grabbed the two rabbits by their cloaks and pulled them down into the snow. 'You're going to give us away.'

'But what if . . .' Podkin said. 'We have to . . .'

'We *have* to get back to Crom,' said Mish. 'He needs to know about this. Maybe he can come up with a plan.'

Podkin knew that was right but he couldn't pull himself away, not if his mother might still be down there. In the end it was Paz who made him leave, taking him by the hand and gently pulling him, all

the while staring him in the eyes with a look that told him they would be back. Absolutely, definitely, they would be back.

*

'There's no way you're going back,' said Crom. He had folded his arms and was looking as stern as possible (which was actually pretty stern). 'Twenty Gorm? It would be suicide.'

'But we'd have *you* with us,' Podkin said. They were all sat by the fire after a paltry dinner of acorn bread and dried mushrooms.

'Doesn't matter,' said Crom. 'I could take out one, maybe two at best. That still leaves eighteen. Are you going to take on eighteen Gorm? With your magical dagger that can't even cut through their armour?'

'We could try,' said Paz. 'We might be able to come up with some kind of plan. We have to do *something*.'

'You don't even know that your mother is there,' said Crom. 'It's not worth the risk. I know how you feel . . . I've lost people before . . . but you'd only end up being caught yourselves. Or killed, even. Would your mother want that?'

There was nothing that could be said. Mish and Mash had already headed off to their beds, exhausted by the long walk through the snow. Pook was quietly snoring in Paz's arms, so Paz and Podkin lit a candle and took him off to their room, leaving Crom to sit and listen to the snaps and crackles of the fire alone.

Podkin waited until the door was firmly shut, and Pook tucked into his little cot in the corner of their tiny room. He set the candle on the shelf between his and Paz's beds and watched as it cast dancing shadows over the earthen walls.

'Well?' he said. 'Do you reckon we could do it without him?'

Paz started to sigh, but in the end it came out as more of a sob. 'Pod, we couldn't even do it *with* him. He's right. We'd just be handing ourselves over to the Gorm.' She sat down on her bed and hugged herself, looking sad and very tired.

'So we're just going to sit here and let them kill our mother too? Or turn her into some kind of slave?'

'We don't even know if she's there, Podkin. We didn't see her, did we? She could be back in Munbury warren, looking after the place like . . . like . . .'

She didn't have to say it. Podkin knew what she meant. *Like Lady Russet.* A hollow-eyed zombie, running her own warren for her new masters. The thought of that woman made Podkin's missing ear give a ghostly twitch. Could that be right? Was there an ugly metal pillar in the middle of Munbury longburrow, watching as Pod's old friends and family cowered before the Gorm? Had their beautiful childhood home become a dead, evil place like Redwater?

'No,' he said. 'No. We talked about that, don't you remember? In the snow burrow, that night before Boneroot. You said mother would never do that. You even laughed at the idea.'

'I know I did, Pod.' Paz sob-sighed again. 'But maybe I was wrong. Or maybe she managed to escape – get clear away from Munbury and the Gorm. Or she might have told them where to go and they could have ...' She couldn't bear to finish that thought. She hugged herself tighter, trying to make her brother understand.

'The point is, we have no idea *where* she could be. And we don't have any way to find out. Not

unless we want to charge into a Gorm camp and end up as a bunch of skulls dangling from Scramashank's belt.'

Podkin sat and stared at his sister for a while. She was right, of course (why was she *always* right?) and so was Crom, but it didn't make it any easier. He couldn't understand why they were both so ready to just give up. Was that something that happened to you when you got older? You grew up, became sensible and gave up hoping for anything?

'I *know* she's there,' he said, eventually, in a quiet voice. And in saying it, he realised that he *did* actually know. Somewhere inside him – in his heart, maybe – there was a hard little nugget of certainty. He *knew* his mother was in that camp as surely as he knew carrots were orange.

'You don't really, Pod.'

'I do. By the Goddess's curly whiskers, I do. And I'm not just saying it to be difficult, Paz. Not this time. I swear to you she's there, and we have to save her. Her and all those other poor prisoners. You have to trust me on this. Please.'

Paz stared at him long and hard, her eyes glinting

in the candlelight. Finally she shrugged and flicked her ears at him.

'Fine. If you can come up with a plan that can beat twenty Gorm, I'll be right there with you. And it'd better be a good plan, mind. One that doesn't end up with us all getting skinned. Goodnight, Podkin.'

And with that, she blew out the candle and snuggled down in her bed, leaving Podkin staring at a dark ceiling.

Twenty Gorm. He couldn't rescue his mother because there were twenty Gorm in the way. He couldn't fight them; he couldn't outrun them. What did he have that could get rid of them without getting himself or his friends killed?

It came to him in the last few seconds of wakefulness, just as he teetered on the edge of sleep. He never knew if it was a dream, an idea of his own, or a special thought sent into his head when he most needed it. It was important, though, and he clung to it all night, so it wouldn't be lost come the morning.

He had two things that would help him beat twenty Gorm: he knew where their food came from and, most importantly, he was friends with a witch.

CHAPTER FIFTEEN

The Battle of Camp Gorm

It took Podkin several days to convince Crom that his plan would work, and then several more for them to find Brigid's house again. They knew she was somewhere west of Boneroot, along the outskirts of Grimheart forest, but he had been in no fit state to take much notice when he was last there.

So they had to set out on daily expeditions, marking the trees as they went, heading further and further outwards. Eventually they went so far that they had to camp out overnight in another snow burrow, but were rewarded the next day when

they stood before a huge gnarled oak that looked a little familiar.

'Could this be it?' Podkin said to Paz. She shrugged, looking over to where a bored Mish and Mash were doing backflips in the snow.

'Well, don't just stand around on the doorstep,' came a voice from deep in the woods. 'Walk up and give the door a knock.'

Mish and Mash both squealed in shock and landed flat on their faces. Podkin and Paz were less surprised when a cloaked figure stepped out from among the trees. Brigid had been there all along.

She watched Mish and Mash pick themselves up from the floor with her blue eyes twinkling. Podkin thought they looked much brighter than usual. Brigid's face also seemed less lined, her back not so stooped.

'Not very agile for acrobats, are they?' she said.

'How did she—' Mish began.

'Know that?' Brigid interrupted. 'I know lots of things, dearie. Come on inside. I've got that potion Podkin's about to ask me for.'

With Mish and Mash staring as though their

eyes were about to pop out of their heads, they all sat around Brigid's fire and shared a pot of stinging-nettle tea. She had mixed something up in a leather pouch, which she gave to Podkin. He slipped it into his belt with a nod. 'For sweet dreams?' he asked, just to check. Brigid winked.

'And also,' she added, 'I've got that thing you two acrobats were after as well. "Bang dust", don't you call it?'

Mish and Mash gaped. They had only had the idea of using the explosive powder that very morning and hadn't even told Podkin yet. Brigid went over to one of her cupboards and brought out two little barrels, one for each of the dwarf rabbits.

'Stinky stuff,' said Brigid. 'Mixed it up a few months ago. Had to call in a few favours from an old friend of mine to get the sulphur and saltpetre. I hope you two know what you're doing with it.'

It was Podkin and Paz's turn to look surprised, but before they could say anything, Brigid took them both by the hand.

'There's one more thing,' she said. 'I'm going to be coming with you.'

'Back to Darkhollow?' Podkin said.

Brigid waggled her ears. 'Yes, but also on this little expedition of yours. You're going to need me.'

'You can't do that!' Paz cried. 'It's too dangerous.'

'Oh, I can take care of myself,' Brigid smiled. 'Especially lately. I've been growing stronger and stronger every day.'

Podkin was about to ask what she was talking about, but Paz already had an idea. 'Because of the Balance you told us about? The picture of the snake?'

'Yes, dear. Very good.' Brigid patted Paz on the head as if she were a clever student. 'The Gorm have been growing far too powerful. The Balance doesn't like that. It's beginning to swing the other way. And I plan to help it.'

Podkin wasn't sure what that meant, but it couldn't be denied that she looked like a new rabbit. And even though he didn't want to put Brigid in danger, the thought of having her along made him feel much better about their chances.

*

The next part was much trickier.

With Mish and Mash both on watch for the

Gorm's supply wagon, it wasn't long before it was spotted again. Wobbling along the rutted, snowy track with its weary guards and exhausted rat, the rabbits managed to sneak along behind it, hiding in the snowdrifts and undergrowth.

Further up the track, Podkin had used Starclaw to slice down a small tree and topple it across the path, creating a simple roadblock.

When the guards stopped the wagon and climbed down to chop the tree out of the way, Podkin and Mash slipped aboard.

Luckily, the sound of hacking wood masked any noise they made as they swiftly added Brigid's mixture to all the sacks of wheat and grain. They poured it into the mead barrels and sprinkled it over the loaves of bread, until everything in the cart had a good dose. All the while, Paz and Mish kept watch, until the guards had almost finished clearing the tree. Then Paz gave a little whistle and the sneaking rabbits hopped down from the wagon and into the bushes.

The guards carried on their way, completely unaware that their cargo had been tampered with.

'Tonight, then,' Paz said, when they were gone.

'Yes,' said Podkin. 'Tonight.' His fur bristled with electric tingles at the thought.

*

It was a full moon with a clear sky, and the stars were spectacular. Podkin could see the Big Radish, Clarion the Bard and the Goddess herself: all the constellations gleaming amongst clouds of trillions upon trillions of twinkling lights. He wondered whether some rabbit had taken the time to name all of them, and if perhaps he should have spent a bit more time studying astronomy instead of sneaking off for naps and games of tag.

The silver glow reflected off the snow all around and glinted in tiny sparkles, like a mirror for the stars.

He sat with Paz, Mish, Mash and Crom. Brigid was there too, with Pook curled up asleep in a papoose under her cloak. They couldn't have left him behind on his own in Darkhollow, and Brigid had promised to stay back, out of the camp and the action (although Podkin had spotted the twinkle in her eye as she said it, and he wondered whether she really would).

Together, they all perched on the brow of the hill, looking down at the Gorm camp. They had wrapped themselves in white woollen blankets for camouflage and looked like harmless lumps of snow. But underneath they were clad in leather armour from Darkhollow, and armed with daggers, swords and clubs. Mish and Mash also clutched the small wooden barrels that Brigid had given them, although they had still not told anyone else what they planned to do with it.

Crom had emerged from his father's old chambers looking especially impressive. He wore a suit of lacquered scale armour, made from toughened, painted layers of leather, and he carried a long shield, a sword and an ash spear. Podkin had wondered if it might be a magic weapon, like his own father's dagger, but Crom had just shaken his head. If there was a sacred treasure in Darkhollow, that wasn't it.

They all sat in silence, apart from Pook's gentle snoring, looking down on the enemy rabbits who were finishing their dinner. The Gorm were sitting around a fire inside the camp fences. Behind them

was a cook's bench. They had all been tucking into bowls of stew and loaves of bread. If their plan had worked, Brigid's concoction should start taking effect any minute now.

Podkin held his breath and waited some more.

The Gorm sat motionless around the fire. None of them moved or even seemed to speak. Surely the sleep potion should have started working by now? *Come on*, Podkin urged. *Fall over. Have a lovely evening snooze.*

As if they had heard his silent wish, one of the Gorm wobbled. He swayed forwards, backwards, and then – like an enormous iron tree being toppled – keeled over into the snow face first.

None of the others moved or even reacted.

Then, just as if a giant row of dominoes had been knocked over, they all began to topple, crashing to the ground and lying there, half covered in frost and snoring like babies.

'It worked!' Paz whispered. 'Podkin, you're a genius! And you too, Brigid!'

'Don't count your carrots before they're grown,' said Brigid. 'You're not even in the camp yet.'

'Give it a few more moments,' said Crom. 'Then we go down.'

*

The walk down to the camp was a terrifying one. They left Brigid and Pook on the hillside and began to crunch their way through the thick snow. Podkin expected a hail of spears or arrows to come down on their heads at any second; they were entering the very heart of the Gorm stronghold and there would be no way for them to escape.

But nothing came flying over the wooden fence, and Podkin and the others soon stood by the gates, an eerie silence all around. Using Starclaw, Podkin sliced a hole through the middle of the doors, chopping out the latch on the other side. He pushed the wooden circle through, and it fell with a thud on to the frozen snow inside the camp.

'Well,' he said. 'That was incredibly easy.'

'Carrots. Counting,' Paz reminded him.

Crom pushed open one of the gates, and they walked inside the camp. They almost stumbled over two sleeping Gorm. Up close the iron-clad warriors looked even more terrifying. It was only their loud

snoring that gave Podkin the confidence to carry on – that, and the thought that his mother might be somewhere nearby.

There were tents to the left and right of them, but all seemed to be empty. The atmosphere was quiet and peaceful. Tranquil, almost, if it wasn't for the shivers of pure terror jangling about in Podkin's blood.

The enormous fire at the centre of the camp cast fingers of orange light across the snow, and sparkled on the mounds of dozing iron that were the unconscious Gorm. *I forgot to ask how long they would be asleep*, Podkin thought, with a twinge of worry. *It must be long enough for us to get in and out, or Brigid wouldn't have let us come. Would she?*

In any case, he hurried his footsteps, tiptoeing past the sleeping soldiers, heading for the prisoners' pen on the far side.

Until, that is, something brought him to a sudden stop.

There, sticking up out of the snowy ground like a rotting, poisonous tooth, was a hunk of metal.

252

A gigantic warped shard of rusted, pitted iron. It reminded Podkin of the statue-like shard they'd seen in the middle of Redwater longburrow, but this one was much, much bigger. It was studded with serrated spikes and jagged nodules, like warts on a toad's back.

And it wasn't just metal. Something was wrong with it. It was deeply unnatural. Evil, even. Podkin watched as the odd snowflake hit its surface and vanished with a sudden hiss.

'What ... what *is* that?' he whispered to Paz. Whispering, not because he was afraid of waking the Gorm, but because he didn't want to draw the attention of that thing. Some part of him wondered why he was stupid enough to think a lump of iron was alive, but every instinct told him that it was.

'It's like that thing we saw at Redwater.' Paz's voice was small and scared. 'But much bigger. And more powerful, I think. See what it's doing to those rabbits.'

Podkin tore his eyes away from the metal and looked beyond it. There, arms chained out to each side, were two rabbits. They had been left,

exposed to the iron, staring at it for Goddess knows how long.

Podkin could see the effect it was having on them. Rusty clouds of blood were starting to cover the whites of their eyes. They were motionless, like statues; they looked unable to speak or think. Unable to do anything but stare at the pillar of metal.

'They're turning into *them*,' Podkin whispered. 'Into the Gorm.'

'This must be what happens – how rabbits turn into the Gorm,' said Mish. The thought made everyone tremble with horror.

'I can feel its power,' Crom agreed. 'I can feel it pulling at me, even though I can't see it. We should move on.'

The rabbits started to back away from the thing, even as it tried to draw them closer. It was a magnet, of a sort. A polluting, poisonous magnet that seemed to take over your mind. It made Podkin feel almost sorry for the Gorm, if that was possible. Once upon a time, they must have been normal rabbits, just like him. Was that the thing they dug up in their

warren? The thing that changed them? He supposed it could have happened to any rabbit. Maybe even Munbury itself, if it had been built near a seam of that warped metal.

As they stepped away from it, Podkin was sure he saw it shudder – a ripple in the solid iron, and something vaguely eye-like blinking out at him. He felt Starclaw grow suddenly heavier – hotter in his hand. As if the blade were angry again.

But, in the next instant, both blade and pillar were still lifeless metal again. Had he imagined the whole thing? *Concentrate*, he told himself. *Get your head together, Podkin. You're in the middle of a Gorm camp, two whiskers away from being skinned alive, for Goddess's sake!*

'Come on! We have to hurry!' Paz hissed. Podkin pulled himself back to the present. They were far enough from the iron that its power was weaker. Holding each others' paws in a line, the rabbits broke free completely and rushed over to the prisoners' enclosure.

As they neared it, the thought of seeing his mother again made Podkin step faster and faster, until he

was running across the trampled snow, dagger held out before him.

He reached the pen and chopped straight through the fence. There were the prisoners, bundled together in a huge mass of bodies, trying to keep out the cold.

'Mother! Mother!' Podkin cried and now the sight of them up close caused Podkin to gasp in horror.

These were starved rabbits – sorry things, more dead than alive. Their fur was patchy and dull; skin hung from their bones, and their eyes were blank orbs in deep shadowy sockets. Even though their pen was broken and they were free to escape, they barely moved. Their heads followed the little form of Podkin as they blinked stupidly at him.

'Mother!' he called again. 'It's Podkin! Has anyone seen my mother? Lady Enna from Munbury? Or Olwyn?'

There were dull groans from the huddle, which didn't even sound like words. And then Paz was with him, both of them calling out for their mother together.

Finally, just when Podkin was beginning to think it had all been for nothing, there was a

muttering from the centre of the huddle. The bodies began to rise, to move aside, and two rabbits came staggering out towards them. Podkin felt Paz grasp his arm and squeeze it, and they both held their breath as the weakened rabbits came closer. They were dressed in rags and blankets. Slowly, the moonlight lit their haggard faces, and Podkin could see brown fur: filthy, matted and patchy, but the same colour as his mother's and aunt's at least. Could it really be?

'Mother!' Paz shouted – the first to completely recognise them. 'Mother!'

A spark of light and recognition appeared in the empty eyes of the starved rabbits, and Podkin saw his mother and his aunt come back to themselves like frozen flowers thawing in the sunlight.

'Children? Is it you?' The voice was cracked and broken, but it was definitely his mother's. Podkin didn't remember running to her, but in the next instant he was wrapped in the fiercest, tightest hug he had ever known, with Paz and his aunt all crushed together as well. He could feel hot tears running out of his eyes, and he heard a wailing and sobbing that

was part joy, part sorrow and seemed to come from everywhere at once.

It was wonderful.

Which made it all the more terrible when it was shattered by the sharp cawing of a Gorm crow.

Podkin's eyes snapped upwards, searching the black sky for the bird. But Mish and Mash were quicker. There was a flurry of *zips* as their slingshot and blowpipe fired in quick succession, and then three or four feathered shapes crashed out of the sky, smacking into the snowy ground with meaty thumps.

Crom had his spear and shield ready. 'We have to go. *Now.*' Wherever there were birds, the Gorm weren't far away. And any second now their sleeping comrades inside the camp might also wake up. If they didn't move quickly they would find themselves surrounded.

But it was too late.

Behind them, beside that awful pillar, the two chained creatures, half-Gorm, half-rabbit, started moaning. A low, tortured sound, as if something was causing them great and terrible pain. Podkin could

feel the thing thrumming and throbbing, growing frantic with rage and excitement.

It was almost as though it were calling out to someone or something, Podkin thought, gritting his teeth so hard he thought they would crack. *But what?*

He had a sick certainty that he knew, but he didn't want to believe it was possible. Instead, he pulled at his mother's arm, hoping to get her away from this terrible place before they were parted again.

And that was when the camp gates burst open.

With a crash and a flurry of snow, a pack of riders stormed through the gateway, the pounding of their iron-clad beasts making the ground shake. They thundered *through* the campfire, sending a tsunami of orange sparks skittering across the snow; they galloped past the jagged metal pillar, which cried out in horrible glee, and finally they skidded to a halt in a wash of steam and melted snow, with a screeching of metal against metal that made all the other rabbits clutch their ears.

'You.' A voice came out of the clouds, cold and flat and metallic. The voice of something that would eat you alive, just because you were in its way.

Podkin knew that voice. He could never forget it. It was the one he heard every night in his nightmares, the voice from the last night he saw his father alive.

He peered out from the huddle of cold furry bodies, looking up to see a huge Gorm rabbit, the lopsided metal horns of his armour twisted up above his head like an evil iron version of Hern himself.

It was Scramashank.

*

'You. Boy.' The voice spoke again, and somehow, even though every scrap of flesh in his little body told him not to, Podkin found himself stepping forward, out in front of Scramashank, with Starclaw held before him in his shaking hands. The dagger was buzzing gently, reminding him of its power, although even that didn't make him feel any braver.

'You must be the runt we have been looking for. The runaway kitten from Munbury. Fancy that – searching up and down the whole of Enderby, and here you are, walking right into our camp with the *real* magic dagger in your hands. Is it a gift for me, bratling? A thank-you present for killing your stupid father?' Scramashank sounded as though he was

smiling behind the iron faceplate of his helm. The kind of smile that used all of your teeth and made your eyes look as though they were about to pop out of your head.

'Leave him be.' Crom's voice came from behind him and, without looking back, Podkin knew the blind rabbit was moving into a fighting stance, ready to give his life. 'Pick a fight with *me*, if you've got the whiskers.'

Scramashank turned his head slightly, and in that instant Podkin knew he would kill Crom without so much as a blink.

'Stay back, Crom!' Podkin moved a step closer to the Gorm riders. 'That's an order! Stay back!'

Despite being bigger, older and scarier than the little rabbit, Crom found himself obeying. He was a soldier after all, down to the bone, and Podkin was a chieftain by right. He stepped back, leaving Podkin standing on his own – a tiny scrap of a rabbit clutching a dagger that was too big for him.

Podkin heard sounds of protest from Paz, his mother and his aunt, but he ignored them. Out of the corner of his eye, he saw the little shapes of Mish and

Mash running away from the Gorm, out of the camp. He couldn't really blame them.

'Yes, I have the dagger!' He wanted his voice to sound strong and unafraid. Like his father's when he had faced Scramashank. Instead it came out weak and shaky, but still he carried on. 'This is it. This is Starclaw. What do you want with it?'

'To destroy it, of course. To destroy all of the Twelve Gifts, like I did the sacred helmet of Sandywell.' Scramashank made a crushing motion with his fist, and behind him the iron pillar groaned in hunger.

'But why?' said Podkin. 'I don't understand. Why would you want to destroy something so special? What good will it do you?'

Scramashank snorted and made a motion towards his sword hilt, as if he were going to kill Podkin there and then. But in the end he couldn't resist the chance to boast. After all, he did have a captive audience.

'The Balance,' he said. 'Have you heard of it? The balance between our master and nature. Neither can become too powerful. But if the Twelve Gifts are destroyed, then there will be no Balance. No more

tribes, no more petty feasts and pointless festivals. There will be only the Gorm.'

It began to make sense to Podkin. The Gorm were like a disease, like a virus. They wanted to spread themselves across all the Five Realms until there was nothing else left. He felt anger like a fire burning in his little belly. Before he knew it, he couldn't stop himself.

'But that's just wrong,' he said. 'What about the Goddess? What about all the other gods and goddesses and spirits and everything else? Who says that being Gorm is the right way? Why should you get to take us all over, just because you've got that stupid iron armour? It's just ... it's just ... not *fair*!'

Scramashank sat atop his mount and stared down at Podkin for a heartbeat, then two. The little rabbit thought, for one hopeful instant, that his words might have pierced through the iron armour controlling whoever was inside. Could the chieftain, or the rabbit he was before, still be alive in there somewhere? Could he be listening, fighting against the poison in his mind and trying to return?

But when Scramashank spoke again, his voice was as cold and heartless as before.

'You rabbits don't understand the glory and strength of the Gorm. How could you? I used to be a pathetic timid failure of a chieftain, always doubting myself, always scared of making the wrong decision. Walking around with that oversized copper pot on my head like a fool.

'Now I have no doubts. No weaknesses. No fear. All I have is power and purpose. You puny things of flesh and fur don't understand. This entire world belongs to Gormalech. He was cheated of it, but he will have it back. It will be washed clean for him in a tide of blood and iron, along with all your tribes, gods and goddesses.'

As though in response to his words, the metal pillar howled. Podkin clearly saw spikes and jagged hooks pushing up from beneath its surface. The Gorm around him writhed on their saddles, some of them cackling and whooping with joy. These things could never be reasoned with. They were pure evil, lost to all sense and blind to everything that was good in the world.

That was when Podkin snapped. Never mind that he wasn't even half the Gorm Lord's size. Never mind that his magic weapon was totally useless against him. He pulled himself up as tall as he could and shouted at the top of his voice.

'Fight me then, *Smell-a-skank*, and you'll see just what real rabbits are made of! Or run me down with your stupid iron monster! I don't care. I am Podkin, son of Lopkin, chieftain of Munbury warren, and you are nothing but a fat, stinking coward!'

With the fiercest roar he could manage, he launched himself at Scramashank's mount and began whacking his dagger against its head-armour, just below the thing's left eye.

Clang! Clang! Clang! Scramashank stared down at him, bemused. 'Your knife doesn't cut through iron, idiot,' he said. 'You won't be able to kill my beast like that.'

Podkin ignored him and kept on striking. 'I'm not trying to kill it ...' *clang!* 'I'm just ...' *clang!* 'showing ...' *clang!* 'my friend where to throw ...' *clang!* 'his spear!'

There was a whistling sound, followed by a wet

269

squidgy *thunk*. One second the beast was glaring down at the frenzied Podkin below, the next there was a two-metre-long ash spear jutting out of its eye socket. With a strangled yelp, it collapsed to the floor, sending Scramashank toppling into the snow.

There was a cheer from Podkin's family and the prisoners behind them, which was quickly cut off by the other Gorm raising their own spears. That and the horrible sight of Scramashank rising slowly, unstoppably to his feet again.

His red eyes flashing, the Gorm Lord came striding around the body of his dead mount. In his hands was his huge broadsword, and he looked more terrifying and murderous than any rabbit ever has, before or since.

Oh whiskers, Podkin thought. *What shall I do now?* In his imagination, Scramashank should have been trapped underneath the iron beast, and then they could somehow all have run away. He'd never thought he'd actually have to *fight* the monster.

Remember. A voice rang in his head. It sounded a lot like his father – that gentle, lecturing voice he used to use when he was trying to tell Podkin how

to be a good chieftain. *Remember what Crom taught you. You can't cut his armour, but you can block a little. And you're much smaller and faster. Now, quick! Duck, roll and jump!*

Podkin didn't need to be told twice. With a yelp, he dived right between the legs of Scramashank and rolled out the other side, ducking low as the Gorm Lord swung his sword round behind.

Armour clanked, and Scramashank spun to face Podkin. Pod flipped backwards, out of reach, and the sword thudded into the ground.

'You can't jump around forever, rat-maggot.' Scramashank sounded almost amused, sure of his eventual victory. 'Soon you will get tired, and then I will peel you like a parsnip.'

'Not yet, you won't!' Podkin dashed left and right. He hopped and sidestepped and feinted, all the while keeping just out of reach of the deadly sword blade. From the corner of his eye, he could see Crom and Paz hefting their weapons, ready to jump in and come to his aid.

Boots! That voice again, only this time more urgent. He rolled under a particularly low

sword-swipe, wondering what his mind was telling him.

Boots? What about them? And then it came to him.

Scramashank's boots weren't iron. They were leather. Big black leather boots. That meant Starclaw could . . .

He just happened to be standing between the Gorm Lord's legs. Without a second thought, he swung the dagger sideways, aiming for the spot above Scramashank's ankle. It *swished* through, as if it were nothing more than a blade of grass.

There was a roar of agony somewhere above his head, and something splattered all over the snow: crimson on white. Podkin smelt a hot iron stink and heard the hiss of rapidly melting ice. *Blood*, he thought, and then Scramashank collapsed in a heap, clutching his leg and screaming so loud it hurt Podkin's ears. For the first time, he sounded like a real animal.

The little rabbit looked up to see the rest of the Gorm riders turning towards him, spears raised. *This is it*, he thought. *I'm going to be skewered like a hedgehog.*

But instead there was an explosion from the direction of the iron pillar. A flower of orange light and a roar that drowned out Scramashank's howls. It was followed by another, and another.

The glare made Podkin's eyes water, and the noise rang in his ears. For a moment he thought the world itself was ending, and then he saw Mish and Mash running amongst the Gorm, waving lit torches and shouting. *Of course*, Podkin realised. *'Bang dust.' Their plan was to blow up the Gorm camp. His friends weren't fleeing – they were setting up bombs!*

The effect on the Gorm mounts was dramatic. With their riders clinging on for dear life, they turned and stampeded across the camp, crashing into each other with great clangs of iron.

'Well done, little one.' Crom was beside him, one big paw on his shoulder, and his sword drawn. 'But we are not safe yet.'

'Wait!' Mish was pointing out of the camp, in the direction of the hill where they had left Brigid and Pook. 'What's that?'

All eyes turned up to the hillside, where the silhouette of a tall robed rabbit could be seen,

her arms raised high. Brigid! As they watched, a bank of rolling mist swept up behind her like a cresting wave, and then crashed on to the hillside, flowing up and over the camp walls and covering everything within.

Podkin and the others stood, transfixed, as the fog washed over them. It was cool and sweet, and Pod could smell fresh pine sap, spring leaves and summer dew, all mixed into one.

But the Gorm weren't so keen. As soon as the mist touched them, they fell to the ground, choking, gasping and clutching at their throats. Their already terrified beasts toppled over, trampling and crushing them into the snow.

Podkin looked across to where the iron pillar stood, now lopsided after Mish and Mash's blast of bang dust. He thought he saw it writhing and twisting. As the fog continued to wash over them, he *might* have seen the soil around the pillar burst open with bright green roots and brambles that reached up their thick hungry tendrils to wrap it and drag it down under the wet dark earth.

Whatever actually happened, when the mist

cleared a little, the horrid thing had gone, leaving nothing but a scar on the ground.

And then Paz was shaking him, shouting in his face. 'Podkin, you were amazing! Just like a real chieftain!' She grabbed him in a quick, fierce hug, and then there was a blur of everything happening at once.

The prisoners were properly awake now, all running for the camp gates with Mish and Mash trying to herd them in the right direction. Crom had Podkin's mother under one arm, his aunt under the other. At some point, Brigid and Pook had come down from the hill; there they were, holding hands with Mish and running along with everyone else.

Someone had brought over the wagon tethered to the mangy rat, and they were loading it with prisoners too sick to walk, and then they were all running and stumbling out of the camp and back in the direction of the forest.

Podkin looked back, still not sure whether he was dreaming. Scramashank had stopped moving, passed out cold. The body of his iron beast was

nearby and, on the ground in front of Pod, his boot, complete with foot inside.

I should probably take that with me, Podkin thought, half in a daze. *Might be lucky.*

'Did I really do that?' he managed to say.

'You did, little brother.' Podkin looked up to see Paz gazing back at him proudly. It was the first time he could remember her looking at him like that. 'Don't let it go to your head, though,' she added. 'You're still an annoying little weasel-brain.'

His mother safe. His father avenged. A new home waiting for them all in the forest ... Podkin's feet were as light as moonbeams and his grin as bright as starlight as he sheathed his magic dagger and ran south with his sister beside him, both of them faster than the wind.

CHAPTER SIXTEEN

The End of the Beginning

The bard finishes speaking, and then places his hands together and bows – the sign that the story is done.

At first the little rabbits cheer, happy that Podkin has triumphed, and the adults around the room clap; but then the questions begin, tumbling out one over another as the rabbits rush to speak.

'What happened next?'

'Was Scramashank dead?'

'Was Podkin's mother all right?'

'Was that the end of the Gorm?'

'Did they all go back to Darkhollow?'

The bard lets the questions wash over him, before raising his hands. Gradually, the little rabbits stop chirping and sit in silence again.

'Those are all good questions,' he says. 'But the stories that answer them are for another night. I believe it's time for little ones to be abed, or the Midwinter Rabbit won't be visiting this warren.'

'Will you be here tomorrow night?' one tired rabbit asks. The bard looks over at Chief Hubert, who claps his hands and nods his head, smiling broadly.

'It appears I will,' says the bard. 'And perhaps a few nights longer. At least until the winter solstice is done.'

The little rabbits cheer, and one by one get up from the hearth and go to find their parents. In the end, just two are left: the inquisitive rabbit and the sensible one.

'I still don't get it,' says the inquisitive rabbit. 'All the stories about Podkin are about how brave and strong and powerful he was. In your one he was just a scared little rabbit. Just like one of us.'

'That,' says the bard, 'is exactly what he was. Just

like one of you. You don't have to be brave or strong or powerful to do incredible things.'

'And what's the point,' the little rabbit continues, 'of just telling that bit of the story? I want to hear about Podkin's ragtag army, and how he beats the Gorm for good, forever, and everything else.'

'Stories have beginnings, they have middles and they have endings,' says the bard. 'That was just the end of the beginning.'

'Well, I think it was a good story,' says the sensible rabbit. The bard smiles his thanks. 'A *very* good story.'

'Kind of you to say so.'

'It was realistic.'

'I like to think so.'

'It was *very* realistic. Almost too realistic . . .'

'Are you getting to a point?' the bard asks. 'Only, I'd like a flagon or two of mead now, and perhaps some more soup.'

'My point,' says the sensible rabbit, 'is that you know an awful lot of details about Podkin. More than anybody should know unless they were *actually there*.'

'What are you saying?' says the bard, a mischievous smile playing on his face.

The inquisitive rabbit's eyes turn as wide as soup bowls. 'What? Really? Do you think the bard is Podkin? Do you think Podkin's become a wandering storyteller?'

The bard doesn't say a word.

'Well,' says the sensible rabbit. 'He hasn't taken his hood off since he got here. Why else would he keep it on, unless he was hiding his missing ear?'

The bard gives a chuckle and reaches up for his hood. The two rabbits hold their breath as he pulls it back to reveal . . . two normal ears, tattooed in blue swirls like the rest of his dyed fur.

'I'm flattered you think I could be Podkin,' says the bard. 'But I'm afraid I'm not he. The story was told to me, and my bard's memory filled it with little things that made it real. Everyday details. Feelings and sensations. Nothing but a piece of storytelling magic.'

The sensible rabbit's face falls and his friend punches him lightly on the arm for being so stupid. Despite their blushes, the two disappointed rabbits

remember to say their goodnights and shuffle off to sleep in their burrows. The bard receives a hearty slap on the back from Hubert and a fresh flagon of mead, and then makes his way to the edge of the longburrow. The musicians have the fireside now, and it is time for the parents to dance the Bramble Reel and sing the old songs. No place for an aging storyteller.

He picks his way through the shadows until he finds a bench tucked away in an alcove. There is already another rabbit there. An old one: sitting, whittling a piece of wood by the light of a candle. The bard takes a seat next to him and raises his flagon in a toast.

'Midwinter blessings.'

'And to you,' says the old rabbit. 'Nice story.'

'Thank you,' says the bard.

'You didn't have to make me sound like such a brat, though.'

The bard looks at the aged, wrinkled rabbit with his greying fur and wispy beard. He takes in his watery eyes, trembling hands and the faint marks of old scars here and there. He looks like any ancient

old warrior that could be found in the corner of any warren throughout the whole Five Realms.

Except he isn't.

The bard laughs and pulls his older brother to him in a fierce hug, careful not to dislodge the false ear tied to the side of his head. 'Your memory is fading, Pod. You were the biggest brat of all.'

'I suppose I was. I'm glad to see you, Pook.'

'I'm glad to see you too. It's been too many Midwinters.'

'That it has.'

The two brothers sit together then, listening in silence as the music fills the longburrow and the singing and dancing run on into the night. They sit and hold hands and think about Midwinters past, the stories in between and how, on a night like this – once upon a time – everything changed forever.

1/17

HUT
11/19

D0261085

Books should be returned or renewed by the last
date above. Renew by phone **03000 41 31 31** or
online *www.kent.gov.uk/libs*

Children's Fiction

CUSTOMER SERVICE EXCELLENCE

CSE

Kent County Council
kent.gov.uk

Libraries Registration & Archives

the carrot

th

C334020052